the OAK
and the
MOON

the OAK and the MOON

KAY CAMDEN

THE OAK AND THE MOON
Copyright © 2015 Kay Camden

This is a work of fiction. Any similarity to real people, places, or events is coincidental.

Editing by The Polished Pen
Cover art by Damonza
Book interior design & typesetting by Bookery

ISBN-10: 0-9910044-4-2 (paperback)
ISBN-13: 978-0-9910044-4-7 (paperback)
ISBN-10: 0-9910044-5-0 (eBook)
ISBN-13: 978-0-9910044-5-4 (eBook)

For more information about Kay Camden go to kaycamden.com

the
ALIGNMENT SERIES

The Alignment
The Two
The Oak and the Moon
The Catalyst
The Warrior

CHAPTER 1

SUMMER, 1964

WE ARRIVED IN our prison on the summer solstice. The shortest span of darkness seemed fitting for my first night in that house. It was a comfort from Mother Nature herself, a promise of morning sunlight as quickly as she could bring it. With no idea what our kidnappers had in store for me and my two-week-old son, I prepared for the worst.

The house was an expanse of stone and glass rising from a plot of land large enough to hold a city. Dusk had fallen, heavy clouds smothering everything in shadow. The surrounding forest stood too far away for refuge. Too many men had watched my every move on our trip from Chicago to here for the idea to linger at all. Even after they dropped us in an upstairs bedroom—alone—the thought of escape kept itself far away. I couldn't run with an infant. After days on the road, I didn't even know where we were. All I knew was we were somewhere across the Virginia state line.

Once I settled in the bedroom on the edge of a chair, little Trey stirred in my arms, fists flinging, and my heart broke for his sister with whom I was only able to spend two weeks. I'd have spent less time grieving their father if I had known I'd soon be grieving my baby girl—abandoned, but in a safer place than her brother. These people didn't know about her, and I couldn't speak of her; they couldn't know she was left behind.

The door to the hall opened and I stood, cradling Trey tightly against me. From my position I couldn't see who'd entered the sitting room. I took a deep breath to steady my racing heart. No amount of time spent with our kidnappers could subdue my unease around them. They weren't just a mob of strange men, they were something else, something I needed to figure out.

A gray-bearded man in coveralls appeared in the doorway. "Evening, ma'am. Just here to install those locks. I'll be out of your way in no time." He set his toolbox on the floor by the wall of French doors and began to unload some tools.

Locks on the balcony doors meant this really was going to be my prison. They weren't prepared for me. They thought they'd only be dealing with a newborn baby. I looked down at Trey, his tiny fingers curled against tiny lips, his baby-fine dark hair in such contrast to his fair skin.

Who would have been holding him right then if I hadn't demanded to come along? Would he be crying alone in this room?

I sat with Trey in an armchair facing the French doors. There were more chairs in that room than I had in my whole house in Chicago. The cherry-wood bed piled high with pillows wouldn't have fit in my own bedroom. The ceilings were taller than my house itself. A cavern of empty space loomed ten feet above me, and I felt about an inch tall. The locks went in, each one like a shackle on my limbs. My family had to be worried. I promised to reach them, but each night of the drive when we stopped to sleep I was too terrified to make contact. I was too terrified to close my eyes.

A man-sized shadow darkened the wall, and I knew who it was before I saw him: the one named Pierce. The skin of my cheek crawled with the memory of his slap. I had been weak with relief when he'd climbed in the other car in Chicago. I wouldn't have lasted the days in the car with his eyes on me.

He walked straight to the handyman who was cleaning up his tools. I moved around the armchair, placing it between me and him, for no reason but my own false security. He had the power here.

"All done, Master Pierce."

"Key?"

The handyman handed him the key and picked up his toolbox. Once dismissed, he left the room. Pierce locked every new lock before facing me. He tossed the key once in the air then dropped it into his pocket. He sat and rested back in the facing armchair with his right ankle on his left knee and his fingers making a tent in front of him.

"The locks are a formality. We'll know the second you step foot out of this house. You're not going to be any trouble for us, are you?"

I swallowed to clear my voice. I would not cry. "I don't know what business my husband had with you. I wasn't involved."

"Fearghus Donnelly. I can finally cross that name off my list. We've been looking for him a long time. I can't take the credit, though. My brother found him."

My heart throbbed, bringing tears to my eyes.

"We thought we got him in time, but we had to watch you to make sure. We were wrong. So here you are." He dropped his foot to the floor and leaned forward. "You're good at playing innocent. Do you like to play innocent?"

There was a subliminal meaning in those words I didn't like. The urge to flee weakened my knees, giving my legs a mind of their own.

He stood. "I know it was your idea to come here, but I wish I'd thought of it. I might have a use for you."

Little Trey squirmed against me, kicking out of the blanket. I hugged him to my chest. He took a baby's breath then released it in a monster's cry.

"You pretend you don't know why we want your son, but I think you do."

I longed to ask him why, but I refused to allow him that power over me. And truth would not have come out of this man, unless truth could be used as a weapon. I couldn't trust anything he said. I could only trust my Fearghus, and he was gone forever. The image of his body—the bruises, the blood. It was the backdrop of my vision; sometimes it was all I could see.

"So innocent. But you're not tricking me. At least Fearghus Donnelly had good taste in women. I also prefer blondes. I'll have to thank him for that when I see him in hell."

A maid hovered in the doorway. He cocked his head and frowned at her like she'd just crashed his party. When he turned back to me, he was smiling that same smile he gave me at my house when I demanded to come with Trey. I'd wanted to run from it then, and I wanted to run from it now. He turned to leave.

"Can I get you anything, Master Pierce?"

"Help her shut that baby up. And send the masseuse to my room. The new one."

The maid watched him leave then put a stack of linens on the bed and came to me. "Let me have that sweet baby. He wants to bounce. See?"

Trey quieted in her arms, his cries dwindling on each gentle bounce. She angled his calmed face toward me.

"I need to change his diaper. I don't have any more diapers. They made me throw the dirty ones away and—"

"Oh, there now, if you need to cry, just let it all out. You have that right as a new mother. Just don't fret about diapers. I'll bring anything you need." She surveyed the room. "No one's brought your luggage up yet?"

I looked at my little bag packed in five desperate minutes before they shoved me into the car. "I just have the one ..."

Her expression held a moment of surprise before she smiled. "You must not take after them. They all travel with enough luggage to fill a ship."

"I'm not one of them. I know nothing about these people. I—" *My baby was kidnapped. I demanded they take me too. We want to go home.*

She pressed her lips together so hard they turned white. "I see. You tell me what you need, and I'll get it. First, diapers." She handed Trey back to me. "I'll be right back." Her accent was similar to the handyman's: slow and soft, every word a sigh. None of the men who brought me here had this accent.

I settled into a chair to feed Trey. As soon as his full belly had put him to sleep, the maid returned with a stack of diapers and a tray of food.

"Don't get up, dear. I know this is late for dinner. I hope you'll forgive me on your first night."

She uncovered the food and poured a glass of wine. The waste of it grated against me. I wouldn't be consuming any of it.

The silence pushed me to speak, but I didn't. My words needed to be sparse until I found out who these people were, what they wanted with my newborn son, and why they killed my husband. Every person in the house was suspect. If I wanted to find a way home, I needed to watch, listen, and keep my mouth shut.

With the bed stripped, the maid started pulling on clean sheets. "You have to eat something. Skinny thing like you and with a baby to feed, you'll need all the help you can get."

I wanted to correct her. *Two* babies to feed. One here with me, one I abandoned. Two babies I was afraid to give their father's name. My beloved husband, who died not knowing he was a father. Beaten and murdered by the people who employ you. You can serve me their food, you can dress the bed in their sheets, but I will not poison my body with anything they provide.

"Bless your heart," she said, standing in front of me. She offered me a handkerchief.

I shook my head and lowered my eyes. Tears dropped onto the baby blanket, spreading as they hit the fabric.

"My room is in another building, but I'm happy to sit with you as long as you need me. What's your name?"

"Sloane."

"My name is Fran."

I stared at a knot in the wooden floor. "I think I'd rather be alone, but thank you."

She released a long sigh, drumming her fingers on her hip. "You call for me if you need anything. No matter the time. That sweet baby will no doubt keep you up all night. I'll check on you first thing in the morning."

When the door clicked shut, I carried Trey to the sofa and lay down with him curled between me and the back cushion. If they'd come for Trey because they knew what we could do, they should have wanted me, or Mam. Or my brother, my sister. Why did they want Trey? He was only two weeks old. He had no power.

The house creaked and groaned all night while I failed to sleep on the longest summer solstice of my life.

CHAPTER 2

After three days of removing untouched food from my room, Fran told me they'd caught on to my hunger strike. They weren't happy, and she wasn't sure what they planned to do. When I explained I had no appetite, she told me I needed to find one and eat for my baby.

Now Trey cried every time I tried to nurse him. My arms and shoulders ached. Holding him became tiring. Fran brought me pillows to prop him up so I could rest my arms. So I sat, and he cried. All day, and all night.

"I'm putting my foot down," she said in the morning on the fourth day.

I'd been on my spot on the sofa, watching the stream of sunlight grow on the floor in front of me for as long as Trey had been crying.

She uncovered a large serving bowl of oatmeal and handed me a spoon. "Give me that baby, and I'm going to stand here and watch you eat every last bite."

I placed the spoon back on the tray without taking my eyes off the sunlight.

"Your milk is drying up, if it hasn't already. Eat, or you won't be able to feed him at all. Is that what you want?" She bounced Trey, but all he did was cry harder.

I was of no use to him. I should've stayed home with his sister. With Mam. He was unhappy here when I was with him, and he'd be unhappy if I was gone. There was no difference to him.

"They're going to take him away from you if you don't eat. He'll be lost without his mama." She turned him toward me so I could see his face, red and blotchy from hours of crying. Real tears stopped coming long ago, but they left behind a dried white line on each temple.

If they took him away, maybe I could go home. I looked at my bag still sitting in the same spot I dropped it when I arrived. I imagined picking up that bag, putting on my shoes, and walking out—away from these people, away from his crying.

He'd be alone. I came so he wouldn't be alone.

The glint of new locks on the French doors caught my eye, although the sunlight coming through the glass was much brighter. The doors' function now disabled, they became stationary panes of glass that displayed a live mural of a hundred-year-old black oak reigning over a wide lawn and the forest beyond. Those locks kept me company at night. I could see them in the dark. Like me, they were also new. They didn't belong. Although we had those things in common, the locks held only menace for me, as did every living and nonliving thing in this house.

That oak, though, it was outside. I could see its limbs wiggle in the wind, the sunlight linger in its leaves. The locks were between us, but they weren't a wall. I could still see that oak.

I couldn't leave him here.

The oatmeal burned my tongue, but I shoveled it in my mouth. When the bowl was empty, I drank the glass of water, the orange juice, and the milk. Fran refilled the water from the bathroom faucet, and I drank it all again.

A snake wriggled inside my stomach at the sight of lunch a few hours later, but I ate the food anyway. The snake gave birth to babies when dinner arrived. Fran ran for the bathroom trash can and slid it between my knees just in time for me to throw up.

After Fran cleaned me up, she said, "You feed the baby. I'll cut up your food." She pulled up a chair and began to cut all the food into child-sized pieces.

I didn't eat until Trey's head rolled to the side, a dribble of milk running across his cheek. He was limp with sleep, and if I didn't know better I'd have sworn he had a smile on his face.

Fran eased her arms underneath mine and took him from me. She laid him in the crib she'd brought but I hadn't used, and sat next to me on the sofa. She watched me eat for a few minutes until I looked at her.

"Sloane, I can't know what you're going through. I don't even know why you're here. But these people have a lot to offer you, and while you're here, you should take it."

My fork paused in my mouth. I knew why I was there: to accompany my kidnapped infant son. What I didn't know was why Trey was, or why they wanted him.

"If not for you, then for your baby. Make the best of things. They have the finest chef in Richmond. They probably spent more on that bed than most people spend on a house. They're offering these things to you. Use them."

"I will not sleep in their bed."

"Yet you'll sleep on their sofa? The sofa probably cost more than the bed. It's from Paris."

Fearghus must have owed them money. We had so little. But greed would furnish houses with sofas from Paris; it must have been their greed for the little money we had that killed him. I can't imagine why my husband would owe money to people who lived halfway across the country. I needed to talk to my brother. Arthur had known Fearghus longer than I had, and if Fearghus was in trouble, Arthur should've told me.

Fran patted my leg.

She had gone out of her way to be kind to me, to care for both of us. "Thank you for making me eat. I'm sorry to be so much trouble."

"You are trouble, but don't apologize. I think I'd be trouble myself if I were in your shoes. Now get some rest while the baby's asleep." She took my dishes and closed the door behind her.

I should've tried to contact Mam that night. She expected to hear from me days before, and with no word from me, she probably thought I was dead. Dream contact required strength I did not have, courage I couldn't find. If they found out, they'd break my only means of communication with the family I left behind.

"The mistress of the house wants you to go outside today," Fran said the next morning. "She thinks you need fresh air. But between you and me, she needs to take her own advice. She hasn't felt the sun for years."

So there was a woman in the family. Someone to appeal to, to explain I had another baby at home. She could release us. She could also send them back for Tara. But my ignorance of my situation made the risk too great. Using Tara as our ticket home could so easily put her in danger.

Fran talked me into a bath. She called a younger maid, Eleanor, to hold Trey. Eleanor sat on a stool in the bathroom and sang "My Guy" to him while I bathed. I'd never seen him so calm. He lay still in her arms, gazing at her face with an intensity that reminded me of his father. He'd never looked at me like that. I should've been happy he was so content, but all I felt was failure.

"Oh!" Eleanor said, interrupting her song. "The little man just wet his diaper. Can I change him?"

"Let me help you. I'll be right back, madam." Fran set a towel on the tub and pulled the plug on the drain.

Their voices carried to me from the other room as I stood and dried off.

"Everyone's saying Pierce is the father, but he looks nothing like him."

"Shh," Fran said.

Eleanor lowered her voice. "He looks nothing like any of them."

"I don't think he's one of them."

"What's his name?"

"I don't know yet. She's only said a few sentences since she came here, and I'm not going to push her. And neither are you."

I wrapped the towel around myself and stood in the middle of the bathroom. The last bit of water gurgled down the drain leaving an abrupt silence. A chill rushed against me, like no warmth could remain in that room for long. The sheer size of the space, surrounded on four sides by marble, didn't hold heat well. I wouldn't have wanted to have to bathe in that room in the dead of winter.

Fran returned and draped a bathrobe on my shoulders, so I dropped the towel and tied the sash around my waist. She patted the chair by the dressing table. "Would you like me to do your hair?"

I sat in front of the mirror and stared at my reflection. Eleanor took her spot with Trey on the stool, his eyes fixed on her face. He liked her more than me. I could've asked her to take care of him. A baby wouldn't know she wasn't his real mother, that her skin was too dark, that she might be a little young. She'd give him love and he'd take it without question. I could have left that house, and he'd have never missed me.

Fran combed the water out of my hair then braided the strands at each temple and tied them together behind my head, leaving the rest free.

"Eleanor, would you bring the blue dress? It will look so pretty with Sloane's blond hair."

Eleanor handed Trey to me. When he looked at my face, his little brows pulled together, creating a dimple in his forehead. Maybe it was best that he didn't like me. My leaving would be easy for him. A cleaner break.

The baby-blue sundress was something I'd have picked out myself, although it felt wrong to mention aloud. "Can't I just wear the dress I came here in?"

"Oh, madam, that dress is being laundered. This one will have to do today. We'll bring more clothes for you soon."

I couldn't help but like the delicate blue and white flowers, or how the hem hit my knees just right. I wondered who they'd borrowed it from, or if someone bought it for me. I wanted to wear my own clothes, not be dressed up as if I were a doll.

Fran showed Eleanor how to swaddle Trey. She handed him to me and led me down the grand staircase those men had brought me up my first night here. Lit by the day, the foyer was two stories of elegance: white marble floors below a tiered ceiling painted in vibrant colors set off by gilded medallions. Had the chandelier taken a seat on the floor, it would have been taller than me. I tried not to gawk as I followed Fran through a parlor with ornate furniture and lush curtains, then through a library with floor-to-ceiling bookshelves and windows as large. A door opened onto a porch that stretched around the front corner of the building. Fran took us down to the lawn. The fragrance of freshly-cut grass wafted around us, and Trey squinted and winced in the sun. I turned him against my chest, shielding his eyes from the light.

We walked through a perfect English garden and down a gentle slope to a lake where a flock of ducks hopped one by one into the water to escape us. The breeze blew my hair around my shoulders just enough to coax out the last bit of moisture. I watched insects dart across the surface of the water, wondering how deep it was, how far I could dive to escape the house towering behind my back.

"I think he's worried about you." Fran pointed at Trey's forehead dimple, visible again as he stared at my face. "He's such a little thing, but he knows you're upset."

He had Fearghus' hair and my eyes. Neither had changed from the day he was born. Mam said if I taught him everything I knew, he'd be the strongest Bevan who ever lived.

Footsteps brushed the grass, and I looked up to see who was coming toward us. It wasn't Pierce. It wasn't any of the men who had come to my house. Pack all their evil and all their menace into one person, and the man walking toward us was the man who would have been created. I felt it inside every part of me. An ache spread through my blood, into my bones, sounding that alarm I have that I can never seem to turn off.

He stopped behind Fran, cutting into me with a gaze so fierce my eyes lost focus. "Fran, you are dismissed."

"Yes, sir."

I glanced at Fran, but she'd already turned. I watched her walk away, and my limbs shot full of electric current, willing me to move. To get away.

The man spoke. "*A chroí, chuir tú iontas go duine orainn. Ní fhacthas dúinn go mbeifeá comh toilteanach seo bheith linn.*"

My eyes widened before I had a chance to stop them. It was my own family's language, yet so out of place. He was either mocking me, or he spoke Irish himself. I wasn't sure which idea was worse.

He snickered at my reaction, like he expected my shock. "My men went for one and came back with two. Your ancestors would be proud of such commitment. You've accepted a life sentence here to protect their most special of children." His English had a slight accent, just like Mam's.

He paused for me to respond, but my throat had seized along with every muscle in my body.

"This isn't the arrangement we expected, but now we see the advantage. He'll grow up with his mother. He'll think he's one of us." He took two steps toward me. His cologne stung my eyes as he leaned into my face. "I'll tell you this once. His life is ours now. If you ever speak or act in such a way to suggest anything else, we'll execute you both."

Trey squirmed in my arms. Heat poured through me, collecting heavily in my chest. Fearghus' broken body came into view, and I was there again, on our front stoop, falling to his side, cradling his head. His wet hair—his bloody hair. His blood all over me.

"Even a monster like you could never kill a baby."

The man squinted and took a step back. My words echoed in my head. I hadn't meant to say them aloud.

Trey was ripped from my arms, and I reached, but it was too late. The man turned Trey upright and out to face me, one rough hand across his miniature chest, his blanket floating to the ground. Trey's face contorted, his mouth open wide. Pink toothless gums and a flattened tongue released a cry so surprised, so anguished, it was silent. I covered my own mouth to keep my scream inside. Trey's soundless cry choked him, then he gasped, and the world filled with his scream. His unsupported head lolled to the side. His legs kicked the open air.

"I could kill him right now," the man said, cupping Trey's forehead and straightening his head toward me.

His neck was so weak. It would take nothing. Tears overflowed, noise invaded my head, and blackness crept into my vision. I bit into my own hand to keep myself from lunging.

"Father, I thought we decided not to kill him."

The voice of another man. Someone had joined us. But I couldn't tear my eyes away from my baby.

A different pair of hands closed in on Trey. One hand slid under his body, the other cradled his head. He was laid in my outstretched arms, and I squeezed him against my chest. His scream ripped through my body. I wanted to crumple to the ground and cry with him, but I stiffened my legs to the point of pain.

"They're waiting for you in the library," said the younger man who saved my Trey.

"Good. This here is your mess. Next time, plan your schedule better so you're in town."

The younger man nodded but stayed where he was while the older man walked back to the house. Trey's tense little body collapsed into that of a rag doll. The remaining man plucked the blanket off the ground and gave it to me. My arm was shaking when I took it, but I didn't care.

He loosened his tie. "My father," he said, nodding toward the house, "expects to be listened to, not spoken to, by people like you."

He wouldn't meet my eyes while handing me a handkerchief. I shook my head, and he put it back in his pocket. I wiped my cheeks with Trey's blanket before wrapping it around him. His face was buried into my arm. I didn't know how he could breathe, but I was too afraid to move him.

Finally, the man looked at me. "Mrs. Donnelly—"

"It's Bevan now."

He watched me for a moment. His face showed not one emotion. "Why is that?"

His father had just threatened to kill my two-week-old baby, and now he wanted to make small talk?

"Answer the question."

"Someone murdered my husband and left him on my stoop. I was afraid having his name would kill me too."

"Miss Bevan, then. Welcome to our home. Have you settled in?"

I wanted to scratch out his eyes. All that cold formality offended me more than anything, especially after what had just happened. "Do I have a choice?"

He put his hands in his pockets and turned to look across the water. In the face, he looked to be a few years older than me. Twenty-five, maybe. His shortly-clipped hair and perfectly-pressed dress shirt and slacks made him look older. The businessman of the family. His part in their game was civility, and he played it well—but not well enough to convince me.

"Just a warning, Miss Bevan. That mouth of yours won't get you into trouble with me, but it will get you into trouble with my brothers, and with my father, as you've just seen. I suggest holding your tongue at all times." He faced me and took a step forward. "And never go anywhere without Fran or Eleanor. Do you understand?"

A shred of emotion seeped from him on this last question. I saw true concern, wrapped in careful, good manners. It scared me more than anything had so far.

"I'll give them the order not to leave you."

I watched him climb the slope and go inside. A minute later, Fran came through the door and hurried down the hill toward me. Her cheeks were flushed, eyes damp.

"Let's get you inside, madam." She took my arm.

"Who was that man?"

"The master of the house."

"No, the younger one."

"The master's oldest son. Martin."

Avoiding the man who had threatened to kill Trey would be easy. Instinct. Avoiding the one who had saved him would be more difficult, but it would be twice as necessary. For he was the one with the intent and the skills to manipulate me.

CHAPTER 3

A FTER DINNER IN my room, Fran gathered my empty dishes and wished me a good night. The earlier trauma had left a hush on me and the baby, for different reasons. Trey was simply worn out from the experience. Not me. My ease was due to the clue I'd been given, the unveiling of my place with these people. I had direction now—to learn their game so I could beat them. It was the only way I was ever going to get us home.

How I missed home. My cozy little bungalow, so empty since Fearghus died. Now, in this gloomy old estate, I understood the true depth of emptiness in a house. I'd put off contacting Mam for long enough, and I was sure she could help me. I had to reach for her that night, if Trey would stay asleep long enough for me to do it.

I dragged the crib next to the bed, resigning myself to Fran's advice to make myself comfortable. When Trey fell asleep, I laid him in the crib. I slid between the sheets and stared at the ceiling, focusing on memories of familiar items in Mam's house until I knew she'd be asleep in Chicago. Mismatched pots of herbs crowding her front steps. The porch swing creaking in the wind. The cuckoo clock in the hall inside. The yeasty smell of baking bread. When I closed my eyes, my sleeping mind followed the memories laid out by my waking mind, stretching across forests and rivers and mountains to find her.

"Madam, it's past ten now."

I shoved myself up. Trey was curled up on the bed next to the imprint of my body, and Fran was standing at the bedside.

"I've been unable to wake you since eight, yet you look like you haven't slept a wink. Are you feeling okay?" She felt my forehead.

"I feel fine." I rested my hand on Trey's back. He never slept this soundly. I must have had to feed him through the night, but I didn't remember doing it. He'd somehow made it from the crib to the bed. Yes—he had interrupted me. I jerked my hand away from him.

Mam.

"Sloane? You look like you've seen a ghost."

Mam said it was time I knew. She told me things I shouldn't believe. The fabric of dreams, yet I knew they were her real words.

"I'm okay." It came out in a whisper.

Fran sat on the bed next to me, lowered my frozen hand to the bed, and stared at my face until I looked at her.

"I'll call for Eleanor. She can take care of the baby today. You need to stay in bed."

Mam told me I had to stay with these people, the Moores. I had a duty now, one that had been in the works for centuries. A duty foretold in prophecy and sealed by the magic of our most powerful ancestors. A duty that, if I failed, would mean Fearghus died for nothing.

"Madam, can you hear me? Your hands are shaking."

These people wanted Trey because they were afraid of him. He would be responsible for ending them. They wanted him here, under their control.

I clasped my hands in my lap. "I'm okay, Fran. Just a little tired."

They wouldn't kill him; they were afraid to. The consequences of killing him would have been far worse than anything he could have done to them himself.

"Would you like me to call the doctor?"

My duty was to teach him the ways of his real family, and learn the secrets of his adopted family, so when his time came he'd have the resources to defeat them.

"No, I'll be fine once I eat something."

"I'll bring you a new tray. Please stay in bed, madam."

Fran rushed out the door. What would she think if I told her I was tired from talking all night with my mother in a dream?

I lay down on my side to watch Trey sleep. His tiny chest, rising and falling. Dark eyelashes on a soft cheek. Eyelids taut, eyebrows slightly raised in the most peaceful way. His future had been predetermined, and he didn't even know. What would happen when he found out? Would he accept his duty?

Would I be able to accept mine?

They had killed his father, hoping to prevent his birth. My fear of giving him his father's name had been for nothing. The people I'd been trying to hide him from already knew about him.

They needed to remember what they'd done. I couldn't allow them to forget who my son was, who his father was, and what crime they committed out of fear. My son was a Bevan, but he carried the memory of his father in his middle name. From then on, I would call him by the name I'd first chosen for him: Fearghus.

So they would never forget who he was.

When Fran returned, Eleanor was with her. Eleanor took Fearghus from me with the brightest smile, and for the first time I noticed how young her face was. She couldn't have been any older than fifteen, only five years younger than me. Two weeks before, I wouldn't have noticed the expanse of such a small age difference.

I asked Fran if she could bring me some unneeded fabric and a needle and thread. She brought several choices of material, and I selected the most plain, although it was fancier than anything I would've bought myself. I sewed a little pocket on the front of one of little Fearghus' shirts. Once Fran gathered what I was doing, she joined me with her own needle and thread and worked beside me in silence.

I couldn't believe she followed along without asking me the purpose for such a thing. When you worked for a family like the Moores, you must learn to get by without asking questions.

Eleanor wrestled Fearghus' four wild limbs out of his romper and added it to our stack. After all the baby clothes had been altered, I slid out of bed while Fran cleaned up our mess. I opened the bag from my house and removed the most important item I'd brought: my family's protective amulet. I held it until the metal warmed in my hand, the magic of the age-worn motif vibrating hot against my palm. Once Eleanor had Fearghus redressed, I tucked the amulet into the new pocket and secured it with a safety pin.

"A perfect fit. Good thing he doesn't sleep on his belly," Fran said.

I looked up at her. "Maybe we should have done both sides."

She nodded. "A future project for a rainy day."

My breath caught in my chest, and I started to cry—angry, fierce tears that didn't belong there. I dropped to my knees at the bedside, buried my face in the mattress, and tried with all my might to stop the assault, but the tears kept coming without mercy.

My brother Arthur had come back from that last trip without Fearghus. Arthur had told me Fearghus got hung up, that he'd be home soon. All those trips they went on together, and that last one was the first time they didn't come back together. Arthur, my brother whom I could always trust, had lied to me. It was two weeks before Fearghus' body was dropped on my front steps. These people had my Fearghus for two weeks.

What did they do to him for two weeks?

A hand rubbed my back, but I wanted to shove it away. Inside my head, I screamed, *I have another baby at home who needs me. A baby who will never know her father, and will now never know her mother. I can't stay in this place!*

When the sobbing stopped, my body folded to the floor, my face hit my knees, and I drew air into a shuddering chest until I could breathe normally again.

"I'm sorry," I whispered to Fran.

"Let's get you back in bed."

I was too drained to complain. Pillows were tucked behind my back, and Eleanor laid a sleeping baby next to me. Seeing the calm in his face soothed me in the most perfect way. Made me whole again.

There was a knock on the door, and Fran went to answer it. I couldn't mistake the voice that carried through the little sitting room leading to the hall. My palms pressed into the bed, ready to move me if he came into the room.

Fran's face was strained when she came back into view. "Master Pierce wanted to see you, but I told him you're resting. It's not proper for him to come to a lady's room. I'll have to speak to someone about that."

Pierce was already after me. I couldn't have him burdening Fran too, not after everything she'd done for me. "No, it's okay. I can see him here."

"No, madam. Master Martin told me to come to him with any problems. He'll set things straight." She brought a basket of clean laundry to a chair and started to fold.

There was no reason for Martin to care about my well-being. He was the oldest one of them, the one most likely to follow in his father's footsteps. His agenda seemed different from Pierce's. It was indirect, buried behind good manners, and quite sneaky. I could never let my guard down for him.

"Martin," I began, but I realized I didn't have a question to ask.

Fran glanced at me but didn't pause her folding. "Yes, madam. Martin, Jr."

"Junior?"

"Yes, the oldest son. The one you met on the lawn."

He was even named after the father. With the little I knew about this family, premonition told me Martin was a key player in this game. I was sure he thought I was blind to his tactics, that I'd be easy to overcome. He didn't know I was already onto him.

Mam had said Arthur knew more than she did. I needed to talk to Arthur. But how? The telephones were surely tapped.

"Fran, can I make a phone call?"

"They removed the telephone from this room."

"Is there a private phone in another room?"

She stopped, a towel half folded, to look at me. "You'll need to speak to Master Martin or Master Pierce about that."

I pushed the bedspread aside and dropped my legs to the floor. "I'd like to see Martin."

Fran helped me get dressed then left the room to ask Martin if he'd see me. While she was gone, Fearghus woke up, so I sat down to feed him. Through the windows, the trees blew around like they were playing with each other in sunlight that dimmed and brightened with the irregular roll of the clouds. I kept my eyes on those trees, trying not to think about whom I'd just asked to speak to.

The thoughts that came instead were worries about my baby girl. Was her belly empty? Did she miss her brother? Mam had probably closed up my house and taken Tara home with her, like she'd wanted me to do when they were born. She said I shouldn't try to care for twins on my own. Would these people have found baby Fearghus if I'd moved back home with Mam?

"Madam, Martin will see you in the library. He's there now." She swaddled Fearghus and led me down the hall to the staircase.

Halfway down the stairs, the tingle of panic hit. I'd initiated a formal meeting to ask a simple question, and I didn't want to face him at all. Why hadn't I asked Fran to talk to him?

At the bottom of the stairs, I stopped. Fran touched my elbow. I looked down into Fearghus' eyes. I knew I must be strong for him. Everything I did from then on was for him, and only him.

Martin folded his newspaper and stood when I entered the library, his gray suit jacket slung across the back of his chair. He was dressed for a business meeting—maybe that's what this was.

Fran deposited me in front of him and left the room. Her order to never leave me apparently didn't apply to him. He motioned to the chair next to him, but I stayed where I was. I didn't know how he managed to acknowledge someone without looking at them once. Arrogance came naturally to these people. They made it look so effortless.

"Can I get you a drink?"

I shook my head. He picked up a tumbler and took a sip.

"What can I do for you, Miss Bevan." There was no inquiry in his voice.

"I need to talk to—" I couldn't give him any information that might put my family in worse danger. "Someone at home."

He looked directly at me. "Who?"

I didn't answer him.

"Your brother?"

I couldn't decide if he was being straightforward, or flaunting his knowledge of my family as a threat. Or was he baiting me for a name?

When I didn't answer, he took another sip of his drink and turned away to look out the tall windows. "No."

"You can't expect me to have no contact with my family at home."

"Yes, I can. And I don't think you should involve Arthur Bevan any more than he already is."

"If I write him a letter—"

"Any mail addressed to you will be opened."

"That's illegal."

"Illegal is my specialty."

I wondered if he spoke my family's language. If he'd understand an insult when I gave him one.

He unbuttoned one sleeve and started to roll it up. "I see you wanting to push things. There's a bit of a lull now that we have Trey. If I were you, I'd let things be."

I looked down at the baby in my arms, then back up at him. "His name is Fearghus."

He stopped rolling his sleeve and looked at me. "His name is Trey."

"Is amadán tú."

He threw his head back and laughed. It was the weakest insult I had. With the amount of adrenaline surging through me, I was glad I hadn't chosen something stronger. He'd said my mouth wouldn't get me in trouble with him, but I couldn't trust anything he said. Things would change if I caught him on a bad day.

"What's so funny in here?" Pierce's voice from behind crawled up my back. "Sloane Bevan is a few things, but none of them are funny."

I imagined what his eyes were doing to my backside, but I didn't turn around to prove it.

"You should go back to your room now, Miss Bevan," Martin said.

I took the long way around the sofa to avoid close range with Pierce.

"Pour yourself a drink. I need to talk to you about Boston."

Pierce rubbed his hands together and shot a devil's smile at me before I made it past his gaze. "Boston."

When I reached the door, he growled and snapped at me. His imitation of an attack dog might be fitting. But no animal could ever be as cruel.

CHAPTER 4

ARTHUR COULDN'T FIND me through dreams, and I couldn't find him. After a week of trying every night, I told Mam I'd lost too much sleep and I gave up. She would have to be our medium. It was an unsuitable arrangement; he'd never be candid to Mam about Fearghus. It was obvious their business had been kept from Mam for the same reason it had been kept from me: they wanted to spare us the worry. My questions about Fearghus would have to go unanswered.

You also have a sister. Why not try to find her? Mam asked one night.

Enid and I had tried our whole lives to connect in our dreams and it had never worked with her either. Maybe

Enid and I could try again. She'd have better luck extract-
ing information from Arthur. And I missed her so much.

How many weeks have I been here? I asked Mam. She
told me it'd been almost a month. All the days in that room
had combined to become one long day that never ended.

I stalled my goodbye to Mam, desperate to ask about
Tara. Her silence about her meant something was wrong,
and I couldn't find the strength to find out what. Tara had
lost the only two comforts she'd ever known: her mother,
and her brother—her companion since her life began inside
me.

Fearghus woke me as soon as I lost connection to Mam.
I switched on the nightlight and changed his diaper. He
wailed and sucked his fingers until I sat in the chair next
to the bed and he knew he was about to be fed. His eyelids
fell as his belly filled. I closed my eyes and relaxed into
the chair.

Shouting from the lawn sent a jolt through me. I went to
the French doors to look outside. Light from the first-floor
windows below me spilled onto the lawn halfway down the
slope. Shadows jerked and moved until my eyes made out
the individual bodies in a struggle. Someone being shoved,
being forced to walk. His hands were behind his back.
Another person got knocked down. Several others held
him, then he was yanked up and his hands were behind
his back too. The group moved out of sight.

I looked at the clock. Half past three in the morning.
Did they have a problem with break-ins here? I didn't need
another thing to fear besides the Moore family itself. The
towering iron fence they'd escorted me through on that

first day looked like it would discourage most criminals. I wasn't sure who would voluntarily come to a place like this.

Fearghus' body drooped with sleep, so I laid him in the crib and climbed back into bed. The police were probably going to come and take those two men away. They should hope the police come for them. Unlike this house, real prison had rules for the guards and a standard of human rights.

The police. They'd be there. Could they help me?

Even if they could, I would never be safe from the Moores. If I returned to Chicago, they'd find me. And they'd find Tara and Mam, Arthur and Enid. I'd end up back at the Moore estate and my family would be dead.

Maybe I couldn't appeal to the police, but it might help me know what was going on. The more I knew about the business of the Moores, the better chance I'd have planning my release.

I put on a housecoat. A glance at Fearghus showed a serene face, splayed arms with open fists, parted lips releasing a baby's snore. He'd be out for a while. The hall was dark. Trailing my fingers along the wall for guidance, I found the stairs and crept down to the first floor. Voices reached me, but they were too muffled to understand. I walked toward them, keeping against the wall, straining for voices that may belong to policemen.

Pierce's laugh cut the air. My blood had its normal reaction to his voice—a sudden freeze cycling at once to a surge of power to get away. I stopped to breathe, to listen. From my spot in the parlor, I could see light spreading into the library from the opposite end of the room. They were in the room beyond. I followed the parlor's wall to its opposite doorway and peeked around the door frame into the half-lit library.

"End it." It sounded like Martin.

A shuffling sounded against the floor, then footsteps toward me. A dull thud from the other room. Martin came through the doorway, opened the door to the balcony, and went outside. He walked along the outside of the house, past the wall of windows, until he was out of sight.

"*Go raibh do chorp ina fheis ag mic tíre.*"

That voice—I knew it but couldn't place it. I'd never heard it full of such rich anger. Spoken so low, that curse was more ominous than if it had been screamed with force. *May your body be a feast for wolves.* It didn't just wish death, but torturous death. And I knew that man. Not Martin—he'd left. Not Pierce. Someone else who spoke our language.

I hurried along the wall of the library to the opposite doorway, grabbed the door frame, and looked inside.

Two men on their knees. Pierce above them. Several other men standing around. Pierce slammed one of the kneeling men in the face with a gun. The man's head jerked to the side.

Matthew. My cousin.

The other man struggled. Pierce shot him in the forehead. He fell back so I could see the half of his face that wasn't a mess of red.

Freddy. His little brother.

Matthew screamed and tried to get up. Pierce shot him in the head.

I stumbled backward into a table. My vision blurred. I ran up the stairs to my room, grabbed a pillow, covered my face, and screamed.

Oatmeal for every meal, every day for a week. It was the only food I could keep down. Fran brought fruit, cookies, crackers, and ice cream, but they rode the tray back out of the room, untouched. I only bathed and dressed because Fran helped me. Fearghus hadn't been out of that room, breathed any fresh air or felt any sunlight since the night they killed my cousins. And neither had I.

One day, my tray of dishes remained longer than Fran had ever left it. The strawberries she brought became my focal point of concentration instead of the usual lone oak tree outside. If I touched one to my tongue, would I taste it? Three pieces made it into my stomach successfully before my stomach cramped. I reached for the trash can that had become my companion and released the strawberries into it.

The door to the hall opened. I thought it was Fran coming for the dishes, but the footsteps were wrong.

Martin came through the second set of doors. He dug behind the desk for the loose phone cable, twisted it onto the loose end on a telephone, and slammed the telephone onto the desk. He looked at my food tray, then the trash can.

"You have your phone call. A private line. Everyone has been told not to disturb you." He finally looked at me. "This is between you and me. You have one hour." He was out the door before I could form an answer.

A hysteria climbed up my body. Not having an opportunity to call home had left things simple. It made sense to me under the circumstances, and I'd dealt with it. Now that I could make a call, it opened a new connection back to my family. I felt ready to break into a million pieces.

In no way was I going to believe it was a private line, but I was dialing Arthur's number before I could think.

"Arthur," I said when his voice answered. I clenched my jaw to keep from crying.

"Sis. Are you okay?"

"Yes. No. Arthur, you have to call everyone off. Matthew and Freddy—"

"I know."

"You'll call them off?"

He was silent on the other end. I wished I could see his face. He couldn't hide anything from me in person.

He sighed. "It's not that easy."

"It *is* that easy. Call them off! There's no way any of us are going to win against these people. They have what they want. They aren't going to come after us anymore unless we come to them."

"Is the baby okay?"

"Don't change the subject. You can't save us. We're here to stay. If there's a way out of this, it's up to me to figure it out, and it's going to take time. Sending anyone else here will just get more of us killed."

"Matthew and Freddy went on their own."

"But you didn't discourage them."

He went silent. No doubt he felt guilty about Matthew and Freddy. "We want you home. We can't let them—"

"I know. But coming here for me is not going to get me home. Please. Fearghus would listen to me, why won't you?" Bringing Fearghus' name into it seemed low, but it was all I had.

His voice darkened. "Fearghus would be the first one storming in there."

"And Fearghus is dead! And so are Matthew and Freddy! Don't you see?"

He was quiet for a long time before he said words that almost broke. "I'm so sorry, Sloane."

"It's not your fault." I wished I could believe it myself.

"He—"

"Don't tell me," I choked out. "Not now. They could be listening in."

"I already figured they were. Are you comfortable? Are they feeding you?"

"Yes. They … treat me well."

"You'd tell me if they were treating you badly. I know you'd tell me." Although he was saying this to me, he was also saying it to himself, as if trying to stave off his helplessness. Trying to come to terms with the time he needed to give me to figure a way out of there.

I could've tried to help him with this task, but I didn't answer. I was unable to give them any praise. Speaking positively of my room, or the food, or the gardens outside felt like a sin. I wouldn't do it.

"Sloane …?"

"My maid cares for me like I'm her own daughter. Like little Fearghus is her own grandson."

"Little Fearghus?" He chuckled. "I like that. *He* would like that."

I took a deep breath to ask the question I shouldn't have asked. "All those trips you took with Fearghus …" Something stole the rest of it from my mind.

Every word of his answer held a world of meaning inside it. "I can't talk to you about that now."

"Does Mam know?"

"Mam doesn't need to know."

"Mam can ..." *See everything.* I willed the words to him. They couldn't be spoken on their phone line.

"Not that. Not any of it."

"Someday we will talk about it."

He inhaled a breath then released it. "Maybe. Or maybe it's best for you to remember him how you do now."

Nothing could have changed how I felt about Fearghus. His soul could've been charred black and I would've still loved him with every piece of me, forever. Arthur of all people should have understood that.

"How is Mam handling ..."

"Fine. Don't worry."

"How is she?" I knew he understood I was asking about my baby girl.

"She's fine."

"She's lost me."

"And she's gained all of us. She doesn't spend a second alone. You worry about you and little Fearghus, and only that."

Sounds filtered under the door from the hall, and I flushed cold then hot. I sat up straight. "I think I have to go."

"Will you call again?"

"No. I believe this is a one-time thing."

He scoffed. "Like a true prisoner. One phone call."

"And this is my only chance to tell you. I have every-thing handled here. Call everyone off. Tell anyone who thinks they're going to be a hero that they'll die. Enough people have died already. Be patient. And trust me. Can you trust me?"

"You know I can trust you."

"Then it's up to you to make everyone trust me. If you start to get worried, ask Mam to check on me. It's hard enough to be here. If anyone else dies—"

"I know, Sis. I'll do my best. You know I can't control everyone, but I'll try. For you."

"Tell everyone I love them and miss them. Tell her every day."

"I will."

"Bye, Arthur." I hung up the phone before my voice broke. I didn't know how much of my hour I used, but I didn't have the strength for another call. I got back in bed and lay down with my back to the door so I didn't have to see him when he returned for the phone. The pillows only muffled part of my crying. When the door opened and his footsteps entered, I bit my lip. Silent tears ran while he removed the phone and left the room. I couldn't give him the satisfaction of witnessing my despair.

CHAPTER 5

AUTUMN, 1964

Selecting books from the library had become a longer process each time. Eleanor liked to walk Fearghus around and read him all the titles while I browsed for something to hold my interest. I'd never had the time for reading, and now it seemed to be the only activity that aided the passing of the days. If someone had told me years before that someday I'd be longing to mop a floor, I'd have laughed myself to pieces.

Now, I hadn't laughed for months.

Avoiding the Moore family was easier than I expected. The staff outnumbered them at least ten to one. The family had the freedom to leave the stagnant gloom of the house and keep themselves busy outside of the estate. My anxiety over running into the master had eased. I hadn't seen him since the day he threatened Fearghus. And I'd never seen the mistress. What Fran had said about her must've been true.

On the chance I did see Martin, he never met my eye, but I always felt him watching me. Pierce's gaze crawled over me like I was a royal feast and he couldn't quite decide which dish to try first. It was so predicable it had become boring.

One late October day when the copper leaves swirled against the library windows, I saw Pierce enter the library from my reading spot on the sofa. I knew what to expect. Eleanor stopped reading book titles to Fearghus, and the abrupt quiet forced me to raise my eyes to Pierce. My good manners refused to die, even in that household, even with that snake of a man.

He crossed the room toward me. Instead of seeing the familiar predator's gaze, I saw something closer to wicked mirth. I wished I'd stood when he'd entered. It was too late to stand now. He sat next to me on the sofa and extended his arm along the back of the cushion, behind my neck. A few of my hairs caught on his arm, and I fought the urge to move away.

"Dickens? Sounds like something you'd like."

I glanced at the book in my lap. Had I picked any other author, he was sure to find some sexual reference with which he could harass me.

He turned his body to face me. "It's been too long since we've talked."

He knew I never talked to him. I doubted he really wanted to hear what I had to say. Out of the corner of my eye, I saw Eleanor start to bounce Fearghus. He was ready for a nap, but if I got up and walked away from Pierce, he'd take offense, and my easy escape from this meeting wouldn't be possible.

"There he is," he said, looking at another man coming toward us. "My baby brother wanted to meet you. Lewis, Sloane. Sloane, Lewis."

Lewis stood in front of me, hands on hips. He wasn't a baby. Bigger than both Martin and Pierce, he was all hard muscle, like a racehorse. The wicked mirth had moved to him and left Pierce casual and smirking. Lewis' narrowed eyes and harsh jaw combined with his teenaged features suggested something unpredictable—something I didn't want so close to me.

Where had he been for the months I'd been here? I assumed the two other sons were older, moved out, living in houses of their own. Lewis plopped down on the sofa on the other side of me.

"You see this?" He pointed to a scar near his eye that pulled his eyelid at a slight unnatural angle. "That's from your dead husband. I don't care much, I just thought I could repay the favor."

He grabbed my chin and jerked my face toward him. Eleanor rushed out of the room, Fearghus still in her arms. I swallowed hard. I didn't want Lewis to feel my frantic heartbeat, or see the fear awakened inside me displayed on my face. *Thank you, Eleanor, for taking Fearghus away from this.*

As he studied me, I looked through him. I imagined the wall on the other side, the windows giving a view of that lone oak tree I could see from my room upstairs.

"Such a pretty face. It's a shame to do this," Lewis said, still so close to me.

Pierce laughed, pulling his arm from around me and dragging some of my hair with it that tugged at the root. He dug into his pocket and tossed something to Lewis. Lewis caught it then opened his palm so I was sure to see the pocket knife.

This is what they'd done to Fearghus. This and countless other things too horrible to imagine. They tortured him for two weeks, then they killed him.

Footsteps closed in on us from behind. A newspaper smacked into Lewis' chest.

"You need to check your stocks."

Lewis released my chin to catch the newspaper. "Now? I'm a little busy."

Martin came around the sofa and stood in front of us.

Lewis groaned, dropping his head back.

I was too afraid to speak, but somehow it happened. "How old are you, Lewis?"

He smiled, all teeth. "Sixteen."

Younger than I'd thought. "I'm angry with Fearghus. He knew better than to pick on children."

Pierce stood, jerking me up with him, his grasp on my arm tight enough to shatter bone. Each finger was a tourniquet. My arm tingled. My hand went numb. He slapped me, harder than he did at my house. Blood rushed to my head and darkness crept to the edges of my vision. I filled my lungs with air. I would not pass out. If I did, I would be defenseless.

"Pierce," Martin said, monotone. It echoed in my head with the rhythm of my heart.

"Woman needs to learn not to talk back."

"Did you forget the directive?"

My mouth filled with the taste of blood. A hot trickle slithered from my nose to my lip. I sucked my upper lip inside, tasting more blood. Pierce raised his hand to me again, glanced at Martin, and chuckled. Instead, he shoved me against Lewis, who caught me and turned me to face him.

"I'll deal with you later. When there are no witnesses." He somehow managed to grasp my arm in the same spot where Pierce nearly broke it. The throb of pain was enough to make my eyes lose focus. I turned what should have been a cry into a deep, choking breath.

"Let her go and sit down. I need to have a talk with both of you. Now." Martin grabbed Pierce by the back of the neck and shoved him onto the sofa.

Pierce laughed. "Make us some drinks, Lew."

Lewis sarcastically put both hands in the air. I fell away from him, resisting the urge to cover my throbbing arm.

The look in Martin's eyes was impossible to decipher. "Miss Bevan, Eleanor is waiting for you in the kitchen."

I'd never been allowed in the kitchen. I didn't know where to go. Martin jerked his head toward the door Eleanor had fled through. I picked up my book from the floor and put one foot in front of the other until I was through the doorway. Once out of sight, I steadied myself on the wall with both hands in the room where they killed my cousins. The print on the wallpaper spiraled, like water down a drain. My legs gave, and I felt the wall slide past my palms. Then I was up and moving, supported by Fran and Eleanor. The light of the kitchen shot into my head. They sat me in a chair.

"Ice," Fran said. She dabbed my mouth with her apron. Eleanor placed my book in my lap and hurried away.

"Where's Fearghus?" My swelling lips got in the way of the words.

"Grace took him upstairs. He's sleeping. She'll stay with him for now."

"I want to go upstairs. I want him with me." I couldn't trust any of these people. Not Grace, not Eleanor, not Fran.

"Hush. He's just fine. We need to get some ice on your face. Oh my."

I pushed myself up. This could've been their plan, to get Fearghus away from me so they could hurt him.

"Sloane, dear, you must sit down. You're going to have a nasty bruise. Let's see if we can do something about that."

"I can't leave Fearghus up there!"

Fran placed a rag full of ice on my cheek, and I took it from her. She moved aside as I pushed by, headed toward the room I just left. The door swung open, and I stopped. Lewis blocked my way.

They'd split up.

"Whoa. That's worse than I thought it'd be. Pierce always leaving his mark." He lowered his voice. "The mark I leave will be permanent."

He expected me to cower. I wouldn't cower to him. The most important thing was getting upstairs to Fearghus. Maybe I should have cowered. Maybe he'd let me go.

Fran took his arm. "You know I don't like you boys in here. Go outside, I'll bring you a snack."

The room with the wallpaper blurred by. Inside the library stood Martin, but no Pierce. No Pierce. Martin took a few long steps toward me before I commanded my legs to move again. He took my arm, turned me toward him, and studied my face. He opened his mouth as if to say something. Looked into my eyes. Pressed his lips together.

I yanked my arm away from him and rushed to the parlor, then up the stairs to my room where Grace was cleaning the windows.

"Where is he?" I gasped.

"In the crib, madam." She pointed.

"No. Pierce. Where is Pierce?"

Her eyes widened. "Not here, madam. He was last in the library. Would you like me to fetch him?"

I clutched my chest to keep my heart from beating through the skin.

Fran came through the door, breathing hard. "Let's lie down." She led me to the bed and helped me lie down on my back. The ceiling twirled, undulated. She pulled up a chair, took the rag of ice out of my hand, and put it against my cheek.

I sat up and leaned toward the crib. A tuft of almost-black hair, a tiny fist, a chest rising and falling. I lay back down and closed my eyes.

The tinkle of glass upon glass woke me. Eleanor's singing moved from the background of my mind to the foreground. I could hear the words, along with Fearghus' fussing which grew more impatient by the second.

"I'll take him," I said, sitting up.

Fran helped me sit and removed my pillow stained with blood. She fluffed the other pillows and slid them behind my back.

When Eleanor put Fearghus in my arms, he released a wild cry. "Why didn't you wake me up?"

"You needed your rest." Fran sat on the edge of the bed. "Forgive me if I'm being too forward, madam, but I ..." She turned away from me to look out the windows. "I don't know your relationship with Pierce. But—"

"I have no relationship with Pierce."

She smoothed her apron. "I understand. But you are here, and so is he." She stopped for me to reply.

"Yes, I know." A situation that couldn't be helped by me.

"And as long as you are here, and he is here, I think it might be best to let him have his way. I've known him since he was born. He's the most difficult of all of them, and all of them are very difficult."

"Difficult?" I hoped she was kidding.

"Vicious." She put her hand on mine, as if to ensure this single word remained between the two of us. "You won't win against him, madam. This will happen every time." She touched my chin, tilting my face to the side for a glimpse of what he did.

"It happened when I was talking to Lewis." I'd expected the strike to come from him. I'd had no indication Pierce would react in such a way, even though he'd struck me the first day I met him.

"Lewis is almost as bad, madam."

"It was none of Pierce's business."

"They stick up for each other. Always have, always will."

"And Martin?" The oldest. The ringleader.

"Martin is … different. He wouldn't do this. Not himself."

"He'd just have someone else do it for him?" And then leave the room. So he wouldn't have to witness two young men murdered. One brother killed in front of the other. My cousins, killed in front of me.

"Martin has a softness to him the others don't. Now let's get your dinner before it gets cold."

CHAPTER 6

MAM TUGGED AT my mind three nights in a row, but I closed myself off. I couldn't trust myself to hide what Pierce had done, and if she found out, Arthur would too. I didn't need more of my family trying to save me and dying in the process.

Fran's advice came from a different time when women didn't stand up for themselves. If the Moore brothers continued to confront me, I'd defend myself every time, for I knew they would soon bore of the game, and I'd still have my self-respect.

Being locked up in a house had its advantages. When you're wearing bruises and swelling, you don't have to worry about being seen in public. I watched my fingers poke my eye in the mirror, still not believing it to be my own face reflected back at me. With a few ingredients from the kitchen and some wording from my texts at home, I could've made it all go away, but I refused to erase their crimes. Whether they comprehended their wickedness or not, they needed to see the manifestation of it, even if it pleased them. They needed to be reminded who they were. I could not hide their evil when given the opportunity to throw it at them.

The hot air in the house clung to my skin. Temperatures like these were a rarity for fall in my Chicago home. I stripped Fearghus down to his diaper and laid him on the bed. Kneeling at the bedside, I rested my chin on the mattress next to him. He turned his head to gaze at me, reaching eager fingers toward my mouth, my hair, my ears. The world was cruel to birth a baby so similar in likeness to a father he'd never know. A man I'd never be able to forget. Every time I looked at this baby, I was reminded.

Perhaps this baby had given me a reason to never forget. Time wouldn't be able to dull my vision of my husband. A part of him would always be right in front of me. Somehow, I needed to figure out how to get us out of this house and back with the people who loved us. A child could not grow up in the home of the family who murdered his father.

"Madam, I demand you go outside. Put some clothes on that babe and I'll go with you. I need some air myself."

I offered my finger to his fist. "He seems comfortable this way."

"The sun will burn him to a crisp. But very well. We'll stick to the shade."

Outside, the breeze that must have been banned from the house caught my hair, so I gathered it up and twisted it into a knot. Fran situated Fearghus on her hip, facing out, and wrapped a light blanket around him open in the front so he could kick. He had a strength to his frame now. His efforts to touch everything within reach transformed him into a grabbing, struggling creature who'd learned to steer his human carrier wherever he chose to go. We walked along the edge of the rose beds. The tinge of fall touched my skin with every other breeze, mixed in like a cold spring pumping into a sun-warmed creek. I picked a few blooms to dry, to start a collection I could hide in my room. Someday I'd find the nerve to do something with it.

Fran wandered down the line of roses to allow Fearghus to see all the colors. A tingle ran along the back of my head, but it wasn't the breeze. I turned around. Martin was sitting on the small patio, staring right at me despite the expanse of lawn separating us. One elbow leaning on one armrest of his chair, he absentmindedly stroked his chin back and forth. His legs were stretched out and crossed at the ankle.

I dropped eye contact. His gaze remained a heated beam focused on me. Reflex caused me to look at him again. He reached for his drink and took a sip without looking away from me. His rudeness shouldn't have surprised me, but he needed to avert his eyes. Why was he staring? Did he not want me picking the roses?

I walked across the lawn and stepped onto the patio with legs fired up to kick him off that chair. The far-away look I had hoped would prove a daydream instead of a shameless stare wasn't present. He continued to stare straight at my face, stoic and emotionless and impossible to read.

"Here." I tossed the rose blooms into his lap. "If it means so much to you, you can have them back."

He looked at the pile with only the slightest tilt of his head. "I don't care if you pick the flowers."

I became aware of Fran hastily crossing the lawn toward me, but I ignored her. "Then what? Do you have something you'd like to say?"

He shrugged. Raised his eyebrows. Shook his head. Three separate, unconnected movements.

"Your prisoner, enjoying the last bit of summer. It just irks you, doesn't it?"

"You should be outside on a day like today." One of the blooms caught the breeze and fell off his lap. He looked down at it, but picked up his glass and took a drink instead.

He was drunk. I shouldn't have been confronting him. He had warned me about my mouth, but he excluded himself as a threat in that warning. I wondered if that exclusion carried over to him in a drunken state. Was that really something I wanted to find out?

Fran placed her hand on my arm. "Madam …"

I shook her off. "Care to explain what's so interesting about me today?" I asked.

He shared a look with Fran, then he scratched his eyebrow and looked away, chuckling under his breath.

"Madam, perhaps we should get you inside—"

He stood up in front of me, forcing me to look up at him. The rose blossoms scattered at his feet. "Miss Bevan, I don't hand out warnings to everyone. So when you don't heed them, what happens as a result becomes your fault and your fault alone." His gaze wandered around my face at the black and blue that mottled my temple to my jaw.

"It's not my fault I've been taken prisoner by a family of monsters."

Fran drew a fast breath next to me. Maybe I shouldn't have said that. But he could do whatever he wanted to me. I wouldn't take it back.

"You can leave this house whenever you want."

"I'm not leaving without Fearghus."

"Trey stays here."

My thoughts turned to poison and all I wanted to do was shove him—hard—into the chair. I needed to breathe, to find my calm. He was twice my size. He could've killed me.

"Fran, I'll send Miss Bevan into the kitchen in a few minutes. I need to speak with her alone."

Fran patted my arm. I took Fearghus from her and settled him on my hip. He took a loose lock of my hair in his fist. Fran walked across the patio and into the house, but I maintained eye contact with Martin. He wanted me to be afraid of being left alone with him. I wouldn't cower. Not to him, not to any of them.

"Have a seat, Miss Bevan."

"No thank you."

He took my shoulders and forced me into the chair next to his. He sat, leaned back, and crossed his ankles like he had before. "I'll be out of town for two weeks. My brothers aren't coming with me. They've been ordered to leave you alone, but I can't promise they'll follow that order if you provoke them."

He took a sip of his drink and looked at me for a response. I watched him instead. He could force me to sit there, but he couldn't force me to talk.

"He has your eyes."

I followed Martin's gaze to Fearghus, who was uncharacteristically still and staring straight into Martin's face. Like animals, babies could sense evil. I was sure of it.

Martin stood abruptly. "Go inside and find Fran."

I tried to stare him down as I walked past, but he'd already shifted his attention to the lawn as if I wasn't there. I didn't need him around to protect me from his brothers. He and his brothers could all go to hell.

Inside the kitchen a team of cooks swarmed like insects. The familiar kitchen staff worked along with them. Seeing me enter, Fran wiped her hands and came to my side.

"Have a seat, madam. You can take your lunch in here today, if you don't mind the chaos."

"Who are all these people?"

"They always bring in help for a big occasion." She saw the question on my face. "Master Lewis' homecoming. They use every excuse to celebrate. Lewis was in Europe for six months. He planned to return at the end of the year but must have decided to come home early."

"Why?"

She looked away and smoothed her hair. "I don't know. I can't keep track of these boys anymore. It's hard for me to believe they are all men."

Eleanor appeared with my lunch. She set the table, relieved me of Fearghus, and sat next to me. She watched Fran join the swarm at the counters. "Lewis is a first-class jerk and a real drag."

I almost wanted to laugh. She made it so simple, so understandable it made my fear of him seem like an exaggeration.

She smiled into Fearghus' face. "We used to play, when we were little. We had the same teacher. He's a year older than me. He used to be nice."

"I don't believe any one of them has a nice bit of *dirt* on his shoe."

"Martin can be nice."

"He just hides himself better than the others."

She cocked her head, pondering. "You think so?"

"I know so."

"Maybe." She kissed Fearghus on the forehead before planting his feet on the floor so he could walk around, aided by her. "Sometimes when I pick up Martin's laundry, his shirts have blood all over them. At least it looks like blood. Why is that?"

The food in my mouth turned to glue. I forced myself to swallow. "I don't know."

She giggled at Fearghus, who had latched on to the leg of the chair. "Maybe he always runs into women having babies. He delivers babies. Lots of babies." Her eyes got wide and she glanced up at me. "Did he deliver Trey?"

I laid down my fork and pushed my plate away. It wasn't her fault how quickly my appetite could flee from the mention of one man's name. "No, he did not. Do you ever pick up Pierce's laundry?"

"Nope. I'm never on that side of the house."

If Martin's shirts had blood on them, Pierce's must be soaked with it.

"My daddy used to go on trips with Martin, but after I was born Martin gave him a better job so he wouldn't have to be gone so much. My mom thinks Martin is nice. My daddy does too."

Grace was Eleanor's mom. Grace's work around me was quick and efficient and not bogged down by conversation. She recognized my disinterest in talk, and I recognized hers. It was a mutual understanding. It was what I liked about her. "Where does your daddy work now?"

"Oh, he works here with the cars."

"He met your mom here?"

"No, my mom didn't always work here. People are mean to my mom because my daddy's white so she works here now."

If Eleanor saw my surprise, she didn't let on. She was probably used to a worse reaction from people when hearing this detail. The difference in her skin tone compared to her mother's now made perfect sense, but what had me baffled was Martin's place in all of it. He *wasn't* nice. To him, people were disposable, to be used until they were no longer *of* use, then to be cast aside. Or killed.

"And Martin told my daddy to bring me here for school. Lewis was the same age, already had a teacher. So that's why I go to school here." She leaned closer to me. For the first time, I recognized the uncommon mix of her features: the green tint to her otherwise brown eyes, the rosiness of her bronze cheeks. "He *is* nice, madam. Cross my heart and hope to die."

Fran came over to remove my plate, pausing when she saw how much food I'd left. "Not hungry, madam?"

"Not really."

"I'll bring you a piece of lemon pie."

I put my napkin on the table. "No thanks."

She put her hands on her hips. "We're not going to start this again, are we?"

Just the mention of it brought it all back. The raw threat of tears touched my eyes. The wall I'd built around those memories shuddered, taking a hit from a cannonball. The hole gaped and out crawled the worst thought of all: I'd wanted to leave Fearghus here, to go home without him. I almost did it.

I straightened my back. "Okay, bring one slice and I'll share it with Eleanor."

Fran took my plate, watching me with that careful look she got when she was onto something. As soon as her back was turned, I dabbed my eyes with my napkin.

Fearghus had hold of Eleanor's finger, and he was trying to climb her, chewing her shirt in the process. "Oh, must be hungry." She handed him to me. "I wish you had a television set in your room. Ed Sullivan is on tonight. There used to be one in that room, but they took it out just before you came. Don't you like television?"

"I don't mind it." But I didn't miss it either, not like I missed music. How I longed to lie on the floor with Fearghus while he played a stack of 45s. He used to say we would die like that, and I'd laugh at the image of the two of us, old and gray, lying on the floor listening to Miles Davis and John Coltrane. I didn't change the record after he died. The last one he put on was still there. I couldn't bear to change it. That was always Fearghus' job. "I do like music."

"You do? You should ask for a record player in your room. Want me to tell Fran? She could ask Pierce or Martin."

"If you'd like." It'd be more for her than me. I couldn't listen to music anymore. It summoned a sadness I couldn't endure. "You'll have to bring your own records, though."

Her eyes lit up. "What do you like?"

"Anything you like."

She was off the chair and lost in the kitchen chaos before I could change my mind. When she returned, she had our pie. I sat Fearghus up to burp. Eleanor started with the tip of the pie and I started with the crust.

"Fran's going to ask Martin. Oh, I'm so excited!"

Her excitement found a way into me, and for once I had something to look forward to. She'd bring the Beatles, the Beach Boys, the Supremes. Maybe Ricky Nelson. Nothing that would touch anywhere near those beloved records I shared with Fearghus. Fran carried over a stack of crisp white napkins for Eleanor to fold for the party, and I helped her with one hand while Fearghus napped in my arm.

When we finished the stack, my conversation with Martin outside popped back into my head. It had been missing from my mind. Busy work and distraction and time spent in a bustling kitchen might serve me well.

Eleanor and I took Fearghus up to my room. My picked rose blooms waited in a small wicker basket in my sitting room, and when I saw Grace changing my towels in the bathroom I thanked her for bringing them.

"It wasn't me, madam. Master Martin brought those up for you. He said they were yours."

I wanted to tell her he was mistaken. They were not mine, and he needed to come take them back. He'd touched them; I didn't want them in here. But all I could do was stare at them, the silky pink, the creamy white, the red so deep it was almost purple. Curling green leaves holding the petals together, everything arranged as if by a florist.

Something poked my arm. I looked up into Eleanor's smiling face.

"Told you he was nice."

"He's playing a game."

Her smile widened. "You should play back."

"Not that kind of game."

She wrinkled her forehead. "Then what?"

A pulse traveled up my legs, my chest, settling in my head before shooting down both arms like something potent and out of control was about to be unleashed. I ground my feet and pulled it in, but with nowhere to go it went back to my head, tucked away, shrinking into a concentrated ball of unexercised will. It roused Fearghus in my arms, so I laid him in his crib and tucked the blanket tightly around him.

I felt an intense urge to be alone. "I think I'd like to take a nap."

Eleanor moved the basket of roses to the chest at the foot of the bed. I lay down on top of the bedspread. When I was certain both Grace and Eleanor had left the room, I opened my eyes. The lemon pie was working hard to eat a hole through my stomach. Coming back up the way it went in would've been too gracious, too civil. Like everything else in the house, its goal was to torture me.

A gentle knock sounded on my door. I got up and stood in the open doorway to the sitting room, staring at the closed door to the hall. A maid would have already come in. Pierce wouldn't have bothered knocking.

Another knock. Then the door opened. A cart holding a record player rolled in, pushed by Martin. He stopped the cart in front of me, but I remained in the doorway, blocking entry to my main room. Maybe they had a spare one lying around, but something told me it would've taken longer to locate one not already in use in one of the rooms.

"I don't want your record player."

He brushed off his slacks. "I never use it. It's yours."

"I don't want it."

He pushed the cart an inch closer. "Okay, then it's not mine. It came from storage."

"Is it that easy for you to lie? You must have a lot of practice."

He exhaled hard. "Where do you want it?"

I saw no reason to answer. I'd already told him I didn't want it.

"Are we really going to do this? You're being childish."

"I'd rather be a child than what you are."

He chuckled. "And what am I?"

Monster. Murderer. Kidnapper. Liar. Con artist.

"Okay, don't answer that."

"Why didn't you have one of the staff bring it to me?" I laced the question with accusation so he knew I could see what he was doing. He wanted me in his debt. He wanted to bully me. He wanted to make himself look good, sweeten me into trusting him.

Still holding onto the cart, he leaned forward, bowing his head. When he looked up at me, I saw an unfamiliar man. "Because they're all too busy setting up for tonight, and I wanted to see it done before I leave in the morning."

So much bare truth seeped through the words that I'd moved aside for him before I could stop myself. He wheeled the cart toward the fireplace. I picked my sleeping Fearghus out of his crib, went into the bathroom, and shut the door.

That hysteria I'd cast away weeks before filled my stomach with hot oil, boiling my organs and rising through my chest. I clutched Fearghus against me, buried my nose in his sweet-smelling hair, and breathed.

Abuse and intimidation were an expected, straightforward custom in this house, and didn't leave me with anything but my hate. Favors and compassion, no matter how false, opened doors to a maze of questions that would never be answered. It left me with a puzzle complex enough to chip away my sanity so slowly I'd never see myself going crazy.

He had a reason to be nice to me. And that reason must have been too deranged for me to understand. I wished it wasn't going to keep me up at night, but I knew it would, and I was sure he knew it too. As long as I remembered it was part of his game, I'd be okay.

CHAPTER 7

"Madam?"

I couldn't ignore Fran, even though I knew Martin hadn't left my room yet. I opened the bathroom door.

"Is everything okay?" she asked.

I nodded, feeling like the coward I was. I walked into my room and laid Fearghus back in his crib. He twisted against the bedding and released a harsh cry. The shock of a cold mattress after being held in warm arms would've upset anyone. I stroked his hair until he settled down, then I faced the room.

Martin seemed to have the record player set up. He watched while the arm went through the motions of playing an invisible record.

Fran smoothed my bed. "Madam, the kitchen needs to know your plans for dinner tonight." She looked at Martin for a response instead of me.

"She'll be joining us in the dining room." He replaced the cover on the record player but didn't look at either of us. "Or she can make a dinner of hors d'oeuvres on the patio."

"I'd rather stay in—"

He looked at me. "Wherever you're most comfortable."

"—my room."

He slid his hands into his pockets and grinned. "That's not one of the options."

If we were in a movie, I'd have been able to spit in his face.

"And bring Trey. It's time you start integrating him with us. We've given you long enough."

Fran moved away to straighten up the items on my bedside table. I faced Martin, unable to form words that fit the twisted politeness of his conversation.

"Miss Bevan, you know if you're unwilling to take part in this, we'll have to send you home alone."

My fingernails stabbed into my palms.

"Dinner in the dining room is formal. The patio is more casual. I'd be happy to accompany you to either, if that'd make it easier."

Blinding white hit my eyes. A sketched image took shape. Black and white flashed to oversaturated color, then the color dialed down, and I could see it. It started to move. Me. Martin. Walking together, arms linked. My other hand on his arm. A little boy ran up from behind and shoved between us, laughing. Dark hair, almost black. Green eyes. Like mine. Fearghus.

The colors ran off like rain down a wall. The canvas behind it was white. A new image appeared. My room, Fearghus' crib, the wall of French doors overlooking the oak tree. The sound that had been missing, now returned.

"Madam?!"

And touch. Pain. My knees.

"Keep her down. I don't think she passed out, but she might." Martin's voice. His face, so close to mine.

My palms peeled off the floor and pressed against his chest to shove him back, but he caught my arms and all my power was diverted. I bumped onto the floor as my knees slipped out from under me. Fran pulled my skirt down to cover my thighs.

"Should I call the doctor?"

"No. Bring a glass of water."

Fran's footsteps moved away. Martin's hands shifted from my arms to my jaw. He tilted my face toward the light. His eyes were gray with a sunburst of blue. I tried to break away from him, but he was too strong.

"Your pupils are dilated. They don't react to light. Can you hear me?"

"Let me go!" I slid my legs around, preparing to kick myself away from him.

He released me and pushed back a few feet, still on his knees. His face wiped clear of all expression—so much expression it would've been impossible to identify even one. It was too late anyway; they were all gone. Fran knelt next to me and handed me a glass of water.

"I'm fine," I said, but I accepted the glass and took a sip anyway, hoping it would distract me from the image still alive in my mind. I'd rather be dead than stroll the grounds with Martin like that twisted daydream had portrayed. So casual and friendly. Affectionate even. My easy smile, it sickened me.

Martin looked at Fran. "Has she ever done this?"

"Not that I've seen." Fran touched my arm. "Madam, do you have a history of fainting spells?"

"I didn't faint."

"No, but you fell down, and you wouldn't respond to us."

I rubbed my knees. "Just to my knees. I didn't fall down."

Martin chuckled and sat back on his heels. "You have a funny way of getting out of dinner."

"I'm not trying to get out of dinner."

"Oh yeah? Well, you have. You're pretty damn convincing. I'm a hard sell and you've convinced me." He rose to his feet and brushed himself off. "Fran, when dinner is served, bring a few of the courses up here." He offered his hand to help me up.

I got up myself. They each grabbed an arm, but I pulled away from both of them. He thought I played games to get out of things? Of course—that's what he'd do. They wanted me to be one of them. They wanted Fearghus to be one of them. Neither one of us would ever be one of them. Going to their awful party wouldn't change a thing, whether they thought so or not. "I'm going. You want me to go, I'll go. You can't change your mind now."

Blankets rustled in Fearghus' crib. Thankful for the distraction, I turned away from Martin and Fran to tuck the blanket tight around his contorted body. He wrestled his arms free, released an angel's sigh, and settled into the mattress.

"Can you do something about her face?" Martin asked.

His guests needed to see what kind of people the Moores were. I had the evidence right on my face, and I was not covering it up to protect their reputation.

"Of course, Master Martin."

"I'll come for her at six-thirty." Martin left the room as I threw invisible daggers at his back.

Fran proved her loyalty to me over Martin by helping me get ready by six o'clock so I could go downstairs by myself, although I had to compromise by allowing her to apply makeup over some of the bruises. She looked pleased I wanted to go on my own. Putting me in a yellow chiffon dress seemed her way of buying me a bright mood for a joy-filled evening. She pinned my hair up, fastened a string of pearls around my neck, handed me my sweater and white gloves, and shooed me out of my room.

With Fearghus in his navy blue jumper and little brown shoes, I descended the stairs into a sea of people and avoided every set of eyes on my voyage through the parlor and library, out the door to the porch, and around the house to the backyard patio. At an empty table farthest from the house, I turned a chair so I could view the garden. It may not have been Martin's idea of integration, but it was all he was going to get out of me willingly.

All I had to do was get through the evening. As soon as I could go to bed, I could find Mam and ask her what had happened to me that day. I hadn't fainted. Consciousness never left me. Awareness of my surroundings did, but it was replaced by a new awareness with a weight of importance I couldn't deny. Mam's visions arrived smoothly, like a memory, or a riddle finally solved—not with a kick strong enough to knock a person to her hands and knees. Perhaps more troubling was the subject of the vision itself. Without an explanation, it resembled a hideous curse. Mam's visions were never wrong. But mine? Without past experience I couldn't make that claim. I couldn't imagine what those people would need to do to me to make the content of that vision true.

I had to find a way for me and Fearghus to escape that house.

"I'm starting to learn. The more information I give you, the more you can use against me." Martin took the seat next to me, but I didn't look at him. "Can I get you a glass of champagne?"

"I'm a nursing mother."

"He won't mind if you drink." He snapped his fingers and a waiter came over with a tray of assorted bite-sized foods. He selected a few things and set them on the table next to me. "Eat. I'll get you a drink. Champagne? Wine? A cocktail?"

"No thank you."

"This is a party."

"This is a prison."

He laughed. "Not bad for a prison. Makes me want to do some time."

Maybe I should've asked for champagne, just so I could've thrown it in his face. Fearghus squealed and kicked off one of his shoes. Martin reached down, lightning fast, and picked it up before I had a chance. His hand then went for Fearghus' leg to put it back on him. I turned

Fearghus away and snatched the shoe out of Martin's hand. "Don't ever touch him."

He raised both hands in the air. "Reflex. Sorry. I'll get you a cola."

I picked at the food while he was away, knowing if I didn't, he was going to insist, and he was going to win. If I didn't put up a resistance to eating, there'd be nothing for him to win. Guests trickled on to the patio from the house, and before I knew it, my table wasn't empty anymore.

"What a darling boy! What's his name?"

I felt the need to make something up, but there was no time. "Fearghus."

"Oh my, dear, what happened to your face?" The woman got a scold from the man next to her, but she waved his comment away.

Such satisfaction of my ineffective makeup should've made me feel guilty for all the work Fran had put into it, but I couldn't have been more pleased. "Pierce Moore happened to my face."

She gasped and covered her mouth with a silk-gloved hand adorned in diamonds bigger than her eyes. Several other people turned our way. Fingers clutched my shoulder and squeezed hard.

"My klutz brother and his six iron. Don't get too close when he's teeing off." Martin handed me a bottle of pop.

The woman lowered her hand and smiled sweetly up at Martin. The others around me shared a few glances, a few raised eyebrows. Not everyone was convinced. I started to shrug out of Martin's grasp just before he released me. He was trying to tell me something with that grasp, but I pretended to miss it and took a sip of my pop.

I looked directly at Martin and said, "Don't get too close to Pierce, ever."

The woman rested her arm on the table and leaned close to me. "You shouldn't be so hard on Pierce. Especially since it was an accident."

"Martin didn't say it was an accident."

Her eyes widened in Martin's direction.

"Miss Bevan's imagination gets away from her when she's had too much to drink. This is why she's drinking cola now."

Oh, how the lies rolled off this man. He was smearing my name, when it was Pierce's name that should be smeared. I opened my mouth to reply, but Martin leaned toward me, and the look on his face froze me in place. Muscles rolled in his jaw, and his eyes became twin points of madness. His control, such an effortless part of him until then, had separated from him, creating a new man on the verge of breaking.

He took a quick look around before leaning in even closer. "*Stad as anois.*"

He was the one who'd put me in this situation, and he wanted *me* to stop this? Well, what would happen if I didn't? "'*S mura stadfad?*"

He checked the faces around us, now all absorbed in conversations of their own. "I have a bag of tricks. I don't have to make up lies. I can make all these people think I'm reciting Shakespeare. But I don't like to use it if I don't have to, and I really don't like to be pushed to use it. Understand?"

"I have a bag of tricks too." One that was bulging from underuse, waiting for any excuse to explode in my hands.

He took a long breath, exhaled. "There's another baby here, in the parlor. He's about Trey's age. Maybe Trey would like to play with him."

I refused to look at him. "We're just fine right here."

He lowered his voice. "This is going to happen whether you like it or not. I'm trying to make it easy for you. Do you want it to be hard?"

"You're trying to make it easy for *you*. It could never be easy for me."

He looked away. "Jared is the baby's name. His mother is Sharon. If you come with me, I'll introduce you."

As if on cue, a woman with a baby on her hip stepped out of the house past Martin's shoulder. She noticed my gaze before I could look away, and Martin turned in his seat. "What timing. See? It's even easier than we thought." He stood and she came straight for us.

Martin kissed her cheek before resting a hand on her back like he was presenting her as a gift to me. "Sharon, this is Sloane and Trey. Trey is … how old?" He looked at me.

He knew how old. My baby's age was the length of our sentence in that place. I could always measure how long I'd been stuck there, held away from my family, by the age of my son. "Four months."

"Oh, how perfect!" Sharon said. "Jared is six months. They'll be best friends. How long will you be here? We visit often."

"She'll be here permanently," Martin answered for me.

"Oh." Sharon's face soured with the look of a woman whose territory had just been threatened. She was either a girlfriend feeling slighted by not being married into the family, or she was a wife with an insecure marriage. She'd found a threat in me even when there was none.

Martin gave his now unoccupied chair a slight turn, and Sharon took a seat. She sat her baby on her lap facing Fearghus, who stared in awe of this little creature in front of him. Did he remember his sister? Did he miss her? He could find a friend in Jared. If he could fill the void of his sister, was it right for me to deny him that? I knew who these people were, and I hated them for it. Fearghus was too young to know. I may never be happy here, but Fearghus had a chance, and I needed to give him that chance.

"Is Jared your first?" I asked.

"First of many, I hope. I wouldn't mind a girl. This family already has enough boys. And now you and I have added two more!"

A boulder fell out of the sky onto me, crushing my response to the pit of my stomach. All those people must have already thought Fearghus was one of them. Whose did they think he was? Across the guests' heads on the lower patio, Martin had joined his brothers on the porch. Three sets of arms leaning on the railing, each holding a drink. Pierce in the middle, talking. Martin watching the ground, nodding along with Pierce's words. Lewis studying the crowd and smoking a cigarette.

"It must be so hard for you," Sharon said, brushing invisible lint from her knee. "Still being single. At least they're letting you live here. A lot of women get nothing, just the baby and all the bills and no man in sight. Your baby will have a father. That's a good thing."

My baby would not have a father. Those devils had killed his father.

She patted my knee. "And with what everyone says behind your back ..."

Her words turned to static as that compressed ball of will in my head went supernova. Every light fixture on the side of the house exploded. Broken glass sleeted over the crowd. The three brothers on the porch straightened up in unison, looking straight at me. Martin and Pierce shoved their drinks toward Lewis and headed to the steps.

I surveyed the crowd. Women screamed and covered their heads. Men cursed. No children in sight, aside from Jared who was close enough to me to be safe. I absorbed the flame from each candle on each table. Pulled each flame's power inside me and held it. Combined them. I released my breath, along with their multiplied power. A ball of fire erupted on every table but mine.

Bodies collided into one another in escape, running for the house against the two men coming straight for me. Lewis was a few paces behind them. Pierce reached me first. Fearghus was ripped out of my arms. His cry carried over the sound of the crowd fleeing into the house. I reached for him, but Martin grabbed my arms. Lewis was behind me. One hand clamped over my mouth, one hand clamped over my eyes. I kicked and clawed. It was wasted effort. Fearghus' screams faded.

"Get her upstairs."

Lewis' arms tightened around me. My feet grazed the ground sliding by below them. His hand slipped higher and covered my nose, trapping the air inside me. The need to flail overtook me, but I relaxed my arms. I would not fight him. Even if I resisted, he'd win, and his victory would only be more satisfying. I refused to give him that.

"Lew! Ease up."

The seal over my nose and mouth broke, and I gasped for the air that now reached me. I was half dragged, half carried into the house and up the stairs, but with his hand still clamped over my eyes I couldn't see where we were going. I knew it wouldn't be to Fearghus. I couldn't hear him. If he was nearby, I'd have heard him.

"Put her there."

My eyes were freed as Lewis tossed me into a chair in my room. I looked at the crib. No Fearghus.

"You're not getting him back," Lewis said, jabbing a finger in my face.

He and Martin stood in front of me. Pierce was nowhere to be seen. I looked at Martin. It was all I could do. Hot tears ran down my cheeks, building a fury inside me because their eager escape displayed a weakness I did not feel.

Martin watched me. So calm, so still. But I saw it. Something about to snap.

Pierce burst through the door behind them, empty-handed, and joined his brothers. "Should we flip for it?"

"Shut up," Martin said.

Pierce turned to face him, but Martin didn't move, didn't take his eyes off mine. I sat straight and held in a sob. The tears streamed freely without my consent. He'd brought me my roses. He'd brought me a record player. He had to bring my Fearghus back. I pleaded with him through our connected gaze. I willed him to.

Pierce took something from his pocket and tossed it into my lap. I knew what it was before I looked down. My amulet. The one I tucked inside Fearghus' shirt every day. He was without it now, unprotected. They'd have to take it off him before they could hurt him. They were hurting him right now.

Lewis cracked his knuckles. Pierce turned away from Martin, exhaling hard in disgust. He walked a few steps away then turned back around and looked at Martin. "If you don't, I will."

"My assignment. My call."

"You screw this one up you can bet this is your last assignment."

"Thanks for your concern."

"She knows too much to let her go home."

Martin looked at Pierce. "You shouldn't have let her come in the first place."

Pierce stepped closer and pointed his finger in Martin's face. "You even try to pin this on me—"

Martin's swift movement was distorted in my teary vision. Clothes rustled and a large mass hit the floor. When everything was still again, Pierce was down, and Martin was standing over him. Lewis walked over to offer his hand to help Pierce up.

Martin returned to face me. "You see what you've caused."

I'd caused nothing. I didn't want to be in that awful place. They'd caused it all. They'd stormed into my house to kidnap my baby boy. They'd killed my husband. My reaction today was a tiny fraction of what was due them.

"A predicament," he said. "You can't stay here now after what you've done tonight. We can't send you home since you've been here so long."

If I fell to my knees and begged him for Fearghus, would he give him back? "It was an accident," I said instead.

He crossed his arms over his chest. "An accident."

"The lights. I didn't mean to do it. It just happened."

"So you couldn't control it. It could happen again, and next time, it could be worse."

"It won't happen again. I can control it now that I know. I swear."

Pierce snickered. Martin looked at him and said, "Where's the baby?"

Pierce's smile dropped. "Secured."

Martin looked at me. "Bring him to her. We're done here."

"You're out of your mind."

"The original plan stands. She knows not to do anything like this again. Bring her the baby and then meet me downstairs. We have a house full of people who need to lose a few memories, and I'm not doing it all myself." Martin left the room.

Pierce and Lewis stared at each other. Lewis threw his hands in the air. Pierce turned a murderous gaze onto me. "You can go get your little bastard yourself."

I shot off the chair. "Where is he?"

Pierce shrugged. Lewis tilted his head back and cackled. They strolled through my sitting room and out the door. The door closed, and I rushed to it. A key clicked into the outer lock and turned the bolt. I was locked in.

CHAPTER 8

I RAN TO THE windows and banged on the glass. Someone had to be outside. If they saw me, they'd send someone up. The slope of grass looked barer than ever. Trees beyond stood motionless—an evening so still while chaos surrounded me.

Summoning a power strong enough to burst a lock would surely bring Martin right back here to reverse his decision to trust me. I couldn't be caught using magic in this house—I needed to break the lock without it. Objects flew off shelves and tables, as if running from my frantic search. I needed something to pry the door, something thin and metal. I rushed into the bathroom. The towel rack wouldn't budge from the wall. The floor register snapped loose from the tile, so I ran to the door and shoved the corner of the register between the door and the jamb. I planted my feet and pressed all my weight against it. It popped out and sliced my forearm before hitting the floor. Blood welled but there was no time for that. I banged the door.

"Fran! Eleanor! Grace!"

I put my ear to the door. No sound. Then a small thud far away. I banged again.

"Fran! Eleanor! Is someone there?!"

I put my ear to the door again. Footsteps coming closer. I banged.

"Madam?"

"Fran! Please! I'm locked in. Get the key. Pierce took Fearghus away. I have to get to him!"

The doorknob turned but the door didn't budge.

"Your side isn't locked, madam?"

I locked and unlocked my side. "No! Pierce locked me in. Please find Fearghus. Ask Martin where Fearghus is. Pierce took him from me outside, took him somewhere. Please hurry!"

"I'll find him. I'll be right back."

Her footsteps retreated. My pulse throbbed in my arm. I turned my arm over. The skin was sliced long and deep, the blood dripping down my yellow dress onto the floor. I hugged my arm against my stomach and paced in a circle. With all those guests still downstairs, she'd never find Martin in that crowd.

My amulet—I'd lost it. It had been in my lap. I darted back to the chair in my main room. I checked beside the cushion then dropped to my hands and knees and put my cheek on the floor. It glinted in the sparse light underneath the chair. Clutched in my palm, the amulet sang to me. I sat back on my heels and closed my eyes. Fearghus would be with me soon. He was coming right now. He was in Fran's arms, content. Smiling. Reaching for her face with those tiny, forceful fingers. Watching the handrail of the staircase passing him by, turning to reach for it instead.

A piercing cry shattered my imagined peace. It was far away, yet getting closer. I jumped to my feet and ran to the door. Turning the handle again did nothing but remind me of being helplessly locked in. His cry gained on me like an invisible force prepared to plow me to the ground. If Fran didn't have the key, I might claw through the door.

Her voice now carried with his cry, trying to comfort him but failing. I could hear the heave in his little body, the muscular response to such desperation that cut each cry and started a new one. Please, Fran, have the key. She wouldn't have come back without the key.

Metal inserted into metal, then the click. I was already turning the handle. His face was a mess of shiny wetness, fists clamped so tightly his fingers made stripes of red and white. A little body normally so soft against me, now as stiff as a plastic doll. Arms and legs molded straight, and the voice box skipping, playing the same brutal cry.

I started to sing the first thing that came to mind. Anita O'Day's "Memories of You," the last record Fearghus played for me before he was killed—the one still sitting in my record player at home. I swayed and sang, moving into the bedroom to the windows so Fearghus could look outside. His fists unclamped and clawed for my face. I leaned into him, let him tangle his fingers in my hair. His cries broke in rhythm, turned to a choke, then a breath and a whimper, then just a breath. A rasp sounded deep in his chest, like he'd cried so hard something inside him had come loose, had separated from him. His innocence. His trust in the world.

When he was asleep, I looked up. Fran was sitting on the chest at the end of the bed, hands folded in her lap.

"Would you bring me a warm washcloth?" I asked.

I wiped down his sweat-soaked hair and tear-streaked face. She helped me slip off his sweaty clothes, and we wrapped him in a blanket as best we could without moving him away from me. She paused, holding his foot. She leaned closer and ran a finger over his heel.

I took his foot out of her hand and turned it toward me. A large open gash, no longer bleeding but recent enough to have smeared blood up his leg. They had bled him. For a purpose, or just to torture him?

"And you, too, madam." Fran studied my forearm.

"From the floor register. I tried to use it to pry the door open. Where'd you find him?"

"He was in one of the unused rooms in the east wing. One of the maids on that side heard him crying."

"Who was with him?"

"No one when she found him."

Maybe it was best I didn't know. I wasn't sure what I'd do to the one who did this to him and left him there all alone. "I think I just want to go to bed."

"First we need to clean and bandage that arm. I can't let you go to bed with a wound like that."

I held Fearghus while she saw to our wounds. She pulled down my covers and piled pillows on the opposite side so Fearghus wouldn't roll off. Still holding Fearghus against me, I undressed, stepped into a gown, and slid into bed. Fran turned off all the lights and closed the door to the sitting room. When I heard the door to the hall close beyond it, I gave in and cried until I fell asleep.

Fearghus woke me every hour. It was hard to blame him for being afraid he'd be taken again, for wanting to make sure I was still there. At two in the morning I got out of bed, put on my housecoat, and walked to the windows. Tomorrow the moon would be full. It looked like a tiny edge had been sliced off, like someone just wanted a small taste. The still trees, the cloudless sky, and a sleeping baby in a quiet house. The heartache of the day had also gone off to slumber. I could no longer feel it.

A rap on the door. I turned to face it. Another rap—a definite knock. Who would come at this hour? Fran or Eleanor? A guest from the party who lost his way to his room? The stillness of the night even took the danger out of Pierce. I opened the door to my sitting room. It was too dark to recognize which brother he was until he spoke.

"You're up," Martin said.

I tied my housecoat. "Yes."

"I need to talk to you. Come walk with me outside."

With the tranquility in my mind, the request settled on me like it would in a dream where the most unusual of ideas are acted on without thought. And I so missed walking at night, under the twinkle of stars. It'd been months since I'd been outside at night. If he wanted to kill me, he wouldn't have bothered taking me outside to do it.

"You'll need something heavier. It's chilly."

I went into my dressing room and pulled on a pair of wool pants under my housecoat. My feet stayed bare. If he was planning to do something to me, I'd have more power with my bare feet against earth.

Martin was standing by the windows, looking out as I had been a few minutes before. Fearghus whimpered when I picked him up. His eyes blinked at me, watery and startled, and the little wrinkle appeared between his eyebrows. I wrapped my *siol fagu* around me and tucked him inside the shawl the way Mam taught me. Now warm and secure, he released a sweet sigh and closed his eyes.

Martin zipped his jacket and headed to the door. "Your shoes?"

"I prefer to go without."

"I'm not letting you go without shoes. It's too cold."

I followed him to the door and brushed past him.

"I'm not going to hurt you. Please, you need shoes." He put his hands in his pockets and waited.

I returned to my dressing room for stockings and shoes. Closing both doors, he led me down the hall to a hidden staircase that dropped us into the kitchen. After checking the room, he put a finger to his lips, and I tiptoed behind him to the door and outside.

Moonlight caught in the dew on the grass, like little stars that had fallen from the sky. With Fearghus sleeping soundly, I followed Martin across the lawn to the trees where a dirt trail began, just wide enough to walk side by side.

He slowed to my pace but walked as if he was the only one out there. "Everyone wants you dead but me. I don't know why that is."

It sounded like he was talking to himself, reciting lines he'd memorized. I said nothing.

"I'm going to Europe tomorrow. I have three meetings and four people to kill. More people to kill than I have meetings. Yet I can't order you killed." He stopped walking, took hold of my arm, and turned me to face him. "If you've done something to me, now is the time to come clean."

"I've done nothing to you." I wanted to pull away, but I didn't. His grasp was loose yet determined, like he was making an effort to be gentle but could crush my bone to powder if he felt the need.

"I won't ask you again. And your execution won't be my choice to make if we do find you've done something to me."

I simply shook my head. I didn't know what he wanted me to say.

"My father supports my decision to keep you alive. If it was solely up to him, you'd have been dead long ago. This is my assignment, and he trusts my opinion. But my opinion will mean less if you continue to cause trouble here."

I tried to read for hidden meaning in his words, but found nothing. The words were bare and honest. The heat of his hand reached my arm through my sleeve.

"I see value in you staying here and being a mother to Trey. I'm working to convince the others of that. But if you're determined to disprove your value, it's my reputation on the line. If my reputation takes a hit, so will you. Do you understand?"

I nodded.

"And from now on, I don't care how hard you have to pretend. You're a part of this family. Trey is a part of this family. He'll learn he was born here. If he ever has any reason to doubt that, then you have failed, and we'll no longer have a need for you."

"What will I tell him?"

He released my arm and turned away. "I'm working on that."

"Everyone thinks Pierce is his father." I tried to control the waver in my voice, but it'd been fueled by too much, for too long, with no outlet.

He spun to face me. "Who thinks Pierce is the father?" He handed me his handkerchief.

I took it and wiped my eyes. "The staff. The people at the party."

"Pierce will not be his father."

"Then who?"

He shrugged. "Does he need a father? His father is dead."

His words froze every part of me. My tears. My heart. They put a clutch on the threatening sobs stronger than the dam I'd built in front of them.

"The truth might be the easiest explanation. His father died. Then we—your family—took you in. How you're related is what I'm working on."

"Can I go back to my room?" My voice shook, but not from the effort to hold back a much-deserved curse so foul my ancestors could've heard it. Instead, it was a broken voice, weakened and too tired to concoct the curse he deserved.

He regarded me carefully. "I think it'd be best if you calmed down first."

A condescending statement that should've angered me only cast a spotlight on the wreckage of my spirit. Like Fearghus, I'd died, yet our ghosts had been banished worlds apart.

"Okay." There was that weak voice again, although I didn't care. I couldn't fix it. Not there.

"Things will get easier. All I'm asking is for you to be a mother. I'll handle everything else."

"And lie to my own child?"

"Just by omission. I'll do the active lying for you. It comes easy for me. You said that yourself."

"I'll never see my family again."

He took a deep breath, let it out slowly. "We'll see. Not right away, but I wouldn't say never."

A knot inside my hate for him unraveled. I was too surprised to stop it. Even though I knew every word could be a lie, it was too precious an opportunity to reject completely. A shred of possibility worth a tower of hope.

"You can't do what you did today. Ever again. And I won't warn you again."

I folded up his handkerchief and gave it back to him. He stuffed it in his pocket.

"There's a bench in a clearing a little farther in. Would you like to go sit for a while before we go back inside?"

My answer must've shown on my face because he didn't wait for a voiced reply. I followed him at my own pace and sat on the bench when we reached it. He sat next to me and stretched his legs out in front of him. Insects brave enough to face the chill in the air sang in rhythm. The cool air settled on me like a cat waiting for me to sit down and offer my lap.

With the stars wrapped around us close enough to touch, it felt like we could've stayed on that bench and time would've stood as still as that night. If we sat there forever, I'd never have to go back into that dreadful house.

At that hour, under the stretch of universe, I felt the earth's pulse, the slow even breath, the throb of life in peaceful slumber. The earth was a sleeping giant our most careful movements may wake.

I was unworthy of every power I had. Each second of that perfect night held more magic than what I'd gather from a hundred lifetimes. What I could do was child's play. A mockery.

He took my hand and pushed my sleeve to my elbow, fully revealing the bandage on my arm. "Who did that?"

I stared at the six-inch line of blood soaked through the bandage, at his fingers against my skin too comforting to be real. In sleep or not, everything at that hour took on the state of a dream. An open, still night could set a stage for us to feel things we may not be open to within the comfort of a house. To do things and to say things we may not do or say while governed by manners and proper behavior of closer-living conditions. The night sky has a way of removing that personal shield.

"Pierce or Lewis?" he prodded.

"I did it."

"You?"

"It was an accident. I was trying to break out of my room to find Fearghus. Pierce locked me in."

He released my arm and looked at the moon. "Asshole," he said under his breath, a word straight from his mind I wasn't supposed to hear, given voice by the lull of the night.

The compassion he'd been dealing had started to feel too authentic. His plan was working. Soon, I'd be too compromised to see the game for what it was anymore.

CHAPTER 9

RAIN WAS PATTERING against the windows when I woke the next morning. My breakfast tray was waiting for me, but my appetite was nowhere to be found. The rainclouds had found a way inside me. Staying in bed seemed more reasonable than facing the day.

Mam knew more than she was telling me. The few details she gave were fed to me as if my mind was as upset as my stomach, a tiny bland morsel at a time, followed by a long wait to see how it settled before giving me more. Every meeting with her left me unsatisfied, and undecided as to how I should play this game with the Moores. Resistance felt natural, but she urged me to see things long term. *Settle into circumstance. Learn what you're up against before you start fighting. Struggling through a thorn bush will only get you more pricks.*

She was certain Fearghus and I wouldn't be leaving that house for years. She begged me to make the best of it and take the good things they offered. Most of all, she asked me to protect Fearghus from the knowledge that could hurt him. Give him the best childhood a child could have until the day he needed to be told the truth. She insisted when that day arrived, I'd know.

She told me I could find happiness in the Moore estate if I opened myself to it. I hadn't had the heart to tell her that was easy for her to say. She wasn't the prisoner.

Fearghus arched his back, straightened his arms, and yawned. Something dark sat on his tongue. I opened his mouth with my finger and turned his face toward the light. A large purple stain marked the center of his tongue. They must have given him something when they had him the day before. I sat up, as if to help myself think of what I've used that dyes the skin purple. I ran through my memory of my shelves at home, but there were too many options, too many combinations of herbs and flowers and vegetables that could go purple before or after being put over flame.

I took Fearghus' hands to examine them. Two finger-nails on his right hand were torn on the end. On their own, or due to his struggle? A surface scrape on the back of his hand could've already been there, could've been from any-thing. It could've also resulted from someone holding him down. I stripped off his clothes. Matching bruises on each shoulder stared back at me. My imagination turned each into an adult-sized thumbprint from rough hands holding him against a table.

I looked into his questioning eyes. "*Tá brón orm, a chroí.*"

He didn't deserve this. He didn't choose to be born with this life, as this person destined to be so special he was hunted by those determined to keep him as their own. I picked him up and turned him over to examine his back. A large chunk of hair was missing from the back of his head. The room must've been too dark for me to have noticed the night before. Had they ripped the hair out, or cut it? A good mother would have inspected her baby. Would have made sure he was okay.

They were trying to scare me into submission. Whatever ritual they'd performed on him had no lasting effect—of that I was certain. Its purpose must've been to frighten me, to teach me a lesson. Spending the day in bed would only reward them.

I was up and dressed by the time Fran came to remove my breakfast tray. "Martin left a few hours ago, but some guests from the party are still here if you want to join them in the library."

"I think I will." I didn't look at Fran, knowing the pleasant surprise on her face would only make me feel rotten for tricking her. I didn't want to be friendly like she thought. I wanted to show the Moores I had no fear.

"Let me braid your hair, madam."

After she left the room, I practiced a smile in the mirror. Never had I felt so false. I picked up Fearghus and faced him toward the mirror next to me. He reached for his reflection, straining into the full extension of his little arm, then reached for mine, and when I showed him my smile, he cooed, turning my smile real.

Pierce appeared behind us. My smile dropped. He wasn't supposed to show up in my room like that anymore. Rules must've relaxed when Martin was out of town.

"Good morning," I said.

He glanced at his watch. "Afternoon."

"It's morning to me. I slept in. I was up late. I'm sure you understand."

He held my eye in the mirror, seeming to be unable to process my excess of words. "I'm here to check Trey's heel. Turn around."

Mam's words filled my mind as if she were standing beside me. I turned around and held Fearghus' heel out. Pierce remained focused on my face, too dazed by my compliance to perform his duty. "You've finally learned."

"Hurry up. I want to go downstairs."

He looked me up and down, amused enough to give a sly grin as if I'd just agreed to go to bed with him. Not even a bathtub of bleach could've cleaned that filth from my body. He bent toward Fearghus' heel and examined the wound. I bit my tongue. So many things I wanted to say, and none of them were allowed out of confinement.

He straightened up.

"Done?" I put a buoyant cheer in the word, trying to remain as pleasant as possible. What on earth was so interesting about a cut on a baby's foot?

"This good mood you're in today, after a night like last night, it makes me think you like to be roughed up."

I walked to my slippers and stepped into them. He was going to do this the whole time Martin was gone. I was sure of it. This was Pierce's game, like Martin had his own. On the surface, Pierce's was more threatening.

But if I could ignore him, remain calm and agreeable, he wouldn't advance. Martin couldn't be ignored. He needed to be watched and analyzed at all times. He'd stacked the deck; he had cards in his pockets and up his sleeves, and to win against him I could never look away. I needed to learn to be as conniving as he was.

Leaving Pierce in my room alone brought a sick tingle along my skin when I reached the top of the stairs, but I forced myself to walk down knowing whatever he wanted to do, he could've done at any moment, day or night, even with me in the room. Muffled piano tinkled far away, and Fearghus cocked his head as I walked toward it.

I'd never been to the east wing of the house. The rain pounded the windows at a more direct angle. I might've been trespassing, but no one had ever told me where I could and couldn't go. I wondered if I was near the room they took Fearghus last night.

I stood in the doorway of a large ballroom with a grand piano near another set of floor-to-ceiling windows. Tufted, upholstered furniture in gold and royal blue clustered in several sitting areas at the edge of the room nearest me. The piano was the only thing to interrupt an expanse of parquet floor, shiny with fresh wax. On the opposite end, a rounded bar swelled into the room. It was no surprise I could hear the music from the main stairwell halfway across the sprawling house. The room seemed to amplify the sound.

The player was bowed over the keys, eyes closed, fluid in arm and shoulder as if the song was coming from within him. I took a few steps into the room. He remained too intent to notice me. A man lounging in a chair waved me over with his half-full tumbler. Did these people ever stop drinking? I didn't want my child around them. Fearghus never drank at home.

When I took a seat across from the man in the chair, the song abruptly stopped. The man looked in its direction and threw up a hand, perturbed by the sudden break. The pianist had twisted on his bench to stare straight at me. If these two were guests from the party, they must've been inside. I didn't remember seeing them outside.

"So it's true. 'Music hath charms to soothe the savage beast. To soften rocks, or bend a knotted oak.' And draw the reclusive spider from her cave." The pianist slid off the piano bench. "Although, that's a misquotation. 'Beast' should be 'breast.' But 'beast' makes more sense, don't you think?" Somehow he'd already made it across the floor to me, and he'd offered his hand, and I'd already placed mine in his. He leaned and kissed my knuckles, gentle enough to be kissing the air above them. "Miss Bevan. A pleasure."

The man in the chair across from me tossed back the last of his drink and stood with his empty glass. He shook it to make the ice clink, eyebrows raised at the pianist.

"Can't—doctor's orders. Miss Bevan, this is my drunk of a cousin, Patrick. I'm Paul." He watched the other man walk to the bar. "Martin called me home to keep you out of trouble while he's gone. Our brothers seem to bring out the worst in you, I hear."

Our brothers? Was he a fourth brother? How many of them were there? My hand was in dire need of a scrubbing.

Patrick returned with a full glass and collapsed into his chair. "That's quite a job for one man. You didn't see what she did last night."

Paul sat on the sofa next to me. "Pity I missed it. I didn't get into town until this morning. You'll have to redo it now that I'm here."

I fiddled with the buttons on Fearghus' suit. "It was an accident."

"Are you prone to accidents? Maybe I should move into your room with you, to be on guard all day, and all night. How about it?"

In looks, he was similar to Martin and Pierce. Medium-blond, a tight build in an average man's height. Add an intimidating amount of muscle, and he'd look like Lewis. But this easy, joking nature didn't fit with any of them. "Are you second oldest?"

He clasped both hands behind his head and reclined into the sofa. "Third oldest. Martin, Pierce, me, Lew. Surprised you don't know that. All the ladies around here should be talking about me nonstop." He paused for effect, just enough time to give me a grin. "From the way Martin talks about you, I pictured an older babe. Miss Bevan." He chuckled. "I'm going to have to call you Sloane. Martin has the manners of an old geezer."

"Where'd Martin go?" Patrick asked.

"Europe. Well, Wales. I think he's hitting Germany too."

"Interesting choice of words."

"Chosen intentionally, my friend." Paul rapped the cushion on either side of him in a mini drum solo then turned to me. "So, any requests?" He cracked his knuckles.

"I liked what you were playing before."

"Chopin it is." He gave the bandage on my arm a long look before returning to the piano. "Nocturne in C Sharp

Minor, for the lady." He placed his fingers on the keys. "And for the newest addition to the family."

The last comment brought reality down around me, turning my politeness toward him into a sickness twisting in my stomach. He deserved a rebuttal—and many were already cycling through my head. But then he began to play, and Fearghus' eyes went wide, and I forgot what was said that turned me so sour.

The music gave meaning to the openness of the room, playing along the air like the swirl of a breeze. I walked Fearghus to the windows to watch the rain slip down the glass. Tiny rivers of water dancing to the sound it could never reach. If the music played long enough, it would've carved designs in the ceiling and walls of the room like water does to rock. I wished I could play piano like that.

I wished I could see my baby girl.

Escape was impossible. Even if we made it out alive, freedom would be temporary until they found us again. The only way we could have left is if they chose to release us. If I could somehow convince them Fearghus was not who they thought he was, they'd no longer want him.

They knew he was a Bevan because I'd given birth to him, but they could never be sure he was a Donnelly. If I claimed he wasn't my husband's son, his bloodline wouldn't satisfy prophecy. If I proved this and swore my silence, they'd have no use for him.

Could I go through with a betrayal of my husband, even if it was a lie? Even if it was the only way to save us? I'd decided to call little Fearghus by his middle name so they would always know whose baby he was. And now I had to reverse it—I had to convince them he was not Fearghus Donnelly's son.

A woman appeared in the room's reflection in the window, but I kept my attention fixed on the water streaming down the glass. If I succeeded, and the lie could remain in the Moore household, imprisoned within its walls after I was free to leave, it would be an answer I could live with. But if that lie was released on my family, or on the Donnellys, my betrayal of my husband would be real to them. Could I live with that?

The last note hung on the air, and the woman in the room clapped. I recognized her from last night. Sharon, the one with the baby, the one who inspired my outburst.

She held out her hand to Patrick. "Can I borrow your bankcard? We're going shopping."

"Where's the baby?"

"One of the maids has him."

"Which one?"

She waved away the question. She glanced at me, seeming to notice me for the first time.

Paul rested his elbows on the back of the sofa. "Sharon, this is Sloane."

"We met last night," I said.

She furrowed her brow. "We did?"

Patrick handed her cash from his wallet. "Honey, you met so many people last night. It's okay if you don't remember. Have a good time shopping."

Paul leveled his gaze at me and held it. He wanted me to drop it, to go along with Patrick's obvious distraction. It felt like a test, and I wasn't sure if it was in my best interest to fail or pass. Sharon smoothed away her puzzled expression but raised her chin just the slightest. Making a judgment about me, like she had the night before, all over again. They'd erased her memory of what happened. She was meeting me for the first time again. I wondered if her judgment was the same.

"The driver is ready for you, madam," Fran said from the doorway.

Sharon tucked the cash in her pocketbook and left the room. Fran circled us, fluffing pillows and asking if we needed anything. On her way out, she came to stroke Fearghus' cheek, an excuse to give me a thorough appraisal. She squeezed my arm, her unspoken offer of aid in case I needed her help to get away from these two men. I smiled at her, hoping to put her at ease. I could handle myself now.

Paul watched her leave. "Is she your bodyguard, or your warden? Here to protect you from us, or us from you?"

"What could I possibly do to you?"

He pointed at Fearghus. "You've already done it."

CHAPTER 10

Some days Paul's piano playing roused a focused spirit in Fearghus I'd never seen, and I could only watch him in awe while he watched me in awe of the music. Other days it knocked him asleep so fast I barely had time to settle into our chair. The rest of the house seemed indifferent to the music. So used to having classical piano filling the cavernous spaces of that house, they'd lost the appreciation held by new ears like Fearghus'.

When I started taking my meals in the ballroom, my appetite returned. How long it would stay this time remained to be seen. Yet, with the amount of harassment I was getting from Pierce with Martin gone, I'd have expected my appetite to have flown to Europe itself. That it hadn't was an indication that Pierce could never hurt me. Everything he did and said revealed the workings of a madman. None of it had anything to do with me.

"I'm going to have to start charging you admission," Paul said to me one day when the light slanted through the windows in that way it does when fall is about to give up its seat to winter.

"Then you'd lose your only fans. I have no money."

He looked surprised. "They don't give you an allowance?"

"Why would they give me an allowance?"

He stopped playing and spun on the bench to face me. "Aren't there things you need to buy? Things for yourself?"

"I don't really need anything."

"What about things you want? There isn't anything you want?"

Going without things you want—an unfathomable idea to a man raised in luxury. Fearghus and I had gone without electricity one month we couldn't pay the bill.

"Come on. If there was one frivolous thing you could have right now, what would it be?"

Having my husband, my baby girl, my family back was not frivolous. It was not a want—it was a need that left me choked and unable to breathe when I woke at night with no distraction from the cold spot in my heart where they should've been. So I pushed my needs away and said the first want that came to mind. "Piano lessons."

He straightened up. "You don't need money for that. I could give you lessons."

My body plunged into ice water. "No. I can't ask you to do that."

I didn't want piano lessons. I didn't want anything from him. I stood; Fearghus' blanket slid to the floor. I leaned to retrieve it, and when I stood up Paul was in front of me.

"I won't take no for an answer. It's the perfect thing to do, to keep you out of trouble, and to keep me busy. I get bored easily. I've been bored stupid since I got home."

"I'm sure you have other things to do."

"What I'd like to be doing is going out and partying every day, but Martin would butcher me alive if I left you alone. Come on. It's for me, not you." He cracked his knuckles and winked at me.

"Fearghus needs his nap." I headed for the door. I was halfway up the stairs, convinced of my escape, when he sprinted up beside me and matched my step.

"I'm going to be torturing you worse than Pierce. You can ignore him because he's a psycho. You can't ignore me." His grin practically knocked me down the stairs. "First lesson, tomorrow. If you're not there, I'll find you and drag you there."

We stopped at the top of the stairs. I stared up at him. I wondered if he'd ever killed anyone, if he was there when they killed Fearghus.

"Madam?"

Paul and I turned toward Fran standing at the bottom of the stairs.

"You have a telephone call. You can take it in the library."

A telephone call? They'd never let a call through from Arthur, or from Mam. Would they? Neither Arthur nor Mam would be foolish enough to call, unless something was very wrong at home. They wouldn't risk a call for good news, but they wouldn't burden me with bad news when I was here, helpless and alone.

"It's Martin, calling from Europe. He wants to speak with you first, madam."

Disgust pulsed through me, souring the hope of speaking to my family. I didn't want to talk to Martin. "I was about to rock Fearghus to sleep."

Fran started up the stairs toward me. "I'll take him. You mustn't keep Martin waiting."

I stayed put, unwilling to give up Fearghus. It could be a ploy to get him away from me and repeat what they'd done to him the last time, but they had no reason to create a ploy. They could take him from me whenever they wanted, and there was nothing I could do to stop them. If I could find out what they'd done to him and why, perhaps I would know if they were likely to repeat it.

Fran took Fearghus, and I went down the stairs to the library. The telephone handset waited off the hook. I sat in an armchair and picked it up, stifling the urge to ask if he'd killed all four people yet. "Hello."

The line crackled. Voices filled the background, then a dull thud silenced them. "Miss Bevan. Where are you?"

I felt my forehead wrinkle at the strange question. "In the library."

"Is someone with you?"

I looked around. My heart skipped, and I wasn't sure why. He must've been trying to unsettle me. "No."

"How are you?"

It took a moment to adjust to the question.

"Sloane?"

It took longer to adjust to him using my first name.

His voice lowered. "Tell Fran to put Pierce on *now*."

"No, it's fine. I'm fine. I just … didn't expect a telephone call."

"I need your honesty."

"I'm being honest. I'm fine."

"Trey?"

"Fine."

He sighed into the phone, and I heard him inserting more change. "I got hung up here. I should've been on the flight home today, but I had to stay a little longer."

"Did number four get away?" I made a fist and squeezed hard. Why had I said that?

He laughed. "Yeah, how did you know?"

It seemed so obvious now, like I had known. Had Paul told me?

"Wait, don't answer. Paul told you. He likes to hear himself talk, but I'm sure you already know that."

I almost dropped the handset. Paul hadn't told me— he couldn't have—but hearing Martin voice my thoughts wasn't something I wanted to repeat.

"What did they do to Fearghus that night?"

A long moment passed before he answered. "Why do you ask?"

"I want to know."

"You don't want to know."

"Are they going to do it again?"

A buzz built on the line, crackling the beginning of his reply. "… Fran to put Paul on. I'll talk to you when I get back."

I laid the handset on the table and went upstairs to my room. Fran put a finger to her lips when I entered. Fearghus' wispy moans meant he was about to give up the fight against sleep. We traded places, switching her arms for mine in the most subtle of motions, Fearghus fussing until I resumed rocking him.

Martin had unsettled me—but how? I went over our conversation again, but as usual, the words themselves had no teeth. With him, the attack came from underneath those pacifying words. I couldn't shake a strange regret, like there was something I should've said. Like our call had ended unexpectedly, before I'd had the opportunity to tell him something important. I had nothing to say to him. So why did it feel like I did?

That night I told Mam about the stain Fearghus had on his tongue the morning after they'd stolen him from me. I described the missing chunk of hair, the bruises on his shoulders, and his ripped fingernails. She said the same thing Martin had said. *You don't want to know.*

After breakfast the next day, I couldn't find anyone willing to go for a walk with me in the chill of a rainy November morning. Fran talked me out of it, Eleanor was with her tutor, and Grace was too busy for me to ask her to drop work she'd have to stay late to finish. With all the lights on in the house, it felt like dusk instead of the middle of the day. My mind was stuck in the sunny days of summer, refusing to admit so much time had passed since I'd been brought there.

From my bedroom windows, I watched until the puddles became unmoving mirrors of the gray sky, then I bundled up, wrapped Fearghus against me, and sneaked outside through the door in the library so no one would see me. Surely Pierce was included in those unwilling to accompany me in that weather. Tormenting me would lose some of the fun if it included his own inconvenience of being outside on a cold, rainy day.

I wandered the garden, ignoring all the spent blooms I could've gathered, the roots I could've dug from ground that would give effortlessly after all that rain. If I had a safe place to store a collection without them seeing it, I might've been tempted. The risk was too great, even if I had a secret hiding place. If they found it, they would assume I'd been planning something. And they'd have been right. I needed more time before making plans of that nature.

Mist began to fall around me. I undid my scarf and covered my hair. The drops were so fine it couldn't pass for rain. I had to squint to see it against dark foliage, and even then, it wasn't falling like normal rain that had weight to it. It was hanging in the air. Suspended. Like there was so much moisture in the air itself, the air had turned to water.

I laid the back of my hand against Fearghus' head. His hair was damp, but his warmth reached through the fabric between us, warming a spot on my skin like a hot water bottle. I wondered how long I could stay out there before they'd notice I was gone, or how far from the house I could go. Would Fran get in trouble when they found me missing?

At the farthest edge of the garden, I turned around to look at the house. A sprawl of horizontal blocks and vertical spires made of white stone, its details blurred by the mist. Lights in the windows glowed like real flames, each surrounded by a halo. They could've been watching me at that moment. I walked along the edge of the lake then crossed the lawn. When I reached the edge of the woods, I joined the trees without a look behind me.

My own rapid heartbeat acted as an alarm, increasing in frequency as the distance grew between me and the house. I passed sycamore, their abrupt white branches like skeletons mingling among an assembly of brown wood surrounding us. Oak covered in moss so green and spongy I had to show Fearghus to let him touch. Maple, fiery at their edges but holding onto a few remaining green leaves, tucked close inside. In a small cluster of young pine trees, I stopped walking. It was too far. It had been too far fifteen minutes before. They'd find me, and when they did, I'd pay. Fearghus would pay. How close was I to the edge of the property? What if I could just walk off of it? Find a road? Flag down a car? I could go home. I could see Tara. I could see Mam, Arthur, and Enid. I could sleep in my own bed.

And they would find me. They'd find Tara and Mam, Arthur and Enid. Even if we packed our bags and fled the moment I arrived home, they'd find us, and we would all pay for this day.

Dogs yipped in the distance. It sounded like a pack of them, excited to be on a hot trail. They'd released their dogs on me. I turned around and lengthened my stride toward the house, hoping to make it back before the dogs caught me. I wished someone had told me about the dogs. With a threat like that, I would've stayed in the house. Avoiding a piano lesson wouldn't have turned into a reckless escape attempt.

A yelping, panting mass tore through the underbrush close enough to jolt me into a sprint. I hugged Fearghus against me. Tree limbs slapped against my arms and face. I could see the edge of the woods as a lighter area ahead, but

I knew once I was out there I'd have no cover. How could I have brought Fearghus out here?

A whistle split the air. I slowed down too hastily and slipped on a pile of wet leaves. I went down on one knee, bracing one hand against the ground while holding Fearghus with the other. The yelping and panting began to retreat back toward the house. In the open air I heard a man singing a Simon and Garfunkel song. I checked Fearghus, all eyes in a bundled face with cheeks flecked with rosiness. All my exertion had warmed him even more. I pulled the cover off his head and tried to catch my breath.

Rain sprinkled the canopy above me, taking a moment before pattering all around like it was giving me a hint to go inside—as if the dogs weren't enough of one. I set a good pace, quick enough to get us to safety but slow enough for the slippery ground, now getting even wetter. It wasn't long before Fearghus' hair was soaked and plastered to his head. When I neared the edge of the woods, I spotted a figure of a man through the last line of trees. It wasn't Paul Simon, even though the man was singing his lyrics like he wrote them himself. It was another Paul.

I had less than a minute to come up with a story, a way to play this situation that wouldn't expose the escape I'd almost made. Was I enjoying a leisurely walk and didn't even notice the attack dogs? Did I get lost? Should I be angry he sicced a pack of dogs on me and a defenseless baby?

I emerged from the trees and walked straight for the house without looking at him. Raindrops tickled my scalp. I covered Fearghus' head. My own hair hung in thick wet ropes against my back. Paul stood, arms crossed, in tall rubber boots but no jacket. His shirt was soaked through.

"No escape today?" Like a statue on the hill, he loomed above me.

No amount of preparation could change what came out of me after that. I veered off my path to stop in front of him. "You disappoint me. You let me get farther than I expected."

Weighted by water, his hair made strips on his forehead that hung in his eyes. "You can scale the fence for all I care. I love a challenge."

I headed up the hill past him. A chill had taken hold of me, whether from the rain or the aftermath of the adrenaline rush, I needed to get inside. His boots squeaked in the wet grass behind me. He sang all the way back to the house. Fran opened the door for us, and I stepped onto the rug she'd thrown down.

"Madam, you're soaked." She took one end of my *siol fagu* to unwrap me.

"I didn't realize how far I'd gotten."

Paul laughed. "You've had months to escape the awful Moore family. Yet one mention of a piano lesson from yours truly and the next day you're halfway to the interstate. I'm trying not to take it personally."

I stole a look at him. He stripped off his shirt before I could look away. Fran tossed him a towel. "Where are your manners? Go upstairs."

"Not a chance. If I have to hunt her down again it will cut into my dinner." He went for his belt, and I turned away, the heat of embarrassment flushing the chill right out of me. He was the one being crude. Why did I feel ashamed?

Fran unwound the shawl, and I held Fearghus as the heavy wet fabric fell to my feet. "You're soaked all the way through. Let's get you to your room in a warm bath and some dry clothes. I'll send someone up to light your fireplace."

"I'll be waiting for you in your sitting room," Paul said as I left the room. I tried to ignore his reflection in the wall of windows, drying his hair with a towel in nothing but his underwear.

CHAPTER 11

IN MY ROOM I dried Fearghus off then nursed him to sleep. His head fell back, his mouth still dropped open. A baby's sweet inhale and exhale, the purest form of relief. All that excitement must've exhausted him. While I watched him sleep, Fran filled my bath. I lay Fearghus on his back on the bathroom rug and lowered myself into the water, my arms shaky and my legs weak. She left a blouse, skirt, and underthings on my dressing bench and hovered at the door before she left. I hoped she wasn't worried about me again.

I washed my hair and stayed submerged until the water cooled. I got out, dressed, combed my hair and twisted it up. Fearghus choked and cried out in his sleep, rigid and reaching, clawing the air. I picked him up and hummed until he was limp again. He was long enough to wrap around my body now. He used to tuck inside one of my arms like a little animal. His memory of his tight world inside me must've been fading with the freedom to straighten his body into open air.

I opened the bathroom door and laid him in the crib. A fire glowed in my fireplace, and Paul was stretched out on my sofa, arms crossed behind his head, staring blankly at the ceiling. Waiting in my sitting room must've been too polite for one of the Moore boys. At least he was fully clothed. "I thought you were going to wait in my sitting room."

"After three hours I needed a change in scenery," he said to the ceiling. He sat up.

"Did you enjoy releasing a pack of vicious dogs on a defenseless woman and baby?"

"Defenseless?" He laughed. "In case you haven't heard, that defenseless baby of yours is a plague on my entire bloodline." He held up both palms facing me. "No hard feelings."

"Prove it."

"But we really need to forget these things." He stood, offered his hand. "Come, my dear, I would like to introduce you to my old pal, Beethoven."

"Fearghus is sleeping."

He glanced at the crib. "So?"

"So I can't leave him alone."

"We'll get someone to watch him."

I crossed my arms on my chest. "No."

He crossed his own arms, mimicking me, and made a low growl in the back of his throat. Goading me, as if I were one of his brothers so ready and willing to butt heads with him. I wouldn't do it, nor would I back down. If he didn't comprehend why I was unwilling to allow Fearghus out of my sight, then he'd just have to be left wondering. It was easy enough to figure out. He finally smiled big, his joking smile—the one that crinkled his eyes and changed his whole face. "I think I'm starting to understand."

"What?"

"Martin."

Had I missed something? The conversation had become an unfamiliar neighborhood in which I just made a wrong turn. I narrowed my eyes. "What about Martin?"

He nodded slowly, drawing it out. "I think I need to have a talk with Martin."

"That's good, because I need to have a talk with Martin too. When he gets back, we can have a little meeting." I dropped into my armchair.

He sat on the sofa and crossed his legs. "I'd rather you not be there. The subject matter might make your presence a bit awkward."

A clamp tightened around my chest, compressing my lungs, closing my throat. Were they planning on killing more of my family? Had they found Mam and Tara? I clasped my hands in my lap, afraid they might shake. I thought back to that turn in the conversation I missed. I refused to leave Fearghus in here alone, then we were suddenly talking about Martin. I saw no connection.

Martin must've left Paul in charge of mind games while he was gone. Either Paul was better at it, or he was ahead because he'd caught me off guard. I thought he was just there to babysit me.

He waved his hand. "Never mind. Let's change the subject. I hear we're having steak for dinner."

I picked my book off the coffee table and found my page. He snatched it from me, snapped it closed, and put it back in its spot. I propped my elbow on the arm rest, my chin on my fist, and gazed out the window. Raindrops clung to the glass, turning the lone oak tree, the lawn, and the forest beyond into a Monet painting.

"Are you always like this?"

I ignored him.

"So aloof. Too good for conversation."

"I am *not* aloof."

"You come off that way."

"To people who harass me, maybe."

"Do you want me to leave?"

The familiar throes of loneliness hit me from nowhere. I was too shocked by it to answer. Of course I wanted him to leave. It was my room, and I could tell him to leave, and Fran would support me. Martin would support me. But I couldn't form the words. Was I so lonely as to crave company from one of my own captors? Fearghus would have been furious to know I'd given in so easily. The fury might've been powerful enough to raise him from the grave.

Paul scooted to the edge of his seat. "What did I say?"

"Nothing." My eyes burned.

"What is this?" He picked up my book. "Ah, Thoreau." He held the book against his chest. "'Only that day dawns to which we are awake. There is more day to dawn. The sun is but a morning star.' There, I just ruined the end for you."

I took it away from him.

"So how long does that baby normally sleep?"

"Anywhere from ten minutes to five hours."

"Shit." He surveyed the room. "Got a deck of cards in here?"

"I miss my family." I was choking, crying into my hands. No warning, no ability to stop it. My family was all I had holding me together after Fearghus died. Now I had no one but a baby who conjured the image of Fearghus every time I looked at him, whose very presence had caused my imprisonment there. The only person I had left was responsible for the hole in my heart. And he was a baby. It wasn't his fault. My blame of him was a knife twisting in that hole. I couldn't take it anymore.

I regained my breath and lowered my hands. "Tell me what they did to Fearghus."

Paul had moved to the coffee table. His knees touched mine. He watched me, his expression neutral. He must've not known which Fearghus.

"To Trey," I said.

"I wasn't there."

"But you know what they did. I need to know if they're going to do it again."

"I don't know specifically. They're going to do a lot of things to him."

"He had a dark spot on his tongue."

He glanced away, then back at me. "Poison."

"He had a cut on his heel."

"Blood sample. And to see how he heals."

"Why?"

He shrugged. "You need to be talking to Martin about this, not me."

"I will talk to Martin. I need to know now."

He stood and took a handkerchief from my desk, dropped it in my lap, and sat back down on the coffee table. I wiped my eyes and my nose.

"That's all I know." He looked quickly at the door. "In case you haven't noticed, I don't get involved in a lot of stuff they do. I get roped into it, but I don't volunteer. It's too much work. Martin, Pierce, and Lew are better at it anyway." He placed his hands on my knees. "Better?"

Two concentrated points of pure comfort radiated from his touch. I could've denied it, but why? I couldn't lie—a man's solid strength was comforting in the most primal way. Maybe it didn't matter who it came from. My husband was dead. He was not coming back.

"Can I say something?" Paul asked.

I nodded. He didn't need my permission. These people did what they wanted.

"You miss them, but why? They're fine. Living their lives. Look where you're living now. Like a queen. Why make us force you to join the family? Why not just do it? Many people would kill to be one of us. Many people have."

I twisted in the chair, knocking his hands off my knees.

"Just hear me out. They're still your family. We can be too, for now. Everything will be so much easier if you just accept it. Why make it hard? You're only hurting yourself."

"Did Martin put you up to this?"

He straightened his back, looking very surprised. It was an expression I'd never seen on him. He was the only one in the family with brown eyes, as rich and varied in tone as rain-soaked tree bark. Maybe he got them from his mother, but I hoped I'd never know. The mistress of the house frightened me more than all of them combined, even though she'd been hiding in her room since my first day there. If I'd given birth to the Moore brothers, I'd have probably been doing the same thing.

Fearghus bleated in his crib. I released Paul from my question and went to him. He gummed his fist while I changed his diaper, then I latched him on and draped a blanket over my shoulder.

Paul was standing. "Ready?"

I sat. "I have to feed him now."

"Woman, this piano lesson has turned into a day-long event." He fell to the sofa.

"You don't have to do it."

He rolled onto his back and covered his eyes with both arms. "Wake me when you're done."

He never had a chance to fall asleep because he wouldn't stop talking. Fearghus lost interest in me quickly, too captivated by the newcomer in our normally quiet room.

In the ballroom Paul coerced me to sit on the piano bench next to him. He eyed Fearghus on my lap then turned around and whistled so loudly I instinctively covered Fearghus' ears. A man appeared in the doorway.

"Bring us a blanket for the baby. And some toys."

"What did you have in mind, sir?"

"I don't know. Rattles and stuff. Whatever babies dig."

The man left and Paul went to the bar. He returned with two short tumblers of iced alcohol. So weary of rejecting drinks in that house, I'd succumbed to saying nothing. Pouring drinks was such a formality to them, and it'd become a custom for Paul to bring me one but end up drinking it himself.

The man reappeared with a blanket. Paul spread it on the floor, stepped back, and frowned at it. "That's not going to work. It needs to be softer. Bring one of those fluffy bed covers."

"A bedspread, sir?"

"Bring two of them."

After the man left Paul noticed my raised eyebrows. "The longer the baby is comfortable, the longer we have, right?"

I watched him take a long drink from his glass, unsure if I should voice my thoughts.

He tapped his temple. "See? I'm catching on."

"I don't know why anyone would go to such lengths to make the plague of their bloodline so comfortable."

"But, sweetheart, that's just it. The more comfortable he is, the less of a plague he'll become."

Fearghus would see through these games. I knew it. Deep down, he'd know who he was. It didn't matter I was gagged against telling him the truth. He'd know.

Once Fearghus was lying on his back, happily kicking two socked feet on a plump fluff of blankets, Paul and I sat together on the bench, his drinks on the piano, my hands in my lap. He showed me the notes on the keys, the notes on the music, and when he reached for my hands to place my fingers on the keys, a voice assaulted the room. "Son."

Paul stilled. He released the tiniest of sighs, withdrew his hands from mine, and stood. "Father."

The master was too far away to be a threat to Fearghus, but it took effort to keep myself seated. Jumping in his presence awarded him satisfaction, displayed a weakness I refused to possess.

"When do you plan to tell me you've dropped out?"

Paul was again at the bar, refilling his drink. "I'm just taking a break."

"You lying shit."

"Okay, then I've dropped out. How's that? Harvard is shit. Cambridge is shit. Yet when I'm there I'm bored shitless. Go figure that one out."

The air in the room seemed to fold. As I snatched Fearghus from his little bed on the floor, the master crossed the room to Paul and seized him by the hair on the back of his head. "Get out of my house. I don't want to see your worthless face again."

Held at an awkward angle that twisted his body to the side, Paul stared at nothing, his face smooth. The master released him, shoving him into the bar. Paul braced both hands on the counter as if preparing to leap over it. The master calmly crossed the room and left. Paul's gaze remained fixed on empty air. I was afraid to speak. To move. I couldn't stand so still for much longer.

Fearghus fussed. Paul looked at us. His eyes focused and he chuckled under his breath. "You know how many times he's said that to me? He doesn't mean it." He walked toward me then stopped. He looked at the table behind the sofa. "*To hell with him!*" he shouted, kicking the table so hard it shoved the sofa several feet toward me. The table crashed to the floor. Fearghus' wide eyes watched my face, waiting for a cue of danger, a cue to cry. I hugged him against me. Don't cry. Please don't cry.

I ran around the piano. Paul stomped the downed table. Wood splintered and cracked. He stomped again. He picked up a lamp from the floor and hurled it on top of the mess that had been the table. Someone had to have heard the noise; someone needed to come in and stop him. He'd transformed into a wild animal. And I didn't know what he was going to do next.

He hovered over the pile of wood and glass, chest heaving, watching it like it was a fallen opponent he was daring to get up and attack him. He drained his glass, still in his hand by some miracle. He strode to the bar, took a big bottle of liquor, and left the room as if he were the only one there.

I took a few uneasy steps away from the piano. The mess of broken furniture on the floor seemed to claim me as its owner now that I'd been left in the room alone with it, but there was no easy way for me to clean it up. Before I was able to call for help, the room turned jagged, like every object had splintered and cracked to create tiny puzzle pieces that slowly became more granular then brightened to white.

A thought reached me from far away: *it's happening again.* I was holding Fearghus. I couldn't drop him. I sunk to my knees, feeling for the floor with one hand, blinded by that white. The pieces fell off, the splintered curtain of white spilling away to reveal a new scene. My room. A little boy jumping on the bed. Me, standing by the windows, bouncing a baby with hair blonder than mine. A man appeared in my bathroom doorway, razor in hand, shaving cream covering half of his face. Martin. His lips moved, and the little boy jumping on the bed plopped onto his back. Fearghus.

"It's not real."

The cracks in the wood floor pressed into my palm. The dizzying silence faded; the sounds of the house resumed.

"It's not real," I said again.

Fearghus' sage-green eyes filled my vision. The little forehead dimple appeared between them. I sat flat on the floor and lowered him into my lap. He withdrew his head a bit, like he was trying to assess me. I couldn't possibly have another baby. Even if one of them forced himself on me, there were ways to prevent a child. This house was haunting me, embedding visions in my head to make me agreeable. Complacent. Accepting of a life I did not want. But a house couldn't do that. Only a person could.

Martin was with me when I had the first vision. He must have planted a seed to mutate in my mind, even while he was gone. He'd accused me of affecting him. But all along, he'd been the one affecting me.

CHAPTER 12

DAYS OF RAIN and Paul's absence made me realize how reliant on him I'd become for entertainment. Fran moved my meals from my room to the kitchen to encourage my appetite and also keep an eye on what went into my stomach. The bustle of cooking was a world I missed, yet instead of reminding me of the pain of my stolen life, it seemed to cradle it, to tuck it in and keep it safe where the torment of memories couldn't turn my stomach and smother my heart.

I missed Fearghus less in this life. Nothing about that house could've ever reminded me of him. The Moores had forced me into a new world, had taken the task of my moving on as their own. At my little house in Chicago, I'd thought of Fearghus every minute of every day. I'd thought of him in the morning, when I had the bathroom sink to myself. In the evening, when I set one place on the table for dinner. When I ate I'd watch his empty spot where he should've been hunched over his plate, devouring a dinner in five minutes that had taken me an hour to prepare.

I'd think of him when I'd pull down my side of the bed but not his. When I'd lie like a cold stone under the covers, remembering his warm hand sliding around me, settling on my belly, pulling me against him, even when I was mad at him. That smell of wet dust he could never seem to scrub from his skin, missing. He worked so hard at the job I'd known about, and at the job I hadn't. The job that killed him. He might've died in the house where I now lived. I had found comfort in the kitchen that fed the people who killed him.

And no matter how many times I'd gotten mad at him, he never argued with me. Had he known he would die young?

If I claimed he was not Fearghus' father, they'd need proof. They'd have ways to test for it, and Fearghus would have to pass the test for my plan to succeed. I had to remove the Donnelly part of him. There was a way. I would get the wording from Mam. The ingredients could be gathered or grown myself. Collecting and hiding them wouldn't be easy, and it'd take time. The hardest part would be destroying the only part of my husband I had left.

Eleanor included me in her small kitchen tasks and helped me with Fearghus, and with each passing day I found myself more included in the work of the kitchen. My longing for any domestic task was met with something new each day: potatoes to peel, sauce to stir, cup-cakes to ice. When Paul materialized at the counter one day, I tried to ignore the rush of his comforting familiarity in my new space.

He planted his elbows on the counter and leaned toward me. "I leave you for a few days and this is what it's come to?"

"I like to keep busy."

He lifted an eyebrow. "There are other ways to keep busy."

"Where'd you go?" I shouldn't have brought any attention to that day, to that hideous monster that had possessed his body, but it was too late.

He swiveled on the stool away from me. "Nowhere important."

I scraped my carrot skins into the trash can. I had to change the subject, think of something else to say. "Want a carrot?" I looked up, but it was Pierce's face I saw. He plopped down onto the stool next to Paul, who was still staring across the room.

Pierce elbowed Paul. "Doesn't she look foxy in that apron?"

Paul spun slowly toward me and smiled big.

Pierce plucked a carrot off my cutting board and held it in front of his mouth. "We should've put her to work a long time ago. I can think of a few … things I'd like her to do for me."

"Hose you down outside like a dog?" Paul asked. He looked like he wanted to apologize for his brother, but I knew he wouldn't. Not in front of him. I should've told him not to bother even thinking it. Nothing he could've said would be a suitable apology for Pierce Moore.

Pierce caught my glance at Fearghus happily snuggled in Eleanor's lap across the room. "Speaking of dogs, I'm not here to do anything to your little *maistín*. Not today, anyway." He bit the tip off the carrot and chewed.

I went back to chopping. The tip on down to the end. Small and round, just like Ruby wanted for her soup.

The sound of Pierce's chewing built a chaos in my head, smothering the buzz of activity and voices in the kitchen behind me. He stopped chewing. "I still have Fearghus Donnelly's wallet. Do you want it back?"

My knife paused on the cutting board, but I compelled it to move again.

"Not much in there. His driver's license. A cute picture of you. I took the cash as repayment for the bullets we lost to his skull. And his leg. And both his feet, if I remember correctly. Right, Paul?"

Paul said nothing. I blinked away the blur. Words couldn't hurt me. All words from him were lies.

"And the cleanup. That room, both the cars. He bled everywhere. What a mess."

Our porch. His blood all over our porch, even though he was already dead. Arthur couldn't get it clean. He had to paint it.

Paul grabbed Pierce's sleeve and yanked him halfway off the stool. "Did you forget what Martin told you?"

Pierce twisted free. "That little *maistín* can't understand what I'm saying. We have years before we have to watch what we say."

"You want to explain that to Martin? He'll be back tomorrow night."

"Tomorrow night? Shit." Pierce leaned over the counter toward me. There was no humor in his smile. "I didn't get a taste of her yet."

A hush settled around me. Several pairs of eyes shifted toward us, then quickly away. These Moore boys said and did what they wanted and no one complained. If I stabbed him with my knife, what would they do to me? If I killed him, maybe it wouldn't have mattered what they did to me. He'd be dead.

But they wouldn't just hurt *me*. They'd take it out on Fearghus.

Paul grabbed Pierce's sleeve again. Pierce was busy digging in his pocket, unable to defend himself. Pierce tossed an object in front of me before Paul shoved him toward the door.

Fearghus' wallet, the one I'd given him for his birthday before he died. Hot tears stung my eyes. I tried to breathe but the air had turned solid. Maybe it was a vision like the others. It wasn't real. I needed to return my attention to what I was doing. Cutting carrots. Small and round. My fingertip ignited. A hand closed over Fearghus' wallet and then it was gone.

"Sloane!" Paul snatched the knife and clutched my hand. "You're supposed to cut the carrots, not your fingers. Holy earth!" He'd spun me to face him, my index finger clamped between his two hands like a sandwich. Blood trickled between his hands and spotted the tile floor. Paul glanced down at the drips that were already making a puddle, then back up at me. "My god did you cut it off?" He released pressure on my finger to take a peek. My finger pounded—

hot, wet, and open. The room darkened at the edges, swirling. "No, but you got it good."

Someone held my shoulders from behind. "Sit her down."

Paul backed me to a chair at the table, still clamping my finger in both his hands. Someone pushed a chair against the backs of his legs, and he sat facing me. "Pressure. It will stop in a minute."

Towels and bandages landed on the table next to us.

"Wrap it up, Master Paul."

"Nah, I got it." He grinned at me. "But you'll probably get a horrible infection. I never wash my hands." He addressed the room. "Did someone call Jo?"

"On her way."

"She used to be a nurse," he said to me.

Eleanor came around the table with Fearghus so he could see me. He tangled a hand in my hair, and she went to work prying his fingers free.

I'd seen Jo around the house but I'd never learned her name. She replaced Paul and examined my finger. "Not as bad as it looks. I think you'll be okay without stitches. Let's get you cleaned and bandaged up."

Martin was due home tomorrow night, and Pierce would retreat. It was easy to attach my warm relief to Martin the person, and I was sure that was part of his plan. I had to keep it separate. Relief followed Martin due to the power he held over Pierce, the simple protection he could offer me. This arrangement served him first, to preserve his plan to steal my child and force him to become one of them. It only served me as a side effect. He was going to have to think of a new way to trick me. Now that I knew the visions were his doing, they weren't going to work anymore. Just like the torment from Pierce couldn't hurt me. What he said they'd done to my husband was made up. Nothing they said was true, therefore nothing they said could hurt me.

Jo looked up at me. "I know it hurts. Please don't cry."

She didn't know how insignificant the pain in my finger was compared to everything else. I felt like I was falling backward in time. I was stepping into this house for the first time—terrified, jumpy, the prey in a predator's lair. So close to losing control. I'd never be able to live there unless I could be strong despite what they threw at me. I had to live there for Fearghus. His life needed to be normal. If I couldn't give him that, I'd fail.

Back in my room I sat at my desk. Fearghus lay in his crib, working the blankets in his fingers while cooing at the ceiling. And I wrote:

> *I live for Fearghus*
> *I will not cry*
> *I am a Moore on the outside*
> *I am a Bevan on the inside*
> *I will make the most of this life*
> *I will teach Fearghus to be strong*

Six simple goals, given life with paper and pen. To succeed would be to keep us both from falling victim to the Moores. To beat the Moores at their own game.

In the morning Fran brought my breakfast into my room instead of walking me down to the kitchen which had become the norm. I felt no need to speak up until I realized how quiet she was being, how gentle her movements were.

"Fran—"

She raised a quick finger to her lips.

"What?" I whispered.

"Paul's asleep in your sitting room," she whispered back.

"He is?" I said too loudly, since she shushed me mid-sentence. "Why?"

"I thought *you* might know that, madam. His breakfast is here too. Please call for me if you need help dressing." She slipped out, closing the door to my sitting room behind her.

I put on a housecoat and peeked into my sitting room. Sure enough, Paul was crumpled on the little sofa there, snoring softly. Fearghus screamed from the other side of the room. I cursed and shut the door, but unless Paul was a sound sleeper I knew it was too late. Fearghus wouldn't calm down until I carried him to the windows to look at our oak tree, stripped of most of its leaves and shivering in what I imagined to be a cold late November wind.

"I smell food." Paul came through my door, rubbing his hair. He yawned.

I became aware of my own tangled hair, but I couldn't put Fearghus down to smooth it.

"Could I have a few minutes to get dressed?"

Paul waved a hand and went for the food. "You're fine. Let's eat. Ah, pancakes and eggs. Perfect."

"Is there something wrong with your bed?"

He already had a mouthful. He exaggerated his chewing then swallowed. "Just playing bodyguard. Stop talking. Eat." He patted the sofa next to him.

I took the chair across from him, settled Fearghus in the crook of my arm, and picked up my fork. "Paul?"

He halted his attack on his pancakes for a brief look my way. Fearghus reached for my bandaged finger, captivated by it.

"Will you buy me some music?"

He straightened his shoulders. "That I can do. Anything specific?"

"Jazz. Miles Davis, Coltrane, Anita O'Day."

He held up a finger and went to my desk to jot them on my paper pad. "What else?"

"Just that for now. Maybe some more after a while?"

"Tell me what you want and I'll get it." He returned to his food, but the fork paused midair and his eyes focused beyond me. "You were supposed to be home tonight."

I turned around. Martin stood in my doorway. His clothes, normally pressed to perfection, were creased and tired just like the man who wore them. With a rolled newspaper and hat tucked under one arm and a briefcase in the other hand, he looked like he'd just stepped off his plane. His attention shifted from Paul to me, then back to Paul.

I waited for him to speak, but it was Paul who spoke again. "Did you catch an earlier flight?"

Martin said nothing. The day's growth of fuzz on his face reminded me of the vision I'd had of him shaving in my bathroom, of me holding the blond-haired baby. I turned away from Martin, wishing they'd both leave so I could flush all the food down the toilet and go back to bed. My heart beat in my ears, in my head, like I'd just been caught doing something wrong. Paul took a bite and chewed, watching Martin.

"We'll talk later," Martin said, and I heard him leave the room.

Paul cleaned his plate and set it down, smiling the whole time. "You know what he's thinking?"

I shook my head, but from his pleased smile I had an idea.

He pointed at me, pointed at himself, and nodded. "I'm just going to let him think it for now. He's always so collected. It's nice to see him squirm once in a while."

I felt a sudden need to squirm myself. I wasn't sure what bothered me more—the suggestion that Paul had spent the night with me, or the idea that Martin would've had a problem with that. Of course Martin would've been disgusted if his brother had gotten together with a Bevan, but Paul's reaction told me Martin's problem might not have been so simple. And there was nothing simple about the flood of emotion driving through me without warning. Or the unwanted pang reminding me of Martin's disheveled appearance. Why would I be worried about *him*?

"He looked tired." The words were not mine, but they came out in my voice. And I hated them.

"He looked like he was about to blow his cool." He crossed his arms behind his head and leaned back. "And so do you."

CHAPTER 13

The air in my room pressed on me more than it ever had. None of my books held my interest. When I found myself sitting at my desk tapping my pencil, I decided to call Eleanor to watch Fearghus sleep so I could stretch my legs and pick out a better book. Winter hadn't even begun and I was cooped up in that tomb of a house like a one-hundred-year-old ghost. I hoped to find Paul to ask if he'd go walking with me outside if I promised not to run away.

As I neared the doorway to the library, I spotted a woman sitting on the sofa, gazing outside. She was dressed for a party with a bright red skirt and heels, a silk blouse and fur wrap. Her white-gloved hands rested on her lap.

Just as she started to turn toward me, I slipped around the door frame out of sight. So much for a book.

My walk took me to the ballroom where Paul was on his knees on the floor in a puddle of scattered paper. He waved me over.

"Help me out," he said, holding one page of music and sifting through the others on the floor. "I need to match these all up."

"What happened?"

He looked up at me, his biggest, best smile crinkling his eyes. "I love to spill music on the floor so I have to waste my day putting them back together. What do you think happened?"

I kneeled down to help.

"Where's Trey?"

"Sleeping."

"Wow. Getting brave leaving him alone."

"Eleanor's with him."

"You know what I mean." He went back to his search. "What brings you out of your cave?"

I picked up a page and read the title. "I wanted a new book, but there's a woman in the library and I didn't want to interrupt her."

"Yeah, that's Martin's girlfriend. She found out he's back and came running. She hasn't yet figured out Martin just likes to work, work, work and doesn't have time for women."

Martin didn't work. He gallivanted around the world on a killing spree. I shuffled the pages on the floor, looking for a matching title to the one in my hand, but then I realized I'd forgotten the title. I looked at the page in my hand again.

"Oh man." Paul sat back on his feet, shaking his head at me. "This is bad. Real bad."

"Maybe you should invest in a folder for your music."

"I'm not talking about the music."

I looked at him. From his wry smile, I'd have expected him to be making a joke, but if he had, I'd missed it.

"Don't worry. You're prettier," he said.

I went back to matching pages, and after another shake of his head and soft laugh, so did he. When we'd matched about half of the pile, Martin entered the room and went straight to the bar.

"Do you know you have a visitor?" Paul said to the mess on the floor.

Martin took his time finishing at the bar then walked over. "I handled it. Come sit with me. We need to talk."

Paul made a dramatic removal of himself from the floor and followed Martin to the facing sofas. I continued piecing together the music. If they needed me to leave, they'd ask me.

"So it's official. You've dropped out," Martin said.

"Oh, you're siding with him now? Pierce can get away with not even starting college, and I'm getting hell for dropping out?"

"Pierce is busy."

"You mean, Pierce does whatever you and the old man want him to do. Pierce is a slave for the family, so he's off the hook."

Martin glanced at me from across the room. I felt it before I saw it, and even then I couldn't suppress the reaction of meeting his eyes.

Paul said, "Sloane, come join us."

Martin didn't look away from me. "I think she's better off leaving us right now."

"Why? You want her to be one of us, so she should hang here while we talk. Maybe you should tell her what you've been doing for the past few weeks."

"What happened to her finger?"

"An accident."

"You were supposed to prevent accidents."

"She cut herself chopping vegetables. It was an accident."

"Why was she chopping vegetables?"

"I don't know. Ask her."

Martin turned his whole body toward me. I curbed the defense so eager to escape my lips. I'd done nothing wrong. If he wanted to ask me, he'd need to verbalize it instead of bully it out of me with vicious silence. But neither one of us spoke, and the moment became almost unbearable until Paul saved me. "Sloane, why were you chopping vegetables that day?"

"I was helping. I like to help in the kitchen."

Martin didn't release his glare. "You don't need to be helping in the kitchen."

"I like to."

"You're bored."

I got up and walked toward them. I was a prisoner in that house. They'd tortured my baby and claimed him as their own. They'd captured and killed my cousins. They'd killed my husband. And he was concerned about my boredom?

Paul laughed. "You sound surprised. Someone who isn't allowed to leave the house, and she's bored? Call the paper. This is front page news. But you know I can fix this easily. I'll take her out and entertain her. Just say the words."

The last sentence, spoken so slowly, so deliberately, meant so much more than the simple words themselves. The muscles in Martin's jaw clenched, and he looked away from me to stare at Paul. If Martin had been any other person, the tension in the air could've only come to blows, but I knew Martin would keep his cool as he always had. I wasn't so sure about Paul. That day he lost control felt like a dream, but I knew it had happened, and it could happen again.

Paul placed both hands on his knees and leaned toward Martin. "Look at you. You've become too wrapped in this, and you know that. You've fallen hard."

"I'd watch what I say right now if I were you."

"If I didn't know better, I'd think you were turning soft."

"Don't provoke me."

"Not following in daddy's footsteps anymore, are you? When are you going to break the news to him? When are you going to tell him that you've fallen for—"

Martin stood and jerked Paul off the sofa by his collar. A movement so fast I felt dizzy just witnessing it.

"Leave," Martin said and released him with a shove backward.

Paul steadied himself. "My pleasure. I'd rather kill you in your sleep." He gave me a long look. I shouldn't have claimed to know him well enough to recognize the bundle of concern, regret, and resignation tied tightly with unwilling surrender. This wasn't a family. It was a political structure, and not a fair one. Paul's soul was bare enough then for me to see how it was suffocating in that house nearly as much as mine. He left the room, and I was alone with Martin, caught in a net, unsure how to escape.

Martin dropped to the sofa. "You look worried. I'd have thought you'd like to see me killed in my sleep." He paused to take a swig of his drink. "It's nothing. We do this all the time. Please, have a seat."

As much as I wanted to flee that room, my need to confront him about the visions was greater. I sat across from him.

"I'm sorry I was gone so long," he said.

"You owe me nothing."

He snorted and looked past me out the window. It was shocking to see him all at once look so much like Paul. It was more shocking to see how close I'd gotten to Paul, how I was able to recognize his features in his brother, dwell on his characteristics when he wasn't in the room.

"You look like you need to say something."

Yes, I needed to say something. But where did I begin? "I know what you've done to me, and I'd like you to reverse it. It's not going to work."

He closed his eyes and rubbed his forehead. "You'll have to be more specific. I can't reverse something unless I know what it is."

"You know what it is."

"Then remind me. I'm still recovering from jet lag."

"The visions. You planted them. Whatever your goal is, it's not going to work. I'd like you to reverse whatever you've done to me."

"Like I said, I can't reverse something—"

"You accused me of affecting you before you left. But it was you, affecting me. That's manipulative on top of how wrong it already is. Remove it, or give me the means to remove it myself." I stood, all at once conscious of the time

I'd been away from Fearghus. I needed to get back to him. "I'll be in my room."

I walked past him but he was already standing, grasping my hand. I yanked it away. He took hold of my shoulders. "Sloane, I've done nothing to you."

"You've affected me with false visions." Maybe it wasn't him. Could it be someone else? Pierce? "I know it was you. You were there when the first one happened."

He released me, his fingers grazing my arms on their retreat. "I was?" He looked away, scratching an eyebrow. "That day you collapsed—you had a vision?"

If he could remember that day so easily, he had to be guilty. Weeks had passed. He'd traveled to Europe and back. He'd no doubt killed several people between then and now. A simple fainting spell wouldn't be so poignant in the memory of a man with a life like his unless it had been his doing.

"Where's the baby?" The strain in his face built a panic in me before I remembered Fearghus was safe with Eleanor. He turned to survey the room behind him.

"He's sleeping in my room with Eleanor."

Martin returned to me, his expression cleared like a true professional. Surely he wasn't worried about Fearghus. A faint pink line crossed his cheek—a recent wound, almost healed. One eye held a shadow under the skin. There was a slump to his shoulders, a heaviness to his stance. He must've met some trouble in Europe. Although he deserved it a million times over, I felt a responsibility, like there was a power inside me to prevent these things if only I could discover it.

"I'm going back to school in January," he said. "I'm taking a break from traveling. From work. My brothers are going to have to take up the slack for me. If I don't finish school now, I never will."

Something about the casual disclosure of information, or the softness of his voice, beckoned me to return the courtesy. "What school?"

"Harvard Law. But I'll fly back for the weekends."

He didn't need to be around to protect me. "I'm not afraid of Pierce."

"Pierce wants to take the room next to yours."

I walked over to Paul's mess of music and started gathering the sheets. Martin knelt down next to me. "I told him to forget it."

"It doesn't matter to me."

"It should."

He helped me collect the rest of the music and we stood up together. He handed me his stack. "A lot's going to change around here. They're converting the two carriage houses into living quarters. Paul's going to move into one. A new building is going up behind them, for an indoor pool, and another for a large garage."

"That doesn't matter to me either."

"You'll have to start joining us for family dinners. Both you and Trey. The next one is tonight." He was straining to find something that would get a reaction from me.

I am a Moore on the outside. "We'll be there."

My compliance was another goal of his. I turned and quickly left the room so I didn't have to see his victory. His silence was enough to prove it.

I am a Bevan on the inside.

I had some goals of my own: to gather or grow the ingredients I needed to purge Fearghus' father from him; to perform the rite, then convince the Moores I was unfaithful to my husband, that Fearghus Donnelly was not the father of my son; to allow them to test my statement. I had to accomplish all this with a calm mind, with a gaze toward the future. Destroying all I had left of my husband was the only way to save us from that place.

When I saw Paul sitting on the bottom step of the main staircase, I noticed the stack of music still in my hands that I should've left on the piano where it belonged. So did he, so I handed it to him.

"Thanks," he said. He hesitated like he had something else to say.

I wasn't in the mood. I brushed past him, but he caught my arm. Human touch became more special with each day it was absent. A tingle scattered through my chest. *I will not cry.* I faced him even though I needed to get upstairs to Fearghus.

He lifted my hand and ran his thumb across the bandage. "I'm really sorry about your finger. It was my fault. It shouldn't have happened."

All I could do was shake my head. I should've pulled my hand away, but the idea dissolved on its way to make my muscles move. The only compassion that dwelled inside a Moore was false—to be used for some kind of gain, to win someone over, to overpower. Martin's compassion I could expect. I could see its purpose. But Paul's? What was he trying to gain?

Footsteps came toward us and Paul looked away from me to the opposite end of the room. I started back up the steps, but not before seeing Martin with the same fixed gaze focused right on Paul.

CHAPTER 14

FRAN HELPED ME dress for a dinner in the formal dining room. I allowed her to choose from the wardrobe, since wearing a gown to dinner in one's own home was such an outlandish notion I couldn't trust my own opinion. When she nudged me toward the mirror, another woman was standing in my place, adorned in baby-blue silk with princess sleeves and a low neckline, her bare neck accented by a diamond necklace, her hair in a French twist. She was elegantly distant. Someone who was not what she seemed.

I couldn't behold myself like that, so instead I looked at Fearghus who was also already dressed. "What if I need to feed him during dinner?"

She fiddled with the sash on my gown even though the bow was already perfect. "Then you excuse yourself, and I'll come help you. I'll be right behind you the whole time. Now I'm needed downstairs, so don't touch your hair, and don't sit down, and I'll see you in the dining room in twenty minutes."

She handed me my white gloves and left. I moved to the window. Frost sparkled on the lawn. The swirl in the air was accentuated with snowflakes almost too tiny to see.

"Knock, knock."

I focused on the reflection of the room in which I could now see Pierce standing in the doorway to my sitting room. I continued looking outside.

"I like your hair up like that, to see the back of your neck. It's my favorite spot on a woman."

If my hair had been done in pigtails with pink ribbons he'd have found a way to sexualize it. Like Martin and I, Pierce also had a goal: to degrade me. He'd do it no matter what I looked like, no matter what I was wearing.

He took a few steps toward Fearghus' crib. I turned around—the reaction he probably expected by the way he grinned. "You could thank me for the compliment."

"Thank you for the compliment."

He was visibly surprised and not so pleased. He didn't like it when I went along with him. My compliance was Martin's goal, but not Pierce's. Pierce liked to overpower me.

"I'm here to escort you down."

"You're too early."

He dropped onto my sofa. "So we chat until it's time. Or, you can just stand there, and I'll look at you." He wiggled into the cushions as if getting comfortable for a night of entertainment. "Did you hear I'll be moving in next door to you?"

"I thought that was up to Martin."

"It's up to tonight. I'm fighting him for it. He only wants that room because I want it, but it's in the bag, baby. He hasn't been in the training room for months. I train every day. I can't believe he agreed."

"Agreed to what?"

"To fight me for it." He patted the sofa cushion next to him. "Come sit by me. We need to get better acquainted. Pretty soon we'll be having breakfast together every morning."

"You won't be happy in that room. Fearghus cries all night."

"I'll shove a sock in his mouth. I have something for your mouth, too."

"Get out of my room."

He rushed me, grabbed me by the back of the neck with one hand. I straightened my legs and held still. I didn't want him to see how afraid I was, although I knew he could feel my raging pulse.

He leaned down to me. "I think you should kiss me."

The only man I'd ever kissed was Fearghus. I would never allow my memory of that to be tainted by this devil. "I'll tell Martin."

"By then it will be too late."

"Maybe. But once he finds out, you'll never get the room next door. Even if you beat him."

His fingers eased their grip on my neck, and he seemed to consider my words. He cursed on his way to the door.

Even after he was gone, it took time to steady my breath, and the angry flush that had crawled up my neck to my face still burned with no sign of retreat.

If Martin didn't win that night, my life here until that day would have been heaven compared to the new torment that awaited me. If I hadn't been locked in that awful room, I'd have gone outside to pray to the sky for something that seemed so utterly illogical on the surface: for Martin to win that night.

I stepped into my shoes and picked up Fearghus, who was frowning so intently I was afraid he might cry. He couldn't have seen or understood what had just happened. If he had any cognizant powers, Mam either didn't know or hadn't told me. I was certain she hadn't told me a lot of things. Probably not as many as I hadn't told her, like the newest: I was living in a house of violent criminals who planned brawls to settle disagreements. But first, let's enjoy our family dinner.

Paul met me at the top of the stairs, his brow furrowed and jaw tense. "Where's Pierce?"

I shrugged, tried to play cool. He offered his arm, and I accepted it and all the comfort and protection it allowed.

"Just so you know, he's up to something," he said.

"I know."

"You need to stay with me. He's all ramped up. You heard about tonight?"

"Briefly."

"Martin can't just tell him no. He's always trying to make it fair. Like Martin doesn't know he's king around here, always has been and always will be. Like we don't know. We know."

"Pierce doesn't seem to know."

He scoffed. "He forgets. He'll remember after tonight." We stopped at the bottom of the stairs. I dropped his arm, even though I didn't want to. He looked away, biting his thumb. "You know, that's why Martin's doing this. Not out of fairness, but to remind him. Pierce only learns things the hard way."

Could this have meant Martin would win for sure? Tears flooded my eyes, a mix-up of sorts. Good news shouldn't bring tears like that, but I couldn't deny how ready they were to spill at the slightest suggestion of Pierce's defeat. I shifted Fearghus higher, settling his cheek against mine in a much-needed tactile distraction of soft, warm baby skin. Footsteps came up behind me on the marble floor.

"Can I borrow Sloane?"

Paul did an elaborate bow with a roll of his hand and left me with Martin.

Martin gave me the most direct amicable gaze he'd ever given me. It was a rare thing, to receive eye contact from Martin so perfectly aimed when it wasn't a glare. "Your hair looks good like that."

That flush burned its way back up my chest, my neck. "Pierce said the same thing."

He turned his head away, and with that simple motion all friendliness was replaced by his mask of neutrality. He exhaled hard before facing me again. "I don't like being compared to my brothers."

"You should be used to it. You're just like Pierce. Except, he's honest about what he is. You hide it."

"Maybe we should talk about what you're hiding."

"You mean, how I'm hiding my son's whole family from him? My son's own imprisonment?"

"What you're hiding from me. From us. On second thought, don't tell me. I like to figure things out myself. It's more gratifying that way."

"It's always all about you, isn't it?

"Most of the time." He smiled. It was so unexpected it had me taking a step back. "That could be an advantage to you."

I turned away from him. I wasn't sure where the formal dining room was, but I wasn't going to stand there with him for one more second. Where had Paul gone?

"Sloane." Martin closed the extra step between us and handed me a record. "I bought this for you in Europe. I thought you'd like it."

I took it cautiously, reading the cover. *I Surrender Dear* by Django Reinhardt and Stéphane Grappelli. It seemed familiar, but the artists' names gave me pause. They certainly weren't American, and I wouldn't have been able to guess what music people listened to in Europe.

"All those forty-fives Eleanor plays for you don't seem to be your type."

He couldn't have known that, unless Paul had told him—but Martin was already back from Europe when I'd asked Paul to buy me that music. Martin had to be lying. He'd bought it here; it wasn't from Europe.

I flipped it over. On the back was a price tag, not in English.

"French?" I guessed.

"Yes, do you know it?" Pleasure lit his face.

"No." So he had bought it in Europe. He'd known I was craving a change from Eleanor's music before I'd known myself.

He reached to take it back, but I hugged it against me. Again, he shocked me with that smile so wide, so casual, so uncharacteristic of his usual mask of stoic politeness, I had taken another step back before I'd noticed what happened.

"I was only going to take it up to your room for you," he said.

I handed it to him and watched him sprint up the stairs and disappear down the hall. I wasn't sure if he expected me to wait. Surely I should've, after he'd given me a gift like that. I wanted to listen to it right there. What could it be? Rock? Folk? Blues? Was it sung in French? The music I'd asked Paul to get for me had weighed on me since I'd spoken the names aloud. I knew how much those songs were going to remind me of Fearghus, and I wasn't sure how strong I was. But this music was new. There would be no challenge to pull the record from the sleeve, no struggle to set the needle and keep my heart from breaking.

Martin returned, and I took his offered arm, too giddy to use better judgment and walk on my own. He was still the person he was. I knew what he was doing. But in that moment the feather of relief lifted from the tower of rocks felt more equal to the weight of a boulder. He did it all too well.

The dining room waited inside normally-closed doors beside Paul's piano room. We stepped into chilly air filling a space as grand as the ballroom and disturbingly quiet. Several members of the staff lined the opposite wall, hands clasped in front of them. I looked up at a ceiling too high for light to reach. Martin pulled out a chair for me near the middle of the long table and took the seat to my left. On my lap, Fearghus reached for the table. A piece of my silverware clattered against the floor and echoed through the room. I shifted Fearghus so I could retrieve it, but Martin placed a hand on my arm. Another piece appeared in front of me.

"Thank you," I said, but the man had already returned to his spot against the wall. The fallen silver fork lay on the marble floor.

"Leave it," Martin whispered, watching Pierce take his seat across from him. Pierce smiled at me. I lowered my eyes, swallowing a shame that should be his, not mine.

People shuffled in and took their seats. Lewis a few seats down from me. An older woman—probably the master's sister—sat across from him. Fran told me she was visiting with her two daughters who sat next to her. Paul sat on my other side, secretly patting my knee after scooting in. The master removed his suit jacket, handed it to one of the staff waiting to receive it, and sat at the head of the table. The opposite head of the table had no place setting. The mistress of the house apparently wasn't joining us. Months of living there and I was starting to wonder if she even existed.

With wine poured and soup served, still no one had spoken. Fearghus took it all in, and I dipped my soup spoon and deposited the broth into my mouth and tried to think of nothing else. The chill from the marble all around me seeped into my bones, crippling my movement and making me long for my room which now seemed like a cozy haven. I appreciated it now that I had this cold, hostile room, this unpleasant surrounding of people for comparison.

The soup bowls were removed, and when a salad landed in front of me, I noticed the master looking in my direction. My skin crawled. I shifted Fearghus to the opposite arm, and Eleanor popped up on the other side of the room on tiptoe and raised her eyebrows high. I gave her a slight shake of my head.

"Martin, tell us about Europe," the master said.

Martin nodded, but took his time finishing a bite and taking a sip of wine. The master continued to stare, probably watching Martin, not me. I didn't meet his eye to disprove it.

"Successful. It took longer than expected. We lost two men and had to regroup. Some of our France information was incorrect and I had to improvise. I'll fill you in with details once I get my notes in order." Martin aimed a pointed look at the women at the end of the table. "I can't bore you all with the rest of it."

"What are your plans?" the master asked.

"Back to Harvard in January. I'm doubling up to finish faster. I won't have time for much else. Lew, get ready."

Lewis glanced up from his bowl like he hadn't been paying attention. "Ready? I'm always ready."

"Lewis will be busy with his own schooling," the master said. "We're going to have to count on this family's rubbish to keep the machine oiled until Martin returns. Paul, are you ready with that oil can? Can you spare some time away from babysitting Miss Bevan, or would you prefer to be her full-time girlfriend and nanny?"

Martin cut in. "You can blame that on me. That was my call."

"I'm aware of whose call it was. I'm not sure it was necessary, but I'll overlook that. I can't overlook how my third son is a leech on this household while making no effort to be anything but useless and seems to enjoy babysitting *Bevans* more than supporting the family endeavors."

Paul drained his wine glass like a man dying of thirst, and I placed my hand on his knee, returning the comfort he'd given me when he'd sat next to me. I didn't need it as much as he did. One of the girls snickered; her mother hushed her. Paul faced her, but he had that unfocused look in his eyes.

"I've told him to leave the house. So he's decided to move into one of the converted carriage houses." The master swirled his glass, addressing it instead of Martin. "I find that quite suitable. Perfect for the family's livestock."

Martin set his fork on his plate. The metal hummed against the china, a single sound in a cavernous room.

Paul seized the edge of the table with both hands and shoved back in his chair. I winced away, covering Fearghus, and then Martin was up and around me, shielding us from Paul. Fearghus twisted, opened his mouth, and screamed.

Martin's body slammed stiffly against mine, almost pushing me out of my chair. I recovered in time to see him shoving Paul away from the table. Lewis charged to his side, but Martin threw an arm out holding him back. I hugged Fearghus against me and rocked, smothering his cries into my chest. Paul raised both his hands in the air, like he was the criminal and Martin and Lewis were the police. He backed up a few steps then turned and headed toward the door. The master was chewing slowly, enjoying the last bit of his salad.

Martin and Lewis returned to their seats. Paul's seat was a gaping void next to me. Entrees were served. If my plate had contained a live scorpion surrounded by cockroaches, it would've been no different to me, but I stabbed and chewed like I hadn't seen food in years and tried not to look at Paul's half-eaten salad. Fearghus squirmed and fussed, wanting away from that room as badly as I did, but I repositioned him continually and worked to gather my calm and pass it to him.

Dessert then coffee. Fearghus started a low, groaning song, worn from the struggle but unwilling to give up the fight. When Martin dropped his napkin on his plate and offered his hand, I clasped it like he was the fireman at my window and the flames were licking my back. He offered to take Fearghus, and I handed him over, too relieved by my rescue to refuse.

CHAPTER 15

MARTIN STOPPED AT the bottom of the stairs and looked at the landing above us. I reached for Fearghus, but Martin kept his gentle hold on him.

"I'm thinking you should come with me instead of going back to your room," he said.

"Come with you where?"

"To find Paul. You can help me calm him down before we lose any more furniture." He loosened his tie. "You can't just go back to your room after such a wholesome family dinner."

Now distanced from that unbearable dining room, my urge to flee to safety had waned enough to expose a lump in my stomach. Paul.

We found Paul in the kitchen, leaning against the counter and shoveling in food from a plate raised to his mouth. His eyes followed us as we closed in on him, but as we got closer it was clear he wasn't looking at me. He seemed more interested in Martin and Fearghus. I took Fearghus and sat in a chair at the breakfast table. The work area of the kitchen was a fast-moving mob of staff members cleaning up our dinner service.

"Glad to see you got your dinner after all," Martin said.

Paul's burst of laughter made me jump and Fearghus' eyes widen.

Martin picked up a wine bottle from the counter and held it up to the light. "Was this full when you started?"

Paul shrugged, closing his eyes lazily.

"Guess I shouldn't expect your help in the morning."

Paul snorted. "My help." He laughed and slapped the counter. He pointed at Martin. "You're good."

"You like throwing up? You're going to puke your guts out."

Paul patted his belly. "Can't wait." He stumbled over to me and fell into a chair. "So, Miss Bevan, how was your dinner?"

"You're drunk."

He looked around at a pretend audience in the room. Everyone was too busy to take notice of us at all. "I am?" Bone struck wood as his elbows landed on the table and his chin settled in his hands. He gave me a boyish grin. "Can I sleep on your sitting room couch again? I like sleeping on your couch. It's not technically in your room, so I think it's okay. Do you think it's okay?"

"You need to sleep in your own room." Martin's voice had turned mechanical.

"We could have breakfast together again," Paul said to me.

"You let him get to you, he wins. Do you want him to win?" Martin asked.

Paul's smile flattened. His jaw clenched, and he stared through me. I shot a look at Martin. It wasn't the time to bring that back up. Was he doing it on purpose?

Pierce burst through the door in his undershirt, pants, and bare feet. "Are we doing this?"

Martin squinted at him. "Now?"

"Chicken?"

"Okay. Now." Martin yanked off his tie and tugged his shirttails out of his pants. "Sloane, if you could—"

"I'll make sure he gets to his room." I couldn't look at him.

Martin shoved Pierce through the doorway, and Pierce laughed like an evil clown. The house had turned into a funhouse of horrors right before my eyes.

Paul stood and steadied himself on the table. "My room like hell. I'm not missing this for anything." He followed them out. I was not joining him in that madness. He was on his own.

I went up to my room, changed into a nightgown and housecoat, and sat in the rocking chair with Fearghus. The chair and the floor sang a creaky lullaby as I nursed him to sleep. I tucked the blanket tightly around his body after moving him to his crib. With his fists raised above his head on the mattress, he appeared to be jumping for joy. Would he ever find joy in that house? Would he become a part of the violence, or could I find a way to protect him from it?

What if Martin didn't win tonight?

I stood with fingertips against the cold glass of my windows. The gibbous moon laid a sheet of light on the land. It was an hour earlier in Chicago. Tara might be sleeping, just like her brother. I wanted to slip out of the room like a ghost and sail across the stars to stand above her crib and watch her sleep. To see, in person, what she looked like now. To stroke her baby-soft cheek. If my plan were to fail, if I were unable to escape that place, perhaps they'd let her come live with me and Fearghus. It would be a better alternative to stealing Fearghus' father from his being, but I doubted I'd be able to find the bravery to tell them about her.

My outer door opened and closed. Paul appeared in my doorway, holding onto the wall. "Sloane," he whispered. He took a quick glance over his shoulder.

I peered past him, fear ripening inside me. Something must have gone wrong.

He stumbled toward me, landing in my arms like a heavy, wet towel, but I couldn't hold him up. He slid halfway down my body then suddenly bolted straight and gripped the lapels of my housecoat with both hands. "You have to hide me." His eyes were all pupil.

My heart thumped. "What?"

He swallowed hard, like there wasn't one drop of moisture in his mouth. "And then it was yesterday. Yesterday? Was it yesterday?"

His hair was wet. I placed my hand on his forehead, as if a fever might explain the strange behavior. "Paul?"

"Then. It. Was. Yesterday." Each word was a sentence itself.

He was burning up and clammy, but not in a feverish way. I could see his pulse in his throat. He looked like he'd just run up and down the stairs fifty times. "Paul, what's wrong with you? Where's Martin?"

"Martin. My brother. He won, you know. Against my other brother." He started laughing—so hard he doubled over before falling to the floor on his hands and knees.

"Did you drink more wine?"

His joints gave. He smacked against the floor and rolled onto his back. "Not wine. It's much better than that."

"What?" I kneeled next to him. I needed to call Fran. Someone needed to call a doctor.

He gasped and pointed past me, toward the ceiling. "It's not all there. Look! It's dissolving!"

"Paul. What did you take?"

"Little. Slimy. D—" He looked into my eyes with sudden focus. "What starts with D?"

My hand flew to my mouth. "Paul," I whispered. "I'm calling Fran."

"No!" he yelled, and I clamped a hand over his mouth and looked at Fearghus' crib. His mouth formed an *O* under my hand, so I pulled it away. "Got it," he whispered. "No Fran. Promise me, Sloane."

Overcome by pity and understanding, I nodded. "Martin?"

"No Martin. No one. Promise." He reached for my cheek, but I turned away.

The news of Martin's victory hit me then, a drop of relief in a pool of sour anxiety. I couldn't help Paul by myself. I had no idea what to do. He was full of poison, and I had no ingredients. I didn't have my family's texts. Even if I could improvise a brew, I would've never remembered the proper wording.

He choked, gagged, and looked at me wide-eyed.

"Do you need to throw up?" I was already hauling him up. He made it to my toilet just in time. I ran the sink faucet to cover the sound then filled my cup when he was finished. He leaned against the wall, drinking the water, eyelids half-closed. If Martin would come on his own, he could help me and I wouldn't have broken my promise.

"Did Martin …" I wasn't sure what to ask.

"Martin isn't here."

I sat on the edge of the tub.

"Martin took Pierce to the hospital," he said. His eyes were closed.

"What happened?"

"It's hot on the inside, but cold on the outside, and there was another place I shouldn't have been. It was all in that place, but I can't talk about that. Do you know about that place? If you know about it, maybe I can talk about it."

"What place?"

"The place where the sea changes into stone. There is a sea around us, all the time. If you stop and listen, you can feel it." He slid down the wall to the floor.

I helped him up. His weight almost pulled me down on top of him, but I managed to get him into the other room to my long sofa. He tugged me down next to him. "It's like heaven and hell combined. You want some? I have some more."

"No." I scooted away from him. "What happened to Pierce?"

He laughed, high and airy, like his throat was tight. "Martin did. I told you."

"Martin did what?" I shouldn't have asked. I wanted to take the question back.

He broke an invisible stick over his knee. "It's not the subject today, though. The subject today is why doesn't your clock shine like the moon? It's looking at me like the moon." His face darkened. "It's looking at me," he whispered. "I don't want it to happen again." He buried his face in his hands.

I didn't know if it was the drugs and alcohol talking or the real Paul talking, but it didn't matter. Both the poison and Paul's troubles had a grip on him that had extended to me, and even though he was who he was I wanted to help him. But I didn't know how.

He lay down, his head in my lap. My hand hovered above him, undecided. It wasn't his fault he'd been born into that family. If he'd been born into my family, he'd be a normal person just like me. He *was* a normal person just like me. His circumstances had warped him, had slathered twenty years of dirt and grime onto a man who had grown from a baby just like my sweet little Fearghus. This could've been Fearghus lying in my lap. Even if he was as bad as Paul, as bad as Martin, as bad as Pierce, how could I not have comforted him?

I stroked Paul's hair. He sighed—prolonged, defeated. Wetness seeped through my housecoat from where his mouth lay against my leg. He scratched his arm incessantly, digging in too hard. I stopped his hand and held it. He shuddered. His legs twitched. He mumbled, a mixture of Irish and English, the babble of a madman.

When I opened my eyes, Martin was prying Paul off the sofa.

"Sorry," he whispered. "I didn't know he was in here."

I rubbed my eyes and looked at the clock. It was midnight. "What happened to Pierce?" I blurted before it occurred to me how close I was to the border of a dream. It was hard to determine what was real.

"Pierce is fine." He paused to look at me. "He broke his collarbone."

"*He* did?" The first word emphasized itself, like it knew something I didn't.

He heaved Paul up by the arm. "*I* broke his collarbone."

I watched him drag Paul out of my room, then I climbed into bed and closed my eyes. I should've told Martin about the LSD, but I wouldn't break my promise. And I doubted it would've mattered if I'd told him. Martin knew everything.

Paul's well-being was not my responsibility. Knowing this did not prevent me from waking up every hour until the morning sunlight warmed my room, and as soon as Fearghus and I were up and dressed, I asked the first staff member I saw to lead me to Paul's room.

CHAPTER 16

Five minutes of knocking on Paul's door, then waiting, then knocking again did not rouse Paul. Martin could've taken him to one of the numerous other bedrooms in that house, but I had to eliminate Paul's own room first. I turned the doorknob, and the door opened into so much light my eyes watered.

"Paul?" The morning sun beamed harshly through uncovered windows of his east-facing room. I entered and closed the door behind me, then thought better of it and opened the door wide. Closed doors made things too familiar.

His bed had a body-shaped dent in the bedspread, but no body. I walked around the bed and found him lying facedown on the floor.

Martin should've left someone here to watch him. I tapped his leg with my toe. Nothing. I gave him a harder push. His body rolled then recovered its position, like all his bones had liquefied.

I lay Fearghus on the rug to kneel next to Paul. I held my breath, waiting for evidence of his. The lift of his ribcage was so slight I had to place a hand on his back to make sure I wasn't imagining it. At the contact, he giggled.

"Are you playing a game?!"

He giggled again. Into the rug, he said, "They're all around you. You don't even know it." He scratched that same arm he'd been scratching the night before with a driving purpose. There was a darkened circle on the rug under his head. Whether it was drool or vomit, I needed to get him off it.

"Let's get you up in the bed." I tugged hard on his arm, but he seemed to be fused to the floor. "Paul, you have to help me."

"Love to help you." He gathered his limbs underneath himself, pushed up to all fours, and climbed the bedspread to the top of the bed like a lizard who'd been sunning himself too long. With the bedspread now piled on the floor, I was able to pick it up and cover him with it. He didn't bother to make himself comfortable, just stayed plastered to the bed with limbs in awkward positions and a silly smile on his face.

I tugged his arm out from under him so it wouldn't lose circulation. I stepped over Fearghus, happily playing with the edge of the bedspread, and closed the curtains. When I returned to Paul, he was scratching that same spot on his arm again, so I gathered the quilt from his sofa and wrapped it around his arm three times.

Fearghus rolled against my leg. I picked him up and watched Paul, wondering if that stuff would ever wear off or if he'd be forever seeing imaginary creatures and speaking gibberish. When I turned to leave, I jumped at a figure standing in the doorway.

"I'm sorry to startle you, madam."

"It's okay. I was just leaving. I wonder if someone could keep an eye on Paul?" I noticed the bottle of wine in her hands.

"Sure, madam. The master wanted this brought to Paul. Where should I put it?"

I was aware of my wide-open mouth, of the question I should've been answering, of the prickling fury clawing up my chest and back, but I couldn't seem to focus on anything except that bottle of wine. The master wanted it brought to Paul. So Paul could poison himself again. Because the master knew Paul couldn't resist it.

"Madam?"

My hand shot out. "I'll take it."

She handed it to me slowly, like she was expecting me to do something other than take it from her. It had no cork. It was ready to go. A welcome sign for someone who didn't know his own weakness.

"Thank you." I waited for her to leave. I dumped the wine into his bathroom sink and returned to my room to nurse Fearghus, to breathe, and to try hard not to cry.

When I'd succeeded in calming the shudder in my chest and the ache behind my eyes, I settled Fearghus on a blanket on the floor to play and put on the record Martin bought for me in Europe. The needle popped on the record and the music began, notes traveling through the air, into my ears, rolling through me, over me, around me. A bubbling warm bath of sound quenching a ravenous thirst, and instead of breaking my heart it mended it, from the bottom up, one stitch with each note, almost to the top, and then I glimpsed a motion in the reflection of my windows, and I turned around.

"You like it?" Martin was smiling that wide, unmasked smile, the sincerity of his rare straightforward gaze like an arrow through me.

I crumpled, and he caught me, and those damn, desperate tears ripped me in half.

Martin and I alternated turns keeping Paul company so he didn't have a moment alone when one of the many bottles of opened wine arrived in his room, the ballroom, the kitchen, or whatever room he happened to be in. Paul was aware of his father's ploy and found it plenty amusing, but Martin and I had come to an unspoken agreement that Paul couldn't be trusted on his own. Not for a while, at least.

Our other unspoken agreement concerned the night I'd fallen apart in his arms. We didn't speak of it. It had been struck from the record. I was glad we hadn't agreed to strike it from our memories, because I would've been breaking that agreement every day.

I was warned of the family dinners usually the morning of, and although I hadn't been able to decode the pattern of their schedule, their agenda had become predictable after the second one. After the soup and salad, the master quizzed his first, second, and fourth sons about school and work and received answers too vague to be meaningful to anyone. Then he spent the remainder of the dinner publicly berating his third son who, in turn, drank too much wine and became silly or violent, depending on the day. The more guests present, the more involved and comprehensive Paul's torment became. Martin played negotiator, Lewis played dumb, and Pierce enjoyed it all far too much.

One evening we arrived to a new seating arrangement with one place setting next to a highchair on the mistress' end of the table, if she were to ever join us. I knew the new place was mine—the highchair made it obvious. I tried to position Fearghus in it, but his back wasn't yet strong enough to hold him without slumping to one side, and when I looked to the staff standing along the wall for help, Martin was the one who came to my aid. He took off his dinner jacket and rolled it into a cushion to prop Fearghus in the chair.

"It'll get ruined," I whispered, but he just shrugged.

With the master and the four brothers seated, it was chillingly clear Fearghus and I had been banished to the end of the table which customarily sat empty unless guests were present. Our segregation should've been a comfort, a much-needed relief, but in that bone-cold room, under the scrutiny of an audience of staff lining the wall, all I felt was a flush of shame. My inferiority to them was alive in that room for all to see, whether it was true or not.

"It seems appropriate to remove the leaves in the table when our party is small." Martin had stood.

"Sit. There's no need for that," the master said, and watched Martin until he returned to his chair. The master launched into his usual itinerary, and I was grateful his torment of me was strictly visual instead of vocal like Paul's.

At the next dinner, my place was again set at the far end of the table. After helping me with Fearghus, Martin sat in the chair to my left as he used to, and Paul sat across from me, causing two members of the staff to jump from their positions against the wall and relocate their place settings from the other end of the table. By some miracle, the master pretended not to notice. Paul told me later he liked the view better there. Martin didn't say a thing about it.

In the evenings when the main parts of the house were dark, Paul and Martin played chess in the bedroom next to mine, which had been cleaned and refurnished as Martin's new room—a front, mostly, since I heard him leave every night, and he was never there in the mornings. After Fearghus fell asleep I found myself wandering in there more often as the nights came earlier and chillier. It was a convenient change of scenery where I could still hear Fearghus if he cried in his crib. And Martin left a quilt on his armchair just for me, so I could wrap it around my shoulders when the winter wind sneaked through his windows and pawed at the circle of warmth radiating from his fireplace.

His room was my room's twin, with the same wall of French doors leading to a wide balcony, only his doors weren't bolted shut like mine. His bed, covered in a ruby-red bedspread and mounds of matching pillows that retained their exact positions night after night, was on the far wall by his bathroom, a long walk from his fireplace and lounging area that had enough seating for a party. Other than the lounging area, the only part of his room that appeared to be in use was the stately mahogany desk holding neat stacks of files and paper. His sitting room shared a door with mine. It remained locked. I wasn't sure who had the key.

I don't remember why we started speaking Irish during these evenings, but I was grateful to speak it with adults again. I feared losing my family's language now that I was without them. The same sad thought occurred to me every night I was there with Martin and Paul speaking Irish and playing chess: how could our families share such an uncommon language yet hate each other so? Were we not the same people?

One December evening Fearghus was fussier than he'd ever been. Nothing I did comforted him. Instead of wearing himself out, he became more frantic. His normal bedtime passed by, and just when panic began to nip at my heels, someone knocked on my door. It was just like Fran to come when I needed her. She had a sixth sense.

When I opened the door, it wasn't Fran. It was Martin.

"Is it too late to bother you?"

I glanced at the clock. It was almost nine. Normally, I would've said yes, but with Fearghus in that mood I didn't think it mattered what time it was. I wouldn't be getting any sleep that night. "We're up." I noticed Martin's coat draped over his arm. "Did you just get in?"

"No. There's a total lunar eclipse tonight. Did you know?"

Fearghus balled his fists and cried harder. I shifted him to my other arm and bounced him. I'd learned of the eclipse from Mam. Without another source of information, I had to pretend not to know, and Fearghus' noise filled the space of what should've been my answer.

"I'm going outside to watch it. I wondered if you wanted to come with me."

"I can't leave Fearghus like this."

"So bring him." He draped his coat on my sitting room sofa and reached for him. "I'll hold him while you get ready."

Fearghus' eyes were squinted so tightly I was afraid he was going to hurt himself. Fresh air might've calmed him down. Maybe Martin's arms would offer something new to distract him from whatever was bothering him. I handed him to Martin and went into my dressing room for heavier clothes. Martin helped me bundle Fearghus, and I followed him outside.

The chilly air offered an immediate distraction, but we weren't halfway across the lawn before he started crying again. The new intensity of it stopped me cold. I wished he could have told me what was wrong. I couldn't read his mind. A better mother could. A better mother wouldn't be working so hard to subdue her own tears—she'd be working to soothe her child's. I needed help. I needed Mam.

"What's wrong with him?" Martin blew on his hands to warm them.

I had to turn away from him to compose my face. "I don't know. Teething?"

"Did you call for Fran? She raised all of us."

I cuddled Fearghus close, his cheek against mine, and wrapped his blanket around him. He stopped crying, but his breath was ragged. He was only taking a break. It would soon start again.

"Look," Martin said, and we both looked up at the moon, partially in shadow.

In my recent dreamtalk with Mam, she'd mentioned the eclipse and told me to keep Fearghus close. It seemed to be a broad statement at the time. I needed to ask her what she meant by that, if anything at all. If she knew there'd be something wrong with Fearghus on that night. As if to prove it, Fearghus took a breath, stiffened his body, and screamed. I turned him to face out and bounced him.

"You have something …" Martin dabbed my face with his handkerchief then pulled back and squinted at a dark spot on the cloth. He peeled Fearghus' blanket away from his face. "His ear is bleeding."

Blood trickled from Fearghus' ear, onto his blanket. Martin exposed his other ear. "Both sides."

The panic from earlier reached me, sunk itself into my heels and climbed my legs.

"Let's get him inside," he said.

We crossed the lawn and entered the kitchen, Fearghus screaming the entire way. The kitchen was dark and vacant. Martin turned on every light, and I unwrapped Fearghus and sat with him on my lap. His crying mouth was open so wide I could see all the way down his throat. His eyes were shut so tightly they could barely pinch the tears out.

Martin brought a kitchen towel wetted with warm water, dabbed my cheek then dabbed Fearghus' ears. "It'll stop. It probably already has."

"Why are they bleeding in the first place?" I whispered it so I wouldn't yell.

Martin shook his head.

"Can I call my mam?" A question balanced on the head of a pin suspended over a deadly fall.

He stopped dabbing to look at me. "How about if I call a doctor?"

"A doctor? Is he like us? Will he know about us?"

He exhaled hard. Looked at the phone on the wall, then back at me. "I'll go talk to my mother."

I closed my eyes. If Fearghus would quiet for two seconds, I could think.

"To talk to my mother, I'll need Fran's help. We'll wake her up if we have to."

"What does *your* mother know about *my* baby?" From the tight wad of anger pressing on my chest, I was surprised it didn't come out as a yell.

He looked straight into my eyes. "She knows a lot of things about him."

I slapped him. My hand, still chilled from the air outside, could've shattered and I wouldn't have known the difference for the pain it caused. I shoved myself back, afraid he'd hit me back or hit Fearghus, but the chair teetered and clung to my legs and I lost my balance. Martin caught me and Fearghus before I stumbled. I struggled. He released me, and I took a quick step back. He righted the chair as Fearghus wailed.

"I'm sorry. I just—" My heart beat wildly. It was obvious I was more surprised than him. He must get slapped often.

"No need to apologize."

Heat surged to my hand and my palm prickled, itchy and crawling. I wanted to look at it, make sure it wasn't bleeding. Martin's cheek was splotched with red.

"I didn't mean to—"

"Yes, you did." He wouldn't stop looking at me.

I pressed the palm against the middle of my forehead, bearing down. If the crying didn't stop, I didn't know what I'd do. How long could a baby cry? Hours? Days?

"I'm calling a doctor. Go to your room. I'll send Fran up to help until the doctor arrives."

"Don't wake Fran. She works too hard." I walked past him toward the doorway.

"I'll give her tomorrow off."

I turned to face him. "Paid?"

"Of course."

"Two paid days off." I should've asked for a week. It'd give more room to bargain.

He looked away, but I caught the smile that touched his eyes. "Done."

On my way upstairs I imagined the trail of noise Fearghus was dropping through the house. If Martin grabbed hold of it in the kitchen and tugged, Fearghus and I would've come bouncing down the stairs, returning to him like a yo-yo. It was a lesson to me, to appreciate Fearghus' normally content manner. I wanted to plant my feet on sacred earth and pray his demeanor wasn't changing, that this wasn't the beginning of a new time in which he'd become aware of his situation and had started his protest.

Fran came to me wearing her housecoat, a frown, and a furrowed brow. "I can hear him all the way down the hall. And blood? Martin said there was blood."

I removed one of the cloths I was holding against his ear and held it up for her to see.

"Oh, you poor dear. We'll get him fixed up. Don't worry."

His screaming ramped up, so I went back to humming "*dTigeas a' Damhsa?*" while Fran fussed around us, repositioning Fearghus, replacing bloodied cloths with new ones. I finally got him to nurse, but it only lasted a few minutes. Fran took him, tried to distract him, cradled him, rocked him, rubbed his belly, patted his back. Nothing appeased him.

Martin arrived with the doctor who was so collected at that hour I wondered if he was nocturnal. He examined Fearghus on my bed while Fran held my hand and Martin stood behind me—three people desperate for news that could only be bad. How bad it would be was the question.

The doctor straightened up. Fran tightened her grip on my hand. I watched the doctor's back. I wasn't sure what he was waiting for, unless he was taking time to phrase bad news.

He turned around, looked at me, then at Martin. "He checks out fine."

Martin stepped forward so he was next to me, his arm brushing mine. "He doesn't look fine."

"I'm aware of that. The crying and discomfort would most likely be due to teething if it weren't for the blood from the ears. The blood—" He shook his head. "I'll be honest. I've never seen it before with no other symptoms or some kind of trauma. We can do more thorough testing at the hospital. You should come immediately." He started to pack away his things.

They'd never let Fearghus or me leave that house. Even if Martin accompanied me, even if they sent an army with us. We were their prisoners, and on that principle alone, we couldn't leave. They didn't care if Fearghus suffered; they'd made him suffer themselves. He could've cried like that forever and they would've looked the other way.

I picked him up. Martin walked the doctor out and Fran just shook her head. She was thinking the same thing. If a doctor couldn't help Fearghus at the house, there was no help for him.

Somehow I'd have to find a way to force myself to sleep. I needed to talk to Mam.

"Madam," Fran whispered. She pointed to Fearghus.

His eyes were closed. His ear was clean. No new blood since the doctor wiped it to examine it. I swiveled his head. The other ear was clean as well. Air seemed to flood into the room. I'd been suffocating and now I could breathe.

Fearghus released a big sigh. Fran covered her mouth, holding her breath along with me. He collapsed in my arms, finally quiet. We were both staring at him when Martin rejoined us, preoccupied, like he didn't notice the noise had stopped.

"We have a bit of a predicament here," he said without meeting my eye.

I almost didn't want Martin to notice the quiet so I could hear what he'd offer to do, or if he'd allow us out of the house to help Fearghus.

"No, Master Martin, look. He's better now."

Martin came to me. He checked both of Fearghus' ears, examining him almost as thoroughly as the doctor. When Martin looked at me, the unprotected relief in his face was like a burst of electricity through my blood, and I was the metal rod grounding it into the earth.

CHAPTER 17

JANUARY, 1965

WE MANAGED TO get Paul into the new year without another near lethal consumption of booze. Paul seemed to know when to stop, but I worried it was only because he felt the pressure of Martin's and my careful watch. Pierce's broken collarbone had healed along with his overactive mouth, but only for the time being. Paul told me this cycle was as predictable as the sunrise: Pierce's behavior would deteriorate until Martin deemed him too far out of line, then Martin would break him, achieving a more obedient Pierce for a few months before his decline would start all over again. I was living with a pack of dogs.

It was hard for me to talk to Mam. I had to be careful with the things I said. If she found out I'd joined up with Martin to help Paul, she'd be seeing only one frame of a long and complex film. My situation with the Moore brothers wasn't something I could explain through a dream. It wasn't even something I could explain to myself, or wanted to explain. I already knew I was a traitor. I couldn't have Mam knowing it too. Not so soon, at least. Mam had a way of knowing everything.

Mam had no answers for me about that night of the eclipse when Fearghus got sick. She said she'd ask the others, but nothing came. Either no one knew, or what they knew was too heavy to drop on me with everything else I had to handle.

One January night while the snow softly piled on my balcony, I put Fearghus to bed and headed next door for our chess night to find Martin alone on his sofa with his feet resting on the coffee table and his arms crossed behind his head, staring at the ceiling. A fire danced in his fireplace. Dropping his feet to the floor when he saw me, he leaned forward to pull the chessboard in front of him.

"*Mise agus tusa*?" he said.

Me and him. No Paul.

"I don't know how to play." The doorknob slipped back into my hand and I paused there, not opening that door to return to my room, even though I knew I should.

"You've been watching us play for weeks." He stood and dragged my armchair opposite his spot on the sofa. "Sit."

"Is Paul coming?"

"Paul went out." He regarded my expression, which was probably more worried and protective than it should've been for a twenty-year-old man whose family had committed countless crimes against my own. "He's fine. He's over it for now."

"In this snowstorm?"

"Would you like to be white or black?"

I didn't answer, but my legs carried me to my chair and I sat. Being alone with Martin was a better fate than staring at the walls of my room until sleep found me.

"How about you're white? Ladies first." He spun the white pieces to my side.

I advanced a pawn.

"Difficult move."

He rarely joked like this, but I supposed someone had to do Paul's job when he was absent. Martin's hair was due to be clipped. He never let it get even slightly long, even though all three of his brothers had let theirs go shaggy. Eleanor said as long as Martin kept trimming his hair they would always be one Beatle short.

"You're even prettier when you smile." He held my gaze while advancing his own pawn.

My mind raced for a change of subject. "If I had some of my things sent here from home—"

"What kinds of things?"

I pretended to study the board to cover my hesitation. I considered what my answer would give away and decided I was safe. "Books."

His eyes raised from the chess board, but only made it halfway to my face where they paused to address my hands in my lap. "They'll check every page."

Knowing Mam could disguise them, I told the first of many lies I'd have to tell. "I have nothing to hide." My toes curled in my slippers. I wasn't adept at lying, and he'd see it.

He returned his attention to the board, but I could tell his focus had waned from our game. We played through a few moves while the suspense nearly burst the room. He owed me an answer—he knew that as well as I did. If I asked the question again, my polite request would become a plea. He wouldn't satisfy a plea. It was below him, as pleading was below me.

Capturing my rook, he set it aside, put both hands on his knees, and leaned toward me. "Wait until I go back to school. You can have them sent to my Cambridge apartment. I'll bring them home to you from there."

A question borne of my surprise escaped before I could squash it. "What?"

He closed his eyes. "I'm not repeating it."

"Why would you ... do that?"

"It's just easier. Your move."

I studied the board, suddenly forgetting how to play. Getting my family's texts was the first step of my escape from the estate. With them, I'd be able to do more than remove Fearghus' father from him. I could make my now limited time there more comfortable for both of us. I would be armed.

A knock pounded the door. Martin glanced at me, then at the door. "Come in."

Two men dressed all in black entered.

"You know not to come to this room."

"Yes, sir. Mr. Moore directed us here."

"Did he." It wasn't a question, or a request for verification. It was laced with too much disgust, too much offense. Like Martin knew this would happen. A hint of a line appeared between his eyebrows—the subtlest break in his mask I wouldn't have noticed a month before. "I'll meet you in my other room in five minutes."

"It can't wait five minutes, sir."

"Take it to Pierce."

"Pierce is ..." Both goons looked at me.

"Out of the room," Martin barked, standing up. They followed him out the door.

When I felt a strain in my neck, I realized I'd been staring at the door far too long. It didn't matter what was going on, and I was better off not knowing if they were downstairs killing more of my cousins. I faced forward, the chessboard leering at me. Martin was either letting me win, or he was dragging out his victory to make it seem harder won, to make it look like I had a chance of winning. He was playing a game while playing a game. I didn't know what I was doing. Why I was in there.

I moved all the pieces back to their starting positions with more hostility than needed. It was a stupid endeavor that would erase the evidence, but it wouldn't erase the time I'd spent with him, or recover the slice of my soul I'd lost in that room, tonight or any night. Just because Paul was normally present didn't make it right. I shoved my armchair back to its spot, folded the quilt, and headed for the door.

Martin and I nearly collided in his sitting room. "You're leaving?"

"Yes. Sorry." Why was I apologizing?

He held up a bottle of wine in one hand, two glasses in the other, their stems crisscrossed in his grasp. "I brought wine."

"You know I don't drink."

"Then more for me. I need it." He didn't move out of my way. "We have to finish our game."

"You mean you have to finish letting me win."

He took a breath and held it. The eye contact was deepening, becoming too much, and he was so close I could smell his aftershave. He was trying to intimidate me. It was his game, along with everything else, and I wasn't going to back down.

"You're right. I am letting you win."

I laughed, not because it was funny. It was absurd. "Why?"

"Because I like your company."

I watched his face and waited for a grin, a smirk, something to prove the sarcasm in his answer. All I saw was the tiniest raise of his eyebrows, a hopeful expression so slight it was barely there. If this was all an act, he didn't need to be so subtle about it. His acting skills were unsurpassed; he should use them. Dishing out his unmasked self in such small portions only left me guessing, and he knew this, knew how it would twist in my mind. For I was starting to draw a line between genuine and fake, starting to recognize the difference, when deep down I knew everything he did was malicious. It didn't matter whether it was genuine or fake.

"I know you're not used to me being honest. It's been a long day. I'm out of lies." And there was the grin I was waiting for, but there was nothing sly about it. "Plus, it's unhealthy to drink alone. Every hallowed oak knows this family does enough of that." He took a step forward, forcing me to take a step back.

He was going to help me get my texts here.

I returned to the armchair, spread the quilt across my lap. He downed a glass of wine while trying to set the chessboard back to how it was before I'd reset it. My glass of wine sat untouched and ridiculous, as usual. Without Paul there to drink it after my time limit was up, it was sure to sit there untouched all night.

"Was your queen here, or here?" He looked up at me. The flames of the fire reflected in his eyes.

"Does it matter?"

"You have a point."

I picked up my wine glass. The first and last time I'd ever had wine was at my wedding.

"Checkmate," Martin said, watching the glass in my hand instead of the board. There was a purpose to everything he did, and he knew it. But he didn't know the purpose to what I did.

I took a sip. The flavor was fuzzy on my tongue, heavier than I remembered. I took another sip. I set down my glass.

"Turn that into a bad habit and you will be one of us."

"That's all I'm having."

"Oh, come on." He poured another inch into my glass.

Gravity pacified the wine in the glass and six words settled in my mind like the snow on the porch railing outside.

Dhá anam táthaithe ag trí rún.

Three secrets shared bind two souls. How many secrets had Martin and I shared?

Accepting his offer of bringing my texts from his Cambridge apartment was one secret for sure. How many secrets did I have left before our souls were bound?

"Shall we play again?" He started to reset the pieces on the board.

I nodded, but my mind was busy sorting through memories, hunting for secrets Martin and I had shared. There was that phone call—the private call he allowed me to make after they killed Matthew and Freddy. He'd said, "This is between you and me." But it only counts if it was.

"Your move," he said.

"That private call you let me make last summer," I blurted. "Did you tell anyone about that?"

He scratched his eyebrow. "Last summer?"

"You brought the phone into my room—"

"No." He looked straight at me. "I told you."

I shifted my pawn one space forward. That was one secret, plus the new one if I accepted his offer to bring my texts. What else? I'd shared other private moments with him, but I didn't know what counted as a secret. Had we shared a secret that night we took a walk into the woods, the night before he left for Europe?

He slid my wine glass toward me. "You look like you need this."

That family was determined to turn me into a drunk, and I wasn't going to fall for it. I needed all my faculties to spring Fearghus and myself out of that house with a story sound enough they'd have no reason to follow us. And I knew better than to latch onto silly superstitions. Three secrets meant nothing, especially since the person sharing the secrets with me had no soul to which mine could be bound.

I sipped my wine anyway, just for something to do to clear my head. We played late into the night, and when I finally returned to my room, I caught myself in the mirror smiling.

"No more wine," I whispered to my reflection.

While I slept I found Mam and told her to pack my texts and prepare them for a journey to Cambridge in the company of a few harmless poetry collections influenced to take all the attention.

The day Martin left he found me in the kitchen stirring blueberries into Ruby's blueberry bread batter. He surveyed the room to make sure he had no one's attention but mine, then he flipped a folded piece of paper in the air, held between his index and middle fingers. I wiped my hands on my apron and took it. He winked at me and left the room.

I didn't realize I was staring at the door he disappeared through until Ruby told me her oven was ready and I needed to stop dawdling and get to stirring. When I had the batter in the pan, I handed it to Ruby and excused myself to the library to read the note. Written in bold handwriting was a Cambridge, Massachusetts address followed by:

As promised. See you soon.
-Martin

Even though I knew he was pretending to be my hero to situate his pieces for checkmate, I couldn't fathom what he had to gain from this victory. That question became a chisel of doubt chipping away at my armor until he showed up three weekends later with a heavy box he deposited on my desk and left my room, no questions asked. With one of my family's texts held against my chest, a thought sprouted in my mind and I could find nothing at hand to poison it with.

Perhaps he actually did do this out of a wild shred of goodness in his black heart.

CHAPTER 18

Martin brought me a new record every weekend he came home and demanded my opinion of the one he brought the previous week, listening with an intensity that overwhelmed me but somehow pushed me to chatter on about music-related things he knew nothing about. Through trial and error, he learned my likes and dislikes, and with each week I could see my taste change with the added influence of music he chose that I'd otherwise never be introduced to. Sometimes, this new person I was becoming would pull a snag in my heart that spilled a longing for my home and family and old life. My baby girl. My husband.

Time would straighten that snag, pierce my heart and make a new stitch, and I'd wonder what Martin's next record would be.

I found Fearghus' wallet carefully packed in a small blue velvet box in the bottom drawer of my bedside table. I sat on my bed and held it in my lap, remembering that day it was tossed lifelessly in front of me, just like Fearghus had been himself. Paul must've rescued it from the kitchen that day. He knew I'd want it, how important it was. He also knew I wasn't strong enough to take it, so he hid it in my bedside table for me to find on a day I could make peace with it in my own time.

Paul moved into the redesigned carriage house. Pierce moved in on me. Each week the taunts would grow in fervor, only to be stripped of power each weekend when Martin would arrive. It was harder for Pierce to find me alone since I spent most of my time helping in the kitchen. Now my presence there was expected, and Ruby and Grace and the rest of the staff planned tasks that would be waiting for me each day.

Fearghus was crawling. Mam said Tara was too. His favorite play area was under the table in the kitchen, a perfect place to keep him out of everyone's way. Eleanor loved to sit with him while he squealed and cooed at the forest of table and chair legs around him. The night he pulled himself all the way up standing, palms pressed on the windows in our room, I contacted Mam to tell her. She told me Tara had done the same thing that day. When my sleeping mind painted her words as a picture, it was like my babies were looking out the windows, searching for each other.

Spring blew in and the landscape mural in my room greened. The lone oak tree filled with leaves, and robins hopped and played on my balcony as if they knew how hard it would make Fearghus laugh. One day Martin came to my room to deliver my latest record and caught Fearghus in his usual laughing rapture with his hands and forehead plastered to the glass. That was the day all the locks came off my doors. Martin had promptly left the room, returned with a toolbox, and removed all the locks himself.

"It's a shame to have such a balcony go unused," he said. "I'll have someone come up and install some barrel bolts you can use to keep Trey from wandering out." He opened all three sets of doors, picked up Fearghus, and carried him outside.

The breeze rushed against me as I stood in the middle of my room, silently cursing the tears that always seemed to reveal me at moments I preferred to appear impassive. I should've accepted the tears and gone outside with them, but since I hadn't, Martin came back in, took my hand, and walked me outside himself. I stood on that balcony next to him and held his hand while he held Fearghus and the robins chirped and the sweet air swirled around us. My shackles were gone. A trust had been established. My heart pounded, angered by my betrayal of my family, aware that I wasn't pulling my hand away because I liked it, and I didn't want it to stop. It had cracked the hard, dry shell around me, just enough to get the tip of a finger out and feel the warmth of the sun waiting for me.

That evening I didn't go to Martin's room for chess at the normal time. I had no way to know if Paul was in there. I didn't want to be alone with Martin.

Settled in my chair, I read the same page in my book three times, but I knew the book wasn't at fault. It was one of my favorites. I put it down and went out on my balcony for some fresh night air, and when I returned inside, someone was knocking on the other side of my wall. It was a Paul move for sure. Martin would never do something so casual, so impolite. I still couldn't go over there without knowing if Paul was staying for the game until the usual late hour to fill the room with more than just me and Martin.

Several minutes later, the knock moved to my door.

It was Paul. "*Cén mhoill*?"

"I think I'll stay in my room tonight."

"Are you sick?"

"Just a little tired."

"You don't look tired. Come on. It's not fun without you." He put his hand on the door to push it open wider.

"How late are you staying?"

He shrugged. "Depends."

"On what?"

"Is this an interrogation? I feel like I'm at the dinner table with Martin Moore, Sr. at the head." He stepped aside and made a sweeping gesture toward Martin's door. "Now let's not leave Martin Moore, Jr. waiting. Being on *his* bad side is just as dangerous."

"Aren't I already on his bad side?"

He chuckled then dropped his smile. "No."

I allowed him to walk me into Martin's room and help me into my usual chair. Martin was leaned forward, studying the chessboard. He didn't look at me, and I was relieved I didn't have to think of something to say to him. I noticed an opened bottle of liquor on a table behind him. Somehow he knew I was looking at it even though he hadn't taken his attention off the board. "I'd offer you a drink, but I'm sure you don't drink whiskey."

"No, thank you." I looked at Paul. Martin rarely drank around Paul anymore.

"Paul isn't drinking," Martin said.

"Don't need to," Paul said. He held up something next to his face, a small cube perched between his thumb and index finger. "I have this." He popped it into his mouth.

Martin grabbed him by the throat. "Spit it out."

Paul managed to swallow anyway. Martin shoved him back against the sofa and stood up. "Want to get your stomach pumped?"

Paul rubbed his neck. "Relax. I made it myself. Nothing illegal."

"That's probably worse." Martin sat and looked at me, and I felt a tug deep inside.

The feeling warned of another secret between Martin and me, possibly the third secret. But that was a silly idea with no merit, and I wasn't about to go along with it. What was more important, and more disturbing, was the commonality we shared. Our mutual concern for the well-being of one person was more binding than any superstition.

"Not at all. It does have one possible bad side effect, though. Temporary blindness. So I might need some help back to the carriage house tonight."

Martin continued looking at me. "Sloane, would you be mad if I walk him halfway to the carriage house and leave him there?"

"Yes, I would."

"Then it would be like old times." A playfulness touched his eyes, but the only evidence of a smile was the slight dimple at the corner of his mouth that only appeared immediately before a grin.

Paul didn't go blind, but he did find everything Martin and I said to be funny. Even simple exchanges like, *Are you cold? Do you want the chair closer to the fire? No, I'm fine*, drove him to fits. I had to take over his game because he couldn't be serious long enough to put together a move.

Fearing more discomfort in Martin's presence, I tried to play hooky the following night as well, but Paul fetched me again and promised he had no legal or illegal mind-altering substances on him. Fearghus woke just as I was settling into my chair in Martin's room, so I returned to my room to nurse him back to sleep.

When I rejoined them, Paul said, "We were just talking about you."

"*Paul* was talking about you," Martin corrected, giving Paul a sharp look.

"Easy, boy. I'm not going to …" Instead of finishing the sentence, Paul laughed. He captured one of Martin's pawns before looking at me. "It's just strange you seem so attached to your family after they lied to you your whole life. Yet you resent us, and we've been nothing but honest."

Were they serious? It couldn't be that easy for them to forget all they'd done. And they were comparing their family, to *mine*? "You know nothing about my family."

They shared a look so smug a tremor rose from the ground and overtook me. "Your family stole my baby. Killed my cousins." I was standing now, and so were they. The tremor's epicenter moved to my heart, and my limbs surged with adrenaline. "Tortured and beat my husband to death and left him on my porch!"

"But what I said is still true," Paul said.

Martin looked at Paul. "Enough."

My nails dug into my palms. I wanted to hit them both. "Don't ever talk to me about my family."

"Why not?" Paul said. "It seems we know a lot more about them than you do. We could enlighten you. Hell, you probably know more about *us* than you do about them."

Martin picked up my quilt from the floor at my feet, and I ripped it out of his hand and threw it on my chair.

"I do know about your family. They're a gang of murderers who abuse booze and drugs and each other. Your mother hides in her room, no doubt she's too disgusted to face the devil she married and the monsters she bore. Either that, or this family has driven her mad." I scrubbed the tears off my cheeks with my sleeves. "My family may have lied, but they did it to protect me." I tore my attention away from Martin, still as calm as he was when I first sat down in there that night. When my eyes settled on Paul, a current lit my system. His wild mask was on like it was for every family dinner than featured his violent exit. I wanted to back away. Instead, I pointed at him. "You're the only one with a speck of decency, but in ten years, you'll be confined in your room, crazier than your fruitcake mother."

Paul seized my armchair and flung it to the side, its leg grazing my shin on its way. I had gone too far. He walked against me, too close for anything but a physical reaction from me, and I wasn't going to give him that. I turned my face to the side. I was finished speaking to him anyway.

"Paul," Martin said behind him.

Paul's breath beat against the top of my head. "You think I'll go crazy? I'll take you down with me."

I said nothing. I knew wild Paul would switch off just as easily as he had switched on.

"Maybe I'll get Pierce to help. He has some good ideas."

I swallowed, the sound of it pounding in my head.

Paul spun away with a momentum that wasn't his own and toppled over my fallen armchair. Martin took over his space, his back pressing against me. "He's going to apologize to you, but not right now. I think you should go back to your room." He turned slightly to look at me, and I could see Paul stand up, straighten his clothes, run a hand through his hair. Like a dog shaking out its fur and licking a wound after just losing a fight to the alpha.

I tried to catch his eye, to see which Paul inhabited his body at that moment, but he was too fixated on Martin to notice me.

"Go," Martin said to me.

I went back to my room and watched my closed door. There should have been shouting, but there was no sound at all. I couldn't tell what they were doing, or if Paul had left. I reached for the lock on my door, and when the metal clicked, so did a perception in my brain.

It had been a setup. Paul had provoked me so Martin could save me. Martin the hero, to whom I owed everything. He used to work alone. Now he had a partner. He chose the person who had the biggest claim on my sympathy. I unlocked and jerked open my door, expecting to find them toasting the success of their little charade. The room was empty. The chess set forgotten. My chair still upturned.

It was too late to call for Eleanor to watch Fearghus while I hunted them down, so I went to bed sick with the idea of them celebrating my conquest. The anger wasn't enough to silence the little voice that urged me to answer Paul's question that started it all: how could I still love a family who lied to me? A family who withheld so much about who I was, who my son was, the true reason my husband was killed?

A dozen white roses arrived in my room the next morning. I didn't want to read the card, but it was stuck in the middle of the bouquet and open to the world.

We're both sorry.
-Paul and Martin

I opened one of my French doors, took the vase of roses outside, and tossed the whole thing onto Martin's balcony. It was too heavy to make it far enough for a display in front of his French doors, but the weight did make a satisfying crash. I went back inside leaving the door open to enjoy the warmth on the breeze.

Martin's voice carried in to me. "You don't like roses anymore?"

The next morning, I got white tulips. This time, I dumped the water out of the vase before returning it to Martin. The sound wasn't as dramatic without the violent splash of water, but I was able to throw it farther. It landed as a scattered mess right in front of Martin's closest set of doors. One of the doors opened, smearing the mess on the tile, and I returned inside and slammed my door before he could speak.

Eleanor told me how much Martin kept asking about me. No one was safe from him. He was taking advantage of her good nature to relay his fabricated concern to me. She told me someone overheard him and Paul arguing a couple nights prior, and Martin had come inside with a bloody nose but Paul hadn't had a scratch on him. Rumor was Martin let Paul hit him. Everyone knew Paul wouldn't have gotten a hit in otherwise.

On the third day I got chocolates. I tossed that overboard too, but I forgot to open the box first so it simply landed with a thud and all the chocolates still safe inside. I was spared on the fourth morning, but when lunch arrived to my room so did another apology—only this time it was in the flesh. I would've thrown him out if he wasn't so much bigger and stronger than me.

Paul reached for my hand, but I backed away.

"Just hear me out," he said. He glanced around my sitting room then looked past me into my room. "Can I come in?"

I remained planted in the doorway. If he wanted to come farther in, he'd have to move me out of the way.

"Okay, I'll make it quick. I'm sorry. I was out of control. And what I said about Pierce—I'm not like that. You know that. Right?"

I wanted to tell him he was sick in the head, just like all of them, but his eyes looked wetter than usual, and he hadn't shaved, and what his father did to him, continued to do to him … it was no excuse for him to torment others, but it did explain the disconnect inside him. Compassion could have turned him wholly good, but I knew I was the only one to give it to him. Was it enough?

"You don't have to forgive me. Just know I'm not like Pierce. And if he tries to do anything to you, I'll cut his throat." He stuck out his index and middle fingers, kissed them, and pressed them against my forehead.

"I forgive the good Paul," I whispered, but he was already out the door.

Another delivery surprised me the next day. After Paul's in-person apology I assumed they were finished trying to win me over. This time it was a basket that mewed. Martin must have thought hard to come up with something I couldn't fling onto his balcony. Or maybe this was the murderer coming out of him.

I opened the lid and two white paws gripped the side. The kitten's puff of a head followed, and his big yellow-green eyes conquered me. I'd never win against Martin. He was a professional manipulator.

With Fearghus on my hip, I tucked the kitten inside my other arm and stormed Martin's room, but it was empty, so I went downstairs and found him in the library, smoking a cigarette. "Since when do you smoke?"

He looked at me quickly, like I'd startled him, but the stoic calm didn't falter. "I don't." He stubbed out the cigarette in an ashtray.

I walked over to him and held out the kitten. "Animals aren't gifts."

"It's not a gift. Since you're not talking to me anymore, I thought you might need a friend." He plopped onto the sofa. "It's only fitting for a witch to have a cat."

The kitten squirmed, grazing my skin with prickly claws. I set him on the floor. Fearghus grunted and pointed, so I put him down too. "Is that a compliment?"

"Of course." That dimple appeared. Now that he'd picked a gift I couldn't throw back at him, he knew he had won. He'd make the perfect lawyer.

"Why aren't you at school?"

"I'm off for the summer." He watched Fearghus scrambling toward the kitten on all fours until it escaped under the sofa. Fearghus dropped to his belly, but his head wouldn't fit under the sofa. Martin laughed. "Looks like Trey needs the friend, not you."

I scooped up Fearghus. Martin stood and blocked me between himself and the sofa. With a day's worth of stubble and what appeared to be yesterday's clothes, he looked worse than Paul had the day before. One eye had a web of red in the corner.

I averted my gaze. "Get away from me."

"I need to talk to you."

"Go get some sleep."

He backed up a step, pressing his palms against his eyelids. "Is it that bad? I was up all night dealing with something."

I pushed past him. "I'm not interested."

He touched my arm. "I never asked you how you sent my Cambridge address to your family so they could ship your books."

A cold wind blew through me. It had been a trap. A trap I unknowingly set, but he baited. And I had walked right into it.

I kept my back to him. "Okay, I'll keep the kitten." I headed for the door to escape before he could see my hands shaking. If he severed my contact with Mam, I'd lose all I had left. The day those texts arrived, he gained the information to blackmail me. This was his warning.

"That's not the reason I bring it up. I've been given approval to take you and Trey somewhere."

My feet stuck to the ground.

"Cambridge, to be specific. But we can take a detour."

He was a liar. It was a setup. I'd have rather rotted in that house than go anywhere with him. The floor creaked, and he was behind me.

He lowered his voice. "If you can keep a secret, that is. They hear we go anywhere but Cambridge, we're both done for."

Into the ground I sunk. I fought a foot free, then another. I took a step toward the door.

"Just think about it," he said. "Cambridge. Chicago. I'll be blind and deaf and get amnesia as soon as we leave."

I left the room. The kitten was nothing. Nothing at all compared to what he could really do.

CHAPTER 19

JUNE, 1965

FEARGHUS WOKE UP smiling on his birthday. He rolled to his belly, slid off the bed, and staggered over to the balcony doors faster than short legs should safely move. Chubby hands slammed the glass, and he turned to me. "'*Mach!*"

I'd been speaking so much Irish to him, all his first words had been Irish. Fran worried he'd never pick up English. I thought she was just disappointed she didn't know what he was saying, and I couldn't blame her. Witnessing my child suddenly begin to talk was more magical than anything in my texts, now safely hidden among the other books on my shelves.

I wrapped myself in a thin housecoat and followed Fearghus outside into the bright June morning. Martin was leaning on his railing, drinking his coffee. He nodded, like he always did, not expecting a reply since I hadn't talked to him beyond a *thank you* or *excuse me* for months. He didn't press me, unlike Paul, who was in the kitchen with me every day chatting me up in a one-sided conversation. I learned more about his girlfriends than I cared to know. Ruby said he was trying to make me jealous. I told her he was trying to make me sick. Sick enough to want to change the subject to one of my own and satisfy his need for me to speak to him again.

Fearghus waddled along the railing, sticking his hands through the balusters and talking baby gibberish to the birds in the yard. The kitten trailed behind him, pouncing on his shadow. He still didn't have a name.

Martin came to my side of his railing. "Would you like me to take him to the garden so you can have some time off?"

I shook my head and went back inside. He knew how much help I had. I didn't need his. I took off my housecoat and laid it on the end of the bed. Something swooped in above me. I looked at the ceiling. It was pure white, a million tiny particles of white, swarming, then falling onto me, covering everything in the room. I whirled around to get Fearghus, but the day had been swallowed by night, and my room was dark. A young woman knelt, head bowed, facing the windows painted with a mural of the full moon hanging in line with the trunk of the oak tree. The hair on the crown of her head was gathered in a band, shooting like a fountain from the rest of the dark length spilling past her shoulders. Both palms flat against the floor, she appeared to be listening to something I couldn't hear.

She spun on her knees to face the door in one fluid, athletic motion, her head still bowed. Heavy bangs cut at odd, uneven angles formed a curtain over her lowered face, and one thin braid, longer than the rest of her hair, trailed down her chest, ending in a shining band of silver twine. Someone entered behind me, but I couldn't turn to see. The young woman raised her face to the visitor. Under those bangs sat eyes so wise, a gaze so direct—a combination that formed a fierce composure I'd never seen in someone so young. She stood, slipping a necklace over her head. I knew what it was before I saw it. Fearghus' amulet.

An assault of light hit me and I covered my face. The June morning returned. "Fearghus!"

He was directly in front of me, standing where the girl had been, in his striped pajamas and an expression too austere for a baby. He was one now. My baby was growing up. In two weeks I'd be a prisoner for one entire year. Someday to be replaced by a new prisoner, a young woman who had Fearghus' amulet, or one just like it. There was danger coming for her. Despite her repose, she knew it too.

I took the pencil from my desk and marked the floor between Fearghus' feet. Instead of grabbing for the pencil like I'd expected, he watched me make the mark, then he toddled back out to the balcony like I'd satisfied some request and he could go back to playing. I followed him out to the side of my balcony near Martin's railing.

Martin lowered his coffee mug. "Are you okay?"

"I need a small wood chisel. Can you get me one?"

He looked at my night gown. He set down his coffee, came to his railing, and leaned toward me. "Your pupils look funny again. I'm coming over."

I met him in my sitting room. He peered into my eyes, then he took my arm and dragged me into my room before the windows. "Close your eyes."

I closed them.

"Now open them."

I opened them and pushed him away. "Stop it."

"What happened?" He picked up my housecoat and handed it to me.

I put it on. "Nothing. Can you get me a wood chisel?"

"You haven't spoken to me in months, and the first thing you say to me is you want a wood chisel?"

"Fine. I'll ask Paul."

"Paul can't give you anything without my approval or my father's approval. Especially something that could be used as a weapon."

I stared up at him. "Please" crawled to the tip of my tongue, but I tightened my lips to keep it inside.

"What are you going to use it for?"

"Nothing dangerous."

He watched me a moment longer. Without a word, he left.

Fran came to help me and Fearghus dress, then I took Fearghus downstairs for breakfast. The breakfast nook in the kitchen was filled with balloons. Fearghus squealed and kicked his legs, wanting down. I took in all the faces, trying to figure out who had known it was Fearghus' birthday.

Eleanor pulled out my chair at the table. "The master said no party, so we decided to have one anyway."

"Shh," Fran said across the room. "Eleanor, that's not polite."

"Oh, she doesn't care what he thinks. Do you, Sloane?"

"I'll care if you get in trouble."

"We won't get in trouble. Martin said it was okay."

Of course Martin said it was okay. It explained why he'd given up on trying to win me over months ago. He'd been planning this—a surefire way to gain my forgiveness. It wasn't going to work. "Fearghus doesn't need a party."

"Sure he does." Fran handed me a plate of breakfast. "It's a lunch party, just a few of us, nothing to get all anxious about. Come back at noon and we'll have cake."

Martin wasn't there when we returned at noon, but Paul was, trying to keep a serious face but failing. He even brought Fearghus a gift. I was convinced he hadn't picked it out himself until Fearghus opened it. It was a kazoo.

"So you'll hate me even more," Paul whispered in my ear, and all the family dinners in which Paul had to endure his abusive father—along with my cold shoulder—stabbed through me, and I stood on tiptoe and kissed his cheek without a thought otherwise. I couldn't be mad at him anymore. He needed me, and I needed him.

Martin missed the presents but arrived just in time for cake. He had no gift for Fearghus, but he did have one for me: a brand new set of wood chisels.

As soon as the party was over, I went to my room and removed the smallest chisel from the set. I scratched the outline of the amulet's design in the floor where I'd marked the young woman's position. Fearghus tipped a lamp across the room, and I rescued it before it hit the floor. I put him in his crib with some toys and went back to my chiseling. It was time for his nap anyway. He banged the bars and called to me, impatient and defiant.

"Hush, Fearghus. There's a girl somewhere who will need this someday."

He threw himself down on the mattress, groaning and grumbling until he fell asleep. When he began to stir awake, my rough design was complete. I wiped up the wood shavings and stood back. It was perfect. But how would I tell the young woman this is where she'd need to stand to see the moon aligned with the oak tree and know her danger was moments away?

Who was this young woman, and how'd she get Fearghus' amulet?

It could've been a copy. Anyone could reproduce the design like I had on the floor. But if I was going to trust this vision, I'd have to trust my intuition. My intuition said it was Fearghus' amulet.

Walking with Fearghus in the garden two weeks later, I noticed Martin come out to the patio with his newspaper. Through a lilac bush, I watched him light a cigarette, take a drag, roll his neck and stretch his shoulders. One of the staff came outside to him, and there was a simple exchange. The man left, then he returned with a glass of water which he set in front of Martin along with something too small for me to see. Martin popped it into his mouth and took a drink of water. After two more drags on his cigarette, he stubbed it out then leaned onto the table, squeezing his head between his hands.

I picked up Fearghus and carried him across the lawn and past Martin, who looked up from his paper but didn't say a word. Inside the kitchen I dropped our collection of seeds onto the counter.

"Y'all need a pot and some soil," Ruby said. "Eleanor, fetch Miss Sloane a pot and some soil for her seeds."

Ruby handed Fearghus a piece of cheese and poked him in the belly. I looked outside at the same moment Martin looked in. A pocket of forgiveness ruptured inside me and spread like dye in water. The sudden return of warmth toward him was more profound than it had been for Paul at Fearghus' birthday party. I looked away, trying to shake it off and raise a shield against a feeling that should not exist in my head for such a man. That forgiveness found its way through, and I knew it could not be purged, for it had trailed inside me behind the flavor of anger that only exists for those people who matter more than others.

My world knew I needed him to carry out my plan, and it had shifted oceans and continents to make a place for him. That was easy to understand. But that look we shared spoke of a preoccupation with one another, a mutual concern that had been built on the rockiest of foundations—a structure built on such unstable ground that it would either crumble with the slightest breeze, or last beyond human existence.

Fearghus and I began our garden in pots on our bedroom balcony. Paul brought me packs of store-bought seeds and we started tomatoes and peppers. When he refused to believe I could cook, I promised him I'd make him a stew. The long summer days left me with many idle hours, so I spent more time practicing piano with Paul in the ballroom. We'd open all the French doors and turn on the fans to create a cyclone of cool air to combat the muggy heat outside. Martin made a habit of bringing work into the ballroom when Paul and I were there, but the books and documents would sit on the coffee table untouched while he chased Fearghus around in their own version of hide-and-seek.

One evening Fran took Fearghus to bed and I stayed downstairs. Martin and Paul had polished off every beer in the ballroom bar and had then started on the liquor. I was in the middle of Liszt's Liebestraum No. 3 when they rejoined me at the piano.

"Teach her the one our mother used to play," Martin said.

I took my hands off the keys and looked at him.

"Which one?" Paul said.

"The one she'd play every night. How could you forget?" Martin shook the ice in his glass.

Paul leaned on the piano, bowing his head. "Was it a Liszt?"

"Hell if I know. I don't know who is who. I'd know it if I heard it."

Paul drummed his fingers on the piano. "I don't remember. That's a pity." He raised his head to me. "It was only a matter of time before we'd forget. I'm sure that's what they wanted though. It's all part of the plan." He finished his drink in one long gulp then moved over to the sofa and sank into it, leaving a sour vibe around me. I didn't feel like playing anymore.

"Probably need to cut him off," Martin said in Paul's direction. "Or not. One more drink and he'll probably sleep like a baby until noon tomorrow. Whaddya think?" His grin was crooked, like his lips were half asleep themselves. He sat on the edge of the piano bench. "Scoot over, Miss Bevan. Do you know Chopsticks? I do."

I scooted, but not quickly enough before he slid against me. The sticky heat in the air glued the side of my body to his, but he didn't seem to notice. I inched away to allow some space in between us while he stared at the keys.

"Okay, maybe I don't. I used to."

I showed him his part. His arm grazed mine on his try at the keys, but I was afraid he'd notice if I moved over more. He was too close to me, but I didn't want him to get up. I couldn't stop looking at his hands, his thick long fingers, the bubbled patch of pink skin by his knuckle that looked like a burn scar. I didn't want to smell the morning's soap being sweated off his skin. I missed the scent of a man's skin. Of Fearghus' skin.

"Was it Chopin? Minute Waltz?" Paul asked from the sofa.

Martin turned around. "You'll have to come play it. I don't know the names." He faced the piano again, brushing my breast with his elbow. "Didn't I say that already? You're the sober one. Either my memory is bad or I'm repeating myself. Or his memory is bad. Or he's repeating himself." He looked at me. "What?"

"Nothing. I mean, yes, I think you did say that."

"Where were we?"

"You were getting up," Paul said, pushing between us. "I need to play something up-tempo or I'm gonna fall asleep."

He took over the bench and started a fast jazzy tune. Martin grabbed my hand and twirled me. Before I could decline we were dancing an awkward type of swing, him too inebriated to keep a firm grasp on my hand, my feet too rusty to match his moves. Paul was the first one to start laughing. It caught on to Martin, then me, but he kept twirling me as the laughter stole what remained of our breath. Every missed hold had us laughing harder, making our moves bolder as we became more determined to get them right. Our feet pounded the floor with the music. Martin twirled me under his arm, swung me around him, my feet learning to stay with his on their own. When he slid me between his legs I was too far gone with laughter to keep my own grip on him. I rode my skirt across the floor, ending up with my back against the piano leg. Martin was bending at the waist to laugh and catch his absent breath.

My stomach hurt to laugh so hard. With his hands on his knees, Martin looked up at me, his face flushed and sweaty, his smile wide. And I remembered it was Arthur who taught me to dance. Enid and I had taken turns with him, trying to learn the Lindy Hop in Mam's front room with Fearghus commissioned to change the records because he was too shy to dance.

Paul came to help me up. I curbed the laughter for the strange outburst it was. I wouldn't know what to do with its memory later. It would bring on a guilt I didn't have room for.

"It's my turn next time," Paul said.

"Only after I get a go when I'm sober. I can't leave Miss Bevan thinking that's how I dance."

I reclaimed my seat at the piano and continued Liebestraum No. 3 where I'd left off. Paul fell onto the sofa as if finally resigned to his drowsiness. Martin sat beside me, now even more fragrant with soap and sweat and everything unique to man.

"Why doesn't your mother play the piano anymore?"

He blinked a long drunken blink. "If we're going into that territory, I'm going to refill my drink." He looked down at my hand on his arm.

I jerked my hand back, not knowing how it got there. I played some chords while he scooped ice and poured liquor at the bar. Paul started snoring. Martin started laughing.

"This is my last one," he said when he rejoined me. "I don't want to end up like him." He took a drink and made a face. "I'm into the cheap stuff now. Let's go outside. I can't listen to that noise."

He took my hand. My heart flipped. It meant nothing.

Outside the moon hung low in the sky and the sound of singing insects and frogs came heavy upon us. Martin handed me his glass to light a cigarette. He took a long drag then offered it to me. I took it, dropped it, and stomped it out.

He fought a smile and lost. "Let's walk."

I stepped out of my shoes. I longed to feel the earth under my feet, the cool grass between my toes. After downing his entire drink, he did the same. Then he yanked off both socks and pulled his shirttails out of his pants. "Do you mind? I need to feel some air."

I could see he was wearing an undershirt when he undid the top button, but it still seemed wrong to stand and watch, so I started down the hill. The grass hadn't been cut for a while, and it tickled my ankles. Crickets jumped ahead of me.

He caught up, his white shirt bright in the darkness. Slowing to my pace, he asked, "Where are we going?"

"To the lake."

"Yes, ma'am."

"And you were going to tell me about your mother."

"Right. It's about time you knew." He took my arm and stopped us so he could face me. "Our mother is very ill. It's a curse we can't lift. A Farrelly curse. Do you know the name?"

I shook my head. His eyebrows lifted and he pulled back a bit—a look of surprise he could easily hide when sober. He was far from sober.

"If you don't know the name, you probably don't know the curse."

"What is it? I might know it."

He crossed his arms on his chest and turned away from me so I couldn't see his face. "She can't see or hear any of us—me or my brothers. We're lost to her. When each of us turned fifteen, she became blind and deaf to our presence. We haven't been able to figure out how to lift it, and she's been closed up in her room since the day she lost Lew." He put his hands in his pockets and turned back to me with his stoic calm fixed cleanly in place. "Do you know the curse?"

"No." I watched his face. A curse like that must have had a history. It would've only attached so securely if there was some need for balance, for nature to even out a wrong. A curse like that would either be used by someone evil like the Moores themselves, or by someone casting punishment. And as a punishment, it was strangely humane. She only lost her children when they were grown, when she knew they were safe and strong and happy. The curse would've been devastating had she lost them when they were babies, robbing her of first steps, first words, hugs, and bedtime stories.

"You look like you know something," he said.

"I know nothing. But I can make some guesses. I'd have to know more about your mother."

"Another day." He took off toward the lake and I followed, dying for more information. I needed to know whether I should fear her or pity her, and I hoped to find some reason to dispel the pervasive disdain I felt for a woman I'd never met—a woman who seemed to be as much a prisoner as I was.

CHAPTER 20

"WAS YOUR MOTHER born here?" I asked when I caught up to Martin.

"No. Ireland, like my dad. He's from the south. She, the north."

"Is that why you speak so much Ulster?"

"*Go díreach.*"

My father's family was also from the North. Which county, I didn't know. Mam had said the last letter she received from him during the war was postmarked in Donegal. Frogs plopped into the water as Martin and I drew near, creating ripples that made the reflected stars dance just past our feet and beyond. He picked up a stone.

"Help me find two more. I'll show you how I can juggle. There." He stooped for one at my feet, and I stepped back and found another. He straightened into position, and I was struck by the urge to laugh.

He juggled longer than I thought a drunk man could juggle, and when the first stone fell, he caught it with his foot. I covered my mouth but my laugh rose up and burst out of me. A year of laughter, built up, with no outlet, had finally defied its containment.

"What else can you do?" The lilt in my voice was barely recognizable to me.

He raised one eyebrow. "You sure you want to know?"

"Walk a tightrope? Do backflips on an elephant?"

He took my hand and twirled me as if we were dancing, and I ended up facing what should've been the lake. A lush field of wildflowers spread in its place. I closed my eyes then opened them again. The outermost corners of the field began to cave in on itself, flowing inward like a slow moving wave. He twirled me again, and the lake was back.

I scoffed. "Illusions?"

"They come in handy. Don't worry. I've exploded my share of light bulbs."

"You should stick to juggling."

"Why's that?"

"It takes more skill."

A smile crept to his face, then all at once he turned and flung one of his stones so far into the lake the sound of it hitting the water couldn't be heard over the sounds of the night. An orange glow shone deep below the surface and flickered upward, growing bigger, brighter, and he extended his arm in front of me to force me back several paces.

Water burst in a column out of the center of the lake, throwing a fiery explosion into the sky that sizzled and turned to ash that sprinkled the water. The smell of hot pavement after a rain swept over us, and I could taste the ash on my tongue.

"You shouldn't do that," I said.

He brushed specks of black off his arms. "Why?"

"The wildlife."

"The wildlife is fine. And you asked for it."

"I didn't exactly have that in mind."

He looked down at the other stone in his palm. "Okay, how about this?" He walked away, along the shore. When he turned around, he skipped the rock on the water toward me. On its third bounce, a wave as tall as me sprung out of the water and hit me head on. I wiped my eyes. He was posed defensively, ready to bolt. My focus landed on the earth at his feet. A square yard of dirt crumbled into the lake, bringing him with it. His body made a big splash, then he came above water, choking and laughing.

I wrung out my skirt, and he kicked out farther into the water. "Join me. Let's swim!"

"You're crazy."

"Come on. You're already wet."

I walked to the edge. "Can you touch the bottom?"

He stood up. The water hit him just below the waist. "It's deeper in the middle, but we don't have to go out far." He took several labored steps to me and offered his hand.

I looked at his hand then his face. And as if propelled by some other force, I sat down on the edge of the shore, took his hand, and hopped into the water. My skirt bubbled around me, and I shoved it under the surface. My feet sank into the mud. We lunged into deeper water and both dunked down.

"It's warm, isn't it?" He swam away from me, a blot of white cutting through the black mirror of water.

Slimy tendrils slithered against my legs. I held still, trying to determine if it was plant or animal. I lifted my legs and floated on my back. The moon was higher, swimming in a lake of sky. Wispy clouds wandered past it like the life in the lake around me. The water trembled, and Martin bumped against me. "Awake?"

I turned upright in the water and planted my feet in the mud. His face was inches away. A drop of water scurried down his nose and leaped off. Contact this close would've been awkward on land, yet in a dark lake at midnight it was comfortable. Gentle waves nipped at my chin. He looked like he wanted to say something but was waiting for a cue, an approval from me. The water lapped, the frogs sang, and he looked into my eyes. The night faded around me, and I was in a small room with walls that were closing in, but I couldn't find the door, and my lungs were being crushed, the air pressing out—

I stood; he stood with me. The water stirred against my stomach, unsettled by the disruption. He took my hand and brought it to his lips. He kissed the back, then turned it over and kissed my palm. I watched him do it, with eyes that weren't mine, with a heart that wasn't mine, with a mind that was still with the moon in the sky. He brought my other hand to join the first. He pulled me forward and leaned down.

I pushed away. The water was molasses, the mud quicksand. Somehow I made it to the shore and climbed onto land.

"Sloane!" He burst out of the water behind me. I was halfway to the house, but he was faster. "Sloane, I'm sorry." He was facing me, holding my shoulders. "I'm sorry."

"I need my shoes."

"We'll get your shoes."

Water trickled down my scalp, my back, my legs—tiny worms tickling my skin. I shivered. He released me and pulled me forward to grab the shirt he discarded earlier, which he put around my shoulders. His scent wafted around me. I felt cloaked in it.

"Stay here. I'll get towels." He stepped inside the house and turned around. "Stay here."

I dripped on the patio and wrung out my hair, my skirt. My dripping stopped. I went inside. Paul had somehow made it to the floor, the top of his body on the rug, the bottom half on the parquet floor. Martin came back with a stack of towels, tossed one to me, and put the rest on the coffee table. He yanked Paul off the floor by the arm and threw him over his back.

"Don't leave. I'll be right back," he said to me.

I dried my arms and legs and face, dabbed my hair and my clothes, and took the towel with me upstairs to my room. Eleanor was on her belly on my long sofa, legs crossed in the air with a magazine before her.

"Eleanor, it's so late. I'm sorry."

"I never get to stay up. You're not coming to bed already, are you?"

"I'm afraid so."

"Drat. Why are you all wet?"

"We went for a swim."

"We who?"

"Martin and me."

She flipped her magazine closed and sat up. "Oh?"

I felt like I was under the gaze of twenty eyes instead of two. I turned around and stepped out of my skirt. If my family were there right now, what excuse did I have? None. I could already see Mam's creased forehead, Arthur's narrowed eyes, Enid's averted gaze. The ghost of my husband's cold, impassive silence when he was upset about something, layered with anger and hurt he'd never admit. Arthur was the only person who could upset Fearghus like that, and I was the only person who could talk him back into a good mood. I would never have that silence again. If it were the only part of him I could have back, I'd take it.

"Will you tell me about it tomorrow?" Eleanor had followed me into the bathroom.

"There's nothing to tell," I said to her in the mirror. "Thank you for watching Fearghus."

She bit her bottom lip. It did nothing to reduce her smile. "I'll watch him tomorrow night too. Any night." She lingered in the doorway while I washed my face, then she brought me a nightgown and closed herself out of my room.

I sat on the toilet in my wet slip. There was something I did want to tell Eleanor. I wanted to tell her about the pink and black tile in my bathroom at home, how I'd fallen in love with that tile while house hunting with Fearghus six months after we got married. How Fearghus fell in love with the limestone outside. How he would've been a stonemason even if all the men in his family weren't. His job was in his blood. The long, hard hours never showed in his spirit, and he was always happy when he came home to me. And I was proud and grateful of how hard he worked, even though I never told him.

He wanted to fill our little house with children. Those overnight trips with Arthur always seemed to get in the way. The trips had been a hobby of theirs since we were kids. How could I have known? I'd never had a reason to question something that had been happening for as long as I could remember. He'd been a fixture at my family's dinner table since I was a child. His presence was woven into my earliest memories—him crashing my tricycle into the fire hydrant, him stopping traffic to rescue my doll from the street. Our lives existed in parallel. We unknowingly learned everything together, until the day I realized the five years of teasing I endured from him were simply his immature quest for my attention. That was our first mutual insight.

He was more than my husband. He lived my life along with me. Losing him was like losing my shadow. The sunniest days were the hardest to endure without him—his absence was most obvious, and I couldn't deny he was gone.

His eyes were open when I found his body on our front porch. His eyes were the only recognizable feature. Mam said I was kneeling on the floor inside the wide-open front door when she got there. I had bruises on my knees for weeks. She said I had projected to her, but I don't remember doing it. The last thing I remember was his heavy cold head in my lap.

She took me home with her to the house I grew up in. I found out I was pregnant a week later. Fearghus never knew he was a father.

And he would never know I almost kissed the man whose family killed him.

Once in bed, my mind opened as soon as I fell asleep—an easy effort with the absence of my usual guards. Hiding my betrayals from my family would only make my soul more rotten and my guilt more leaden. I was giving up.

Mam's presence was immediate and strong, like she'd been waiting for me. She probably knew everything. But she had so much to tell me about Tara that my mind climbed to another plane where guilt and betrayal and fear couldn't subsist. Only joy.

After she brought Tara to me, I brought Fearghus to her, then I asked her where my father was born. The abrupt change in subject made no apparent effect on her.

"Don't concern yourself with the past. And don't listen to anything the Moores tell you about your ancestors."

"How old were you when your family moved to Wales?"

"I was born in Wales."

Paul's words from months ago swirled with hers in my dream. Could I trust my mother after she'd withheld the truth about my son until I was captured by our enemy, unable to free him from a future he may not want?

"What was my father's last name?"

"O'Neill."

"Why did you change all our names back to Bevan?"

"He told me to. He wrote to me before he died."

That must have been the letter from Donegal. He asked her to do what I decided to do to my own children: sever their relationship from their father in name. Was his reason the same as mine? For cover? For protection? "Did he say why?"

"I didn't have a chance to ask him. Sloane, if you follow this path, you'll find only heartbreak. The future holds so much for you and little Fearghus. You don't see that now, but someday you will."

"Would you rather I get my information from Martin?" I felt myself cringe, although I knew it was only mental. Even in a dream, I couldn't take back the words that rushed from me before I'd approved them.

She faded away for a moment, just long enough for my guilt to put that slip of the tongue on a silver platter and present it to the traitor inside me. As if the question wasn't bad enough, my use of Martin's name suggested a familiarity with my captors. Mam had to understand it was natural for me to know them as individual people. It didn't mean anything to me, and it shouldn't to her either.

Her full presence washed back in, more lifelike than ever. "You will trust Martin the son."

I broke contact. I woke and sat up in bed, cold with sweat, the room around me blurring with the scenery from my dream. I was prepared for her to recognize my treachery. I was not prepared to recognize hers.

CHAPTER 21

AUTUMN, 1965

MARTIN AND I avoided one another until autumn touched the trees with orange and red and Fearghus learned to run, climb, and put two words together, which often took the form of a demand. He spoke Irish to me and English to everyone else, almost as if his fifteen-month-old mind could already sense a difference between the two of us and the rest of them. We harvested our vegetables from our balcony garden, and I made my stew, which lured all four Moore brothers for a taste test. Paul joked I'd get them all with poison in one go, and Lewis said it was better than Ruby's, who faked offense but beamed with appreciation over my ability to bring all four boys together in the kitchen—a now unlikely gathering, she said, unless fists were flying.

Martin was the first to excuse himself and Paul remained the last, and as soon as the kitchen cleared of staff and Eleanor took Fearghus to bed, I finally surrendered to Paul's persistent conversation and sat down across the table from him. Martin wandered back in minutes later. Another setup, for sure, but my mood was too high to care.

Lightning pulsed against the windows. The kitchen rattled around us. Paul turned around in his chair to look outside just as the rain hit.

"Anyone up for a walk? Sloane, I know you like to walk in the rain."

"I don't know what gave you that impression."

"Seems I caught you out in the rain once."

"'Caught' might be the wrong word, don't you think?"

"What word would you use?"

"I'd say you met me walking freely."

Martin got up and opened the door wide for Paul. Balmy air blew in—a summer storm in mid-autumn.

Paul shoved away from the table. "Am I being kicked out?"

"Yes," Martin said.

Paul removed his shoes and threw them at Martin, who dodged them both. Martin closed the door behind him. Paul's socks came off on the patio, followed by his shirt. We watched the light patch of his skin move across the dimly-lit lawn and disappear into the trees, then Martin turned around. "I need to talk to you."

I wished I'd left with Paul. Martin's and my avoidance of each other was a two-person job. He must've had the day off.

"We should probably go to your room," he said.

"Fearghus is sleeping."

"My room."

There was no way I'd agree to be alone with him there. I shook my head.

He looked around, as if the hanging pots and pans and block of cutlery had ears. "Follow me."

He took me to the covered porch off the room where they killed my cousins and closed us outside. Rain clamored down the gutters and splattered off the roof, creating a fine mist around us. The day's heat was losing a battle, and the thunder cried its victory. The noise would mask the liveliest of conversations. And Paul was out there, half naked, doing who-knows-what.

Martin leaned one shoulder against the house and crossed his arms on his chest. "Have you thought about my offer?"

I thought about his offer every day, but he'd never know it. "I won't go anywhere with you."

"No one else can take you in secret. I'm the only one you can trust."

"You'd know where my family lives. You'd know their names, what they look like."

"What makes you think I don't already know all that?"

"I don't trust you."

"Why not? I've given you no reason not to trust me."

"You killed my husband."

"No, my father did."

"You tortured him."

"I was in London the whole time."

"Then who?" I didn't know why I was running down this path. I didn't want to know what lay ahead.

"Pierce and Lew. Sam, Daniel, Joey." He looked up, toward the porch ceiling. "Charlie, Vince, probably Bernard and Pete."

Grief weakened my knees. My next inward breath brought a tremble inside. "That many?"

"He didn't break, if that's what you're wondering. We got nothing from him."

"You could have called it off."

He looked out at the lawn. "I was in London."

Thunder pounded the air. I stepped out of my shoes. "I'm going to find Paul."

"I'm not finished."

"*I* am."

He stepped in front of me. "If you wait too long, Trey will be too old to go. He'll remember he was there. He'll blow our story. I can take the two of you now."

I backed into a chair and sat. He was right—the opportunity was fleeting. I'd never leave Fearghus alone in that house. If I wanted to visit my family, my baby girl, I had to do it now or never.

Through the railing I watched the tops of the trees sway in the wind, masses of darkness rolling against a sky of the same shape and movement. Raindrops hit my feet then switched direction. A chill mixed into the breeze and skimmed my bare legs and arms. I hugged myself, rubbing away the goose bumps.

"Do you need more time to think about it?"

I nodded. I couldn't look at him.

"There's one other thing." He took the seat facing me. "We've been talking about your story. It's not set in stone, but we're leaning toward you being our sister."

My stomach turned. "That's not going to work."

"We can make it work. People will wonder why you showed up out of nowhere. They'll suspect you're not my mother's daughter. My father doesn't care. He says it's none of their business."

"What about your mother?"

"She has other things on her mind. Everything else will be the same. You married and changed your name. Your husband died. You moved here." He looked like he had more to say.

I stood, and he stood with me. I looked up at him as the moist air swirled around us, reminding me of the water that night in the lake. My ponytail flapped beside my face like a banner in the wind.

"Do you think you can play this role?"

"Do I have a choice?"

"Yes. There are other options. If you don't like this idea, I can pass it along. We're looking for the easiest way to fit you in. It'll be easier for everyone if you're comfortable with it."

"I don't like it."

His shoved his hands into his pockets. "I don't either."

What reason did he have not to like it? What did it matter to him?

"I have a better idea," he said, like I'd spoken the words aloud, "but you'll like my idea even less."

The threat of a worse idea to bully me into accepting the first. It would've been a good strategy if he actually had another idea. I didn't want to play along, but I had to call him on his bluff. "And what's *your* idea?"

"You marry into the family."

Like hell I would. "Anyone in particular?"

He smiled. "Me."

I wanted to set the whole house on fire, grab Fearghus, and run. "You're crazier than all of your family combined."

Martin looked at the door. Pierce and Lewis burst through.

"Oh, a big secret party out here?" Pierce said.

Martin's expression became even more featureless.

"Seen Paul?" Lewis said.

Martin jerked his head toward the woods.

Lewis elbowed Pierce. "Come on. Let's scare the piss out of him." He pulled his shirt over his head. Pierce did the same. They hopped the railing and tore off in the rain, down the slope of the lawn, like two attack dogs on a trail.

Martin brushed the moisture out of his hair. "If you say anything to anyone, we're both dead. Got it?" He went back inside without waiting for my answer.

Winter rushed in hard and spent its time whispering to my idle mind about matters that had been put in storage with my autumn wardrobe. By the time those blouses, skirts, dresses, and gowns would appear back in my dressing room, my time for visiting my family would have run out. Weekdays were spent with the books in the library, or Paul at the piano, or Eleanor in Martin's room, which now held

219

a new television set in the corner by the fireplace. Martin came home every other weekend with a gift for me.

He had trained me to look forward to those weekends.

One warm Friday in March, he arrived for the weekend early, just as I was walking through the foyer. He handed his hat, briefcase, and jacket to the doorman, then he looked at me. That look must have brought the spring sunshine inside, radiating onto me in a rush of sweet warmth. Fearghus arched his back, and I let him down to the floor. He ran to Martin. This scene had become too familiar to be strange, yet its strangeness hit me in a way it had never hit me before, like I was seeing it with my eyes from my old life. Those eyes saw a family. A man coming home, his wife and child greeting him. It couldn't be connected to me. It was wrong.

"You're early," I said. A voice from another time. My voice, but not my voice. From the present, or from the future? It felt like one of my visions, but I was certain I was firmly planted in reality. "Is it warm outside?" The answer I already knew, to a question asked simply to distract my pounding heart. To make this greeting normal again.

Martin flipped Fearghus upside down and shook him by the ankles. Fearghus bit his fist and cackled.

"That's a nice smile to come home to."

At first I thought he meant Fearghus, but he wasn't looking at him. I put my fingers against my lips to cover a smile that wouldn't retreat. "No gift? Have you finally run out of things to buy me?"

He lowered Fearghus to the ground and laid him on his back. "Sloane, I haven't brought you a gift for weeks." He gave me a sideways grin, like I'd just given *him* an unexpected gift. He stepped over Fearghus and came to me. "Your gift," he said. He kissed my cheek. It swept me away. I was a cottonwood seed and that kiss the wind, and when the movement settled I struggled to get my new bearings.

"I'm a little disappointed you're not slapping me right now, Miss Bevan."

If he hadn't brought me a gift for weeks, then why did I spend every Saturday morning wondering when he'd come through the door? I wanted to touch the heated mark left by his lips, but I didn't dare draw attention to it. How did I fall this far into madness? When did I start allowing these things?

He brought my hand up and slapped himself with it. "There. Have you had lunch?" He headed toward the kitchen, loosening his tie.

I took Fearghus outside, behind the carriage houses and new garage, around a cluster of trees, to the plot of land we picked out for our real garden. The groundsman had already dropped off some tools for me to prepare the land, but until now, I'd been afraid to start. I hadn't asked Martin, or Pierce. Not even Fran. The groundsman had obliged me solely on his ignorance of my position. But if Martin could kiss me without permission, I could plant a garden.

Fearghus played in the dirt while I tilled the soil. If I stayed away from the house too long, they'd send someone for me. I needed to keep this garden a secret long enough to confirm it as a safe place to grow what was required for the effect that would remove my husband's blood from my son. I watched the sun's descent and allowed us two hours before we brushed off and headed back to the house.

Paul waved to me from his carriage house patio, surrounded by a harem of women. Fearghus waved back, and I figured it was good enough for both of us. Paul had enough female attention for his ego. He appeared engaged enough with his little party to not wonder where we'd been. We'd need to take the long route home next time to avoid passing in close range to someone who'd wonder why we were taking such regular walks to an abandoned part of the property.

In my room I unclothed Fearghus and put him in the tub. I took off my blouse and skirt and sat on the edge to wash the dirt off my legs. My two-hour limit was a blessing as much as it was a limitation. My back was stiff and my legs felt shaky. Fearghus plunked his fist into the water and held it there, more fixated on his own arm than ever.

"Water. Warm water," I said and reached for the soap.

He giggled. Water swirled around his arm like the drain plug had been pulled below it. He was far from the drain, and the plug was in place. He pulled his arm out and threw his head back to grin at me, then he shoved his arm back in the water. The whole bathtub transformed into a whirlpool so strong he could barely remain sitting.

I pulled his arm out of the water. "Stop, that's too much."

He stood up.

"Sit. You can't stand in the tub. You'll fall."

"Ah!"

"Sit!" I bent his legs to help him sit. He slapped the water with both hands, splashing me. "Fearghus! Time to get out."

He squirmed and fought while I dried him off. Once free, his bare feet pounded out of the bathroom. I kneeled in his puddle on the floor and listened to him tearing his books off the bottom shelf of the bookcase. I held a breath then let it out, and with its release a new fear revealed itself.

His talents were awakening. How would I ever control him?

Motherhood became about teaching restraint, and practicing my own—from locking my darling son in a cage and sinking the key to the bottom of the lake. His energy was put to best use in our garden, but once the seeds were planted I found what little patience an almost two-year-old really had when I turned my back one day to gather our tools. Although destruction had been such a common theme inside the house, creation became his specialty outside. When I turned around to call him toward the house, he had grown our newly seeded garden to maturity in a matter of seconds.

My pause, my shock, only encouraged him, and he fell to his hands and knees, aiming to do more. I rushed to him and pulled him to standing. "No, Fearghus. It's not right."

He was too young to understand the consequences of using his skills to force nature's hand. He was too young to have this kind of power at all.

"Pick!"

"No. We need to put it back. Can you put it back?"

He tried to jerk away, and when I held onto his hand, he whined and fell limp. I couldn't put it back myself, not without triggering an alarm in the house. My magic was still under surveillance. Possibly Fearghus' too, but I doubted they'd be watching him at such a young age. I didn't believe he could do it myself. Guidance from my texts or from Mam could give me a way to do it covertly, but this couldn't wait.

Fearghus fussed and writhed on the ground, so I sat next to him and waited for him to finish. It didn't take long before he realized I wasn't reacting to his fit, and he sat up and pointed to the garden. "Pick!"

"Do you want to go back to the house and have some ice cream?"

"Yeh!"

"Put the garden back to how it was and we can go have ice cream."

He scrunched his face. Picking the ripe vegetables from our balcony garden was his favorite game. Ice cream was his favorite treat. Which would win?

Two chubby hands flattened against the earth between his legs. Before my eyes, the plants on the patch of land we tilled and seeded for weeks experienced a year of drought and a year of decay in such a short moment I would've missed it if the dry, dead stems and leaves weren't littering the ground in front of me.

"That's not what I had in mind, *a chroí.*"

He was already leading the way back to the house. We'd have to reseed the whole thing. The waste of our work and the death of the plants tossed me into a pit of grief, but I followed Fearghus home and rewarded him with ice cream. He was too young to understand the wrongs he committed. How could he be granted such power before he knew right from wrong?

To prevent a repeat occurrence of our garden's unnatural growth and demise, I was tempted to repair and reseed the garden without Fearghus, but I knew there was a lesson to be learned and I didn't want him to miss it. What devastation awaited the world if I didn't teach him responsibility?

A couple weeks later we placed the final seed, and I knelt in front of Fearghus and took both his hands. "If we're patient, in a few days we'll see baby plants sprouting through the ground. Do you want to see the baby plants?"

"Yeh."

"Okay, then let's stop, and wait, and let the plants grow themselves. Okay?"

"'Kay."

I released his hands. He turned and took a few steps toward the garden. I fought the urge to grab him, to hold him down. He'd never learn if I restrained him; he had to do it on his own. If he grew the garden again, he'd have to put it back, and we'd start over and repeat the process. Until he learned.

"Let's go see what Ruby has for lunch."

He took another step and squatted at the edge of the tilled soil. He poked one finger in. I held my breath.

"Baby?" he said.

"Yes, but not yet. Maybe tomorrow?"

"'Morrow?"

"Yes, we'll come check tomorrow. Okay?"

He straightened up and walked to me. I picked him up. My relief swam in a sea of panic. If I could barely control him at this age, how would I ever handle him when he was older?

CHAPTER 22

WHEN THE FIRST sprouts peeked through the soil, Fearghus ran around the garden pointing them out one by one, each discovery more joyous than the last. My shoulders ached from lugging buckets of water—a task more risky than I expected. I had no explanation for that bucket making several trips from the faucet on the closest garage to the land behind the cluster of trees, so I had to avoid all possible eyes, which extended our already questionable time away from the house.

While I watered he lay on his belly with his ear against the ground, like he could hear the roots quenching their thirst through the earth. He'd point out every fallen leaf, every snapped stem, and no matter how many times I'd tell him it was okay, his brow wouldn't unfurrow until I distracted him with the blooms on the lavender or the new fruit on the tomato plants. Our plants were his friends.

The continued secrecy of our garden fed my bravery, and I dropped some seeds in between vegetable plants for my own purposes. If discovered, I wasn't sure how much it would give away, but I was prepared to lie about their purpose. *I am a Moore on the outside.*

Martin, Paul, and I resumed our Irish-only chess nights now that Martin was home again for the summer. The arrangement had changed; Martin and I now played as a team against Paul. When I'd return to my room afterward, I'd lie in bed and try to clear the wicked errant pleasure alive in my brain from sitting next to Martin on his sofa, from laughing at his jokes, from staring into his eyes at a distance much closer than normal life usually allowed. Mam couldn't know.

I wanted him to take me home to visit my family, but every time I tried to tell him, my words lodged in my throat and all I could think about was Fearghus' wallet in the bottom drawer of my bedside table.

One night Paul didn't show for chess at the usual time, so Martin and I started a game without him. It was the perfect opportunity to tell him I wanted him to take me home. While he was pondering each move, I'd gather the nerve, only for it to fall flat each time he finished his turn and looked up at me.

"*Níl tú ag díona' ro-mhaith anocht.*" He took my bishop. "*Tá tú ro-bhog orm.*"

I had to agree—my distraction had made the game far too easy for him. He raised his eyebrows, like he knew I had something to say. Could I say it in Irish? *Tá mé ag iarraidh go dtiúrfaidh tú abhaile mé.*

"*An bhfuil rud eicínt eile uait a dhíona'?*"

Yes, I wanted to say. *I do want to do something else. I want to see my daughter. My mom, my sister, and my brother. If you're the only one who can take me, I'll go with you.*

The door opened and Paul came in and plopped into a chair. His lip was swollen and split in the middle with a line of dried dark blood.

"Paul!" I slipped back into English. I didn't want our Irish time tainted by the violence in the Moore household.

"What'd you do now?" Martin said, unmoved.

Paul leaned back in the chair and closed his eyes. "Just a friendly conversation with Martin, Sr. Remind me not to tell him to kiss my ass again. He doesn't like that."

Martin fell against the back of the sofa, laughing. "Did you hit him back?"

"Are you kidding? If I wanted to die, I'd rather pick a method that's more fun."

I got up and examined his face. He tried to smile at me, but it turned out lopsided.

"I'll get you some ice."

He caught my arm and spun me into his lap. "No ice. Just sit with me and I'll be okay." He wrapped his arms around my hips.

From the closer position I could see blood pooling around the eye opposite the swelling on his lip. "You have a black eye, too."

"Yeah, he hit me twice."

"He hit you twice?" I tried to get up, but he held me tighter. "Your own father hit you twice?"

He raised one eyebrow and nodded. His gaze moved to Martin, then he threw both arms in the air. I stood up.

"You shouldn't talk back to him," Martin said.

"Yeah, yeah." Paul released a breath through his teeth. "He shouldn't hassle me."

"It wouldn't be hard to appease him. Sign up for some classes. Get a job. Go to Baltimore for two weeks and take care of the shit there. Take some of your girlfriends. Mix in some leisure time."

Paul slid lower in the chair. How could anyone be so supine about such a violent confrontation with his father? "Why appease him?"

"So he gets off your back."

"And do what he wants me to do?" Paul scoffed.

"Not necessarily. Just do something. It doesn't matter what it is."

Paul snorted. "You know it matters. Don't be an idiot."

Martin looked at me, but I wasn't sure why. I pretended not to notice, and he returned his attention to Paul.

"He'll never approve of anything I do unless it's something he tells me to do. I have that luxury for some reason. You, Pierce, and Lew get away with murder—" Paul paused for a second before bursting into laughter, unable to collect himself enough to finish his thought.

I stared at the floor. Martin stared at me.

"Never mind," Paul said finally. "Join your teammate, Miss Bevan. Let's play."

Later that night I lay in bed, floating with relief at my inability to ask Martin to take me home. Fearghus' ghost was with me. Protecting me, our daughter, and my family. I could not bring a murderer to my family's home.

A heavy thud woke me that night, and I sat up in bed holding my breath. Fearghus shifted next to me. I put my hand on his back to silence him. Someone stumbled through my door with their hand on the wall then fell down on hands and knees. I looked around for a weapon. I had nothing.

"Sloane?"

"Paul?" I slid out of bed. He reached up and clung to my nightgown as soon as I got to him. His weight pulled me to my knees.

"Sloane, you have to hide me." He took a panicked look behind him. "Someone followed me."

"No one followed you. Everything's fine. Did Martin go back to his other room or is he still next door?"

He dropped his voice to the tiniest whisper. "I don't know."

I tried to stand up, but he kept his hold. His lip was still swollen, and his eyes were two pools of black. "Paul—"

"Don't use my name! They'll kill you if you say my name. They'll kill us both. They cut off my fingers and replaced them with new ones. But I know. I know they're not mine." He held up his right hand as if to prove it.

I took his hand with both of mine. "There is nothing wrong with your fingers."

He jerked away. "See those lines?" He pointed to his knuckles. "That's where they cut them off and sewed on the new ones."

"Let's go to the sofa." I tried to stand, and this time he allowed it. I helped him lie down, pulled the quilt off my bed and covered him. I knelt at his side. "Why do you take that stuff? Is this fun? Does this make you feel good?"

"They make me take it."

"Who?"

"The people in the woods. They pace out there, back and forth. They watch me until I take it."

I smoothed his hair. I was sure the people he spoke of didn't exist until that poison was working itself through his system, justifying its existence by warping his mind. He caught my hand. Held it against his cheek. Closed his eyes. "Why are you so nice to me?"

With the edge of the quilt balled in his other hand, he looked like a little boy. "I have to leave again. Give my old man some time to cool off. But I have nowhere to go. I can't be alone. I don't want to be alone."

"You won't be alone."

"They'll come kill me if I'm alone."

"Who?"

He opened his eyes. A shock surged through me.

"*You* know who."

I pulled my hand away. Either the drugs were talking nonsense, or they were breaching a barrier of confidentiality. Would someone I know really come to kill him?

I needed to tell my family that Paul, the third son, the one with the brown eyes and no intent to do anyone harm, should be spared. That he was an unwilling member of the Moore family. But they'd think I'd been influenced to protect him, and they'd hate him even more for corrupting me.

In the morning Paul was gone. If the quilt from my bed wasn't crumpled on the end of the sofa, I'd have thought the whole thing was a bad dream. I left Fearghus in the bed between two stacks of pillows and went outside to greet the summer morning from the balcony. A doe and fawn were grazing at the edge of the woods. I wanted to wake Fearghus so he could see them, but the still of the morning had fixed my legs in place.

The doors opened on Martin's balcony. He came out with his coffee. "If he does that again, send him over here and lock your doors. If he won't leave, have someone come get me."

"I don't mind it."

He leaned his elbows on the railing and looked across the lawn at the deer. "It doesn't matter whether you mind it or not. He can't sleep in your room. He's a drug addict, and he shouldn't be around Trey."

"He just needs someone to talk to sometimes."

"That someone is not you."

The acid in his voice took me back two years, to that day he chastised me by the lake after the master threatened to kill Fearghus. He hadn't used that tone on me for so long. I turned to go back in my room.

"Don't be mad. You know it's not right for him to use you like that."

"A lot of things about this situation aren't right."

He took a sip of his coffee. "A lot of them can't be helped. Some of them can."

"Some of them don't need to be."

"I'm not arguing with you about this. If you want me to ban him from your room, I can, and I will. Don't push me."

Anger roared into my head. I clutched the balcony railing that separated me from him. Responses swarmed, pushing and shoving each other on their way to my mouth. He was in charge, and he always would be. The freedoms I'd gained in those two years were granted only because of him. I was standing outside on that balcony because of him. It was in my and Fearghus' best interest to remain peaceful, to be grateful for what we had and use it to our advantage.

I live for Fearghus. I will make the most of this life.

I went inside. Fearghus was sitting up on the bed. "Water garden time?"

After breakfast we walked to the lake and followed the shore. I tried to interest Fearghus in the ducks to make our walk appear casual to anyone watching. Fearghus wasn't interested in ducks. He had only his garden on his mind. The sun's heat pulsed against us in clearly defined waves. Fearghus' sweaty hair clumped against his head, but he showed no sign of discomfort as he marched through the grass. We took a different route through the woods toward an unfamiliar rumble that grew louder with each step.

Fearghus started running when the ground leveled out into sparser forest, and I let him get ahead of me, knowing his short legs wouldn't take him too far. The edge of the forest that opened into our garden came into view. A monster of an object moved just past the farthest trees, back and forth, pacing like one of Paul's feared people of the woods. I stopped. The ground vibrated to the motion of that monster. My heart took a plunge. And then I was running. "Fearghus!"

His green and blue striped shirt passed between the final trees and stopped cold. The yellow machine contin- ued its work, and when I reached Fearghus I picked him up. I didn't want to see it—our garden ripped from the earth, overturned, dirt falling from bare roots, stalks reaching through upturned soil in a desperate search for help. Fearghus' eyes, round with horror, stunned by the ease of destruction. Watching his friends being buried alive.

I turned him away from it, but he twisted to face it. He raised an arm to point at what little was left of our garden.

I took a few steps backward. "Let's go back. We'll see if Ruby has any treats."

"No! Down!" He kicked and pushed at me.

I lost my grip, and he slid down my body and ran toward the yellow machine. He collapsed to the ground when I caught his arm, writhing and pulling away from me. I picked him up again. He fought and gasped. At the far end of the garden Pierce stood, smoking a cigarette with a devil's smile pointed straight at us.

Fearghus cried the whole way back to the house. Ruby offered cheese and cookies with no success, and when she got out the ice cream he only cried harder. I dragged him to our room, passing Martin on the stairs, who stopped to watch but said nothing. I couldn't blame him for what happened. I'd set it all up. I'd accepted a risk. This was my fault.

I held Fearghus on the balcony and swayed with him until the cries turned to shuddering moans and his exertion wore him into sleep. I laid him on the bed, tugged off his sweat-soaked clothes, and stroked the ripple between his eyebrows that would not smooth. Guilt overpowered all the anger and I covered my face, bowing against my lap, trying to curb the spasm in my chest but it couldn't be contained. It was finally my turn to cry.

Fearghus and I poured all our energy into our little balcony garden even though I knew there wasn't enough time left in the season for what I'd planned to do. Somehow, I'd have to muster the bravery next summer to grow what I needed, just outside my bedroom, visible for all to see.

The first night I woke alone in bed, my muscles were paralyzed as if they remembered how the empty side of the bed tormented me every night after my husband died. I forced my legs to move, for my arms to work. It was my little Fearghus who was missing this time. I rushed into the bathroom, then the sitting room. I checked under the sofa and under the bed. And then I saw through the window, his curled white back lying against the porch tile, his shock of dark hair given shine by the moon.

I went outside. His cat was stretched against the front of him. Fearghus had named him Friend, and he seemed to live up to his name more every day. I scooped Fearghus up. He turned in my arms to face me and blinked his eyes open.

"You can't sleep outside. Let's get back in bed."

He frowned. "Stay with plants. Keep monsters away."

I brought him inside and closed the door. "Nothing will hurt our plants."

"Yellow monster—"

"That was not a monster, it was a machine. And it will never happen again." It was a mistake. *My* mistake.

He snuggled into bed, too sleepy and calmed by the night to complain.

The second night I found him out there, I brought him inside and locked the barrel bolts on the doors, but I should've known locks would not hinder my child. When he got out there on the third night despite the locks, I stayed awake with my family's texts, searching for some way to keep those doors closed at night. I found nothing that could safely be used in the Moore house without asking Martin's permission, which I knew he would grant, but I didn't want to add to my list of ways I was beholden to him.

The next day Fearghus and I built a scarecrow. We stuffed one of Fearghus' shirts, his pants, and a pair of socks with straw from the maintenance shed. I sewed the clothes together, Ruby supplied a little squash for the head, and Fearghus' teddy bear lent his hat. We put our scarecrow on a little stool beside our row of pots, and I told Fearghus we needed to give him a name.

He named him Martin.

CHAPTER 23

THE REAL MARTIN had been scarce that week I struggled to keep Fearghus in bed at night. Through Paul, he cancelled chess night due to being too tired. From what, I wasn't sure, since Paul's excuse, "He's been training a lot," left me with doubt.

I'd never been in their training room in the basement, and I had no desire for a tour. Every time I imagined what my husband endured in this house, that basement became the most likely setting. I knew this was a coping mechanism that allowed me to move freely in the rest of the house without fear of stepping on the spot in the floor where he died.

One morning after breakfast I let Fearghus loose on the lawn, and I sat on the patio and wondered how long Tara's hair would be by now since her brother's had been cut so many times I'd lost count. They were both born with that thick dark hair. If they hadn't been a boy and a girl, I'd have never been able to tell them apart.

"Come walk with me. I have something to show you," Martin said, coming outside. He offered his hand. "And Trey."

The weight to his words kept me in my seat. "What is it?"

"A surprise."

"I don't like surprises. And he'll throw an awful fit if I cut his outside play short."

He stepped off the patio in Fearghus' direction. "Trey! Want to go for a walk and see a surprise?"

"That's rotten."

"What'd you expect from me?" He shot me a grin before crossing the lawn to Fearghus, who was already running toward him.

I stayed in my seat until Fearghus yelled, "Mama!" and squinted into the sun while looking my way. Martin knew just where to hit an adversary. Martin put Fearghus on his shoulders, and I followed behind them toward Paul's carriage house, but instead of going inside we made a turn and my mind filled in the trail from the direction we were walking.

"Martin, stop. Don't take him back there. Please." He must've heard about the destruction of our garden from Pierce. He couldn't be doing this to us.

He turned around. Fearghus' innocent smile shone above him, full of highest hopes of the promised surprise.

"It's a good surprise. Trust me." He extended his hand. When I didn't budge, he came back to me and took my hand.

He knew I couldn't trust him, but he didn't know the burden of a child's innocence riding on that trust so unworthy of such a gamble. I was a grown person, armored for the trials of this life. Fearghus was open and delicate. Vulnerable to the darkness of the Moore family. The slightest wrongdoing to a child had the capability to scar him in a way that could never scar an adult.

I watched the grass skimming past my shoes and knew if Martin failed us now, my distrust of him would forever be set in concrete. A crew of men digging a trench came into view, and Martin caught me looking at them as we walked by.

"That's part of it."

When we neared the last cluster of trees that once hid our garden from view, Fearghus struggled to get down and Martin lowered him to the ground. He ran ahead, just like he did that last day we made the walk to this spot.

"He's just a baby," I said. It sounded more like a plea than the warning I'd intended to give.

"Are you seeing what I'm seeing? Babies don't run like that."

Fearghus made it past the trees and stopped. His voice carried back to me, too far away to make out the words, then he spun toward us, yelling and waving his arms. I ran toward him. Martin followed. When I got to him, I picked him up.

He leaned into my face. "Babies there?"

"Babies?"

He pointed past me. "Babies!"

I turned. A freshly tilled plot lay before us. Three men were planting tomato plants in the farthest row.

"Down!"

I put him down, and he ran to the garden, fell to his hands and knees, and put his ear against the ground.

"Pierce could only remember tomatoes. You'll have to replant everything else. I know it's probably too late in the season—"

"You can't do this for me."

"Okay, then it's for him." He nodded toward Fearghus. "You'll have irrigation now. How were you watering before? I hope you weren't doing it by hand."

"Pierce—"

"Overstepped his bounds. He won't do it again. I just wish you'd have told me you wanted a garden. It would've saved you a lot of work. We have people to do all of this for you."

"I wanted to do it myself."

He wrapped his arm around my shoulders and walked me toward the garden. "Of course you did." He tapped Fearghus on top of the head.

Fearghus looked up, frowning. "None in there."

"You'll have to put them back again," Martin said.

Fearghus smiled, lighting every dark corner in the world, and when he turned away from us to view his repaired garden again, I saw a tangible joy around him. I felt a weight lift, a peace settle around me. Martin glanced at me, making me aware of how long I'd been staring but I couldn't take my eyes off him. He gave me a polite nod and took a step away, looking uncomfortable in my presence for the first time since I'd met him. Maybe I couldn't trust this man, but I'd never know if I didn't try.

"I want you to take me to Chicago."

Martin nodded without looking at me. If his pulse was thudding as hard as mine, he didn't show it. We watched the men finish the last two tomato plants and gather their tools. I wasn't betraying my husband. It was only hard for me to accept Martin's offer before because I wasn't sure I wanted to go with him. Now I was sure.

"We'll leave in two days. Tell Fran to pack your luggage for a week away. If she asks, we're going to Cambridge."

"Are we also going to Cambridge?" I'd been imprisoned in a house for over two years. It would've sounded appealing to anyone.

"Not unless you want to." He turned to me, squinting in the sun.

I couldn't look at him so I looked at Fearghus, who was on his hands and knees on the other side of the garden, facing the tomato plants with a look of concentration I'd learned to fear. "Stop, Fearghus."

His expression broke, only to be replaced by the most mischievous of grins, and he flattened his palms and bore down even harder.

"Fearghus!"

He shook his head like I was annoying him.

"Trey." The volume of Martin's voice was no higher than mine, but Fearghus looked up, then he sat back on his heels.

"Time to go back," Martin said.

Fearghus stood and took a wistful glance at the tomato plants. My demands so easily tuned out, yet he was standing at attention for Martin? He knew no reason to fear him, although he had many. I hoped he'd never know the fears I knew.

"Gosh it's hot. I could use some iced tea." Martin touched the small of my back, and I turned with him, linking my arm in his like I would've with Paul.

Footsteps pounded behind us, getting closer, and instead of stopping they continued on as Fearghus blasted between us and ran ahead, laughing wildly. My view of the scene detached, moved forward, and spun around, and I saw it again, replayed. I gasped and ripped my arm free.

"What?" Martin said.

My breath was coming so fast I had to swallow to gain control of it. My first vision had just come true. I had now lived it. It was now my past, instead of an envisioned future I never believed, a trick of my mind I blamed on Martin.

"Trey, slow down," Martin said, glancing ahead. He faced me again, his eyes darting between mine. "Can you make it back to the house?"

I nodded and took his arm again like I never wanted to let go.

Two days later Fearghus played with our luggage while I sat in the foyer waiting for Martin's car to be brought around. Martin was in the library on the phone. Soon I'd be in a car next to him, and I'd still be wondering if he'd drive us through in one day. If I'd see my family that soon. Or if that night, I'd be in a hotel—alone with Martin. I couldn't bear to ask him.

The doorman loaded our luggage and helped me and Fearghus into the passenger side, and we sat in the idling car until Martin strode down the steps and got in the driver's seat.

"Sorry. Something always comes up last minute."

I covered my hair with my scarf and tied it under my chin. And then we were moving around the circle driveway, and I squeezed Fearghus and clenched my jaw, but the tears came anyway. If Martin noticed, he didn't let on. Sick with the worst combination of emotions, I stared out my window, happy to be on my way to see my family and my baby girl, but crippled by sadness to know I'd have to leave them again and come back here. How would I ever say goodbye?

The road signs told me we were heading toward downtown Richmond, but before we made it all the way, Martin pulled into the parking lot of a car dealer. He went inside. I wiped my face on Fearghus' shirt. I knew we could escape, and Martin knew that too. He was either a gambler, or much too self-assured.

When he returned Fearghus was behind the wheel. Martin took him out of the car then came around and opened my door. "We're switching cars."

A man came outside to shift our luggage to the trunk of a sleek black car. Martin tipped him, and we all got in.

"What was wrong with the other car?"

"Nothing," he said, backing out. "Except that's the car we're expected to be in."

"Sneaky."

"No, smart. You don't want to see what will happen to us if we're caught."

"Us? This wasn't my idea."

He laughed, although I didn't mean it to be funny. "We have hotel reservations in Cambridge too. They wouldn't expect us to stay at my apartment. Someone matching my description will check in for us."

"Who?"

"A guy who owes me a favor. I need to tell you about Cambridge, about the things we're supposed to be doing there, about my apartment. Do you want to do that now or later?"

We turned onto the highway. Concrete stretched in front of me. I was a bird, and my wings were unfolding, stretching for the first time in over two years.

"Let's do it now," I answered, in need of something to occupy my mind. I took Fearghus' shoes off so he could stand on the seat and watch the city roll past us outside. He hadn't been in a car since he was two weeks old. I hooked my arm around his waist, and Martin told me all about our pretend trip to Cambridge.

Lunch was burgers and fries. Somewhere in the twists of the Appalachians he told me we'd stop in Dayton for the night. I spent the next several hours wondering how I'd sleep in the same room with him. Surely he wouldn't want me out of his sight when I could escape so easily. Night closed in and Fearghus fell asleep on the seat with my lap as his pillow. We drove into downtown Dayton. A tight cluster of light and noise seeped into my window and built an excited panic in me. The unfamiliarity of it persuaded me to believe I was no longer myself. I was so out of place, it didn't matter who I was.

Martin parked in front of an elegant hotel. A man came to open my door, and Martin picked up Fearghus and we all walked inside. He left us on a sofa in the lobby and went to the front desk. The lights were low enough that Fearghus fell back asleep in my arms. I heard Martin check in as Michael and Judy Sullivan. He asked for two adjoining rooms. A pressure against me released. I could breathe again—when I didn't know I was suffocating.

The elevator was a stifling box. I was glad to have Fearghus asleep on Martin's shoulder. His eager inquisitiveness would have added a layer of chaos in my mind when I had too much already. Martin unlocked one of the rooms and we went inside. Our luggage came in on a cart behind us.

"All the bags in this room, sir?"

"The one on the bottom goes next door." Martin flipped the covers down on the bed and laid Fearghus on the sheet.

The bellhop nodded, making nothing of a supposed husband and wife staying in separate rooms. Maybe we were brother and sister. Could I be his sister? Could I be his wife? I watched him tip the bellhop, and it struck me this arrangement of rooms was the same we had at the Moore estate. He didn't sleep in his room next to mine when it was first prepared for him, but he did now. And if my first vision came true, they could *all* come true. Martin, shaving his face in my bathroom one day. Me, holding another baby. A young woman, imprisoned in my room at the Moore estate, just like me.

"I'm going to order a bottle of scotch. Do you need anything? A snack? A glass of wine?"

"No," I blurted. "Nothing."

He propped a chair against the open door that joined the two rooms. "This needs to stay open." He took off his tie. I wanted to look away from him, but I couldn't. "Are you sure you don't want a drink of some sort? You look like you're wound tighter than—"

"I'm just tired."

He tossed his tie into the other room and unbuttoned the top button of his shirt. Looking around, he lingered on the window, then the door to the hall. "You trust me?"

I couldn't turn back now. The draw to see my family was too great despite the risk of exposing them. I had to trust him. "Yes."

"Then I trust you."

CHAPTER 24

EVERY THIRTY MINUTES I woke to my pounding heart, reaching for Fearghus and finding him sleeping sweetly next to me. My eyes would adjust to the foreign room and I'd panic again, thinking I was newly kidnapped until I remembered I was with Martin, my known and familiar kidnapper of two years. His presence next door would then remind me why we were in that strange room, and I'd toss and turn, impatient to see my family yet sick with anxiety over how they'd feel about the new me. The me who didn't grab Fearghus and flee the room as soon as Martin fell asleep.

I was up and dressed before the sun. I sat by the window and watched the dark sky lighten to a surround of baby blue and a low streak of pink clouds—a visual depiction of the presence of each of my children in my life. Fearghus all around me. A tiny hint of Tara hanging low, drawing my eye. Soon I would see her. Soon I would leave her again. The sky would turn blue from horizon to horizon, and those pink clouds would blow away.

Waking sounds reached me from Martin's room. I heard him shower and dress. Fearghus sat up and stretched. As I was dressing him, Martin appeared in the doorway in his slacks, shoes, and undershirt. "Ready?"

I just looked at him. Surely he wasn't going out missing his shirt.

"I'm waiting on my shirt. Shouldn't be too much longer."

He must've sent it out to be ironed. "I could've ironed it for you."

He leaned against the door frame. "I'll keep that in mind."

I picked up Fearghus' shoes and called him to me. He plopped down on the floor on his butt. "No shoes!"

"You're not leaving without shoes. Come here."

He threw himself backward against the floor, arched his back, and whined. It was too early for a power struggle. And with so little sleep, I had nothing in me to fight him.

"Trey, listen to your mother."

Fearghus grunted, but he sat up. He looked at Martin, then he looked at me.

"*Move*," Martin said.

He stood up. That was good enough for me. I scooted over to him and put his shoes on while he stared at Martin.

We had breakfast in the hotel. Martin was in no hurry, which made my job of moving the food around on my plate more prolonged and more difficult.

"You should probably call and tell them we're coming. I'd rather my visit not be a surprise on top of extremely unwelcome."

I'd already told Mam the night after I decided to come, but I couldn't tell Martin that. After checking out at the front desk, he took Fearghus on a tour of the lobby while I made the call. Mam said Arthur was already there. He'd spent the night, in case we showed up early. Enid would be there in a few hours. The three of them were the only ones who knew.

"My brother will be there," I said to Martin when I rejoined him. I felt it proper to give him a fair warning even though I had no idea what Arthur was going to do, or if he'd do anything at all.

"Of course. I'm sure he's anxious to see you."

"My brother doesn't like you."

"Your brother isn't going to be a problem for me."

I chuckled, even though it wasn't funny. Arthur wasn't going to be a problem—he was going to be a catastrophe. "You don't know my brother."

"Unfortunately, I do."

I spent the first few hours of the drive trying to keep Fearghus in the seat and wondering if I should ask Martin how he knew my brother, and whether his answer would bring me comfort or more grief. By the time we stopped for lunch, I'd concluded that any connection between Martin and Arthur would undoubtedly include my husband, and

I couldn't bear any mention of him that might confound the ruckus already alive in my head.

I was being personally escorted to my family's house by Martin Moore. And my brother was there waiting to welcome this man who'd killed his best friend. We should've turned around, headed straight to Richmond without looking back. But if I didn't get to see my daughter, I wouldn't make it back to Richmond in one piece, and then Fearghus would be just like his sister. Motherless.

Martin followed my directions to Mam's house like they were unknown to him, although I couldn't shake the feeling he was pretending for my sake. We rounded the corner on to Mam's street of snuggled-together houses, some two stories, others three, much taller than they were wide and all distinct in their detail. White shutters on one, red on another, a gray roof, a brown roof, chimneys reaching to the sky. I spotted the green door and the white porch. The house I grew up in, once so familiar I could tell I was home by the cracks in the sidewalk out front. Now the house was a miniature replica of itself. I pointed. "That one."

He pulled to the curb. The curtain shifted in the front window. I reached for the door handle, but Martin got out and came around. He opened my door, took Fearghus from my lap, and helped me up. I put Fearghus on my hip. Every muscle in my body quivered. My hands shook. I'd been silently crying since the Chicago skyline appeared on the horizon, but now a second, more forceful wave of tears hit.

"I'll be in the car." He touched my elbow. "Give your brother my regards. And if anyone gets any ideas, remind them what's at stake here."

I looked up at the house. The door opened and I was running up the steps. I collided with a solid block of warmth, and it surrounded me, and then I was inside. The door closed behind me and I couldn't see past all my tears.

"Where is she?" I gasped.

Everyone backed up. I put Fearghus down. A little girl stood holding on to the edge of the sofa and chewing her pinky. Her yellow dress was slightly twisted, and the ribbon in her hair held on for dear life. Her brow wrinkled the way Fearghus' did when he was on the verge of a disagreement, and she trailed her hand along the side of the sofa and situated herself behind Mam's legs.

Mam sat, placing her hand on top of Tara's head. "Let's give her a few minutes to warm up."

I sat on the floor. Fearghus walked in front of me and stood in the middle of the group, sizing everyone up.

"Is your warden staying in the car?" Arthur asked.

None of that mattered now. Fearghus walked to Tara and poked her in the chest. She shrunk back, curling behind Mam's legs.

Enid sat on the floor next to me. "I'm getting married."

I pulled off my scarf and used it to dab my eyes. "He asked you?" I only knew about Enid's Johnny Doyle through Mam. They'd started dating about a year before. I'd never met him.

She showed me her ring. "I'm sorry. I planned to tell you after you got settled, but I just couldn't wait." I hugged her so hard she started laughing, but when she pulled back and looked at me, her face dropped. "What?"

"I won't be able to come."

"We haven't set the date. Maybe you could ask if he'd drive you back?"

Reflex turned me toward the front door, to the path that would take me to go ask Martin right now. Arthur was at the window with the curtain pulled back, watching the street.

"Yes. I'll ask." But Fearghus wouldn't be able to go. He'd be older; he might remember it. He could never know anything of this life, of his real family.

He'd somehow pulled Tara's yellow ribbon free from her hair, and he was busy picking at the loop to straighten it while Tara watched, brow furrowed, chewing her pinky.

"Fearghus, give it back."

He ignored me. I looked at Mam, and she waved a hand at me like she wanted me to let them be. We all watched Fearghus work, and when the ribbon was finally straight, he shoved it back at Tara. She took it cautiously, like he was going to snatch it back, or bite her, or both.

I wanted to say her name, but I was afraid I'd cry. "Want me to tie it in your hair?"

She looked at me like *I* would bite.

I reached out both arms.

She shook her head and backed into Mam's legs. Fearghus came toward me, thinking my outstretched arms were for him, and I was thankful for him to hold. He'd been the single substitute for both my children for two years, and he would continue to be. This visit would soon be over and leave me with an empty spot in my lap the size of this Tara instead of the newborn Tara I remember holding last.

Tara handed the ribbon to Mam who closed Tara's hand around it and pointed at me. Mam stood. "I'm going to invite Mr. Moore in."

Enid gasped and Arthur crossed the room toward us. "I hope you're kidding."

Mam went past him. "I need to speak with him."

"Speak with him outside."

She frowned at him. "Arthur, be polite or sit down and be quiet."

Arthur followed her out the front door. Fearghus noticed the bookshelf and the potential mess it'd make and headed straight for it. Tara followed, trailing her fingers along the sofa.

"Can I try on your shoes?" Enid asked. "How much did those cost?"

I let them off my feet. "I don't know."

"Do they let you go shopping?" She slipped them on and walked in a little circle.

"No, never. They bring it all in for me."

"And you choose?"

I shrugged. "From my dressing room. I suppose you can call that choosing." I leaned to peer out the open front door. Arthur stood on the porch looking down. I got up for a better view.

"Is he really coming in?" Enid whispered.

I could see Martin's hat coming up the stairs past Arthur, who moved aside for Mam to pass into the house. Martin was now level with Arthur and offering a handshake. When Arthur didn't respond, Martin took off his hat and came in. Arthur came in behind him and slammed the door much too hard.

Mam took Martin's hat and jacket, and Martin turned to face Arthur again. "I'm sorry about the awkwardness of our last meeting."

"Let's not bring that up here."

"You're the boss. How about offering me a drink?"

"I would, but we're all out of rat poison."

Martin caught my eye. "A special family recipe? I'm disappointed I'll be missing out."

Arthur stepped close to Martin, who raised both arms in the air, and Arthur patted him down like they do in movies. It appeared to be a common routine between the two of them.

Enid pulled me to the sofa with her and handed me one of my shoes from her foot. When I leaned to put it on, she leaned down with me. "Oh my gosh, Sloane, he's so handsome."

I snatched the other shoe out of her hand.

"He has Paul Newman's eyes! And that expression—you know the one!"

I elbowed her hard. She covered her mouth, eyes smiling.

Arthur still faced Martin. "Fearghus was a brother to me, and you think you can come in here—"

"You should've told him to stay home with his wife."

Arthur's fists clenched at his sides. Mam took Martin by the arm and led him into the kitchen.

"I don't care what Mam says. I have to kill him." Arthur stared after them.

"What does Mam say?"

He glared at me, a face of stone. "I'm not okay with any of this."

"And I am?"

"When you got out of the car, you let him hold little Fearghus."

The accusation could've been a physical strike for the way it lashed me. My chest went raw all at once, popping open all the little boxes where I'd stuffed the grief, the shame, the heartbreak of the last two years. Words of Martin's defense blazed in my mind, threatening to expose the traitor in me. Arthur could never judge me more harshly than I had already judged myself. "You have no idea what it's like there. What you'd do if you were in my place."

He stared me down. "I wouldn't let them touch him."

I turned away. There was no point in talking to him. His thoughts were skewed by the anger and defeat caused by Martin's presence in our family home, and until he either made peace with it or Martin left, he wouldn't be able to talk to me rationally. I couldn't expect him to understand why Martin brought me home if I didn't understand it myself.

All of Tara's little books were now scattered on the floor, thanks to Fearghus' wild arm, so I sat next to them and handed one to Tara. She took it from me and set it nicely back on the shelf, forgetting she was afraid of me until I handed her a second one. We stared at one another, the book in between us. Fearghus took it from me and handed it to her. She put it on the shelf. Her movements were slow and gentle, compared to the yanking and shoving I was used to from Fearghus. Her neck was slimmer and more pronounced. Her hair flipped on the ends, just a bit longer than her chin. Her fingernails were clean and clipped perfectly straight, unlike Fearghus' constantly dirty and ragged ones. She made the child I was raising look like an unruly beast.

As if to prove my thought, just as Tara placed the third book in line with the others, Fearghus' arm swept the shelf sending all three flying. Tara bit her fist and cackled. It was Fearghus' identical laugh.

Fearghus attacked the books on the floor, shoving them all like a bulldozer.

"Stop!" Arthur hollered.

Tara jumped, looked at Arthur, and started crying. I reached for her but she shrunk away. Arthur picked her up and she wailed into his neck.

"I'm sorry," he said. "I didn't mean to yell. *Shh.*"

Fearghus stood straight, arms at his sides, and watched Arthur like he was on display for his personal entertainment. He pointed at Arthur and turned to me. "Like Paul."

I covered my mouth but it was too late. I didn't want to laugh at Arthur when he was so unsettled.

"What's so funny?"

I shook my head. Outbursts in the Moore household were so common to Fearghus that he could calmly make such a matter-of-fact comparison while his rattled sister sniffled in her uncle's arms. And if I explained to Arthur that he was just compared to one of the Moore boys and indirectly insulted by his own nephew, it would only make him angrier.

Arthur jerked the chain on the ceiling fan. The new breeze ruffled Tara's hair, but she was too busy watching Fearghus to notice.

I turned him toward the mess he made. "Let's put them all back now." I looked at Tara. "Would you like to help?"

She nodded and Arthur let her down then held his hand out to help me up. "I can't stand him being in there. It's making me—"

"Forget he's in there. We haven't seen each other for two years."

He hugged me hard, long enough for Enid to get up and join us. We all sat on the sofa. My children took turns returning the books to the shelf like it was an old routine of theirs.

"We should talk, but I don't know what to say," Enid said.

"Me neither," I said.

We watched the kids until Fearghus stopped and leaned into Tara's face. "You have cookies?"

Tara turned away from him to scan the room. None of our faces suited her needs, so she ran into the kitchen with Fearghus on her heels. I followed.

Mam and Martin were seated across from one another at the kitchen table. Mam pushed away from the table and retrieved two vanilla cookies from her cookie jar for the kids. They ran back into the front room.

"The three of you are staying for dinner," she said to me. "I'd like a few more minutes alone with Mr. Moore."

He was fixated on an orange he was turning over and over in his hands. I wanted to know if he'd heard what she just said, if he'd already agreed to stay for dinner. He didn't appear to be ignoring me so much as he was lost in thought and taking it out on that orange. I'd never seen him so preoccupied.

Turning to Mam for an explanation got me nothing but a pat on the arm. I gave her a quick what-did-you-tell-him nod toward Martin.

"Go catch up with your brother and sister," she said.

I returned to my spot on the sofa. After a few false starts, a conversation grew, mundane in subject matter but perfect in function. Those two years became a long weekend, and if my babies weren't chattering and walking around us, we'd have had no reason to think otherwise. Lured by Enid, Tara allowed me to tie the ribbon in her hair, and I took my time to extend the moment. It was a memory I could hold with me back to Richmond and invoke every day until I could see her again.

A light commotion reached us from the kitchen, and I got up to check on Martin. He was peeling potatoes next to Mam, who was slicing and tossing them into a skillet. This time he wasn't too preoccupied to notice me standing there. "I didn't expect to learn something on this trip."

I raised my eyebrows.

He held up the knife. "How to peel potatoes."

"I could've taught you that at home." The words knocked the wind out of me. At home? The Moore estate wasn't my home. Chicago was my home. He went back to his peeling as if my words weren't echoing through the air like they were to my ears. Home was no longer home, but the Moore estate would never be my home. I'd changed too much to belong with my family; I could never change enough to belong to my new one. I was living in the moment when a candle blows out—the featureless, unending dark before the eyes adjust. My place had been yanked away. I was floating in a void.

CHAPTER 25

"THEY'RE MAKING DINNER," I said when I returned to the front room. It no longer seemed right to plop down on the sofa between the two of them like I had earlier. That would seem impolite from a guest. I was a guest.

Enid scooted to the edge of the seat. "What's the matter?"

I sat in the chair by the window and looked outside. "I shouldn't have come back."

Arthur got up and leaned his shoulder against the wall near me. "You tell him to bring you back whenever you want. They can't keep you locked up in that house."

"It's just not worth it. I'll always have to go back. And Fearghus can't come anymore. I can't leave him there alone."

He exhaled hard and brought his fist against his lips.

Enid came over and sat on the floor at my feet. "It's okay if you have to go back. It won't be forever."

"How do you know? I could live there forever. I could die there."

"You won't die there," she said. "And there are worse places to live. Don't you find it a little exciting to live in a huge mansion with a man like Martin?"

Arthur cursed Martin under his breath.

They had opposite views of my life in the Moore estate, and they both couldn't be more wrong. Perhaps combining their ideas would come closer to the reality, but the thought of defining it at all gave me a sickness and a chill, and I couldn't decide if I wanted to laugh or cry. I'd done both within the hour and I feared I was coming unglued. "You don't know—"

"I *don't* know," Enid said. "I'm just asking you to see it from someone else's eyes. It's a temporary stay in a mansion with a handsome, mysterious man and all the money and clothes you could ever want. Any girl would love that. We'll always be here when you do get to come home. Someday we'll all be together again."

"That's almost exactly what Martin's brother said."

Arthur stepped directly in front of me. "Don't listen to any of them. They're all just as bad as he is, or worse."

"Two are worse. One of them—"

He pointed at me. "Don't defend any of them."

"—could be good. But he has no chance in that family. They've corrupted him. I worry so much about Fearghus." My hand went to my chest, a reaction to hold the words inside. I'd never thought those words, but somehow on this day they were given life. The monster of grief that had been living inside me had just been torn from the shadows and given a name. With this new recognition, could it now be subdued, or would its power grow?

"*Is treise dúchas ná oiliúint,*" Enid said. "He'll always be one of us. They can't change that."

"They have a strong influence."

"Don't let them. Keep him away from them," Arthur said, as if it were that simple.

Martin's manners at dinner remained flawless, even under Arthur's pointed questions and killer glare. The expert dance around the interrogation was too natural an act to be taught in law school, and I wondered how much of his talent had been used on me without my knowledge. I knew my brother noticed every twist, every avoidance, but with Mam and the children present there was little he could do. Arthur's ease in attacking Martin fed my discomfort. They had an obvious history. How long or how involved was an uncertainty that was best left alone.

While the table was being cleared, Martin caught my elbow and led me into the hall. He leaned into my ear. "Do you want another day here?"

I stared at the knot of his tie. Yes I wanted another day. But at what cost? Could I possibly get more beholden to him? Did it matter?

Tara and Fearghus stampeded down the hall. Martin pressed against me to move out of the way as they passed. If we stayed another day, they'd be harder to rip apart. Fearghus wasn't floating in a void like I was. He was solid in the world he knew. He'd go back to his life with the Moores—his home—and this trip would be filed in his memory as a fun outing that would fade with time and new experiences. The familiarity of returning to the only home he'd known would be as much a comfort to him as returning to this home had been to me.

Martin touched my chin. I looked up at him.

"I can't leave you here for the night. I'd like to, but I can't."

I knew it was too good to be true. "We can go. I didn't expect to have a long visit."

"I meant we can get a hotel room tonight and come back tomorrow. Do you want to come back tomorrow?"

Goodbyes were easy that night. Fearghus fell asleep on our drive downtown. Martin circled the Loop, passing several hotels before settling on the Congress Plaza. The energy off the streets combined with the glow in my heart, and when Martin parked at the curb and smiled at me, I smiled back—a gesture meant to be a fleeting acknowledgement of his own, of his offer of tomorrow, of his prolonged risk in order to satisfy me. But my smile wouldn't fall, and neither would his. The only passage of time were the beats of my heart, heavy in my chest, throbbing in my head.

My door opened. "Good evening, ma'am." The valet offered me a hand.

Martin slid his arms under Fearghus, freeing my legs, and I got out of the car. We walked inside together, one woman carried by the height of her spirit, and one man burdened by a slumbering child.

The lobby was encased in marble except for the ceiling where arches of colorful mosaic tile drew the eye upward to crystal chandeliers and an elegant clock draped with two resting gilded women. Martin led me to the central sitting area and passed Fearghus to me.

"I dare you to check in as Ricky and Lucy Ricardo," I said.

"You think I can pull that off?"

He could pull anything off, but it couldn't hurt to make him prove it. "Perhaps not."

The dimple appeared at the corner of his lip. "You're on. But you have to come to the desk with me."

He satisfied my dare with a composure so convincing I decided I must call him Ricky for the remainder of the night. Our suite was as opulent as the Moore estate. My shoes sank into the plush rug as I noticed the crystal lamp that would be Fearghus' first victim if I didn't watch him closely. Martin laid Fearghus on the bed. Then he sat on the edge to remove Fearghus' little shoes. I turned to take in the whole room. There was a sitting area with a sofa and a few chairs, but no other bed.

"I need to call home for my messages," he said. "Do you want anything from the bar?"

I shook my head. My heart thumped, compelling me to speak up about the sleeping arrangement. Just then, the bellhop opened a door to an adjoining room, and Martin asked him to take his suitcase in there. Martin followed him in, closing the door behind him.

After stepping out of my shoes and removing my stockings, I went to the window. The lake spread against the lights of the city, a black featureless void stretching to eternity. From this view, there was no other shore. It went on with no end. If I were a stranger to this city, if I'd never seen a map showing Lake Michigan as a small liquid portion of this vast country, I'd know of no other shore, no end to its black void.

There could be an end to our time at the Moore estate. A map I hadn't seen. Another shore. If that shore was out there, there was no guarantee it was freedom, or even a return to the life I'd lost. It could as easily be my death.

The door opened between our rooms. Martin stood in the doorway, missing his jacket and tie. He held up a deck of cards. "Join me?"

Had I already reached that shore?

I turned off the light so Fearghus could sleep and followed Martin into his room, a less spacious version of mine. I took a seat on the sofa. He sat on the facing armchair, the deck of cards still in his hand.

"Trey has a sister," he said.

I couldn't speak. He should've been dealing the cards. His eyes remained on me, but I didn't meet them.

"You have a daughter." He opened the box. The cards slid into his hand. He set the box on the table and leaned forward, resting his elbows on his knees. "Why didn't you tell me?"

I took the cards out of his hand. Shuffled them. Dealt us five each. "What are we playing?"

"You should've told me. We could've … arranged something. Sooner."

"I thought you knew everything about my family."

"I do. But I didn't know that. Don't know how I could've missed it. Where was she the day they came for Trey?"

"In the back room with Mam."

"Did they see her?"

"So now what? You're going to go home and tell them? Did you tell them on the phone just now?" I stood, tossing my cards on the table. I'd just made the biggest mistake of my life, and my baby daughter was going to pay for it. I couldn't see her tomorrow. I couldn't face any of my family. They were going to have to leave, to find somewhere to live where no one would find them. I had to go to sleep and contact Mam. They didn't have much time.

Martin caught my elbow and spun me. He lowered me into his chair. I made no effort to fight him. He was too strong. He'd win. He always won. Against me, against everyone.

He knelt in front of me. His hands embraced my thighs, fusing me to the chair.

"I will not tell a soul. I swear it."

Such open emotion had never touched his face so profoundly, as if the whole world was behind him waiting for my acknowledgment.

A dent appeared in the middle of his forehead. "I told you I wouldn't bring anything home from this trip. This included. Do you trust me?"

I nodded, possessed by a power beyond me, fueled by this bared humanity laid in front of me by the most stoic man on Earth. If this was the level of intensity he kept barred behind his usual cool composure, he was an even stronger man than I thought.

He released my legs and sat on the edge of the sofa. "We'll have to figure something out. I thought this was a one-time visit. Now I see it'll need to be more regular."

"We can't. I won't leave Fearghus there alone."

"Fran can watch him. I'll tell Pierce if he—"

"No. I won't leave him there."

He bowed his head and stared at the floor for a long moment before getting up to pace the room. "We'll bring him. I'll leave you at your mother's, then I'll take him somewhere fun. If you trust me with him."

"And what if he goes back and tells them you dropped me at someone's house and went off without me?"

"We'll tell him not to tell." He dropped back onto the sofa.

"And what if he does?"

"He won't. We'll bribe him." He smiled. "Ice cream. Right?"

Sleep was out of my reach again that night, for similar reasons as the night before—along with something new. I couldn't stop thinking about Martin's hands holding my thighs and that glimpse I'd been offered into the barest part of him.

The next morning Martin walked Fearghus and me to Mam's front door then told me he couldn't intrude on another day and he'd be back to pick me up after dinner. The door opened and I stepped inside, but when I turned around to watch him drive off, I felt a part of me tear away like it was attached to that car.

Tara let me hold her and brush her hair. Fearghus made her cry three times, but he made her laugh too many times to count. I promised Enid I'd come to her wedding, knowing now I had a possibility and Martin's sly mind to find a way to hide it from the Moores. Mam let me take some of her vials of herbs and mushrooms I'd never be able to grow at the estate. I buried them deep in my purse, trying to come up with a white lie to tell Martin if he found them.

When Martin rang the doorbell, I took one look around, realizing it might not be the last. I gave my scarf to Tara, hoping she'd remember me. I hugged Mam, Arthur, and Enid, and Martin walked me down the steps and closed me inside the car. Fearghus waved wildly enough for both of us, and as soon as the house was out of sight I scooted against Martin, slid under his arm, and cried. If he promised to forget everything he saw in Chicago, he could also forget that.

Life at the Moore estate continued as if we'd never left. Hateful, abusive family dinners, followed by Paul's drug-induced trips to my room at night and Pierce's taunts during the day any time he found me alone. Fearghus made trouble in new ways every day, accompanied by Friend the cat, who shared in both the fun and time in the corner, voluntarily. Fall swept in and Martin returned to Harvard during the week, spending weekends at home. It was his last semester. We traveled again to Chicago for Enid's November wedding. Martin said it was the last time Fearghus could see them.

Lewis brought a girl to a few of the family dinners before announcing wedding plans of his own. He was the youngest one of them, but he'd be married first. Extravagant wedding preparations began for a spring wedding. Every day samples of wedding cakes, flowers, and decorations could be found somewhere in the house.

Lewis' room was remodeled for his bride, and I realized I'd soon be joined by another woman in the house. Such news would've made me happy, if every comment of mine wasn't answered by her sideways glance or rolled eyes.

Their hands were tied with fronds of fern under a spring sun on the lawn in front of the largest gathering of people I'd ever seen. I couldn't have been the only one to notice the bride's carefully altered dress, ruffled and gathered so perfectly to cover a little bump of baby.

Our garden burst from the ground, growing with a vitality that made me wonder if Fearghus and Friend weren't tramping out there at night to help it along. The day I caught Pierce's smug gaze trained on Friend following Fearghus along the edge of the lake, I decided to use my forbidden skills for the first time. I gathered from the garden that day, studied my family's texts that night, and empowered Fearghus' amulet to reach its protective arms around Friend. Since Fearghus now wore it on a string around his neck, I knew it couldn't help Friend unless he was at Fearghus' side. Their symbiosis was part of the spell. It was the best I could do.

Ruby saved empty jars for me. I told her they were for Fearghus' projects, which was true, but they were also my own. Plants we collected from our garden went into the jars and were hidden around my room until Fran found one cleaning and I knew I needed a more permanent hiding place. On my hands and knees, I checked every seam in the wood floor and found a loose board in the best place for hiding but the worst for easy access—directly under my bed.

Fearghus and I gathered all the jars hidden throughout the room and stacked them by the bed. I wiggled under, pried the loose board free, and began to fill the floor cavity with my collection. Before I'd finished stowing them all, I heard a knock on the door and froze. Fearghus ran toward it. I scrambled backward, bumping my head on the bed frame. "Fearghus!"

I swept the stacked jars still in plain view under the bed. They crashed to the floor and rolled in every direction. Shiny black men's shoes came toward me.

"Do you need help?" Martin's voice. Teasing. Slightly triumphant. He'd caught me. He didn't know at what, but he knew something.

I slid out from under the bed. He offered his hand. I got up on my own and smoothed my skirt. He tapped one of the upturned jars with the toe of his shoe, cocked his head, and raised an eyebrow. I sat on the bed and stared at my hands in my lap. Where was that lie I was prepared to tell?

He sat next to me. Fearghus turned his bucket of blocks upside down and they loudly joined my scattered mess on the floor.

"Do you need some personal storage?" he asked.

I didn't answer.

He got up and closed and locked the door to the hall and the door to my sitting room. He put both hands on my bed, prepared to shove, and looked pointedly at me. I got up. The bed scooted across the floor, exposing the loose flooring and my half-concealed illegal ingredients. He knelt at the hole and unloaded the few jars I'd already stashed. With both palms pressed on either side of the small opening, he bowed toward it. Static filled my head and popped my ears from the discharge of magic.

"There," he said, scooting around the hole to face me. "This is how it's done."

I knelt next to the hole. He slid his hands in the small opening I'd already created, jerked upward, and a section of flooring five floor boards wide popped loose. He set it aside. "All the storage you need. If you don't mind a little dust."

A pocket of warmth gushed through my chest, up my neck, and into my head. He'd done it for me. Not to further his motives, not to feed his ego. For me.

"Why are you doing this?"

He brushed off his pants. Remaining on his knees, he faced me like my mirror image. "I don't know. It's really stupid. If they find out, I better have a good explanation." He looked out the window for a moment before looking straight into my eyes. "You make me do stupid things."

I couldn't breathe. The gushing warmth was a hot wax covering my whole being, seizing my joints, stilling my heart. I felt my lips part, but no words came out.

"Sloane, I've been in love with you since the first day I saw you." He leaned close—so close. We shared a breath, a pause, a possible exit for me as much as it was for him. He kissed me.

My heart rattled awake, pounding in my head. The hot wax cracked, and I was free. I closed my eyes and rose to meet him. He kissed me again, his hand on my jaw sliding to the back of my neck to pull me close. I sunk against him, fearing I'd float away if I didn't find an anchor. His heart beat heavy against my palm, placed to hold him away as his lips drew me further in. He tasted like fresh air. Like a clear spring. Like a man I wanted more of. I thrust away and started to get up, but he caught my hand and kept me down.

"I think you should marry me."

I pressed both hands against my cheeks. To calm my mind. To slow the room from spinning. "I can't marry you."

"Why not?"

"You …" I looked at Fearghus playing with his blocks. "I can't."

"I'll take Trey as my son."

"I can't allow that."

"Why not? It's the perfect answer. He'd have a father. His life here would make sense to him."

"No." I shook my head. "Never."

"I can make you happy. Just think about it."

"There's nothing to think about."

He glanced at Fearghus. "I can make him the strongest one of us. Think about that."

"He'll never be one of you." I tried to get up again, but he gripped my shoulders to hold me in place.

"No, but he'll be as strong or stronger than us. Read between the lines, Sloane. I can't say it aloud."

My breath was coming fast and short, either from my struggle to get up or from the aftershock of what I'd just done. What I wanted to do again. He released my shoulders, and I pushed away from him to find some space, some sanity away from that sunburst of blue in those gray eyes and those lips I wanted against mine again. I had betrayed my family. Was he speaking of betraying his?

"You'll teach Fearghus …" I lowered my voice to a whisper. "To beat them?"

He combed the room with his eyes before they settled back on me. He nodded.

"Why would you do that?"

"Because I don't blindly follow orders anymore."

"That's too—" I shook my head, unable to finish.

He scooted toward me, bringing us as close as we were before. "I want to make things right. And I want you. Fearghus Donnelly can have you in the afterlife. I want you in this life."

I covered my face with both hands. Fearghus. Lying on that altar under that white cloth on his last night on Earth before he was buried in my family's cemetery, in a plot he would someday share with me. Martin was making a compromise. He knew I still loved Fearghus, that nothing would change that. And it was a truth he was willing to accept. He'd been trained to hate me and my family since the day he was born. So why still want to marry me, a woman still in love with her dead husband? He'd gain nothing except a lot of resistance from his family, and a risk of exposing his deceit every day.

How quickly would my family disown me?

I sat while he loaded all my jars into the floor, covered it with the panel, and moved the bed back.

"Think about it," he said. Then he left.

I was paddling toward a new shore with fragments of a map in my hand. Fearghus was dead. Not coming back. My hesitation over Martin's offer made Fearghus feel so far gone to me. Out of reach. An old life, a memory. And the hole he left in my heart was patched with betrayal.

CHAPTER 26

Fearing my new scandalous dreams involving me encircled in Martin's bare arms would somehow intrude into our conversation, I closed myself off to Mam at night. I kept busy in the kitchen, refused chess nights, and buried myself in the latest fiction purchased for the library. Too often I'd pass him on the stairs, meet him on the patio, or enter a room he was in. He was a different man to me. A new, different kind of danger. No amount of distance from him eased a powerful, uncomfortable closeness, or the tingle that raced from my head to my toes.

Enid was right. He was handsome. And well-mannered, funny, and smooth. He was respectful toward the staff even though his upbringing had trained him not to be. He went out of his way to be nice to me, to do things for me that would expose a glaring red flag if found. Fearghus adored him. Fearghus obeyed him. Fearghus didn't know Martin had his father killed.

He was a murderer. A liar. A criminal.

He bought Fearghus a sling shot for his third birthday and taught him how to shoot the highest acorns out of the trees. They practiced while I seeded, watered, and nurtured the last flora required for the spell to separate Fearghus' blood from his father. Soon I'd have the proof I needed to make my claim. At the end of the season I could convince them to release us and leave my family in peace. We would be free. We could go home.

Martin didn't pressure me about my decision to be his sister or his wife, and I pretended to ponder it in order to buy some time. He replaced our chess nights with work, but the law books and piles of documents didn't explain the split lips and bloody knuckles, so I did what I normally did when I needed to know something about Martin but didn't want to ask him directly: I asked Paul.

Paul was perched on a kitchen stool finishing off his cola when Martin walked through, nodding at Paul and me before letting himself outside and plopping into a patio chair with his newspaper. It was in between meals, and the kitchen was empty aside from us and my lemon pudding.

"Try this," I said, handing Paul a spoonful. He wasn't the best test subject. He liked everything I made.

He stuck the spoon in his mouth and pretended to fall off the stool in ecstasy. I turned to hand a spoonful to Fearghus, who was driving his toy car along the lines in the tile floor. When I straightened I noticed Martin leaned over the table outside, rubbing his temples so hard the muscles on his shoulders rolled.

Paul noticed too. "Must be another migraine."

"Migraine?"

"Is it just me or is he getting them more often?"

I wiped my hands on my apron. I wasn't sure how I'd lived there for years and not known about Martin's migraines.

"Maybe it's related to the black eye. Or the bloody knuckles." It was a baited reply. To soften it, I took Paul's empty spoon and started running water to wash the bowl and beaters I used.

"No, he'd get migraines without that."

I busied myself doing dishes, but it did nothing to distract me from prying further. "Without what? He hasn't traveled anywhere lately. Why does he have a black eye?"

"Because they finally found somebody who's a decent match for him in training. You should go downstairs and watch sometime. This guy—he's good. You'd think Martin would've given it up. But he hasn't, and it's only making him better. I didn't think he could get any better."

"I have no need to watch something like that."

"Martin's going to start beating him. Just wait. And Lew's going to owe me a ton of money."

I scoffed. "What do you need his money for?"

He crossed his arms. "It's the principle."

Fearghus got up from the floor, noticed Martin outside, and banged on the glass of the door. Friend dashed to his side. "*A Mháthair*, can we go out?"

"Let me finish the dishes and I'll come out with you."

But the door was already being opened by Martin, and Fearghus tramped out without even a glance at me.

"I'll watch him." Martin closed the door.

Little boy and cat sprinted down the lawn and fell onto the grass. Martin returned to his chair and unfolded his newspaper.

Ruby came in and bumped my hip with hers. "You go outside. I'll finish these dishes." When I didn't move, she said, "Scoot," and bumped me out of the way. "Enjoy this day with Master Martin. Summer won't be much longer."

I wiped my hands and took off my apron. Ruby shook her head, watching Martin rubbing his temples again. "He's got it again. Miss Sloane, be a sweet thing and bring him out some aspirin and a glass of water." She got me the bottle of aspirin. I filled a glass with ice and water and went outside.

"Thanks," he said. "You should be on the payroll."

I walked to the edge of the patio and watched Fearghus rolling around in the grass. "He's going to be covered in grass stains."

"Let him play. It's good for him."

Ruby brought a bowl of peanuts and an empty bowl for the shells. Martin cracked one and offered it to me, but I put up my hand. I tried not to let my gaze linger on his black eye, or the purple bruise running down the back of his forearm from elbow to wrist. Whoever heard of such foolishness?

He folded up his newspaper and tossed it on the table. "Be glad you're not allowed out of here. People in this country have gone crazy."

He turned a chair toward me with his toe, but before I could decide to sit, the sliding glass door rumbled and Martin stood. The master had joined us. He surveyed the yard as if Martin and I weren't there. The bad manners were as much my fault as they were his, but I wasn't going to greet a monster. The master stretched his back and rolled his neck then looked at Martin. "Have you decided which option? The boy is getting older. You have little time left."

"I have a few details to consider—"

The master cut the air with a hand. "Have your decision made before fall." He took a peanut, cracked it in his hand, and dropped the shell on the patio. "It shouldn't matter much to her. I'll be grandfather to the boy either way." The master gave me a sideways look before he stepped off the patio toward Fearghus.

I started to follow, but Martin held my arm. "It's fine."

We watched the master walk down the lawn and stop in front of Fearghus, who looked up, squinting in the sun. Friend's tail lowered, sweeping back and forth against the grass. The master's voice reached us on the patio, but not loudly enough to understand the words. If Fearghus would've responded in some way, my eternity on that patio would've been more easily endured, but he simply squinted, staring up at that man until the master turned and walked toward the side lawn and out of sight.

Martin released my arm. "Sit with me."

I watched Fearghus go back to his inspection of the grass. "Maybe I should—"

"He's fine. And I have one more point to make before you decide. Something hard to bring up on its own, so I'll take this opportunity."

I sat. He took a peanut, tossed the nut in his mouth and the shell in the bowl. He had the manners to use the bowl and not make a mess on the patio for Ruby. His father did not. When he finished chewing and swallowed, he didn't speak, so I looked at him again. He was staring through the table. Then he got up abruptly, shoving both hands in his pockets, and turned to face me.

"If you're our sister, they'll each think they own a part of you. My place with you will be equal to theirs, and I won't be able to keep them away from you." He raised his eyebrows just a bit, asking if I understood.

I looked at my hands in my lap. He knew his brothers better than they knew themselves.

"If you're my wife, they won't be able to touch you."

I straightened my fingers. The sunlight glinted off my wedding band, sending a stab of guilt into my chest at the thought of replacing it with a new one. Martin was right. How could I argue with him? But there was still a fragment of me that would never trust him, and that little fragment ballooned, smothering out all other thought. Even though I knew I'd be gone in a few months, and none of this mattered, I couldn't control the response so eager to be voiced.

"If I'm your wife, you get all the control, instead of them. Don't make me think you're doing this for me. It's all for you, and your place in this family."

He closed his eyes and I fought the urge to stand, to go to him. To take it all back. By the time he opened his eyes, my heart was pounding away and I feared he could see it. He returned to his chair and sat leaning forward. "I have no desire to control you."

"You can't know what they'll do. You're just making threats." The words weren't any truer outside of my mind.

"It's the truth and you know it."

"It's also true that it'd be easier for you." I moved my gaze to the lake, unable to look at him.

He leaned back, crossing his arms on his chest. "Of course. I don't want you as my sister. I've told you how I feel about you."

"That will go away."

"It hasn't for three years." He pulled another chair closer so he could put his feet up. "It's only gotten worse."

I looked at him. He was smiling crookedly, like there was some irony I'd missed.

"Nothing has to change. We'll have a ceremony. That's it. You could even continue to wear that ring." He nodded toward my hand. "You stay in your room, I stay in mine. It's more conventional here, anyway. That's how my parents have always lived. We'd be the perfect TV couple." He uncrossed and recrossed his legs.

A deep sadness steadied my pounding heart. To think I could be married again, but have no love along with it. No intimacy with a man. No human body to keep me warm at night once Fearghus grew too big to sleep with me. The idea struck me harder, hit me deeper, than the idea I'd be betraying my dead husband and marrying his enemy. His murderer.

"Things would change. Fearghus would be your son."

"Either my son, or my nephew. And the same rule applies to him. As my son, he'd be mine. They'd have to go through me to get to him."

"He doesn't need you. They won't do anything to him."

His lips parted to speak, but he exhaled instead then closed them. He looked at me long and hard. "You married Fearghus Donnelly, but you won't marry me?"

"Fearghus was nothing but a good man."

"You really think that?"

I refused to acknowledge the question.

"Fearghus Donnelly was a force to be reckoned with. He had more blood on his hands than me and Pierce combined."

"You're a liar."

"Want to call your brother and ask him?"

"I already asked him."

"And?"

I lowered my eyes. "And he wouldn't tell me anything."

"Good for him. He has more sense than I thought." He pressed his fingertips against his closed eyelids. "I have to go in. This light is killing me."

I watched his back as he went inside. His shirt was wrinkled and damp with sweat where he'd been in contact with the chair. I knew a recipe for a migraine tonic, and all the ingredients were hidden in my floor upstairs. Martin already knew about my collection. It was a simple recipe, one that would be no harm to anyone if I made it for him.

Poking my head in the door, I asked Ruby if someone could watch Fearghus. Once Eleanor had joined him on the lawn, I went upstairs, crawled under my bed, and sorted through my jars. Each ingredient joined to create a small heap on a handkerchief. I folded it up, put everything back, and returned to the kitchen.

Ruby raised her eyebrows at me when she saw me dump the contents of my handkerchief into a teacup.

"It's something that might help Martin."

"I ain't seen a thing."

I helped her peel potatoes until the water boiled, then I let the tea steep and strained it into a teacup. I put a spoon and the sugar with it on a tray which I carried to Martin's room while infusing the mixture with the ancient words I knew from heart. A little help couldn't hurt.

His door hung open a few inches. I tapped the door frame.

"Come in."

He was on the bed, facedown on the pillow. All his curtains were closed against the day, his room only lit by the sunlight escaping around the edges. It appeared as if he fell straight onto his bed. He hadn't even removed his shoes.

"You have a migraine?"

He grunted into the pillow. "If I could throw up, or die, it would be better." He chuckled, but it turned into a groan.

"I made something that might help. I'll leave it here." I slid the tray onto the bedside table.

He pushed himself up on his elbows. "What is it?"

"Tea."

"Lipton?"

"Sure."

"You've been hanging around me too long."

His shoes needed to come off. There was no way to be truly comfortable while wearing shoes in bed. "Do you want me to call someone to help you get comfortable?"

"I'm fine."

I was halfway to the door when I heard him turn over on the bed. The image of those shoes dirtying his nice bedspread that Fran or Eleanor would have to wash compelled me to turn around. He was drinking the tea in one unbroken gulp. I returned to his feet, pulled the laces on both shoes, slid them off, and set them on the ground.

"Thank you." He held my eye. "For the tea."

"You're welcome." I fled the room before either one of us could say any more.

CHAPTER 27

FEARGHUS REFUSED PAJAMAS that evening so I allowed him to sleep in his underwear. I covered him with the sheet, but he kicked it off. Tired of fighting a headstrong three-year-old all day, I surrendered, turned off the light, and went downstairs. I could no longer spend the evenings in my room because even the dimmest lamp would keep him awake, playing and musing and battling sleep. Sometimes I thought he was more nocturnal than his cat, who would stretch out beside him, belly-up, paws curled, snoring.

I found Paul with a half-empty bottle of wine, banging away on the piano. His rigid posture and sweat-soaked hair told me he had succumbed to more than just the wine.

Martin was probably somewhere in the house, but his company was more dangerous to me than Paul in his worst state. I slipped off my shoes and sat on the sofa, pulling my legs underneath me. Paul broke his song, leaving an unfinished movement ringing awkwardly in the air. He joined me, wine bottle in hand. He slammed it on the coffee table. I jumped.

"I think that was louder to me than it was to you. Wait. I said that backwards." He sat on the sofa across from me. I immediately recognized the feral look in his eyes. The urge to leave caused my palms to press into the cushion, to help me up. It was silly. I ignored it. I put both hands in my lap.

"I wish you would drink with me. It could be so … much fun."

My typical flat-out refusal seemed like a bad idea. "I'm tired. I'll probably go to bed soon. Maybe some other night."

"I bet you'd drink with Martin."

The statement came so fast, without meaningful context, that I felt a chunk of conversation had been snatched out from under me. My response fired out before I could stop it. "What makes you say that?"

"I bet you do all the time."

Our chat had turned into a minefield. My moves must be delicate or something would be set off. How dare he lead me into this?

"What song were you just playing? Was it one of my—"

"Who cares?"

"Paul, if you're going to be rude …"

"Martin. What a great guy he is. But there are a few things he hasn't told you. Has he? Has he told you?"

The full-body tingle that had been accompanying any mention of Martin's name mutated into a cold, jagged shock, dragging my fear and distrust out of the corners to which they had retreated so long ago. Only now they were so full of life and raring to be armed with newfound power that I barely recognized them. I didn't want to hear anything. But I couldn't stop Paul.

"Martin's the one who found your husband. He hunted him, and he found him, and he dragged him back here like a trophy."

It wasn't true. Martin said he was in London.

"Martin ordered it all. The torture, and the kill."

"He was in London," I said.

Paul took a swig out of his bottle, and when he lowered it, he nodded like he'd just remembered something. "You're right. He was in London."

I tried to breathe down the flush that had crept up my neck.

"But only for the end. He was here for the beginning. He had to leave in the middle of it. And when he called home from London and found out your husband still wasn't talking, he told our old man to kill him."

The earth had increased its spin. I could feel it pulling me, the force pressing me sideways. I was a helpless mass of flesh plastered on its surface, incapable of freedom. Unable to find rest.

"If he'd been here, he would've done it himself," he said.

"No. He wouldn't."

Cackling, he leaned forward, his chest tipping the wine bottle in his lap almost parallel to the floor. It was too empty to spill. My feet found my shoes and my hand the door. I gripped the frame, trying to clear my head, but it was infected by Paul's mad laughter. I heard it on my way down the hall and up the stairs. Martin wasn't in his room. He was somewhere else in the house he'd been spending all his free time.

I ran back down the stairs and opened all the doors in the east hall until I found stairs leading down to a lighted space. Heavy, rhythmic pounding was the only sound coming from below. At the bottom of the stairs an expanse swept in front of me, but my eyes went immediately to the only movement—a man punching a bag hanging from the ceiling. I crossed the huge room, passed objects I didn't care to see. I stepped onto spongy floor, then off. The pounding stopped. Martin steadied the bag and looked at me. He was shiny in all the light, wet from head to toe. He swallowed, the only break to his panting.

"You told me you were in London."

He squinted. "What?" A fast outward breath—not a word.

"You told me when Fearghus was here, you were in London."

He bent at the waist, hands on his knees, and shook his head at the floor. Like he had no time for this.

"Am I your trophy too? Is that why you want me? You got him, now you want to steal what was his? Claim us as your own?"

"Can you give me a minute so I can talk to you?" It was a sentence too long for the little breath he had. He picked up a towel and wiped his face.

"You don't talk. You lie. Don't ever talk to me again." I turned and walked over the spongy floor, across the room, and ran up the stairs. My head pounded from the change of bright light to dim hall. I ran up the main staircase and went into my room. I changed into a nightgown and wiped my face and neck with a wet washcloth, ignoring the tremble that wanted out of me. I got into bed, pulled Fearghus against my chest, and pressed my lips against his hair. He was all I had. I would never forget it again.

A low hum pulled me from sleep to reality, but my eyes felt sealed shut, and my limbs were under sand. I wanted to turn my head, but it wouldn't obey. Several labored blinks opened my eyes to slits. The light in the room had an odd slant, like it was evening, not morning. I wiggled my fingers and my toes until one arm finally roused. I slid it toward Fearghus. The blanket was pulled back. The sheet was cold.

I opened my lips but my jaw was tight. I heard his name called in my mind. Friend meowed from the floor, incessant and hoarse, like he'd been meowing all day without end. He leaped on me and marched along my body, little paws working the paralyzed muscles through those blankets that were as heavy as sand. If Friend was here, where was Fearghus?

When I managed to get my elbows under me, I pushed myself up, but my head felt five times too big and I gasped to fill lungs that were five times too small. The hum in my ears dwindled away leaving the room far too quiet. I dropped back against the bed and rolled onto my side. My clock displayed half past six in the evening, but it should be morning.

"Madam, you're up?"

It was Fran's voice, but her face was blurry.

"You have us so worried. I don't know what you're coming down with, but when I couldn't wake you this morning I knew it was bad. How do you feel?"

"Where's Fearghus?" My voice was hoarser than Friend's.

She slid a tray onto my bedside table and felt my forehead. "The mistress came to get him this morning. It's the first time she's left her room for so many years. Isn't it remarkable?"

My pulse jumped from my chest to my head, quaking the room around me, and my blankets morphed from heavy sand to a mold of glass. I closed my eyes and willed every muscle to move, to free me from my trap. The mistress had Fearghus. She affected me with this paralyzed slumber, and she took him away.

The room twisted, and I hit the floor.

"Madam!"

Fran knelt beside me, and I latched onto her outstretched arms. My legs had no structure. No bone. She tried to help me up, but my weight kept her down.

"Madam, I need to go for help to get you back in bed." She tried to pull away.

"I'm fine right here. Find Fearghus. Please, Fran, bring him back."

She disappeared through the door. I reached behind me and found the bedspread. I tried to pull myself up, but it came off the bed in my hands. Pressing one palm on the floor, then another, I got my knees underneath me, but the room pitched like a ship on an angry sea, tossing me into the cold waves.

I awoke in bed. The sunlight belonged to morning, and my body belonged to me again. My arm slid to Fearghus' side. Still empty. I sat up.

He was sitting on the farthest sofa in his underwear, staring into the room.

"Fearghus."

He didn't move. Friend was perched next to him like a statue on the arm of the sofa. I threw back the covers and rushed to him. He stared past me with a dead, unblinking gaze. I knelt in front of him and put my hands on his arms. The underside of his chin was scraped deep. He looked through me.

"Fearghus!" I gave his body a gentle shake. It ran the length of him like a wave, and when it reached his head he closed his eyes. "Fearghus, are you awake?"

His eyes were sunken in, surrounded by a circle of dark—an extreme version of how he looked on days he skipped his nap and stayed up too late. I pulled him off the cushion and set him on his feet. He opened his eyelids. His eyes rolled down out of his head and settled back into the same stare.

Dread clutched at me, pinching skin, snapping ribs. The same monster's grip from the day I opened my front door to find my husband's crumpled body. A recognized loss. A love torn away from me. I carried Fearghus to the bathroom. The light stung my eyes, but he didn't even flinch. I set him on the side of the bathtub, filled a cup with cold water, and threw it in his face. He stared. The water dripped down his cheeks, off his chin, and onto his hands lying open to expose a long, fresh cut across each palm. Matching. Deliberate.

There was no room in my world for this. I had been to the bottom. There was nothing lower. It was not possible to lose the last person I had.

I flew into my dressing room and yanked on some clothes. I pulled a shirt over Fearghus' head and tucked his limp arms through the holes. He stepped into his pants mechanically. If his fight against clothes would only return, I'd never complain about it again. He was a rag doll in my arms all the way down the stairs and out the kitchen door. Someone followed us outside, calling to us, but I kept walking down the slope to the shore of the lake where I set Fearghus on his feet. I turned him to face the sun. His pupils remained as they were, consuming his irises except for a thin green outline as if trying to overcome some blindness inside. He didn't flinch from the light. He didn't squint.

"Fearghus, you have to come back. If you don't come back—" I grabbed him and buried my face in his chest. His little heart beat against my cheek. It was the only life in him.

Strong arms pulled me away from him.

"Trey." It was Martin kneeling down to peer into his face, shaking him. "Sloane, what happened? Trey!"

"His palms." I choked, covering my mouth.

Martin turned Fearghus' little hands palms up. The bloody wounds jumped off his fair skin in the daylight. Martin released Fearghus' arms and sank back on his heels. He looked at the house like it was human, like it had just uttered a violent insult straight at him.

"Your mother—"

"My mother," he said.

"She—"

He shushed me. "Listen. This is…" His eyes darted, focusing on everything around us but me. "Damn it!" He put up a hand, blocking my response. "It's going to be tricky. I can fix him. I can't do it here. I can't let on that I know. Shit!"

Fran was coming down the hill toward us. Martin picked up Fearghus.

"Madam! Master Martin, Sloane shouldn't be out of bed."

"I know. Trey's sick too. I'll take them both upstairs and sit with them until someone else is free."

"Eleanor is free."

"No need to rush her up there. Let her finish what she's doing. I have some time to kill. I'll sit with them." He took my arm with his free hand and pulled me toward the house. The last time I saw him, I told him I didn't want to speak to him again. I couldn't trust him, not after what Paul told me—the truth that exposed Martin's guilt in Fearghus' death along with his lie to cover it up. Was that yesterday? The day before? It didn't matter and it couldn't be helped. I needed Martin now.

In my room he set Fearghus in an armchair, backed away, and watched him. "The timing. It's just perfect, isn't it?"

I didn't know what to say.

"After Paul …" He shook his head, exhaling. "You're just going to have to trust me. I know what she did, and I think I can fix it. But I can't let on that I know, and I can't fix him here. I have to take him out of the house."

"Now?"

"Tonight." He touched my arm. "But you can't come."

"I'm coming."

"If you leave this house, a million alarms will go off. They won't know if he leaves. They never figured out how to bind him."

"Then do it here."

He dropped to the sofa, covered his face with his hands, and rubbed his forehead. "I can't. She'll sense it." He looked at Fearghus. "I can't believe this. She went behind all of us. She knew our plan and she—" He ran a hand over his face.

"She did something to me. I've been sleeping for days."

"I know. I heard. But I didn't know …" He paused to stare at Fearghus, registering new surprise like he'd just seen him for the first time again. "She can't know I've done anything or she'll try it again. She'll have to think it didn't work … that he overcame it."

"What'd she do? What'd she use?"

He looked at me, his expression blank. "Nothing you'd be familiar with."

"She cut his palms?"

"I'll have to do that again to reverse it."

I buried my face in my hands. I heard him get up, felt his arm go around me. He led me to the sofa and sat me down next to him. I couldn't allow him to help me, but it would take weeks to figure out what she'd done and even longer to learn a way to reverse it. By then the effect would be permanent.

I had to let him help me. Martin was our only chance.

"Don't worry. He won't even know what's happening until the end, when he starts to find himself again."

"And then?"

"And then I bring him home. Here, let's put him in bed. Eleanor will be up here soon. Everyone must think he's sick, that we think he's sick." He picked up Fearghus.

I pulled down the cover on his side of the bed. Martin laid him on the sheet then leaned down and placed his hand against his little chest. "Trey, you should go to sleep. Can you close your eyes?" Martin touched the corners of Fearghus' eyes, and they closed. "Maybe he'll stay asleep. It'll be easier for you until tonight. I'll come at midnight. Have him ready to go. Don't look like that, it'll be fine."

"I can't stay here if you take him. I can't."

"Sloane, if we don't do this tonight, we lose our chance. Do you understand?"

"Can't you make something up? Another trip to Cambridge? Somewhere else?"

"If anybody knows I took him out of the house, it will get back to her, and she'll know what I've done. They'll all know what I've done. I shouldn't be doing any of this, yet I keep doing it." He looked away quickly, scratching his head, blowing out air. "They find out he's gone, I'm dead, you're dead. So tomorrow, stay in your room, and pick up your meals downstairs but bring them up here to eat. Don't let your maids in, don't let anyone in. And pray to every element they don't insist on checking on you. I'll bring him back in the middle of the following night."

I sat on the edge of the bed. Friend jumped up next to me and lay down with his paws and chest across Fearghus' belly, a position that normally made Fearghus twist and laugh from the tickle it caused.

"You didn't have breakfast."

I shook my head. My hunger must be nothing compared to the hunger of the little boy lying next to me. When was the last time he ate?

Martin went to the door. "I'll send Eleanor up with food."

I found ointment and a bandage in my bathroom for Fearghus' chin. I washed his face and hands with a washcloth and put him in clean pajamas. He slept through it all. Too numb to cry, I couldn't shake the idea I was dressing him for his funeral.

CHAPTER 28

T HE ROOM DIMMED with the fading sun. I took a break from watching Fearghus sleep to pack his little bag with clothes, shoes, a blanket, and some snacks and juice from the kitchen. Friend glared at me from Fearghus' side, like all this was my fault, like there was something I should be doing, but wasn't.

"He'll be okay," I said, petting him. He didn't purr. The tip of his tail came alive, flipping in a chaotic fashion. A communication, if I could decipher it. Fearghus could probably understand it.

I pored over my options for the thousandth time, finding yet again there was only one: to allow Martin to take Fearghus out of the house alone. I fastened his amulet on a string around his neck, knowing Martin would have to take it off to do whatever he needed to do. It lay against his chest, rising and falling with the breath that was the only evidence of life in a boy who should be running circles around the bed that held him.

My bedtime came, but I couldn't sleep. I watched the minutes pass on the clock until midnight. Martin let himself into my room one minute later. I reached for my lamp.

"No lights," Martin whispered.

I withdrew my hand and sat up in bed. Martin sat next to me. "He slept all day?"

"Yes."

"Let's hope he stays asleep for five more minutes. Sloane—"

"Just take him." I stood and walked around the bed to pull the covers off Fearghus. I could feel Martin watching me in the dark, but I didn't look at him. He came around and slid his arms under Fearghus. I handed him the bag I packed.

He paused in the doorway. "I'll have him back here at this time tomorrow night."

He left. I closed the door and sat on the edge of the bed. The silence built itself into a noise too loud for sleeping. I opened the doors on my balcony so the sounds of the night could drown out the silence.

I watched the ceiling until the sun rose. I found Fran in the kitchen before she could make it up to my room. When she spotted me, she put down her towel. "Madam?"

"I was up with Fearghus all night. He's finally sleeping. Could you please tell everyone not to disturb him?"

"Of course, madam."

"For the rest of the day. He's still sick. I'm hoping he sleeps all day." Worried I was overdoing it, I got myself a glass out of the cabinet and filled it with orange juice from the pitcher on the counter.

"You should get some sleep, too, madam."

"I will. I'm just going to take some breakfast to my room, then I'll go back to bed."

"Go on up. I'll bring it to you."

"No—I mean, no thank you. I can get it."

Fran stopped to study me. Ruby turned around, a spatula in one hand and an egg in the other. Both sets of eyes dug into me. I picked up a banana. I was no good at this. Martin could lie with such ease. Why couldn't I?

"I mean, this is all I want right now. I'm just so tired."

"I could have you some eggs in five minutes," Ruby said.

"No, thank you. I'll eat later. I'm just more tired than hungry. I didn't sleep a minute last night." That was the truth. This must be what Martin did—picked out the truthful details and combined them with a lie. As long as his conscience only focused on the details, he could stand behind it. He could say the grass was green, and I'd see a lawn of grass rippling in the wind when all he saw was one struggling blade growing out of a rocky wasteland.

Back in my room I locked my door and ate the banana, every bite turning to glue in my mouth. The orange juice was a bitter acid. I put away all of Fearghus' books and toys, lined up his shoes in the dressing room. I wanted to know where Martin took him. If he was crying. If he was afraid.

I mounded pillows on Fearghus' side of the bed and covered them with the blankets to make it look like his little sleeping body. The doubts mutated into questions lashing me like a whip.

What if it had all been an act? Martin was one of them. He worked for them. He did unmentionable things for them. He was an expert liar, and if he wanted something badly enough I don't think I could see past his lies. He'd found us by the lake so fast, as if he'd already known what was wrong with Fearghus.

What if his goal was to get Fearghus away from me so they could do things to him? Perhaps the mistress hadn't completed her work. She needed more time, so she sent Martin to collect Fearghus. He'd been so quick to sweep Fearghus away. He knew what was wrong and how to fix Fearghus, but he didn't prove anything to me. I trusted him. How could I trust him?

My doorknob jiggled. Then again, more aggressively. Panic rush through me. A heavy knock. I went to the door. "Paul?" It was too early for Paul.

"Try again."

Pierce.

"But you just gave yourself away, sugar. You'll have to settle for me. Open the door."

I glanced at the bed. The pillows were too lumpy to be Fearghus' body. He was long and straight. No one would ever believe it, especially not Pierce.

"Don't make me find my key."

"Fearghus and I are sleeping. We're both sick." My voice shook on the last word, so I turned it into a cough. It was hard enough to lie to Fran and Ruby. I couldn't lie to Pierce, even though I needed to lie to him most of all.

"*Open* the *door*."

I put both hands on my chest to calm the wild spasm of my heart. There was no way to slow it, to appear calm when every nerve was poised to run. Martin could do it. The more heat on him, the cooler he appeared. I envisioned his face, his easily cleared emotion when Arthur was patting him down in Mam's front room. At the dinner table that night under Arthur's rapid, pointed questions phrased with no room for escape, yet Martin managed to get around every one of them.

I opened the door.

"That's my girl."

"The staff has orders not to disturb us. I'm sorry, but I have to include you and your brothers too." I couldn't let him think I knew Martin was gone. "Could you please pass it to them? And I'll see you all when we feel better."

I started to close the door, but he pushed past me into the room. "I think something's off here. Where's Martin?"

Martin's slow drink of wine when his father was on a rampage at the dinner table. His steady glance at Paul when the monster in Paul awakes.

"In his room, I'm sure. You can cut through." I went into my sitting room and opened the adjoining door. With the wall between us, I could no longer see Pierce. But if he was moving to the bed, I'd hear him.

"He's not in his room," he said after moving into view.

I closed the door. "Did you check his other room?"

"Sure did."

"Well, I don't know. I can't help you. So if you'll—"

He looked over his shoulder at the bed before coming at me. He grabbed my jaw, tilted my face up to him. "You're doing both of them, aren't you?"

I swallowed. "No."

"Paul and Martin. Who do you like better?"

I stepped back. He backed me to the wall and was so close I could smell the coffee on his breath, his mint gum. His hand moved to my throat.

"It's only fair to give me a turn." He took a long inhale against my hair.

"I have the flu."

"Nice try." His fingers relaxed.

"Okay, you take the risk. But I warned you."

He snorted, turning away, chuckling. He pointed at me. "If I see you out of this room once in the next week—"

"Goodbye, Pierce." I walked to the door to the hall and put my hand on the knob.

He stared at me, licking his bottom lip, back and forth, contemplating. Then he left. I locked both doors and fell to my knees, propped my forehead against the floor, and breathed until the shaking stopped and my heart was calm. My blood cleansed my body of adrenaline, leaving my limbs loose and my knees weak. I stumbled to my bed and fell into it, asleep in an instant.

I awoke to bold sunlight angled into my room from my western sky. Children's voices carried through the window panes from the lawn below. I got out of bed so my eyes could prove I wasn't dreaming. It was a whole group of them. The Moores from the north must be visiting—aunts, uncles, cousins, second cousins. Too many names to keep track of, and more of them each time they came. Dinner tonight would be a grand occasion, and I had an excuse, but I wasn't sure if the master would accept it. If he demanded Fearghus and I attend dinner, we'd have no choice but to attend no matter how sick we were. Martin wouldn't be there to talk him out of it.

Martin would also be missed at dinner. How would he explain when he returned?

I put on a housecoat and took the private staircase downstairs to the kitchen. A frenzy of preparation occupied our regular kitchen staff plus the extra help hired for these occasions. Fran spotted me in the midst of it all, and she made a tray of snacks for me and Fearghus. I insisted on bringing it up myself, and she was torn away from me before she could complain. I knew she'd send my regrets about dinner, and if they weren't accepted, I'd dress and join them, claiming Fearghus was too sick to rouse from sleep. It was a statement I could defend. It was true the last time I'd seen him.

Back in my room, I watched the sun sink in the sky and tried not to think about Fearghus' little palms. The insects opened the evening with their song, and the sounds of a patio party carried around the house to my balcony. They'd be up drinking all night. Martin would never be able to sneak Fearghus back into the house.

Children burst onto the lawn, screaming and hooting and falling down in the grass. The older ones started a game of tag, and the younger ones staggered around imitating them without understanding the reason of their movements but full of giddy delight anyway. I wished Fearghus could be out there. The entire family was rotten, but at least he could join the children before all their souls spoiled like their parents'.

The sky darkened and the party grew louder. I paced on my balcony. Rain would cancel their party. I leaned over the railing, looking up. Stars twinkled behind wispy clouds. Rain would only bring them inside—a position that might cause more problems for Martin trying to come home. I wished I knew if he'd prefer them to be inside or outside. I could arrange either. The magic would call attention to me, though, when attention was what I had to avoid that night.

I tried to remember what Martin had told me about his mother and the curse upon her. *A Farrelly curse*, he'd said, then was surprised I wasn't familiar with the name. I needed to crack why his mother had done this to Fearghus. Find out what drove her. Whether it was envy or some sick-minded reason, I needed to know what I was facing, and what Martin had held back that night.

Midnight came and I paced my room until one o'clock. The party roared outside. I jumped to Friend jerking awake on the bed. He bolted to the balcony and nudged his basket. I threw the rope over the railing, lowered him down, and watched him streak across the night toward the woods.

Headlights swept the lawn, lighting a panic inside me. Martin was home. From the way my heart lurched it could be no one else. He'd never get Fearghus in the house undetected. What was he thinking pulling up front like that? I shoved my arms into the sleeves of my housecoat and went into the hall. Voices mingled from below, but not close enough for their owners to see me. I crept down the hall, turning off lights as I passed each switch. When I reached the main staircase, I remained in the shadow, watching the door. It opened. Martin came in alone.

A woman squealed. Shoes clicked across the floor, and Martin turned toward the sound and smiled his most guarded of smiles. She ran into him but he caught her by the shoulders at arm's length. He leaned in to kiss her cheek. She took his hand, pulling him toward the library. He looked up, straight into my eyes, and winked.

I sunk down against the wall, and he was out of sight.

Back in my room I sat on the bed, watching the minutes on the clock until twenty-two of them had passed and my door finally opened.

"Where is he?"

He put his finger to his lips.

"Is he okay?" I whispered.

"He's fine. Come here." His hand found mine and led me out on the balcony. "Darn. I was hoping we could see him. I told him to wave."

I followed his gaze across the lawn, but saw nothing.

"I had to stash him in the woods. Who decided to have a party tonight, for crying out loud?"

He took a cigarette out of his pocket. I took it away from him. "Tell me everything. You reversed the curse?"

"Yeah, he's back to his troublemaking self." He looked around. "You need some chairs out here."

I tucked my housecoat under me and sat on the floor. He sat facing me. I slipped the cigarette back into his breast pocket. "And?"

"And as soon as these people call it a night I'll go make him come inside."

"You're not going to tell me what you had to do to him, are you?"

He looked away. "No. But I will tell you, when I finally found him, he was playing with his memory of his sister. They were in his garden. The hardest part was convincing him to come out, to come to me and leave her there."

Something on my face made him move to my side and wrap his arm around me, and for several minutes I couldn't speak. I could only stare at the harsh white balusters of my balcony railing against the darkness of the night beyond. My Fearghus was out there, free in the world, innocent to all the peril there to torment us, and I was imprisoned behind those bars. But if those bars dissolved before my eyes, I knew Fearghus would come back to us, leaving me free to sit here with Martin, under his arm, with more reasons to stay than escape.

"Thank you," I said.

He kissed my temple, and that kiss was the sunlight and rain on the seed he'd planted that day on the porch in that storm when he told me which one of them I should marry. I could still see his smile just before he'd spoken that single word, that seed.

Me.

CHAPTER 29

WE SAT ON the balcony and listened to the summer insects sing until the noise of the party dwindled to a few low voices and finally, the patio lights went off. I sat forward and he removed his arm from my shoulders.

"Let's allow a few more minutes for everyone to find their rooms."

"He's probably asleep out there."

"He's probably built himself a throne and convinced all the wildlife to do his bidding." He chuckled then abruptly looked at me. "Have you ever been in his mind?"

I shook my head. "He's too young."

"I know, but I had no choice. And it's unlike anything … it's the most perfect balance of magic and power. Everything is precise, lined up just so, it's like picking a lock. All the pins perfectly in place, coming together in a way I've never…" he put his hand on my knee "…I see now, what she did must've been an accident. There's no way to change one thing without throwing it all out of whack. And I honestly think she meant to change just one thing. She didn't know what a delicate balance there is inside him. There's just no way to change one thing."

I stood and walked to the railing so he couldn't see my face. *I* was going to change one thing inside his perfect mind. It was our only way to get home.

"Are you all like that, or just him?"

If the mistress hadn't decided to do what she did, I'd have completed my plan and stripped the Donnelly out of my son. *I* would've been the one to upset the perfect balance of his mind. Fearghus would be gone, and it would be my fault.

It couldn't be true. The mistress had a purpose, and the destruction of Fearghus' mind was the key. "What your mother did wasn't an accident. She wanted to take Fearghus from me like her children had been taken from her."

He didn't answer. He'd leaned his head back against the house to stare at the ceiling. "I thought of that myself. I called your brother to warn him."

My stomach sank. "About what?"

"About not letting Tara out of his sight." He got up, brushed off his pants. "I'll go collect Trey. Come inside. It's getting chilly."

I remained outside in the cool breeze. A storm was blowing in. The wispy clouds rushed quickly across the moon, making their escape before the storm clouds pushed in. I imagined the words exchanged in that phone call between Martin and Arthur, their voices very real in my head. Whatever history they shared, they now had to cooperate because of me. I could worry about Tara but it'd do no one any good. She was safe with Arthur and Mam. I had to trust that. Martin's warning to Arthur didn't prove the mistress knew about Tara. Martin was only being cautious.

Fearghus rode piggyback on Martin into my room. Martin threw him onto the bed and pointed at him. "Bedtime." Then he looked at me. "He's a little wound up."

I seized him and hugged him until he squirmed out of my grasp. I combed down a rough spot of his hair with my fingers. He ducked away, just like he should. His amulet hung on its brown cord around his neck.

"*A Mháthair*, I was in a box, and I was stuck, and it was a really long time, and then Martin got me out and I got ice cream!" He smiled up at me, like there was no treat in the world more special. His front tooth was chipped.

Martin caught me looking at it. "It was like that when he came around."

I took Fearghus' hands and held them while looking into his bloodshot eyes. The wounds were so vivid in my memory I didn't need to see them again, but I turned his hands over anyway. Two matching sets of cuts slashed across both palms—one set from the mistress, one from Martin.

"Yeah, got boo-boos. S'okay." He pulled away from me. "Friend wants up."

Martin headed toward the door. "I'll see you in the morning. Get some rest. You both need it."

"Can I get ice cream 'morrow?" Fearghus stared after him, smiling with his bottom lip tucked under his top teeth.

Martin turned around. Whether it was his fatigue, the late hour, or the infectious joy of a child, his mask wavered and the visible effort it took him to stabilize it inflated a bubble of a laugh that rose in my chest.

"You'll have to clear that with your *máthair.*"

I'd heard him say it so many times, but this was the first time I listened. Fearghus had started calling me that because it was what Martin called me. All along I'd thought Fearghus had picked it up himself. He was following Martin. Emulating him. The man who'd just saved him from an imprisonment inside his own head and then rewarded him with ice cream. And even though Fearghus didn't get the answer he wanted, he continued to smile at Martin's back as he left the room. I went onto the balcony to pull Friend up to our room in his basket elevator.

Martin was a hero to my son, and to me. It no longer mattered if winning us over had been his plan from the beginning. It had worked.

I grilled Fearghus about hunger and cleanliness and determined he was more tired than anything, so I tucked him in, moved Friend from Fearghus' pillow to his side, and went into the bathroom. I stared into the mirror. My son was back. Conscious. Himself. My plan to escape this house had been destroyed in the process of saving him. I couldn't change a thing about him without the risk of losing him again. We would never move back home.

With the joining of these two thoughts came another. My answer to Martin's question was ready before I'd realized I had no choice but to answer it.

When I saw Martin awake and dressed on his balcony the next morning, I left Fearghus sleeping like a rock in the bed and let myself into Martin's room.

"Martin," I said.

He turned around, squinting into the room, his suspenders hanging loose. I waited. I didn't want to speak to him outside. He put out his cigarette and came inside, pulling the balcony door halfway closed behind him.

"I want you to take me to see your mother."

"No." The answer was so immediate it had to be premeditated, as if he was expecting me to ask.

"Then I'll ask Paul. Or Lewis, even."

"They know better."

"Then I'll go to her by myself. Her room is in the northeast corner—"

"Did you already forget what she did to Trey?"

"That's why I want to see her."

"And what she did to you? She knocked you out for over twenty-four hours and you never saw it coming."

"That's why it's better if you go with me."

He took a breath and held it. A rare inward focus came over him, like he wasn't seeing me anymore. He was reconsidering. The breeze wandered into the room and ruffled the papers on his desk, reminding me of my second question that'd brought me in there.

"One condition," he said. "You let me take Trey downstairs for a few hours every day."

"Whatever for?"

"To teach him to defend himself."

I was shaking my head, but I wasn't sure why. Soon, I'd be teaching him this very thing. But my lessons would in no way compare to what Martin had in mind. "He's too young."

"He should've started a year ago."

"What will you tell your father? Your brothers?"

"Nothing. They expect it. He's one of us, remember?"

My throat seemed to close up. I swallowed hard. It was going to happen. My escape had already failed and there was no alternate plan. Not even a dream.

"What kind of lawyer are you?"

He didn't flinch. "The kind who gets his family out of trouble."

An unscripted question pushed its way through. "Does being a lawyer retire you from your old job?" He watched me, like I should continue. Surely he knew what I meant. Did he really want me to say it out loud? "Your old job of killing people."

"Do you want the short answer or the long answer?"

"The short answer."

"No."

I wondered what the long answer was, but I knew it didn't matter. I was sure I'd learn it in the years to come. All I needed now was a straight answer, which is what I got. Anything else would cloud this matter that needed to remain as simple as possible until the ends were tied and it was too late to go back. My only motion, from now on, must be onward. "Take me to see your mother while Fearghus is still asleep."

"We have a deal?"

A quiver of dread started in my stomach. I should've been happy. Fearghus needed all the help he could get, but I couldn't see what Martin's help would provide my son without seeing the eventual outcome. My son was to become one of them.

"Yes. A deal."

He snapped both suspenders up on his shoulders and walked past me, expecting me to follow. When I didn't move, he turned around to look at me, and my blood flushed hot and my breath threatened to choke me, but I knew I had to get it out, now or never.

"I've decided I will marry you."

That dimple appeared by his lip, but I didn't want him to smile. I didn't want him to say anything.

"I won't take your name."

He nodded once. "Understandable."

"I won't have any children with you."

"It's not expected."

I stopped there. I had more conditions, but they'd fled, and whatever they were, they seemed trivial compared to the two I'd just given. Any more would've eased the weight of those two.

"Trey will be my son."

I nodded. I couldn't say yes, but I knew it was what had to be. I walked past him, toward the door. He caught my hand and held it between both of his.

"You won't regret it."

I pulled away. "Take me to your mother."

He walked me up one flight in the circular staircase in the tower. I'd never been on the third floor. The hall was wider and covered in a plush royal blue runner. There were fewer doors, which meant the rooms on this story were even larger. The air was warmer and very still. It seemed to compress me from all sides. Martin stopped at the double doors in the corner of the house opposite my room. He knocked and stepped back, hands shoved into pockets, as cool as could be.

I clasped my hands in front of me so they wouldn't shake. When he knocked again, my heart pounded harder and a fear swelled inside me that made me light-headed.

He looked at his watch then glanced down the hall. As the oldest son, someday he'd be the master of this house. Soon, I'd be his wife. I didn't need a vision to show me what future was now possible after the choice I'd made. If Martin inherited the house, I'd be the mistress in this remote room on the stifling third floor. The thought gave me such a chill I turned to leave. Martin caught my arm and returned me to his side.

The door opened. It was Fran. "Master Martin?"

"We'd like to see my mother for a minute."

"Sure, sir. Do you need me to stay?"

His gaze flicked to me. "No."

"Let me tell her you're here." She closed the door.

"You have to come in with me," I said.

"I won't be able to talk to her."

It didn't matter if he couldn't talk to her. I couldn't go in there alone. He stared at me. When I realized I was staring at him, I turned away to face the door with the wreath carved in the wood, the vines, the initial M. I couldn't sleep behind a door carved with their initial. Once I became the mistress of the house, could I safely leave? Would I have to wait until it came to that before I could go home?

I then realized I didn't know her name. Everyone called her 'the mistress.' "Do I call her Mrs. Moore?"

"Her name is Órlaith."

The door opened. Martin placed a hand on the small of my back, and I went into a sitting room that could swallow mine and still be hungry for more. Fran left, closing the door behind us. So he couldn't feel the tremor clamoring through my body, I stepped away from Martin and stopped just inside the double doors to her room.

She stood in a patch of sunlight beaming through a row of open French doors, too many to count in one glance. She wore a cotton housedress. Her feet were bare, her hair long and loose. One shade darker and her blond would be red. Away from this blinding morning light, it probably was red. My dark-haired son would never fit into this family.

"Don't loiter in the doorway. Come in if you want to see me."

She walked toward me and took a seat in an armchair just out of the patch of sunlight. She was wringing a vibrant yellow scarf in her hands. It was wrinkled and worn as if it suffered that wringing all day long.

"Is someone with you?"

"Yes. Martin." He and I stopped outside the circle of furniture.

"Is he beside you?"

"Yes." I took his arm.

"Tell her to look higher, that I'm about a head taller than you," Martin said. "She forgets how tall I am."

She was looking at his chest.

"He's a head taller than me." I placed my hand on his cheek. "Here."

"Will you bring my Paulie to visit?"

Martin shifted his weight and took my hand off his face. "Tell her I'll try. That she knows he doesn't like having to speak through Fran."

I repeated what he said. She played with the yellow scarf. "What brings Sloane Bevan to my room?"

"I want to talk to you about my son."

She dropped both hands to her lap and turned to look outside. Her view spanned the length of the back lawn all the way to the woods. She had an unobstructed watch of it all: the patio off the kitchen, the gardens beyond, the back lawn, the lake, Paul's carriage house, and all the other separate buildings. She spent day and night in this room, watching us, never joining us. She couldn't see her sons, but she could see Fearghus and me. It's no wonder the back of the house always felt like it had eyes.

"Go on," she prompted.

"I ask for very little here. I just want him to be safe, and because of that, I give my son to you. To your family. You don't need to hurt him anymore."

"Hurt him ..." she said to the sky outside.

"He's all I have."

"You're wrong about that." She was facing us again, focused on Martin's chest instead of me.

Defiance took command, squashing my fear and kicking it aside as one thing became shockingly clear: I didn't need to give Fearghus to her. She thought he was already hers, that he was no longer mine, not since he was two weeks old. The futility of this visit slapped me like a cold, wet towel, and I took a step back. I'd hoped to appeal to her, mother to mother. She'd lost all her sons. No woman could wish that on another.

"I was wrong." I started to turn away, angry tears stinging my eyes. When she spoke again, something in her tone planted my feet.

"There's a knowledge our families share which you may be too young to know, unless you've recognized it yourself. Good follows bad follows good. A cycle of neutrality. Of equality. The tide, evening out the sand. Smoothing the beach on which we walk. It's the natural course of things. Our intentions don't matter; they simply play their part in this cycle and the cycle goes on. Your mother, or Martin, can give you the Irish."

"What does this have to do with Fearghus?"

She placed both hands on the chair's armrests like she was going to stand, but she didn't. "It has everything to do with him."

I wanted to sit with her, to listen to her explain everything to me. I wanted to ask questions, get answers, no matter how difficult they were to accept. Find a purpose in a life that had become prey to chaos.

"He's a part of it. He's affected by it. He's the next cycle. He'll be one half of the whole." She curled her shoulders and drew herself down, bowing her head, covering it with both hands.

Martin touched my shoulder. "We need to go."

She began a subtle rock in the chair. Martin took my arm and led me into the hall, closing both sets of doors behind us.

"Is she okay?"

"Yes. She just gets migraines like me."

We were halfway down the hall when one other condition of my voluntary marriage to Martin nearly tripped me and I stopped walking. "Fearghus keeps his last name."

A deep line showed between his eyebrows. "That's going to be hard to convince—"

"Then I'll have to be your sister instead, if that's the only way he can keep his name."

His forehead smoothed. He could see where I had him. "Okay then. I'll figure something out."

I never knew what he figured out, but a judge came one week later and married us in the library in the presence of more staff than family. Martin gave me a ring, but I put it in my bedside table drawer and continued wearing the one I'd worn for years. Fearghus and I had joined the family. It was a sacrifice necessary for our survival, and most importantly, for Fearghus' well-being. If I could succeed in raising him with Bevan morals within the confines of the Moore estate, he'd never need to escape. He would already be free.

It wasn't until a year later when I was descending the stairs behind Fearghus' hopping, lanky, four-year-old body that I understood the mistress' words that day. She affected Fearghus with that awful affliction that almost took him away from me. Martin had intervened to neutralize it, which brought Martin into my heart. I was a married woman again, with countless reasons to question my marriage. But when the mistress' meaning came alight in my mind that day, it was enough to slow my hand on the railing and stop my feet on the stairs. If she was right, my marriage to Martin followed the badness of that spell on Fearghus. My marriage was the next iteration of good.

The same day of this discovery was the day I met Rose-mary.

CHAPTER 30

SUMMER, 1968

FOUR YEARS HAD passed in that house before the day Pierce brought home his bride. Her white-blond hair and blue eyes were the envy of every American girl and a trophy to Pierce. Her accent was as southern as the staff's. Pierce must've picked her like a wildflower from right outside the door. The day I met her she was alone in the foyer, surrounded by bags and boxes just unloaded from the cars outside. A headband colored with the hues of a sunset crossed her forehead and wrapped around her head, and flat-heeled sandals peeked from underneath her ruffled peasant skirt. She looked like she'd stepped right out of one of those war protests on the news on TV.

I interrupted her wide-eyed examination of the domed ceilings above her. Dollar signs should have shown in the eyes of a new bride in her rich husband's home, but the only thing I saw was panic. I held out my hand. "Hello. My name is Sloane."

She tensed a little before taking my hand. She held on, like I'd just promised to lead her somewhere. "I'm Rosemary. You're …"

"Martin's wife. And this is Fearghus."

She took a glance at Fearghus. "Y'all might have to excuse me. If I don't find a chair I just might faint."

"Let's go in the library." I headed toward the doorway. Fearghus ran ahead, but Rosemary didn't budge. She was looking at all the parcels at her feet.

"Do I need to …?"

"Someone will take it to your room for you. Where's Pierce?"

She looked up the stairs. "He went up them long stairs soon as we got inside. I don't know how long he'll be but I'm sure I should wait for him."

I knew in that instant this woman's shy good manners covered a heart of gold too pure to recognize the devil she had married.

"Who knows what he's up to? Let's go sit down. He can find us."

One of the doormen was coming down the stairs with Martin's luggage. Martin hadn't mentioned a trip, not that I should expect him to. Our marriage hadn't changed anything but the terms we used to address each other to company.

Fran met us in the library with lemonade and sugar cookies, introduced herself to Rosemary, and told her to make herself comfortable while they prepared her room. I could see Rosemary's arrival was not anticipated. I wondered if Rosemary's existence was a surprise as well.

I sent Fearghus outside with his cookie and took a seat by the window to keep an eye on him.

"When he said 'house in Richmond,' I'm seein' this cute little thing with a white picket fence and a clothesline out back. Either this is a dream or a nightmare. I cain't figure which." She picked up a glass of lemonade then set it back down. "Promise you'll be my friend. I'm scared enough being married and movin' so far away. To a house full of strangers ..."

She had no idea how much we already had in common. "I think we're already friends."

A tear ran down each cheek, but she grinned despite them and took a sip of her lemonade.

"You're not from Richmond?" I asked.

She shook her head. "Tennessee. Small town you won't have heard of. Pierce'd visit me whenever he'd come through, goin' on a year now. Then this last time, he told me, 'Pack a suitcase. You're comin' with me and I'm gonna marry you.'"

"How long have you been married?"

"Two days. Oh, Sloane, I'm scared stiff. No way I'll fit in here. No way at all."

"Pierce wouldn't have married you if he didn't think you'd fit in." I could've told her Paul was the only one who'd bring an unsuitable girl home to torment his father. And it was Martin, the favorite son, who'd married the most unsuitable girl of all.

I went to the side door to tell Fearghus to get down off the porch railing, and when I turned around, Martin was kissing my cheek. "I'll be back in a few days. Something unexpected came up."

"Just you?"

Someone whistled from the front door. He tapped on the window and waved to Fearghus. "Me and Pierce and a few of the guys."

A few of the guys. That meant something big was going on, something dangerous. He smiled and looked down at my hand clinging onto his. I pulled my hand away.

Fearghus blasted through the door. "Where you goin'?"

"Out of town. You be good for your *máthair.*" He ruffled Fearghus' hair, and Fearghus and I followed him to the foyer where Pierce was standing by the door. Martin jabbed Pierce in the arm. "You going to say goodbye to your wife? She's in the library." He picked up one of his bags. I went outside with him.

At least fifteen men stood around five idling cars. A sixth car was heading up the circle drive to join the others. A few of the guys? This was a gang. I tried to remember the trips he'd taken in the past, and if he'd ever traveled with such a large group. My memory of the past four years couldn't be trusted for details such as these. It was like I hadn't been paying attention. The chaos of the first years made it too impossible.

Now I was paying attention.

Martin ran a finger along my cheek. "Don't make me think you're going to miss me. I'll be holding onto a lie the whole time I'm gone." He caught a set of keys tossed to him.

"I thought you had to finish that contract."

"It'll have to wait. Sorry you'll have to have breakfast by yourself for a few days."

"I like being alone."

"I know you do." He kissed my forehead. Fearghus jumped on to his legs like a monkey and held on. He shuffled to the first car, pried Fearghus off, and put him in the passenger seat before taking the driver's seat. Fearghus waved at me, pretending he was going with him, and the scene became reality just for a second, just long enough to feed me a thought that someday this situation might be real. My son, one of them, part of this gang, heading out into the world to commit whatever heinous crimes they considered their job.

Pierce breezed past me and Fearghus gave up his seat to him and ran up the stairs to me. I held his shoulders, and we watched the line of cars drive off until they were all out of sight. When I returned to the library I found Rosemary, as well as Paul leaning over the back of the sofa on his forearms.

"I can give you a tour," he was saying.

She stood. "It'd be nice to give my legs somethin' to do."

"Have you met Miss Bevan?"

Her brow furrowed. "You mean Sloane?"

"We call her Miss Bevan around here."

"We do not," I said.

Fearghus and I followed them on a tour of the house, which only made Rosemary's wide eyes even wider with each new hall we entered and ballroom we peeked into. She couldn't hide her polite surprise at my and Martin's separate rooms. When Paul turned his back to lead us down the hall, the sideways glance she gave me said she'd be inclined to know more details later when we could talk girl to girl. Unfortunately, there were no details to give.

She asked me later after a dinner on the patio. We walked Fearghus down the hill to the lake. Halfway there, he took off in a run and jumped straight in, screaming all the way into the water.

"Don't shoot me for asking, but how come you and your husband have separate rooms?"

I didn't want to lie to this girl I hoped with all my heart would become my friend. "We just always have."

"How's that? You ain't always been married?"

We stopped at the edge of the lake. I watched Fearghus pretend to fight a sea monster. "We got married because of Fearghus." A truthful lie. Martin's specialty.

"Y'all don't get along?"

"We get along okay."

She sucked her top lip under her bottom lip. "I'm bein' so rude. I have so much time to bug you and I'm doin' it all on the first day." She stepped out of her sandals and wiggled her skirt down her legs. "Last one in's a rotten egg!"

Her splash started Fearghus laughing so hard I was afraid he'd drown.

I sat on the bank and watched them swim, leaning back on my elbows and trying to think of a way to explain my relationship with Martin without exposing my other life. Those thoughts naturally led to thoughts about Martin himself, and I wished I'd asked him to call when they got wherever they were going. Fearghus would surely ask about him while I was tucking him in at night, and I wanted to satisfy his inquiring mind. Martin's role as father to my son had tied a rope between him and me that grew thicker each day.

When they emerged from the water, Rosemary tied her headband around Fearghus' head, and he gleefully marched us up the hill and went to bed with one simple question I couldn't answer.

When's Dad coming back?

Pierce came back first, and he was unexpected, and alone. He burst into the kitchen when Fearghus and I were helping Ruby, pointed at me, and said, "Library. Now."

I wiped my hands. He had a bandage on his temple and bruise on his jaw, which I tried not to dwell on when I came toward him. He grabbed the back of my neck and shoved me through the doorway. We didn't make it to the library. He backed me into the wall in the small dining room, took a knife out of his pocket, and showed it to me before setting it on the buffet.

"Call your brother. Tell him to release him. Understood?"

"Release who?"

He slammed me into the wall. My head cracked against plaster. I saw stars.

"If I find out you're in on this, that you set him up …" He punched the wall inches from my face. "Telephone. Now."

I stumbled forward and caught the table. There was no arguing. Whatever he wanted me to do, I had to do it. We made it to the library. He pushed me into a chair. When I looked into his eyes, I knew.

"Martin?" I almost choked on his name.

He slammed the phone into my lap. "Call your brother."

I dialed the phone. A bass drum pounded in my head. I couldn't cry in front of Pierce. Five rings, then Arthur answered.

"Arthur—"

"Sis?"

"Let him go. You have to let him go."

"It's too late. They've already got him."

I closed my eyes. Clenched my toes. Fought a shudder threatening to rip through me. Pierce shifted his weight above me. I reached for that calm, Martin's calm, which I'd fed and nurtured inside me. I looked at Pierce and put the handset against my chest. "May I have some privacy? I can't convince him of anything with you standing over me."

He took a long breath in. His nostrils flared. And by some miracle, he left the room.

I put the handset back up to my ear. "Arthur, this ends. Let him go."

"You make it sound like I did this. I had nothing to do with it."

I wanted to scream, but it would only make matters worse. "You know about it."

"Of course I know about it. Okay, I was there. But I left."

"You know where he is?"

"He might not be there anymore."

"Find out where he is and make them let him go."

He didn't answer. I could hear him breathing into the phone. There were too many things to say and not enough time. "Please, Arthur."

"Why?!" he yelled. "I don't want to know your answer but I want you to think about it. Why should we release him? Why do you care?!"

My limbs shot full of life with a desperate need to act. I was the only one who knew both sides, the only one who should be making decisions about anything related to the war between our families, yet I was the only one who was never consulted.

"Martin is my husband. Fearghus' father. We need him. You'll never understand and I'm not asking you to. If anything happens to him, Fearghus and I will be so much more lost to you. You have no idea."

"This is—"

"Martin saved Fearghus' life."

Silence took over his end of the line for too long. I imagined what they were doing to Martin right then. I imagined if Fearghus knew, if he was standing there watching. No matter what they were doing to Martin, it would hurt Fearghus worse.

"That's why I married him, and that's why we need him. He makes our lives here tolerable. Take him away, and we'll be living in hell. And it will be on you."

His voice became low, contemplative. "Mam said he'd save Fearghus."

The handset slid off my ear, down my chest, to my lap. There was nothing more to say. Arthur already knew of Martin's importance to us, but he participated anyway, and he was doing nothing to help us. I could hear him talking through the phone on my lap, but I stared ahead at the bookshelves across the room that I relied on for so long before Martin's company eased my days. I picked up the handset when I heard him shouting my name.

"I'm here."

"Tell them Navy Pier at midnight." He hung up.

When I couldn't sleep that night, I got out of bed and went into Martin's empty room. I sat on his sofa in my spot for chess nights and thought about how fitting it would be if the Bevans killed my second husband to avenge the Moores killing my first. Their war was tearing my world apart. I was stuck in the middle. A casualty.

The following day was a numb haze. My sweet and blissfully ignorant son gave up trying to entertain me and moved onto Rosemary. Finally time to go inside for the night, I couldn't decide which one of them was dirtier. I read him three books and knew my mind would not rest, so I tucked him in and slipped downstairs. I wandered the foyer, the hall, the kitchen, and the library, watching the gradual slowing of the day's routine until only Fran remained, closing windows and locking doors.

"Do you need anything before I turn in, madam?"

I shook my head, afraid a restrained cry might escape if I spoke. I let myself outside, crossed the lawn to the woods, and followed the path to the bench where Martin and I had sat that night so long ago. Night overtook. The brightest stars arrived first in a sky with an absent moon. The cool breeze wrapped around my bare legs like a curious being feeling out a stranger. A single toad's croaky vibrato carried along the air until it was finally answered from far away.

Light flickered low through the trees, settled in one spot, then went off. A car. I took off running, back through the woods, across the lawn, and to the front of the house. Men were unloading from three cars parked in a line. Pierce stood by the first, in the open door of the backseat. Another man joined him. Together, they helped a passenger out of the backseat, his arms slung over each set of shoulders, and walked him into the house. I followed them up the front steps. The lights in the foyer flipped on.

Martin's once white shirt was darkened and blotchy, dirty gray stains mixing with rust red. His collar was hanging, ripped at the seam. Hair that should be light was as dark as Fearghus'. Feet normally so solid on the ground dragged and stumbled as he was half-carried up the stairs. In his room I pushed ahead, pulled down the covers on his bed. Fluffed his pillow. And covered my mouth to hold in a scream when I turned around and saw his face.

He was a cartoon. A drawing. Colored by a child with blue and purple crayons, as a silly joke because everyone knows those aren't the colors of human flesh. It wasn't real. It was a nightmare, a memory—of how Fearghus had looked when I found him dead on our front porch. Only Martin was alive.

"You want anything?" Pierce asked, helping swing Martin's legs onto the bed.

Martin didn't answer.

"He's all yours," Pierce said to me. They left.

I walked to the bedside. I was afraid to touch him. One eye was pinched at an odd angle, swollen shut. The other eye looked at me, then closed. I slid my hand under his and sank to my knees. My eyes filled. There were many reasons they'd do this to him. They'd probably been wanting to do it for years. But the most important reason, the most personal, was because of me. And the more personal the reason, the more brutal the abuse.

I took the stairs down to the kitchen and filled a bowl with ice. He was in the same position when I returned. The sheet under his hand still held the indention of mine. I took off his shoes. He flexed his feet. I found a pair of scissors in his desk drawer and cut both sleeves of his shirt from wrist to collar. He was able to lift just enough for me to slide it out from under him. A sickening smell of blood and sweat wafted around me. His undershirt was stained even worse. I eased it out of his pants then cut straight up his chest and down both sleeves. I took both shirts into his bathroom and tossed them in the tub. I grabbed his hand towel off the rack on my way out.

His breathing had slowed, like he'd finally relaxed. I pulled a chair to the side of the bed and filled the towel with ice. "Will it hurt you if I—"

A scratchy whisper. "No."

I wasn't sure if he was answering my question, but I placed the ice against his face anyway. When the ice saturated the towel and began dripping onto his pillow, I got a bath towel from his bathroom and folded it on top of his pillow. I sat with him until the ice melted and he fell asleep. Then I went into my room for my family's text, returned to Martin's side, and read him our most powerful prayer for healing and restful sleep. I sealed each eyelid with lavender oil and a kiss.

He slept for fourteen hours. Fran and I were applying ointment to the cuts on his face when he woke up. She quickly excused herself. Martin stared at the ceiling with his good eye, refusing to meet mine.

When I realized he wasn't going to speak, I sat on the edge of the bed to apply ointment to his knuckles. He allowed me to do one hand before pulling away. "That's enough."

"The other one is just as bad."

He licked his lips. I got his glass of water from the bedside table and helped him drink. He settled back against the pillow. "I'm going to say this once, and then we're going to drop it for good. Your family is—" He choked. It awoke a cough that shook him without end. When he regained control and lowered his hand, his palm was covered in blood.

I fought tears and wiped his hand with a towel.

He continued in a whisper. "They're worse than us. I had a deal with them. And they attacked me, twenty guys to one. My goal was a truce. Theirs was sabotage."

I couldn't excuse what happened, but I had to explain. "You have to see their perspective."

He swore. The worst swear, with no hesitation, no apology. It lit a fire in my blood.

"You took me and Fearghus. They think you forced me to marry you. They're still trying to save me."

"I'm taking care of you. Both of you. If it weren't for me—"

"If it weren't for you my husband wouldn't be dead. He'd never have been found. His son would never have been found."

"They would've found them." He put his hand against his mouth like he was about to cough again.

I didn't want to argue with him but I couldn't stop. "Without your help? You know that's a lie."

"You want some truth? Here's some truth. Whatever comes to them, they've brought it on. I'll give you some names right now. They'll be dead in twenty-four hours. You can start mourning early."

I stood. "Stop it."

He was just angry. He didn't mean it. His defeat hit him harder than every strike to his body combined, and this was his way of coping.

He tried to turn over, but the motion became a wince instead. "Close the door on your way out."

A numbness swept my body and left me cold. My family's attack had defeated more than his physical power, his mental strategy, his knowledge of the game. It had also ripped through his manners and civility to uncover the traits he held deep inside that also belonged to his father. To Pierce. To Lewis. To Paul on his worst days. My shock didn't result from this newly exposed side to the man I married; it belonged to an instantaneous recognition of my expert ability to lie to myself, to mask a known truth, to wholly believe I had married the only good one. Deep down they were all the same. I had crafted my own perfect lie, and I had believed it.

CHAPTER 31

IT WAS A chore keeping Fearghus out of Martin's room. He didn't believe any white lie I told him, and every day he badgered me to tell him when Martin would be better so he could come to training with him. I'd think his training would be a free ride without his drill sergeant father on his case, but when I questioned him, he dropped his gaze to his feet and said he didn't like training without him.

When Martin was finally well enough to leave his room, Fearghus was warned to leave him alone but didn't listen—if he had, I wouldn't have recognized him as my son. Satisfied to see his father well again, he didn't ask one question about his startling wounds and fell right back into his usual independent play. But my avoidance of Martin for anything beyond necessary interaction didn't get by Rosemary.

"Does it bother you so bad to see him like that?"

We were sitting in the shade at the edge of the woods on the far end of the lake. A cluster of mighty sycamore towered above us, their limbs extending far from the woods so we could sit comfortably in clipped lawn. Fearghus had lured the ducks close. They preened under the canopy of the tree Fearghus was climbing. He was too busy conquering the tree to notice the heat.

"I just don't think he wants me around right now. He's upset …" I couldn't put the words together to explain it to her safely.

"Men bellyache at everyone around them, but I really think it's the only way they know to reach out when they're feelin' bad."

"Martin doesn't complain."

She raised both eyebrows. "Well ain't you lucky. You picked the right one."

I stood to tell Fearghus he was too far up the tree and needed to start coming down now. When I rejoined her in the grass, she handed me a bracelet made of clover blossoms. "You'll get through it. You have a good marriage."

"I'm not sure that's how I'd describe it." We watched Fearghus as he lowered himself through the branches toward the ground. If he minded that easily he must be up to something.

"You kiddin'? I've seen the way you look at him. And he's outta his mind in love with you. I've never seen a married couple so sweet to each other. It's like a restraint y'all have with each other when in company of others, like if we saw how it really was we'd all be so sick with envy of y'all we'd just give up on the spot."

I stared at her, astounded by her view of my marriage, when Fearghus reached the bottom branch and jumped, flipping in the air and landing on his feet. He looked at me, first guilty, then smug. He could see he was about to get scolded, and he was already trying to play it down.

"That boy oughtta join the circus," Rosemary said.

With a glance over his shoulder that dared me to complain, Fearghus started back up the tree for a second go. "Our marriage—it's a lie," I said. "I've been lying to myself. I thought Martin was the good one, but he's not. They're all rotten and he's one of them, and I married him."

"Aw, they're not all rotten."

I looked into her eyes. She didn't know. She was just as stuck as I was, and she was stuck with Pierce, not Martin. If I was locked in a cage with a snake, she was locked in with a hungry grizzly.

"Same as any human being, they have faults. But it's not you tellin' lies. Love tells lies. The worst ones."

I shook those words off. Love didn't factor into this. Her earlier words, the ones that accused me of avoiding Martin because I couldn't bear to see his broken nose and black eyes, clung to me for weeks. They started a slideshow of every wound he'd brought home. With each repeat of the show, a pattern came further into focus. Under the influence of time, each lacerated cheekbone, broken finger, and black eye carried a heavier weight inside me. One at a time, those injuries brought an alarm anyone would feel seeing another person wounded. Displayed together, in this unending collection of memories, they proved Rosemary's case.

I couldn't bear to see him like that. Not because he was a human being who'd been violently wounded. Because he was Martin.

The first morning I joined him for breakfast again, he stared at me so long I almost excused myself, sure he wanted me out of his sight. Then he asked me to pass the jam but took my hand instead, kissing it before smearing his toast. I relaxed into my chair and we fell into our normal breakfast routine, although a silent one.

"Pierce almost has me convinced you set me up," was the first thing of depth he said to me a few mornings later. He could've been discussing the weather. He'd had over a month to make amends with his attack, but the matter-of-fact tone for this subject matter seemed so out of place I couldn't answer. "The one hole in his argument is your inability to contact them. And he knows that. But you and I know that's no hole." He picked up his coffee mug but didn't drink.

"I have no way to phone or write to them without you knowing."

"True, but that hasn't stopped you from sneaking them messages in the past." He was talking about when I gave Mam his Cambridge address to send my texts. He hadn't forgotten, and he knew I hadn't forgotten he'd caught me.

"I would never set you up, Martin."

He rested his knuckles against his lips and studied me across the table. If this was how the opposing party in a lawsuit felt under his scrutiny, it was no wonder how successful a lawyer he was.

"I can always tell when people are lying," he said.

"Then you know." I dropped my napkin on my plate and pushed away from the table. It was unfair for him to make me feel like this.

"Yes, I do." He didn't elaborate. If he'd thought I was lying, I'm sure he would have.

I neglected to warn Rosemary about the family dinner routine before I found us in the midst of her first one and the worst assault on Paul I'd seen in years. When she turned her tear-filled eyes to Martin, obviously expecting his help, I realized she also saw him as the good one. Pierce, her husband sitting at her side, should've been the natural person she'd look to for help. But she hadn't.

I wished I'd told her Martin couldn't help. No one could help. So I did what I normally did. I ate my soup and reached for my calm, the calm I'd grown from Martin's steady stare that witnessed his father's vicious undoing of his brother when I knew behind it dwelled the same feelings I had—that each time, a part of Paul crumbled away, and one of those days the person we loved would be lost to us. That Martin was as helpless to intervene as I was.

She caught my arm on the way out of the dining room, and instead of answering her pleading expression, I invited her to chess night—necessary that night so Martin and I could keep Paul entertained and away from his many chemical indulgences. She became Paul's teammate, and for once we were evenly paired. Although she offered no help to Paul whatsoever, he seemed to enjoy explaining the moves to her more than if she'd been an expert player. He didn't drink one sip of liquor.

After two games, she said, "Y'all know how to play Rook?"

"We only play chess here," Martin said with a straight face. I elbowed him playfully so she'd know he was joking.

"I've a deck in my room. I'll go get it."

Paul stood with her. "I'll go with you."

When I realized Martin and I were both staring at the door they'd gone through, I moved my attention to the chessboard and started picking up the pieces.

"I feel like I should've made him stay here," Martin said.

I couldn't acknowledge what he was thinking, even though ignoring his comment meant I was thinking it too. Since Martin and I had nothing to talk about lately, the wait for their return was a life sentence in solitary confinement. I tried not to wonder where Pierce went after dinner, whether he knew his wife was here with us and what he'd say about Paul following her to their room. Maybe he was in their room.

They finally came through the door giggling.

"Did you get lost?" Martin said.

"Is Rook a four player game?" I asked quickly.

Martin and I had to watch Paul and Rosemary play a few rounds before we caught on to the rules. It only seemed complicated until I found myself playing it. Martin had to stop when his scotch left him too relaxed to care about winning. When I kissed his cheek goodnight, his hand lingered on mine. Once in my bed the memory kept me awake, restless and feverish.

The following night I couldn't sleep either. Fearghus and his cat had once and for all captured every square inch of the bed, and I could no longer determine which one of them put off more body heat. I got out of bed and took a pillow to the sofa. A glow illuminated Martin's balcony outside. He must've been working late for a court appearance the next day, or perhaps he'd simply left a light on.

The sofa was cool to my skin. It didn't take long for me to miss the warmth of the bodies in the bed, but when I got up to reclaim my spot, it was no longer there. I went to the windows. Martin's light was still on. A stranger inside me slipped her arms in mine like sleeves, her legs in mine like stockings, and I opened the door between our rooms and entered his sitting room. The door to his room was open. I stepped through the doorway and pulled the door closed behind me.

An abandoned book lay open under his banker's lamp on his desk, the only source of light in an otherwise dark room. He stood at his windows with his back to me. His night pants hung low and loose, like he forgot to tie the drawstring. He also forgot to put on a shirt. His feet were bare. The doorknob clicked in my hand when I released it. He turned around.

A tingle shot from my stomach to my chest, but instead of invoking an expected wild dance in my heart, it calmed it, and my body became charged with a strong sense of well-being. "Are you working?"

He said nothing, just continued to watch me. He had a toned fighter's body—well-defined shoulders and strong arms, a torso shaped like a perfect V.

"Fearghus and his cat are taking up my whole bed."

He opened his mouth as if to speak, but instead of words out came a long, slow breath. I became aware of the short hem of my slip, of the sheerness of the material, of my untidy hair. I closed the distance between us and stopped in front of him.

"Can I sleep with you?"

He looked at his bed, then back at me. "You really want that?"

I nodded. He reached a careful hand toward my ear and removed my hairpin with such gentle ease that if my hair hadn't untwisted and fallen loose against my shoulder, I might not have felt it at all. He took the other pin too, setting them on his desk without breaking my gaze. He slid one hand against my cheek and leaned in, watching my face like he understood how overwhelming a man's touch could be after I'd gone so long without it. Fingertips woven into my hair, the warmth of his palm against my cheek. I had to close my eyes, to limit one sense before the others became overloaded. His lips grazed my cheekbone, my earlobe, and finally rested against my neck. One point of contact, a universe wide. He inhaled slowly. When he pulled away, I found myself gripping the waist of his pants.

He went to his desk and tugged the chain on his lamp. Darkness took over where light had been. My eyes adjusted to the moon casting its soft light through the windows as he walked to the bed and pulled the covers down. He stood beside the bed, waiting. I was on the edge of a cliff, my destination concealed beneath a lush forest canopy below. I had walked along the edge so long hoping for an easy decline, an easy trail down. I could continue walking the edge forever and never get anywhere, never know anything but this same view, this same terrain. And I jumped.

The love he made to me presented an ideal complement to my new life. To the new me. It was a thorough test of my patience, my stamina, my ability to forget the past and the future and move with the tide. I shivered from every sweep of his hands, was lit by every kiss. His restraint was fuel, each touch a spark. He learned every square inch of me.

The night transformed into a life sentence of waiting, a desperate need for the perfect ending. And he took his time. He reveled in it. When he was finally in position to join himself to me, he put his thumb on my chin and forced me to look at him, to grant him permission. I was too breathless to answer. My nod was his welcome. It wasn't until it was over that I could fathom just how sweet the wait had been.

His elbows held most of his weight off me, but he dropped his forehead against my shoulder. His breath cooled a patch of my skin. I closed my eyes for a moment until he lifted his head, and when I opened them I was looking straight into his. He was about to say something crazy, I could see it. I twisted underneath him, and he freed my legs so I could turn onto my stomach. I was afraid to look at him. I didn't want him to see this new layer of my attachment to him. How I needed him even though he was who he was. It would only encourage his feelings made more powerful by this moment. Ours was an arranged marriage. There was no love here.

He lowered himself down, his chest pressed against my back, and his lips touched the back of my neck. His heart pounded against my skin as if it was inside me consuming my own heart. Conquering it. I was more beholden to him than ever. After having this, I couldn't be without it.

He rolled onto his back and remained that way until his breathing slowed, then he got up, pulled on his pants, and went out on the balcony. I heard the flick of his cigarette lighter, the creak of the railing under his elbows. I thought of Fearghus lying in his grave. I'd just gone to bed with the man I had married, yet I couldn't have committed a greater sin. My eyes filled, but I smeared the tears away with the back of my hand. There was no need to cry. I was a different person then than I was now. The path of my life had been severed and begun anew.

I couldn't sleep in there. I needed to get up and go back to my own bed, but the mattress held me like a bed of plaster and my limbs were too heavy to move. Fearghus was lying in a double grave in the woods of Illinois, waiting for me to join him someday—a privilege of which I was no longer worthy.

Martin came inside, and I wished I'd already left. I didn't want to be seen in just my slip even though I'd walked in there earlier in it. He sat on the opposite side of the bed. It was my cue to leave. I sat up and slid to the floor, but he grabbed my hand. His other arm hooked my waist, and he pulled me back in bed, against him, kissed my forehead, my eyelids, my lips, and held me until I fell asleep.

In the morning I woke up before him. I eased myself out of his bed and stole a look at him before I left. I could still see the imprint of my body with his curled around it. I went into my room, to the bottom drawer of my bedside table, took off Fearghus' ring and put on Martin's. If he noticed it at breakfast, I couldn't tell. He grinned at me for other reasons. After breakfast I went to the kitchen and brewed myself a tea from the ingredients in my bedroom floor. It was an acceptable safeguard against pregnancy for now. I needed to consult my family's texts to find a mixture that wouldn't lose effect with continued use. Asking Mam was not an option.

I promised myself to stay away from Martin's room at night until I did.

Rosemary wandered into the kitchen while I was helping to prepare lunch, and I pulled out the chair beside me and pushed a pile of green beans in front of her when she sat. We always talked best when our hands had something to do. There was enough noise in the kitchen to make our conversation our own.

"Where's Trey Fearghus?"

I stuck my thumb toward the doors leading to the patio. "Out there hunting for worms."

"He's got the better job." She started snapping beans. "Don't ya ever think about what you're missin' havin' all these folks to do the chores? Not that I ever saw myself stuck keepin' a house for a man, but I guess since I was a girl I had this romantic notion of bein' a wife. When I married Pierce, I thought I'd be doin' his laundry and makin' him dinner and doin' the grocery shoppin' and drivin' some kids to school someday. Do the kids here even go to school?"

"Martin wants to put Fearghus in school soon."

"Yeah, but you're different. What about Lew and Caroline's baby?"

I shrugged and snapped a bean. I never even saw that child. Caroline had made it obvious from the day her daughter was born that she was not sharing her with me. Her nannies must have been given the same orders. "I imagine she will too."

"Well that beats being stuck in here with a teacher and never playin' with other kids."

As much as I worried about Fearghus leaving the estate to go to school, I knew Rosemary was right. It'd be good for him. I just wished I could be the one to take him and pick him up every day, not some driver in some fancy car.

"Other stuff too," she continued. "Moppin' the floor, washin' windows, plannin' meals. Not that I want to be my mama. I want my rights, too. But some of that … I just cain't see myself lettin' all these people do all the work for much longer without me bein' bored to an early deathbed."

She had no idea how much of that I missed, what an ache it roused when I thought about it too long. "You do all that if you want. I do. Ruby will let you mop, just pick up the mop."

"Aw, I'd feel so silly. I feel silly enough when my maid tries to do my hair and I have to tell her my hair don't like gettin' done up in a braid."

"You're doing a chore right now." I threw a bean at her. She'd left her hair long, loose, and natural for the last family dinner. It had natural wave, beautiful in an unruly way. Mermaid hair, stroked by sea and dried by sun. I was glad they hadn't made her change it, and glad she hadn't allowed them to.

"'Cause *you* are. That's different."

"It's no different. Whatever you want to do, just do it. Ask for an iron in your room if you want to iron. Come cook with me when I cook. We can kick all the staff out and make the whole meal." Couldn't she see she was the one with the freedom, not me?

Her eyes got big. "When?"

"Tonight. Dinner."

"Don't you kid."

"I'm not. I'll tell Fran right now. Fearghus can help us. We can even get Paul in on it."

She bit her bottom lip and smiled widely.

"Okay, maybe not Paul. He'll just make a big mess and get in our way."

She averted her gaze and went back to snapping beans. "We should still invite him. He's such good company."

My curt glance followed but she didn't notice it, and I felt sick with shame. She'd meant nothing by it. My fear of her husband was building this friendly affection she had for her brother-in-law into something else, almost as if my mind had twisted to see things his way. Perhaps I was becoming too like them: paranoid, skeptical, accusatory. Creating a fault in others in order to gain power.

Or perhaps I just knew Pierce too well.

CHAPTER 32

F EARGHUS WASN'T ON the patio where I'd left him. My anger at being disobeyed was quickly replaced by worry when I heard Pierce's voice coming from the side of the house. I ran to the corner then slowed to a walk as I came around.

First I saw Pierce leaning against the wall, lighting a cigarette. Fearghus was walking away from him, his stride restrained like he'd been told not to run but so much wanted to run. His shirt was crooked; a twisted ball of it stood up near his collar like someone had grabbed it and held on. When he saw me, he started running toward me and ran into my skirt.

"I asked you not to the leave the patio," I said, desperate to get his mind off what had just happened. I held his head against my leg until he pulled free.

"Uncle Pierce wanted me."

"Then you should've come to get me. So I knew where you were going." And so I could've gone with him.

He looked up at me. I picked a piece of grass out of his hair. He wasn't wearing his amulet.

"I just didn't …" He looked down.

"What, Fearghus?"

"Didn't want him to get my lizard." A creature's head popped out of his breast pocket before crawling into his hand. He held the skink up to me.

"Why did Pierce want to take your lizard?"

"He didn't. But he woulda if he saw him. He didn't see him." He grinned at me like he'd just won a game.

"What did Pierce want to talk to you about?"

He shrugged. The skink crawled into his shirt pocket. "He wants to come to my room. Can I take him there?"

"I'm not sure he'd be happy up there. Do you?"

He cocked his head and squinted one eye. "Okay. I'll put 'em back on the rock."

When we rounded the corner of the house, I saw Martin on the patio with his newspaper and my stomach fluttered stupidly. But it wasn't nearly as silly as me pretending not to notice him until he called my name. Fearghus showed him the skink before heading to the cluster of rocks beyond the patio. I paused for Martin, which seemed to be enough since he kept looking at me without saying anything. I finally gave up and went for the door.

"Darling."

I turned around. The flutter in my stomach returned, more like the wings of a hawk than a butterfly.

"Care to sit with me?" Everything had healed but the scar on his eyelid. I still wasn't used to it.

"You might want to ask your brother what he wanted with your son. And why it was necessary to grab his shirt."

"Who?"

"Pierce."

One of the staff opened the door. "Your car is ready, sir."

"Thank you." Martin folded up his newspaper and patted the arm of the chair next to him. "Come sit for a few minutes before I have to leave."

"Where are you going?"

"Philadelphia. It's a simple real estate issue."

I sat in the chair. "Will you tell me when it's your turn to strike back so I can relax until then?"

He smoothed his newspaper hard against the table, like he was making a new crease. "I don't need to visit anyone in your family anytime soon." He leaned back in his chair. "Unless you want to go for a visit. I'm sure your brother feels better after breaking my nose. Maybe he and I can get along now."

I was desperate to see Tara again, but I wanted to wait until Enid's baby was born in a few months. My visits must be timed to get the most out of them. I also wanted Fearghus to be a little older, so he'd be content to be with Martin all day away from me while I was visiting my family. But here Martin was trying to distract me from the conversation I had started.

"No, I already know how this works. They struck last, so it's your turn. You always have to win." It was impossible to know if he was lying about Philadelphia, because all he did was smile. I could feel an anger rising in me, and I did nothing to suppress it. "What's so funny?"

He looked down, but that grin wouldn't go away.

"You think you already won." He had me and Fearghus. The Moores' goal was Fearghus; I was an added bonus. And Martin was the one who'd won us both.

He nodded. "A long time ago."

Fearghus was in front of me, holding out a box turtle. "What about her?"

"No animals in our room, and I won't tell you again. You can play with her out here, but she needs to stay outside where she belongs and I'm not discussing it further."

Fearghus straightened and froze, staring at me like I was speaking some foreign tongue. I started to rephrase it in Irish, but he cut me off. "Friend comes in our room and he's an animal."

"That's different."

"No fair!"

"Trey, you heard your mother. Now go play or go inside and wash up."

I closed my eyes and pressed my palms against my eyelids. The sun beat against my face and arms, and its heat radiated up at me from the patio stone. When I opened my eyes, Fearghus was back in the grass, and Martin was watching a flock of ducks land on the lake.

"Philadelphia," I said. "You're going alone?"

"Yes. And if your bed gets crowded again, you're welcome to mine. While I'm gone, or any other—"

"I'm fine. It's fine, I mean."

"I'll have another bed brought to your room for Trey. He's old enough for his own bed."

"No, it's fine how it is. We don't need another bed to crowd things."

He loosened his tie, which seemed strange since he was about to leave the house. "You're welcome to move into my room with me."

"I can't. I'd have to move all my …"

"We could give Trey his own room. There are many empty ones he could pick from. He can't room with you forever."

"There aren't any empty rooms near mine. He's too young to be far away from me." Especially with Pierce loose in the house.

"I'd give him my room, but I can't leave the two of you alone on that floor all night."

I pressed my lips together. I could see where this was going, and instead of being direct, he was manipulating me into suggesting what he wanted to suggest himself. The leaves in the trees shifted, but instead of a breeze I only felt something like hot breath on my neck. "If you go to Philadelphia and get into trouble again, so help me—"

"I wouldn't tell you it was a simple real estate issue if it wasn't a simple real estate issue."

I wanted to tell him he had a history of lying, and once a liar always a liar. He must have seen it on my face because his eyes narrowed and he put both hands on his knees and leaned forward. "Maybe we should stop before this turns ugly. I don't want to leave on a low note."

"Because you might not come back alive?" I stood and brushed off my skirt.

"Yeah, that's what I said."

"That's what you mean. Don't be a snake with me, Martin. Save it for your family or your clients."

His newspaper ruffled in the breeze then slid off the table, but he had stilled in place and made no effort to pick it up. It flipped and caught the wind, flapping, vying for attention.

"Save it for *my* family," I added, unable to stop myself.

He got up and shoved his chair into the table. Across the patio Fearghus looked up. Rosemary and Fearghus and I were going to make dinner, and he was going to miss it due to some illegal, immoral, or violent business meeting. A thought dove in, claiming that if he knew about our dinner he'd cancel the meeting and stay, and I took a breath to tell him, to ask him to stay. He shoved my chair into the table and stormed past me, and I was glad to see that thought crash and burn.

"What's wrong with Dad?" Fearghus had joined me.

"Nothing. Did you put all your animals back where they belong?"

"Yeah. Did Dad break the chairs?" He squatted for a better look.

"Of course not."

"Is he mad?" Fearghus' face held the expression of someone witnessing a miracle, bringing the abnormality of it to my attention. It was the first time either one of us had seen Martin lose his cool.

I took Fearghus upstairs and put him in the bathtub, unable to stop thinking about Martin shoving those chairs. I wondered if that was the extent of his anger, or if he could be pushed further. When Eleanor came in to deliver fresh towels, I asked her to stay with Fearghus and hurried down the stairs, hoping to catch him before he left. The right thing to do was apologize. Ask him to call me when he got there. See him off properly.

A black sedan idled at the bottom of the steps outside, but it was empty. I waited in the foyer, catching my breath, trying to talk myself into going back to my room and forgetting all about it.

He came into the foyer with a briefcase in one hand and a small black case in another. He stopped in front of me, expressionless.

"I won't tolerate that kind of aggression in front of Fearghus." My words shocked me more than they appeared to shock him. It wasn't at all what I wanted to say.

"For some reason you're determined to pick a fight with me, and I won't have a part in it. Especially when I have to leave." He set down his briefcase and opened the door. "Especially after last night."

"Last night was a mistake." I didn't mean it. But something made me say it, just to see him hurt. Just to see how it would make me feel.

He closed his eyes and turned his head, breathing out. "You make me wait a year," he said, shaking his head. "Screw it. Years. And now you're going to do this."

"I make you wait? I'm not yours to have. I don't owe you anything."

He abruptly looked at me. "So that's it. The recurring theme. If you can reduce it to that, so be it. We obviously have a difference in opinion about each other."

I stood, speechless, in sudden recognition of a pit of hate inside me, growing, gaining power. The hate I'd had for him, for killing my husband, for kidnapping my baby, for imprisoning me, for separating me from my daughter and my family before I had a chance to heal from tragedy. That hate was in there, barking orders, shoving around other emotions and making me its puppet.

"Goodbye, Sloane."

I went to the window to watch him leave. He drove away, alone. About that, he was being truthful.

The most difficult part of our dinner preparation was convincing all the staff to leave the kitchen. Rosemary made fried green tomatoes and mashed potatoes with gravy, and I made chicken à la king and a lemon chiffon cake. Fearghus put his destructive skills to use mashing potato after potato and didn't even take a break to lick the beaters.

It was Rosemary's idea to serve the staff, but we knew they'd never go along with it so we sent Fearghus out to find Paul, who rounded them up and seated them in the small dining room. While they ate I made a second cake because Paul had already helped himself to a large piece of the first one, claiming I'd made him wait too long for his dinner.

"Did you taste this?" he said to Rosemary, offering her a bite off his own fork.

"We should let them off their shifts when they're done," I said. "But they're not going to take it from me."

"Go tell 'em, Paulie." Rosemary poked him in the arm. "I'll bring dessert in."

"*Milseog*," he said.

"*Milseog*," she repeated. They smiled at each other like they shared a secret.

Fearghus hopped down to follow. I started washing our dirty pots and pans. The calm room compelled me to think about Martin, so I started counting backwards from one hundred. I didn't get far before the doorway to the hall filled with Pierce.

"Dinner should be on the table and you're in here alone? Care to explain?"

"The staff is almost finished eating. Then we'll serve everyone else. It will only be a few minutes."

"The staff is eating? Who said you could make that call?"

"It was your wife's idea." As soon as I said it I wanted to take it back. He wouldn't see the thoughtfulness I wanted to attribute to his wife, nor would he understand I was calling him on his mistake—it wasn't the insubordinate decision of his prisoner, it was the wish of one of the ladies of the house. All he'd see was his staff eating in his dining room, causing his dinner to be late. This was a problem to him, and I had just blamed Rosemary.

"My wife doesn't need you to encourage her silly ideas." He took off his jacket and threw it on the breakfast table. The salt shaker toppled and rolled slowly off the edge. He was close enough to catch it, but he simply watched it crash on the floor into jagged pieces of glass. "Clean it up."

My heart climbed into my throat, beating hard. "The broom is in the closet behind you."

"You're brave, considering Martin's gone right now." He crossed the kitchen and leaned his hip against the counter next to me. "I want to see you on your hands and knees cleaning that up."

Fearghus came through the swinging door and stopped. I couldn't send him away without him asking why. I needed a good reason he wouldn't question, but I couldn't think. I groped for Martin's calm inside me. It was long gone, tucked away with all other thoughts of him.

"I wouldn't want your son to be cut by that glass."

I took my hands out of the dishwater and dried them.

"Good girl," Pierce said.

The door swung open and Paul and Rosemary came through carrying stacks of dirty dishes. They stopped behind Fearghus. Their expressions were identical—a frozen transition between giddy joy and abrupt anxiety. Two sets of eyes sliding between me and Pierce, then to the broken salt shaker on the floor.

"Who spilled the salt?" Paul said.

"Aw, hon, did your coat knock that off?" Rosemary handed me her stack of plates. "I'll clean that up. You go relax in the library 'til we get the table set." She kissed Pierce on the cheek. He watched her get the broom out of the closet before he left the room.

Paul moved the chairs while she swept. After putting them back, he took the broom away from her and finished it himself. Fearghus held the dust pan for Paul while Rosemary and I cleared and set the table. Then we rounded up Lewis, Caroline, and the two visiting cousins from California and finished up all the food. I was thankful for all the conversation so I didn't have to speak.

Hours of restless sleep that night forced me into Martin's room. The serenity of the night promised he'd never know I accepted his offer of his bed while he was gone. The next day, Rosemary found me in the library with a road atlas, calculating the mileage from Richmond to Philadelphia. She held a pair of blue jeans she was in the process of embroidering.

"Y'all goin' somewhere?"

"Just Martin. He left yesterday."

She sat next to me and went to work on a purple peace sign on the front leg. "Seems a bit late to be plannin' his route."

"I just wondered how long of a trip it is."

She stopped sewing and looked up. She was putting something together in her head, and I had no idea how, unless she heard about our fight yesterday. "Trey Fearghus just told me his daddy was mad yesterday, like it was bigger news than Bobby Kennedy gettin' killed. I thought that ain't cool. Martin don't get mad."

"No, not often."

"Well, when he comes back you just patch things up and you two can beat me and Paul's socks off in Rook."

"It was my fault. I wanted to make him mad, and I'm afraid I'll do it again." Someone else had control of my voice again, but this time, I gave it up willingly.

"Why on earth would you do that?"

"Because he did something really bad, a long time ago. He … hurt someone I love. I hate him for it, and I don't know what to do." A shaky sickness overtook me. I looked down at my hands, willing them not to tremble. I gathered a breath that stuttered through me. "I think it's making me crazy."

She stuck her needle into the blue jeans, set them aside, and waited for me to continue. I drew another breath and closed my eyes. I'd said too much. There was no point in talking about it, and bringing her into it was an awful idea.

"Know what I think? Folks get so hung up on findin' a way to forgive too fast too soon and 'course that's gonna seem impossible. Peace is out there, it's just gotta find you, and you gotta be open to it. How can you be open to it if you're busy workin' out way to forgive?"

"I don't want to forgive him."

"Aw, Sloane, no one's perfect. You gotta love him for what he is. Even the bad stuff. That's what makes him up. And that's what makes him need you so much. Think, without you, he'd be this dirty ol' lump of coal on the ground with no hope of ever bein' a diamond. But you come along and you pick 'em up and hold 'em in your hand and keep 'em warm and soon you'll have yourself a diamond. And you cain't hate that piece of coal anymore, 'cause it was you that changed it, and it's got a part of you in it now."

The world was cruel to pair an angel like this with a devil of a man like Pierce.

Martin's luggage passed me on the stairs a few days later. Knowing he was near set my heart intent on doubling its rhythm, so I took my time wandering the house until I found him in the kitchen with all three of his brothers. I stopped in the doorway. He didn't look at me or speak to me, but when he shifted his weight, it was enough for me to know he'd noticed me. I couldn't blame him for still being sore with me.

I went down to the lake where Rosemary and Fearghus were swimming.

"Have you ever tried the pool?" I asked when she saw me and got out.

"Nah. If you don't come out covered in gunk, you ain't had any fun." She squinted in the direction of the pool house. "It's over by Paulie's place? I'm over there all the time and I never even seen it once."

I rarely had a reason to visit Paul's carriage house, and I wondered why she would.

"Hey, Mom! Is Dad home?"

I followed Fearghus' gaze. The Moore brothers had come out onto the patio. Fearghus' shorts were so heavy with water he was almost losing them as he streaked past me and ran up the hill.

"Want me to keep him a tad longer so y'all can talk?" Rosemary asked.

"No, I need to get him cleaned up for bed." I started up the hill, but Fearghus was already running back down with Paul on his heels. He stopped at the shore, biting down on a smile, and Paul picked him up and tossed him into the water.

"He needs to come in," I said to Paul.

Paul gave me a serious look and pointed at me. "I think you need to go in. The lake."

I backed away from him. He grabbed Rosemary instead. She shrieked all the way into the water. Then he backed up and took a running leap in next to her, his body balled up to make the most violent of splashes. I used the commotion to steal a look at Martin on the patio, but he was no longer there. Only Pierce remained, staring down at the lake, his cigarette hanging off his lip, forgotten.

CHAPTER 33

MARTIN WAS ABSENT from dinner in the small dining room that night, so Paul moved into the chair next to me to form three couples—Rosemary and Pierce, Caroline and Lewis, and me and Paul. Fearghus finished first and asked to be excused. I knew he wanted to find his dad. He bounded off even though I knew Martin was probably speaking with his own father and shouldn't be bothered. Rosemary had a way of pulling Caroline out of her shell and into a conversation, and I soon realized her technique was to keep the focus on Caroline. She'd participate in a conversation as long as it was about her. The boys were having a conversation of their own. I was too occupied by the many possible exchanges taking place in my head between Martin and myself to pay any attention to either of them.

By the time I'd put Fearghus to bed, everything I could think to say to Martin and every likely reply from him had played out in my mind, and all I wanted was for it to stop. So I wandered down to the ballroom and turned on the smallest lamp.

The piano bench was cold through my housecoat. I placed my fingers on the keys and closed my eyes, playing by feel at first. Missed notes rang harsh in the air, and a deep breath didn't steady the tension building in my arms and legs. I stopped playing and stared at my hands. My silence wouldn't be the first to break. This was Martin's world. It was his job to correct the motion of it. I pulled the lid over the keys and went upstairs to bed.

I woke with a jolt. Large blobs clung to the ceiling, rippling, refracting light. The walls around me melted, exposing a new room full of sun. My room. I was sitting on my sofa, but it was closer to the windows. Another sofa faced me, and behind that stood a man, tall and muscled, in a fitted black cotton undershirt with a gun strapped under each arm. He gripped the back of the sofa with both hands, about to rip it in two. His face was tight, lips pressed, eyes narrowed, like I had just done him wrong. I didn't want to see him hurt like that. He stormed out of the room, and I turned to my side, toward a woman looking as pained as I felt. But there was a calm strength in her, and I had to reach out and use it, but I didn't know how, and she was looking at me with such hope, and nodding, over and over, until she nodded herself away and all I could see was black. I waited for my reality to fade back in, but I was lost in the void until I remembered the young woman kneeling in my room with the moon aligned with the oak tree and how much she resembled this woman next to me on the sofa. Then I heard a voice.

"*A Mháthair?*"

"It's okay. Go back to sleep."

Fearghus was leaning over me. "Are you having a nightmare?"

"No, just a dream."

He propped himself up on one elbow. "You can tell me, you know. If it's bad guys and monsters. I can protect you. I have to when Dad's not here. He won't always be here."

"Is that what he tells you? What else does he say?" I slid his elbow out from under him and lowered his head to his pillow.

"He says when I'm big I have to be strong and protect myself." He yawned. For a moment in his face I saw the baby he once was. The baby I had given everything up to protect. In my mind I saw his father's face. Normally blurred with time, it came brilliantly alive to me, only to be replaced just as easily with the image of that man from my vision, as if that man held the key of a reminder.

In the light from the moon, I watched his eyes close, his jaw loosen, his lips part. His breathing slowed. I hoped he'd never have the burden of protecting himself from these people. If he truly became one of them, perhaps he'd have no need. Could I allow him to integrate so completely they'd never have a reason to do him harm? Was his safety worth selling his soul to them?

I slid out of bed and walked to the windows. Light burst onto Martin's balcony next door, then lowered in intensity, like he'd flipped off the main light in favor of a lamp. It was probably his banker's lamp on his desk. Surely he couldn't be working at one in the morning. He must have finished with his father and come up to his room for bed. But that light—he'd left it on. He wasn't in bed. And like a beacon, it called me to the adjoining door and into his room.

He was sitting on the edge of the bed in his undershirt and pants, gripping the edge of the bed so tightly each muscle in his arm was taut. His gaze remained on the floor at his feet until I stopped right in front of him. Then he looked up, stood up, and started unbuttoning his pants like it was some dare for me to look away, to leave, to give him his privacy.

I reached his zipper before he did. Instead of stopping it, I lowered it, and his pants dropped to the ground and then his mouth was on mine. All the fabricated conversations flushed from my mind, releasing the tension they'd demanded, freeing the space they'd so greedily consumed. I kissed him back, reaching for his face, pulling myself against him. He grabbed my shoulders and held me away.

His voice was a harsh whisper. "Don't do this if you're going to argue with me tomorrow."

I twisted my shoulders. He released me, but it felt more like a shove. I took a step back to keep from stumbling. My breath came fast and hard. So did his. We stared at each other, catching our breath. He stepped out of his pants and kicked them away, not breaking our gaze. It was my move.

I got in his bed. He got in after me. We collided under the sheet like two storm fronts competing for command of the sky. He captured my arms and flipped me over, swept my hair to the side and kissed the back of my neck.

His thumbs hooked the straps of my slip. I scooted away, ducking under his arm until I was facing him again. His hand closed over my shoulder and slid down my arm. His fingers weaved into mine. He closed his hand, forced my arm against the bed and held it there until I looked at him.

He wanted me to say something. He was waiting for it. Perhaps he wanted to know why I came in there. Why I wanted this. But I couldn't divulge an answer I didn't know myself, so I simply looked at him, hoping my expression was as void as I wanted it to be. If he wanted to know something, he'd have to ask. I wasn't going to give up information to someone who thought he deserved my explanation without having to humble himself and ask the question in the first place.

And then I remembered the other night, that look on his face, that thing he was about to say to me before I turned over to prevent it. Heat swept my stomach then spread to my fingers and toes in one beat of my heart. Those words, whether he was waiting to say them to me or wondering if I'd say them to him, they couldn't be said.

My free hand slid up his neck to his head, my fingers combed through his hair, and I rose up to kiss him. His weight settled on top of me, and we both forgot that lingering look and the things that could've been said.

"Don't leave," he said later, when we were both sedate. "I want to wake up to you."

Now that the sky was calm, and a kiss on the forehead and an arm around my belly had become the gentle rain after the storm, I obeyed him. With my back to him, I fell asleep, hoping I'd stay that way and have the image of his room as an easier reminder in the morning before my unsuspecting waking mind saw him. But when I woke up I was facing him, and he was already wide awake and looking at me.

"You talk in your sleep," he said.

"No I don't." Fearghus had never told me that—neither Fearghus.

"Yes, you do. Do you know a third language?"

I turned onto my back as a tingle ran the length of me. There were too many things in my mind I didn't want him to know, and I wasn't sure how much I could trust my sleeping self.

"It wasn't English, or any dialect of Irish I've ever heard. Do you speak Welsh?"

"I'm sure it was nothing."

He picked up a clump of my hair and put it against his lips. "I'm glad you keep your hair long."

"I've been thinking about cutting it short." I hadn't ever wanted to cut it, but for some reason I felt the need to tell him I was.

"That would be a shame."

"It's *my* hair."

He squinted and pulled back a bit. I rolled to the edge of the bed and sat up before realizing I wasn't wearing my slip and didn't know where it was.

"You need your dress?"

"It's a slip."

"Sorry." He reached to the floor on his side of the bed and handed it to me. "You know what could happen if we keep doing this. What you don't want to happen."

I took it and put it on under the covers. "I have it handled." I slid out of bed. And then I remembered the blond baby in my vision, the one I was holding by my windows while Fearghus jumped on my bed and Martin shaved his face in my bathroom. The groundswell that followed carried so many competing emotions I had to sit back down on the edge of the bed to keep from being swept away.

"What's the matter?"

I got up and went to my room. That vision was a lie, a cruel test. To show me a baby I didn't want only to make me want it. How could I not want a baby I've already seen? I couldn't bring another child into this house to be subject to all the things I'd witnessed and endured. I couldn't continue the Moore line. My family would disown me if they hadn't already. *I* would disown me.

Fearghus' slippers were missing, which meant he was already in front of his cereal in the kitchen. I went downstairs to brew my tea. Through the doorway to the small dining room, I could see Martin with his newspaper and an empty plate, waiting for me to join him. Would my blond hair and Martin's blond hair give us a blond baby? Fearghus was still at the kitchen table, humming and coloring a picture in his pajamas. I took a banana and went outside.

Heat swelled around me and pressed harder the farther I walked. It was unfamiliar ground without a companion at my side. Whether it was Fearghus, Martin, Rosemary, or Paul, someone was always filling the air with conversation. Without it, the birds were too chatty and the gusts of wind felt aimed at me. I'd never been to the edge of the estate, and I wondered how long it would take on foot. Surely I should wait for a cooler day. How many acres did they own? A hundred? A thousand? All I knew was a fifteen-foot fence surrounded the property. Both Martin and

Paul had told me that. They hadn't told me how long it would take me to reach that fence.

I walked to our garden, turned on the sprinklers, and watched the birds play in the water. After about ten minutes, I turned the faucet off and walked back to the lake. I stood with my back to the house and watched the wind ripple the water, wondering if I should jump in and cool off like Rosemary and Fearghus were so apt to do on days like this.

"I waited for you."

I'm sure he saw me tense, but what did he expect after sneaking up on someone? "I wasn't hungry."

He came forward and stood beside me. "You could've joined me for tea. Where'd you go?"

"Just for a walk. I didn't realize I still needed your permission for that."

He took hold of my arm. "You promised you wouldn't do this."

Promised? I remembered no recent promises. "Do what?"

"You're being argumentative."

I pulled my arm away. "No, I'm not. You're—"

"You came to me last night. I told you I didn't want to argue with you today."

"Then stop arguing with me."

He smiled wryly and shook his head at the lake, like he and the lake were sharing some understanding at my expense.

"Have I strayed too far from my cage? From your thumb? I'm sorry, next time I'll remember to ask your permission to take a walk."

His expression hardened. "That's enough."

"May I go back inside?"

The look that overcame him sent a pang of fear through me. I'd seen the same look on all of his brothers. My legs obeyed my command to stay in place rather than react to the flush of blood making me step back. I wouldn't cower to Martin even though I was the only thing nearby for him to shove or punch, which is how the Moore brothers responded to disagreement. If he was going to hit me, he'd have my complete cooperation, and I'd have him figured out just like I had his brothers figured out. This pit of hate would be justified for yet another reason.

"I'm not doing this." Each word was a separate and distinct stab, as if the power he would've used physically had been diverted into words. He walked back to the house. I gave him enough time to get inside and out of the kitchen before I went in. For the rest of the morning, I avoided any areas of the house he may have retreated.

To have an excuse to be away from him for lunch, I packed a picnic for Fearghus, Rosemary, and myself. We worked in the garden until it was time to eat. Then we spread out a blanket and passed out the food.

"I'm gettin' a job," she said. "Grocery store clerk. I'm gonna apply tomorrow. Paulie knows just where it is and says he'll drive me."

"What about Pierce? He should drive you."

She glanced at Fearghus, who was standing on the edge of the blanket with his back to us, munching his sandwich and surveying his garden. "I ain't sure if Pierce is gonna be too keen on me gettin' a job. I'd rather get it first, then tell him."

I felt my eyebrows go up. She of all people should know this wouldn't suit Pierce. But she was his wife. She knew him in a way I didn't.

"Shoot, I'd drive myself if I knew my way around this state. You and I need to get out more, learn the land. Cain't be leanin' on our husbands to drive us around. We should go for a drive sometime, just us girls."

I gathered our wrappers and folded them up together. I didn't know how to tell her I wasn't allowed out of the estate without Martin. She'd think I'd need liberating, and she'd have no idea just how much liberation I truly needed.

We worked in the garden then cooled off in the lake, and I was sure to check the patio for Martin before we headed back into the house. I wished Rosemary luck on the clerk job and put Fearghus in the tub. We took turns adding to the end of our ongoing bedtime story until he started to get too wound up, and I tucked him in and turned off all the lights but my reading light.

Every turned page of my book required me to look up and check Martin's balcony for that certain dim spread of light from his banker's lamp. The balcony remained shrouded in darkness. I bookmarked my page, unable to focus on the words any more. I settled on the sofa with a quilt, but that balcony retained its draw. If he hadn't come up by now, he was probably staying in his other room. It was unlikely he was already next door.

His room was dark and empty, his bed was still made. I pulled down the covers and got in between the cool sheets. I imagined shapes in the shadows on his ceiling as if I was gazing at clouds, and I dozed, but woke up every few minutes. Changing positions didn't help. At one o'clock, I got out of bed to look outside.

The moon was high and bright, just a hair short of full. The oak tree gave in to the breeze like a plant in an underwater current. A door opened and closed in the hall. I turned around. Martin came in and stopped, holding the wall. His shirt was unbuttoned all the way, and the outline of his hair was uneven, like he'd run a hand through it and not bothered to fix it.

"I have good reason to throw you out," he said, "but I'm not sober enough to give a shit." Still holding the wall, he stepped on the back of one shoe to remove it, then the other. "And not sober enough to think this is anything but a great idea."

I got in his bed. He took off his shirt and pants and got in with me. He grabbed me and rolled me on top of him.

"This is so dysfunctional," he said.

"Tell me one thing about our situation that isn't dysfunctional."

He put a finger to my lips then kissed me hard.

He was missing from the bed in the morning. He was missing from the house. Ruby said he left without eating breakfast, with an overnight bag and a foul mood.

CHAPTER 34

MARTIN WAS GONE for over a month. In that month I taught Fearghus how to make the bed, sweep the balcony, and use the word 'classified.' All his chores had to remain our secret, which made them more fun for him—an added benefit I didn't plan. He made a game out of it all until he broke his arm while downstairs in the training room. No one would tell me how it happened, not even Fearghus himself, and I wished Martin home so he could find out it was an accident and put my worries to rest. Both Caroline and Rosemary got pregnant, although Rosemary didn't know it yet. I couldn't find a reason to tell her and spoil the discovery for her, especially since I didn't know how I knew myself. She'd gotten her clerk job and worked part-time for two weeks before she quit. She didn't explain why, and I didn't need to ask.

I kept Martin's bed warm for him every night, analyzing the sounds in the sleeping household, wishing each unidentifiable creak was his step on the stairs. I couldn't ask anyone where he was and admit not knowing myself. After weeks of straining to catch his whereabouts in random conversation and hearing no mention of it, I decided no one knew where he was. To Fearghus, his father was working and very busy, and trying to swim and climb trees with his arm in a cast kept him occupied enough not to ask more. His arm was freed after three weeks. Despite Fearghus' delight, I was disappointed Martin would only hear about his son's mysterious accident and not see the visible consequence of it with his own eyes.

Family members from the north came to visit and filled all the guest rooms on the second floor's east wing, compounding my nightly analysis of noises in and around the house. Paul convinced me to join him, Patrick, and Sharon for dinner the first night they arrived, and I accepted in the hope I'd hear something about Martin's whereabouts. Sharon was already seated when I joined them, but when she excused herself suddenly and left the table, I recognized she too would be adding another heir to the Moore line.

Fearghus was thrilled to have a boy his age to play with until Jared joined him one day for training. That day, I found him in the kitchen having dinner by himself, stabbing holes in his mashed potatoes and scowling.

I made myself a plate and sat with him. "Did you have fun with your cousin?"

"He doesn't play fair. And they let him." He looked up at me. Scrapes and bruises were so common on my energetic child, but there was something sinister about the thick split down the center of his bottom lip.

"They let him what?"

"Be not fair."

"Did you hurt your lip in training?"

He went back to his mashed potatoes. "Yeah."

"What happened?" I wished he could wear his amulet during training, but Martin said it wasn't allowed. That it would be nothing but a crutch. That he'd learn nothing.

He dropped his fork on the table. "I'm done. Can I go outside?"

"You didn't answer my question, Fearghus."

He shrugged. "May I be excused?" He hopped off the chair without waiting for a reply.

I watched him tug the door to the patio open then slam it behind him. He stopped and stood just outside the door. His clenched fists relaxed but he remained still, and I wondered if his eyes were open, surveying the land, deciding where he should begin, or if they were closed. To savor the air. His moment of temporary freedom.

He took off in a sprint and I got up from the table and went to the door. It was too cold outside for a swim, but he was headed straight for the lake like the autumn chill hadn't swept in weeks ago and shoved out our sticky summer. That lake would be bone-jarring cold. When I realized he wasn't stopping, that he intended to do it, he was already at the shore, then airborne. I jerked open the door and ran down the hill.

I waited for his head to bob to the surface. I yelled his name. He swam straight to me and I pulled him out by his arms. "What's gotten into you? It's too cold for swimming!"

He hugged himself. His lips had lost all color, causing the green of his eyes to turn his face into that of a wild animal. "I know."

"You're going straight to bed. Come on." I dried his face with my skirt and turned, expecting him to follow. He stayed put. I snatched his arm. "*Deifir!*"

His wild animal eyes shifted to the house but became something more than just brilliant color on a pale face. It was the look of an animal backed against a wall, terrified yet vicious and prepared to fight. I dropped to my knees in front of him. He shuddered. I pulled his cold, wet body against me. He shivered in my arms.

"If you wanted to swim you can go to the pool house. Didn't you know the lake would be cold?"

"I wanted it to be cold."

"Why?"

"So the badness of the cold would take the other bad things away."

I bristled as if pricked by a poisonous thorn, its bane spreading like a fire in my blood. The fuse was lit and burning toward a reaction too large to extinguish. I held him tighter. My fear and anger would only magnify his. *I will not cry. I will teach Fearghus to be strong.*

"What other bad things?"

He squirmed, so I let him go. He wiped his nose with a shaking hand. "When's Dad coming back?"

"I'll call him and tell him to come home." I wasn't sure how, but I would do it. Even if I had to plead with the master himself.

It wasn't until Fearghus was dry and snuggled into bed with his cat under his arm that I understood the shift in my perception that day. My efforts to protect him would never be enough. There were monsters in his life I couldn't see, traps I'd never be privy to. His protection was a dual effort, and Martin's absence left a gaping breach.

That house was a prison to my son as much as it was to me, toxic in ways I'd never know. In the elements he found solace. It's the blood he was born with; it's the one thing they couldn't take from him. And he'd need it. I'd hoped his ignorance of why we lived in that house could ease his life there, but now I understood it only added a cloud of mystery to an undeniable hell.

The walk I'd repeated between Martin's bed and his balcony did not make the wait for night's cover any easier. Neither did the view of the stars which I'd hoped would calm my head. Fearghus had been hurt two times while Martin had been away. Had more wounds been inflicted? Ones I couldn't see?

When the flood of light on the lawn below me blinked out, I put on a housecoat and slippers and followed the wall in the dark hallway to the staff staircase into the kitchen. I let myself outside and walked to the corner of the patio where I'd have a view of Paul's carriage house. A dim light glowed inside. Crickets hurried with me across the lawn, like they were leading me instead of fleeing from me. My slippers were damp when I got to Paul's little porch, so I stepped out of them and knocked on the door. The breeze played with my hair. I turned around to check the house. Every window was dark.

I knocked again. If he was drunk and asleep, he'd never hear me. If he was high, he was probably crouched under a blanket thinking I was the boogeyman. I tried the door knob. It was locked. The third knock rewarded me with a clicking lock, then a cracked open door.

"Paul, let me in. I need to talk to you."

He opened the door but stayed in the doorway, blocking my entry. His jeans were buttoned but not zipped, and his shirt was only tucked into the front of them. "Good grief, Sloane, you had me thinking my old man was finally here to kill me."

I stepped up, against him, forcing him back. He only gave me a foot.

"What's so important at one in the morning?"

"Can I come in?"

He looked like he needed to explain something. I raised my eyebrows. I knew all his vices already. If he'd left his evidence in plain view, he'd just have to let me see it. He should've known it wouldn't surprise me.

He swallowed. "Rosemary's in here. Sleeping."

I felt my raised eyebrows freeze in place. "Shouldn't she be in her room?"

"We were just talking. She fell asleep. She's been so tired lately. I didn't want to move her. I think she needs to sleep."

"Of course she's tired. She's—" I bit my lip to make it stop. No one knew but me. "You better get her back in her room before Pierce wakes up and finds her missing from their bed."

Paul ran a hand through his hair. "Pierce left for Rochester this morning."

I elbowed past him to see for myself. She was on his sofa, a little ball of a woman covered with a blanket, blond hair spilling over the edge of the seat like a waterfall. The frayed hem of her jeans peeked from under the edge of the blanket, and her toes were inside, but it wasn't enough to absolve either of them.

"We were just talking," he said again.

"Talking."

"Playing cards and talking. She gets so tired sometimes. It keeps happening. She said she just wanted to close her eyes, but then she fell asleep."

I shook my head, unsure why I wasn't agreeing with him. Her pregnancy explained why she was getting tired, but everything else I needed to disagree about was getting all jumbled in my head.

"Don't be a spaz. I slept in your room on your couch all the time and that's all it was."

"All what was?"

"Do you want a drink or something? Here you are visiting me and I'm not even offering you a drink."

"Paul, you can't do this anymore. For Rosemary's sake. Nothing matters but what it looks like and if Pierce saw—"

"Pierce can go to hell. What did you want to talk about?" He closed his eyes and worked his jaw the way he did when his father's abuse was about to flip the switch on his personality.

"I wanted to know if you've heard from Martin."

He backed into the wall and crossed his arms. "Haven't talked to him since he left last month. Why?"

I shouldn't have come out here. The only information I'd gained was a clue I didn't want to hold. Not because the picture I'd seen was painted with guilt, but because it planted doubt. It opened a trap door into a new level of fear for two people I cared for dearly.

I needed Martin home now more than ever. "I need him to come home."

"So call him and tell him to come home. You should know you're the only one with the power to order that cat around."

Paul had just allowed me into his quarters to witness the most criminalizing of situations. I had no secrets from him. I took a breath and released the truth. "I don't know where he is."

"You don't? Well I don't think he's doing anything for the old man. He's probably in Cambridge."

"Do you have the telephone number?"

He squinted at me, like he was trying to decide if I was playing with him.

"Do you have it?"

He picked up a pen and wrote the number on the palm of my hand. "Be sure to tell him he's an asshole to his wife. Seems we have a lot of that around here."

"I can walk Rosemary back. Let's wake her up."

"No."

I studied him. He was capable of a lot of things. Was he capable of doing what I didn't want to believe?

"We were *talking*."

"If anyone else in the house sees you and Rosemary *talking* like this …"

He waved my words away. "We do this all the time. No one's seen us yet."

As Martin had said many times, it wasn't my job to save Paul from every one of his mistakes. It was an endless shift without breaks, and he wasn't my responsibility. But this time, he was going to take Rosemary down with him. She didn't deserve the punishment Pierce would so willingly dish out.

"Do you know how many of your relatives are sleeping in that house right now? Any one of them could mistake your door for the pool house door in the morning, and then what?"

"Then I politely direct them to the pool house."

I walked over to Rosemary and pulled the blanket off her.

"Fine," he said. "I'll carry her inside. Don't wake her up."

She blinked and mumbled when he picked her up. He was cursing under her weight by the time we made it to the kitchen. I was thankful her room was on the ground floor, and I was sure he was too. We both must've been too relieved to have her and Pierce's bedroom door in view to wonder why the light was on. I entered the room first; I was too far in to back out unseen. Paul said Pierce was in Rochester, but there he was, one palm against the window pane, head forward and low, shoulders tense. Like someone was out there, someone he needed to kill.

Paul ran into my back and cursed again. Pierce turned around. I bridled my reaction. Held my breath so the blood wouldn't drain from my face, relaxed my shoulders to appear casual instead of caught. In my mind I saw Martin carefully unfolding his napkin at dinner while the master dug into Paul instead of his food, Martin's hand covering mine under the tablecloth when Paul finally broke. Martin grabbing Paul's arm to steady him in the hall afterward, the tight grasp puckering Paul's shirt even though it was a calm being transferred. A calm I could mimic if I tried. A calm I missed.

"Would you mind lowering the light?" I said. "Your wife is very tired." Still leaning against the window, he couldn't seem to take his attention off Paul so I turned on a small table lamp and flipped the main overhead light off. I pulled the covers down on the bed, which prodded Paul to carry her over.

"So much for a four-day trip," Paul said. It was not the time for his mouth. Inappropriate timing only seemed to enhance his sarcasm.

Pierce had removed his palm from the window but remained in front of it in a strange, hunched half-turn. "Thought you might like a surprise."

"Love 'em," Paul said.

With the lighting in the room dimmed, I could now see outside. Pierce's view looked straight onto Paul's carriage house and its one light in the window that had told me he was still awake. There was no trip to Rochester. He'd made it up.

"But this surprise is a real drag, brother. You ruined my night."

Pierce shifted his jaw to one side, then the other. "How's that?"

Paul shrugged and walked to the door. "You figure it out. You're a smart guy."

I looked at Rosemary sleeping soundly on the bed. She'd wake up in the morning, unaware of this exchange. Pierce would ask her where she was all night, and she'd tell him the truth. And now that I saw what Pierce had set up, what his paranoid, conniving mind had prepared, all question diminished and my trust of Paul and Rosemary shone bright. Tonight was innocent and because of that, Rosemary would have nothing to hide. Pierce would put it together in his twisted mind, and two innocent people would suffer.

There was a reply from Pierce, but I didn't hear it. I was already at Rosemary's side. I combed her hair with my fingers and began to braid, a distraction from my real task: a gentle idea guided toward her like the slightest breeze, on particles of air she'd breathe in for her mind to absorb like it had been there all along. She was with me all night, in Martin's room, talking girl talk until she fell asleep on Martin's sofa. The second idea I didn't send to her. She wouldn't have known I asked Paul to carry her if she was too exhausted to rouse.

"Sloane," Paul said.

I went to him and we left the room together.

"I'll find you tomorrow," Pierce said just before Paul closed the door. I wasn't sure if he was talking to me or Paul.

I went straight to the library and called the telephone number on my palm. It rang and rang. Even after I hung up, it rang in my head all through the night.

CHAPTER 35

ROSEMARY DIDN'T SHOW for breakfast or lunch. I helped Eleanor change the sheets on Martin's bed, and when I returned to my room and found Fearghus mixing soaps, lotions, perfumes, and anything else he could find in my bathroom, I made him help me clean it all up then took him outside.

There was a small gathering of men on the patio when we rounded the house. I knew their faces from past visits. The steady stream of visiting family had rolled by me for years, their names the fallen tree limbs in the water sailing by. Occasionally one would stick in my memory until something pushed it along, forgotten. They made no notice of

Fearghus and me as we walked by, and I wondered if any of them knew how to get in touch with Martin.

I'd called his Cambridge number first thing when I woke up and enough times after that to lose count. It rang unanswered every time. I'd copied it to a slip of paper since it had almost washed off my palm, but the paper stayed by the phone in Martin's room. I knew the number by heart.

"Got a nest right about here," Fearghus said. He was on a quest for ants again.

I sat against a tree and watched him scouring the dirt for an ant. He'd only need one. I wished I'd brought a book. I didn't want to sit there and think about Martin.

"Found one!" He drew a line in the dirt with his finger in front of the ant, marking a trail they for some reason wanted to follow. He found another ant and made another trail. Soon he'd have the whole colony marching in a design he'd carved in the dirt, and I'd have to come up with a really good reason to get him back in the house for dinner.

A breeze tinged with the slightest winter chill blew over us, mixing with the rays of the sun that wouldn't surrender. Martin had to be in Cambridge. He'd only taken one bag. Where else could he go that would have enough clothing and work to supply him for over a month? Fearghus' hair ruffled in the wind, showing me a shadow on his scalp. I got up, stepped over his lines of ants, and brushed his hair back. He swatted me away.

"Where'd you get that nasty bruise?"

He paused, hands on knees in a squat.

"Fearghus?"

He watched the moving design of crawling black bodies on the ground in front of him. I couldn't tell if he was too engaged with his ants to hear me, or if he was avoiding the question.

I touched his hair where the bruise was. "This one."

He exhaled. "Hit my head in the dark."

"Did you get out of bed last night?"

"No. Training." He broke into one of his lines with his finger and drew it toward a neighboring one, joining one procession into another.

"Training in the dark?"

He shuffled away from me and started a new line away from the others.

"With the lights off?"

"Yeah."

"Why?"

"So my eyes aren't a weakness." He looked up at me, like he was explaining something I should already understand. "To make my other senses strong."

I stared at him so long he cocked his head and smiled, expecting a game I was playing with him. There was no game, not with him. The game involved his adoptive family, what they were doing to him in the basement of that awful house, and how much I could do to protect him from it. And his senses they intended to make strong—were they wise to *all* of his senses? Enough to exploit them? His senses were still developing. Even I wasn't aware of all he could do.

He looked past me. A boy headed our way. Jared, the boy who didn't play fair.

"Whatcha doin'?" Jared stopped at the edge of Fearghus' lines of ants, hands on hips.

Fearghus gave him a long, hard stare then returned his attention to his work. My son knew better than to rudely ignore others, but before I could reprimand him, Jared jumped into the middle of Fearghus' gaze, stomping viciously on the lines of ants.

"Jared!" I snatched him by the arm and pulled him away. "That's not nice." He smirked up at me, clearly unapologetic. I got the sense nothing I'd say would correct him, that he was too wild and out of my control. I was the adult and he was the child, but I could see he held no respect for that relationship.

His head snapped forward and he fell into me. I caught him against my legs. When I looked up Fearghus was there shaking his right arm like men do after they've just hit another man. "Did you hit him?"

"Yeah."

"What's wrong with you!"

"Didn't you see? He just—"

"I don't care what he did. You don't hit other boys!"

Jared yanked out of my grasp and lunged for Fearghus. Fearghus swiveled, avoiding him and kicking him in the back of the knees at the same time. Jared hit the ground and Fearghus jumped on top of him.

I darted toward the house, losing my shoes in the grass. Paul was the only one left on the patio, smoking a cigarette with his feet up. "Help, Paul! Hurry!"

We both ran down the hill. Jared had gotten on top of Fearghus and had him pinned, but Fearghus continued to twist and kick, diverting all of Jared's effort into holding him down. Paul caught Jared's shoulders and pulled him upright. Fearghus rolled and hopped to his feet in a single motion, studying Jared as if waiting for an opportunity to attack.

Paul twirled Jared away from us and gave him a shove. "Go in the house and calm down."

Jared looked over his shoulder at Fearghus and spit in the grass. Blood trickled out of one nostril, and his forehead and one cheek were mottled with red. He started up the hill.

Paul laughed. "Trey, if you're going to fight someone, don't do it around your mother."

"Paul!" It wasn't the time for jokes.

"And he's bigger than you. Never let someone bigger than you get on top of you. Didn't your pops teach you that?"

Fearghus absentmindedly wiped his hand across his bloody mouth. His eyes were glued to Jared's retreating back. "Yeah."

"Now you know why. It's a death sentence. He'll hold you 'til you wear yourself out trying to get out from under him, and when he starts pounding away you'll be too pooped to defend yourself. *Next* time—"

I grabbed Paul's shirt, too furious to come up with any words.

"What? That little shit has it coming. You should've heard what he called Ruby this morning."

"Thank you for helping." I released my fistful of his shirt, the rough motion of it suggesting how badly *I* wanted to hit *him*. He took the cue to leave. Fearghus had returned to his parade of ants. In a squat with his face close to the ground, he shuffled down the line and randomly jabbed his finger in the dirt. I started to go for him, but then I realized he was putting all the injured out of their misery. The practicality of it tore my heart in two. I wished he didn't care about these things that could only become a burden in our lives here. Affection for something other than himself would afflict him with a weakness these people could use against him. No mother wants a selfish child, but for his own protection, it was the best thing for him. And it was a protection I could not nurture in him.

"Wait until I tell your father about this."

"He doesn't care. He's not even here." Lacking any visible sadness, those words stabbed harder than anything, especially since his father's absence was my fault.

I took him inside and made him sit on a stool in the kitchen and watch the clock. I went to the library and called Martin's Cambridge number again. After five rings, the line clicked.

"Hello?" A woman's voice. An accent I couldn't place.

I stared at the faded number on my palm. I must have dialed it wrong.

"Hello, is someone there?"

"Yes … I'm looking for …" I couldn't have dialed it wrong. I'd dialed that number twenty times.

"Hello?"

I hung up. My hand remained on the handset, shaking it in the cradle. I picked it up again. My finger trembled into each number hole. Two rings, then a click.

"Hello?" The same woman's voice.

"I'm sorry. I'm looking for …" I couldn't let her know I couldn't find him. I couldn't let her know I needed him. "Roger."

"There's no Roger here."

"I'm sorry." I hung up. A rabid animal tore into me, snapping bones, tearing flesh, and I sat still and let it have its way with me. Of course he had a mistress. To not already know this was my own fault, my own naiveté. An ingredient of our arrangement I shouldn't have overlooked. Now so painfully clear, it stunned me more to see how carefully he'd hid it, how he'd even thought it necessary to hide.

I walked to the mirror by the door. Checked my face, my hair, then returned to Fearghus in the kitchen. Rosemary was beside him, wiping his fingernails with a rag. She stopped when she saw me. "Sloane, you okay?"

I nodded. I put on my apron and took Grace's knife out of her hand. She relinquished her potato cutting task easily, sharing a look with Rosemary before moving off to do something else. After two potatoes, Rosemary was at my side with her own knife. Fearghus was coloring a book at the table.

"You got a look on you like you fittin' to explode."

I shook my head. She waited.

"Fearghus is on my bad side right now." She wouldn't buy it. Fearghus was too often on my bad side to make this day anything special.

We worked until we ran out of potatoes. Then she wiped her hands on my apron. "If you ain't gonna talk, I gotta ask you somethin'. Pierce woke me early this mornin' talkin' in that funny language of yours, and it was like I was talkin' back until I blinked my eyes a few times like wakin' from a dream. But I was already awake. Ain't that strange?"

A new sensation spread over the remnants from that Cambridge phone call, like snowfall on a forest fire. "What was he saying?"

"Like I know what y'all are ever sayin'. Why's he talkin' that to me like I'm gonna respond? And funny thing was,

I think I was respondin' but I don't remember what I was sayin'."

"Can you repeat any of what he was saying?"

She tilted her head and looked at the ceiling. "Not what he was sayin' this mornin', but there is somethin' he says a lot." She closed her eyes and sounded out the words, her tongue wrapping awkwardly around a language so foreign to her yet familiar to me, even in this raw form.

The forest fire inside me extinguished and froze, ice settling hard in my heart. "Rosemary, if you ever hear him say that again, leave your room and find me. Or Paul, or anyone. Do you understand?"

"What's it mean?"

"I can't translate it." I wouldn't translate it. I had to tell Martin, but he was out of my reach … with some other woman. If I told him, Pierce would find out fast, and it would only be harder on Rosemary. Martin couldn't be in her room all day and all night to keep Pierce under control. Rosemary was on her own.

Pierce had been dragging the truth from her that morning. He'd masked both his words and hers. She'd been answering in English, but he'd made her hear the Irish, or gibberish, even. It was a simple trick. I had to know if she'd given up the real truth or the truth I'd replaced it with. "So you don't remember this morning at all? What about last night?"

"Last night …" Her eyes lost focus. She took a piece of her hair and twirled it around her finger. "Feels like it's been a coon's age since then. Did I fall asleep in your room?"

"Yes, I had to get Paul to carry you to your bed."

"Shoot, you'd think my life was exhaustin' the way I sleep lately."

I should've mentioned pregnancy could do that. She'd left me with a perfect opportunity to bring it up, but I couldn't do it. It wouldn't be fair to her while I was so distracted by Martin, who had no real children of his own. He only had Fearghus, the adopted child of an enemy family whose mother he married even though she refused to bear any more children. If he wanted his own, taking a mistress was the way he could. He wasn't aware of this blond baby I'd seen in my future. Would I agree to have children with him before his mistress did?

My arm pulsed. I looked down at Rosemary's hand gripping me. "Sloane, your color ain't good at all. You oughtta get upstairs in bed."

She and Grace forced me upstairs to my room and helped me into my housecoat. Their compassion coaxed the anguish from where I'd stashed it, bringing on a fuzzy headache. They thought I was the one who was sick until Rosemary rushed into my bathroom and vomited into the toilet. All my worries fell to the ground as Grace and I grinned at each other over Rosemary's head.

I was right. Fearghus would have another cousin.

CHAPTER 36

CHORES KEPT THE questions silent in my mind the next morning. Thorough scrubbing of our bathroom, dusting and sweeping of our room, and changing of the sheets and bedspread held Fearghus' attention. When we moved to the sitting room his patience lapsed, so we went downstairs for a snack … to a kitchen that held Martin.

Fearghus' holler and wild jump onto Martin's legs covered my momentary inability to walk, my flush of heat from head to toe, my maniac heart. When Martin looked up from Fearghus and met my eye, I'd just regained my composure to ask Fearghus what he wanted for his snack. His answer was a question to Martin. "Dad, will you eat with us?"

"Sure. What are we having?" Martin's gaze was still on me even though I'd locked my focus on Fearghus and refused to move it.

"How about an apple and some cheese?" I asked Fearghus.

"I broke my arm and then had a cast and then it healed and the doctor cut it off."

"How'd you break your arm?"

"And the cast was white and hard and my fingers were stuck like this." Fearghus tensed his arm in the position held by the cast.

I went to the icebox for an apple and the cheese. After making them each a plate I went upstairs, trying to ignore the hot line on my skin drawn by Martin's index finger as my arm reached across to place that plate in front of him. I was as bursting with things to say and ask him as Fearghus was, but it was all confined behind one bitter accusation waiting to fire. He could at least be honest about his affair.

My cleaning moved to Martin's room now accented with a small pile of luggage just inside his door. If I'd gone in there before going downstairs, I could've had a warning. I swept his floor then started on his bathroom. Leaning into the bathtub with my sponge, I heard footsteps enter his room and gain on me. I couldn't decide whether to stand and face him before he yanked me up by the arm.

"What are you doing?" He leaned into my face, the small line between his eyebrows the only indicator of anger. "You don't clean my room. You don't clean anyone's room."

His thumb pressed into the muscle of my arm. I didn't want to flinch, but I couldn't help it.

He looked at his hand and released my arm. "Sorry. God, sorry."

Water from my sponge dripped on the floor. If he was a decent man, he'd tell me now. He wouldn't carry on with his life, deceiving me. Sleeping in our bed after sharing hers. He turned away, toward our reflection in the mirror. He ran a hand down his face. "If you act like anything but a lady in this house, you're just making it easier for them to—"

"Were you in Cambridge?" He was worried about my reputation in this house. Perhaps he should consider what would happen if I had to turn a blind eye to his mistress.

He faced me. "Yes."

"By yourself?"

"Mostly." A direct stare. No change in expression, no averted gaze, no shifting of his weight. A statue. The most expert liar. "How'd Trey break his arm?"

I tossed my sponge into the tub. "You'll have to find that out yourself. I don't know what goes on down there."

"It happened in the training room?"

"Yes, along with a black eye, a split lip, and too many bruises to name. He's four years old. You all belong on a burning pyre."

He spun and headed to the doorway, but as he passed through he grabbed both sides of the door frame, stopping himself. "If I find him now, I'll kill him." His chin dropped against his chest. He let out a breath then turned to face me. "What else?"

I narrowed my eyes at him. I should be the one asking questions. He should be giving the answers. Instead of explaining this to him, I did what I knew would make him most mad: I retrieved my sponge and continued my scrubbing of the bathtub. "Go find Fearghus. He needs you."

The demand hung in the air. I'd never spoken such inflated words to him, and I didn't know how he'd respond. When I allowed myself a glance behind me, he was gone.

Fearghus and I ate lunch on the patio. He noticed Martin through the windows and called to him. Martin came out looking at me, but when I looked away he turned his attention to Fearghus.

"I need to talk to your uncles inside and then we can hang out. That sound okay?" He gave Fearghus the thumbs up. Fearghus returned it. The door opened and the three other Moore brothers came pouring out.

Pierce handed him a beer. "Let's talk out here. She can leave." He smiled into Martin's unamused face.

"She can stay out here until I change out of this suit." Martin went inside and closed the door.

"Trey, go long." Lewis held up a football, aimed for a throw.

Fearghus' mouth dropped open a little before he scrambled off his chair and ran several yards out on the lawn. The ball shot toward him and he reached, but the force of the throw was too much for his little arms. It hit him square in the belly and appeared to take him backwards with it until he was flat on his back.

Lewis cocked his head at me. "Whoops."

I wanted to hit him, dig my nails into him, shove his foul mass to the ground with a force equivalent to that football hitting my little boy. I stepped out of my heels instead and ran to Fearghus. He was choking. Blue in the face. I sat him up and patted his back. He coughed, his eyes watering until tears ran down his cheeks.

"You just got the wind knocked out of you. You're okay."

"*A Mhát—*"

"Hush." I smoothed his hair back and kissed his forehead. I wanted to carry him straight to Martin, but I shook away my own thought. Martin couldn't be burdened with these small abuses. They'd only become an inconvenience over time, and we needed to count on him for the big ones. Some we had to take and put behind us. Knowing I couldn't trust my mouth to obey me, I carried Fearghus around the house to the side entrance, straight to my room, and locked the door.

Two eyes, wetted and dimmed by betrayal, stared up at me from the bed. "He threw it too hard."

"He did. He made a mistake. He was very wrong."

"He did it on purpose. Not a mistake."

"He may have done it on purpose, but it was still a mistake. Do you want to read a book?"

He sat up. "I want to punch him."

I lowered him back to the pillow. "Do you think that would fix things? I don't think it would."

"Dad should punch him."

"Your dad wouldn't punch his own brother." Not in front of us.

He scrunched up his face. "Uncle Lew is not Dad's brother."

"He is." I trailed my fingers across his eyebrows, his eyelids, his nose, his cheeks, encouraging his face to relax.

"Uncle Lew is from a different family."

My hand paused in its stroking of his hair. "Your Uncle Lewis is part of this family."

"Then me and you and dad are from a different family."

I pressed my lips together to keep from crying and screaming at the same time. He'd already figured it out. And just as he'd found this truth, it was my job to undo it, to tell him he was wrong, to make him a respected and trusted member of this family. He would not be safe until that happened. How could I make him a part of this family without allowing his heart to blacken and die like all of theirs?

I watched the sparrows play on the balcony railing while Fearghus napped. I needed a plan to fit Fearghus into this family in a way he could keep his good heart, but my thoughts kept returning to that woman's voice answering Martin's Cambridge phone number. My son's well-being was far more important than my bogus marriage.

Someone knocked on my door. I could pretend not to hear it, but I needed to confront Martin to end this distraction. I opened the door. It was him.

"Hold on to this for next time." He handed me a slip of paper.

I took it before I noticed what it was: his Cambridge phone number written in my handwriting. I'd left it by his phone.

He glanced at Fearghus sleeping on the bed. "Come to my room. I need to talk to you."

I stuck the paper in my pocket and followed him. If he was going to tell me the truth, I was going to take it with one emotion—gratitude for his honesty. It's all I would feel. It's all I would show.

Once in his room with the door closed behind us, he spun around to face me and crossed his arms. It was a stance to confront someone, not admit fault. "He went to training without me. How often." It was a demand, not a question. And when I didn't answer quickly enough, he repeated it. "How often."

"As often as he would have—"

"If I was here? I was gone for over a month. He knew better than to go down there without me."

"Unless another adult in the house tells him otherwise. He's a child, Martin. He does what adults tell him to do."

"You should've prevented it."

"And how was I to have known this? You left without a word. You never called."

"Since it obviously wasn't clear, he's not to go down there without me, until I say otherwise."

I felt a heat rise in me. I wanted to ask who he thought he was telling me what I should be doing with my child. My bargain to allow Martin to take my child as his son gagged my mouth. Our marriage is what sealed that bargain. He was free to break that marriage, but he still expected me to keep my side of the deal.

"My brothers are down there. Anyone down there with them is fair game. With no witnesses. Got it?"

"His teachers are down there."

"Not all the time."

"You should've called." I covered my mouth with both hands. Fearghus had gone down there so many times, for hours on end. I thought it was safe. How could I have thought it was safe? My growing comfort in that house had made me complacent, left me without a proper guard.

"Pack a bag. I'm taking you and Trey to Chicago."

The shift in subject matter without the loss of his confrontational tone gave me pause, and I worried I'd heard him wrong. "You said Trey couldn't go—"

"I changed my mind. We leave tonight." He put a cigarette in his mouth, went out to his balcony, and shut the door with me left inside. If the snake thought I was going to be ordered around like that … well, he'd have to take a trip to Chicago by himself. It would devastate Fearghus if Martin left again.

It would devastate me.

The mix of my emotions was a churning, effervescent potion building pressure with each tick of the clock. I wasn't sure what kind of love I had for Martin, but I couldn't deny its presence. It was like the steady beat of a faraway drum. Always there, in the background, waiting for me to pay attention. I didn't seek it out but there it was, drumming, drumming, drumming. And the stronger the love had grown, the more profound my hate for him had become.

Perhaps if I'd realized this sooner, I'd have thought up a remedy, a small act of willpower to calmly stave off this building clash of love and hate. It was too late now. The pressure was too high, and what would come would do so spontaneously.

When he stubbed out his cigarette and came back inside, I was sitting at his desk. He did a double take, his face grave on the first glance but quite changed on the second. The expression that held was as subtle as all his expressions, but I'd learned the marked differences, the almost non-existent clues. This time, it was all in the negligible tilt of his head, the slight lowering of shoulders. And the eyes, which told me he didn't expect to find me still in his room. He couldn't conceal the look of pleased relief fast enough, so he left it there on his face for me to take in. For it to warm me.

"I'm not so easily dismissed." Words to undo that warmth so I could make my accusation with a clear head.

He said nothing, standing as if braced for a blow.

"I'm also not so easily fooled. If you have a mistress, I'd hoped you'd tell me without me having to ask."

"I don't have a mistress."

He said it so straight, so unflinching, most people would let it go at that. His mastery of lying was a complication I hadn't figured into this exchange. Since I had no recourse, and no real say in what he did in his life, I expected an unashamed confession. My suspicions validated. Easy.

What I was left holding was something more fragile than a marriage with infidelity, something I didn't want to touch, not with Martin holding the other end.

Trust.

"You have a woman there, in your Cambridge apartment."

"I do not. I don't know who told you that—who told you that?" He came quickly toward me. "Paul?"

If I didn't tell him how I knew, he'd surely go after Paul. Whether the threat to Paul was a tactic to draw the information out of me or if he truly thought Paul was guilty of telling, it had worked. I couldn't allow him to blame Paul. "She answered the phone."

He turned away, scratching his head and looking genuinely confused—not an emotion he'd willingly show if he'd been in control of it. "Emilia? She never answers the phone."

Such an easy release of the woman's name meant my suspicions could be very wrong. "I might've called a few times."

"Emilia's the maid. Did you ask for me? She should've given me the message."

"I—no. I didn't."

He sat on the bed, his face in his hands. "Shit, Sloane, you're killing me. If you thought ..." He dropped his hands to his knees, leaning heavily, like all the strength had been sucked out of him and he needed to prop himself up. When he looked up at me I saw a humbling truth. As much as the idea of him having a mistress had hurt me, the accusation of it hurt him more.

"You left for a month, without a word. You didn't call. What'd you expect me to think?"

"That we needed a break from each other."

"We did? I don't remember having that discussion."

I wanted to button my lip, to slap myself. To stop this madness. Another woman was inside me, determined to argue with a man who'd just arrived home after a long absence. A man I missed terribly, a man I wanted to sit with and talk to and feel against me.

He opened his palms to me, like he had nothing left to say. He'd helplessly resigned. I could then see exactly what he was thinking: A month had passed but the time had no effect on us. We'd picked up exactly where we'd left off. Petty arguments and misunderstandings and me lashing out at him for reasons I didn't understand, picking fights just to see him squirm. Something had to change. I couldn't be this person. I couldn't live like this.

I left him there like that and walked down the main staircase and outside, shedding shoes and stockings as I crossed the lawn. I passed my oak, dropping my hairpins next, my hair freeing itself in the breeze. I let my cardigan fall as I headed due west, toward my oak's sister tree deep in the woods. *I am a Bevan on the inside.* Fall leaves crunched under my feet and showered from the canopy with each hit of wind that was stirring up hard in my wake. I bent to scoop a handful of damp earth without breaking stride. I smeared one cheek. Another scoopful, and I smeared the other. I stopped to paint both arms, my neck and upper chest.

When I reached the sister oak I fell to my knees, dug fingers into soil, and bent to the ground. Forehead against earth, I imagined roots unfurling underground, reaching for my fingertips. The connection that formed was immediate and true, and my own roots unfurled in response, sprung from captivity, awakened from a forced hibernation. Forbidden magic felt reckless and glorious and unstoppable. The branches above crackled with the unexpected pull of my power. I withdrew my fingers from the soil, fearing the fire inside me would escape and engulf the forest in flame.

Settling back on my heels, my hands in my lap, I bowed my head. I listened to the wind die down, the leaves find rest, when all I could feel was my own unrest, the dizzying swirl of love and hate. The love had been winning and in response, the hate was mutating into something I could no longer control. It was changing me, splitting my mind in two, reconstructing half of me into someone unrecognizable. This unyielding hate had every right to be there. It was in my blood. It was nurtured by my memories of my husband's lifeless body, my tormented son, my lost little girl.

These reasons justified the hate and made the love feel so devastatingly wrong. My purpose there was to protect my son, to raise him true to his blood. Nothing more. I could not accept love from my most hated.

I scooted on my knees toward the oak's trunk to be closer when I dug my fingers into the ground a second time. I needed to feel its magic ring in my bones, to dedicate its force to memory so I'd have a token to carry back to the house. In the new spot my fingertips jammed against leaden earth. I looked up into the branches of the mighty oak. To grow from this soil, a seedling must've been strong.

Strong. Like love grown from the toxic soil of hate.

And my love for Martin had not just grown. It had flourished.

The man had done unspeakable wrong. I'd never forgive those wrongs or the one responsible for them. That man … did he still exist? Martin wasn't the same man who'd hunted and tortured Fearghus. He wasn't the same man who'd ordered him and my cousins killed. His metamorphosis wasn't complete, but it had begun. He'd already changed in drastic ways.

Acceptance of his love would reward me with an ally, one I couldn't win this war without, one who could protect my son in ways I never could. If I could assign my hate to a different man, the man Martin used to be, perhaps the love could be new. Unassociated and uncomplicated. I could dispel the battle inside me. I could focus on my real enemy. I could teach my son the skills he'd need to survive. To fight. I was a warrior, and so was my son.

I sat back on my ankles and passed a hand down each arm, smearing the soil into my skin along with the design of my family's warriors. A curling, overlapping, unending pattern of lines representing limitless will, dedication to the elements, and good luck. A gust of wind drove through the trees. Leaves rained down. I let them fall in my lap, on my hair. It was a kaleidoscope of motion all around until the wind eased and each leaf swirled to its resting spot. That's when I saw Martin.

He was standing several yards away, slack, yet alert, as if drawn out to the middle of the forest by some mystery force and was just now laying eyes on the culprit. The peace I'd found was plain enough on my face for him to stoop for earth and smear his face as I'd done, shed his shoes, his socks, his shirt and undershirt. He closed the distance between us, going to his knees when he reached me. He only broke eye contact to study my arms, the design he surely knew from his history with my family.

With his remaining handful of earth he smeared one arm—only one. Then he took my hand and placed it on his shoulder. His breathing was fast but slowing with a surrender I could not only see but feel, carried by the ground between us. His eyes relayed the spontaneity of his decision—and the fear that I could so easily decline what he offered. That I could reject him.

Marking Moore skin with the insignia of a Bevan warrior was an unthinkable abomination.

I formed my hand around his arm. I looked at it there, my skin against his, feeling his warmth, his solid muscle. My son was napping inside the house he knew as his home, his comfort so reliant on the man in front of me. My daughter and my family, safe, as long as I stayed here. Martin, the *new* Martin, removing the locks on my balcony doors.

Hiding my herbs in my floor. Pulling me against him in bed. I looked into his eyes, so intent on the decision I was about to make. And I marked him.

The action opened a channel between us. His magic was there pooling in my hand and traveling up my arm, mingling with mine in a push and pull that stole my breath as I jerked my hand away. He'd closed his eyes, reaching blindly for my hands, and placed them against his chest. His magic was there again, pure and liquid and rushing up my arms. I didn't know what he was doing or how. Combining magic was difficult and dangerous without insulating matter, or an honest supplication to a sacred force. The pull was at once familiar, yet so terrifyingly foreign it had me jerking away again just to catch my breath. Since he didn't open his eyes, I took the opportunity to claw the soil around me, gathering enough to smear his chest. Without it, the friction of our magic could kill us both.

His eyes had opened halfway by the time I was done, and I knew he was waiting to see what I'd do. It was more a dare than a plea. He knew what my response would be. He knew me too well.

I laid both palms against his chest, this time making sure to breathe. I drank him in, letting the magic fill me, charge me to double the power. I could see his purpose. He wanted me to feel what it truly felt like to join him, to accept him as my ally. To know how powerful we were together.

Instead of jerking away this time, I let my hands slide down his body and fall off gently. The severing of the connection left me dizzy, and I fell forward, catching myself with a hand on the ground. When I raised up to look at him, he was shaking his head hard as if to clear it.

"Walk with me," he said. "I need to show you something."

I started to tell him Fearghus would wake soon, but he put a finger to my lips.

"He was awake when I left the house. Rosemary was having a snack with him. He'll be fine."

We headed deeper into the woods. The chill in the air didn't touch me due to Martin's warm hand around mine and the heat he was transferring—an effect that should rob the practitioner of his own heat according to what I knew. But Martin had tricks of his own.

We walked so long, stepping over fallen trees and ducking under limbs. The gray sky turned grayer. I feared we wouldn't have enough light left to make it home safely, but our serene, silent companionship was too sacred to break with a question. I trusted Martin to get us back. In the light of day, and in the dark.

"Here we are," he said finally, and I looked ahead toward a pattern through the trees that could only be man-made. We approached a wrought iron fence, the same one that spanned the front of the property. Fifteen feet tall with spikes on the top, it was impenetrable to most. Not to a Bevan, though. Or a Moore.

"See that road?" He pointed beyond the fence to where the road led on our right. "Walk that direction and you'll reach a little town in about three hours."

I couldn't imagine why he'd be telling me this. There was no way I'd go anywhere without Fearghus.

He dropped my hand. The cold rushed against me.

"This section," he said, taking hold of an iron spindle, "is the only one that won't alert me, or my mother, father, or brothers, if it's been breached."

Without his hand I was so cold my teeth would've been chattering if any part of me could move. Standing there with one arm drawn with the mark of a Bevan warrior, Martin Moore was showing me the only escape, my secret door out of there.

"Why are you—"

"Because I want you to know."

"So my decision to stay here is—"

"Your decision."

My teeth were chattering now, activated by not just the cold. That other side of me reared up one last time, surging with the need to run. She hadn't yet learned she had to stay. It was her duty to stay. It was my decision to stay.

"And for one more reason. If anything happens to me … if they find out what I'm doing, what I've done…"

It was as if he knew those were the perfect words to subdue that almost nonexistent side of me. It was easy to forget the sacrifice he was making to help me, how much danger he was putting himself in to be my ally, to protect Fearghus. To love me.

"And here's how you'll find this spot again." He came back to me and pressed two fingertips against my forehead. A spark lit inside my mind, then it was gone, to hide away until I called upon it.

He took my hand and led me home.

Darkness had fallen hard by the time we reached Martin's discarded shirt. With no moon and no stars, I'd have been lost out there without him. I stopped him just outside the library door. "You can't go in there with your arm—"

"I'm about to." He tugged me forward.

As if made bolder by our newfound allegiance, he entered the Moore family estate as one half Moore, one half Bevan warrior. My heartbeat didn't slow to a normal rate until we reached his room undetected. We undressed and cleaned the mud off each other's skin. And there under the shower in a cloud of steam, I asked him if he'd move into my bedroom with me so Fearghus could have his own room. He drew me against him and kissed me so deeply I again sensed the channel that had opened between us in the woods, and that dangerous yearning for a raw, foreign power I had no idea how to control.

CHAPTER 37

Our visit to Chicago marked the first in which Tara wanted nothing to do with me. She only wanted her brother, who'd never be able to visit her again. She cried when she realized he wasn't with me, then she planted herself at the front window to peer out as if she couldn't believe he wasn't coming. I couldn't tell her he was in the car that dropped me off, and I hoped she didn't notice his face through the car's window when Martin returned to pick me up. No one could have stopped her from tearing through the door and running down Mam's tiny city yard to see him.

I cried our entire drive back to Virginia.

My room was promptly rearranged to accommodate Martin's things, and Martin's room was remodeled with a set of children's furniture for Fearghus, who was thrilled to have his own little kingdom. The space allotted for one little boy was excessive and embarrassing, but it was a battle I chose not to fight. No room in that house was suitable for a child to grow up unspoiled. I pledged to find a way to undo it, to teach him gratitude and humility no matter what grand quarters he grew up in.

There was another shuffling of rooms once Rosemary discovered she was pregnant. Pierce moved them to his third-floor room where his wife would have more quiet—and less easy access to Paul's carriage house. Rosemary's loss of freedom didn't seem to occur to her at all. She was too busy being delighted she'd soon be a mother.

Paul disappeared for two solid months I worried more about him than I had about Martin when he'd left without warning. Martin planned to go looking for him, but it seemed each time his bags were packed he'd be hit by an incapacitating migraine that stuck him facedown in bed for two days. After he developed a tolerance to my headache tonic, I found another recipe in one of my texts and tramped down the stairs, smuggling the ingredients in my pockets as well as Fearghus'.

Rosemary was in the kitchen biting her nails. This new habit of hers was often accompanied by a deep daydream—a combination that left her drawing blood. I had a fix for nail biting too, but I didn't like to use magic on people without their consent, and getting her consent meant telling her things she still didn't know about us.

Teas, though, were another thing. I unloaded my pockets onto the counter as she continued to bite and stare.

Fearghus climbed up next to her. She looked at him, recognition momentarily lagged until her eyes focused and she grinned at him, crinkling her nose. The expression was like a spotlight in a garden at night. It couldn't quite take away all the shadows.

I filled the kettle and put it on the stove. A group of children thundered by outside, so I relieved Fearghus' pockets of my jars and told him to go out and play with his cousins. That's what we called all the children who visited the house. It was too hard keeping up with who was a second cousin or a third cousin or a cousin once removed.

"Do you want to talk?" I asked Rosemary as I crushed a bay leaf with my mortar and pestle.

She held up my jar of valerian root to get a better look. "This from Trey Fearghus' garden?"

"I'm making Martin a tea for his headache."

"Another headache? Maybe he should see a doc." She set the jar back down. Each nail was bitten so short, just seeing them sent a throb to my own fingers.

"Rosemary, your nails …"

"I know, ain't it awful? I oughtta wear gloves all day long."

"Maybe you should. Or if there's something bothering you …"

She turned in her chair then, as if startled by a sound I didn't hear. She was fixated on the doorway when in walked Paul. Shaggy-haired and bearded, he opened his arms wide. "My ladies."

Rosemary made a sound like a subdued sob and covered her mouth. Paul's goofy grin fell flat so fast I dropped the pestle. His outbursts had me trained to react at the slightest hint of a mood swing, but I wasn't quick enough to grab Rosemary who had already crossed the room and was shoving him hard.

"I know," he said, catching her arm. "I know, I know."

She was shoving him again, and he was backing up, just taking it, her fury met with such tenderness by a man whose normal reaction was fury of his own. The clash of it draped the greeting with such intimacy I had to avert my gaze. I tossed everything together and thanked my water for boiling so I could set Martin's tea to steep and escape that room that was now so saturated with emotion I didn't want to witness. As I turned toward the door, I caught an image that stayed with me for a long time no matter how hard I tried to dispel it: Rosemary captured in Paul's embrace, Paul stealing a wanton kiss against her hair.

Outside I found Fearghus sitting alone on the patio steps in muddy socks.

"What happened to your shoes?"

He pointed to the group of children throwing rocks at two small objects bobbing on the surface of the lake.

"You threw your shoes in the lake?"

He shook his head and pointed again. "They did. They took 'em. Said dogs don't get shoes, so that big kid held me and that girl took them off me." He squinted up at me, the harsh angle of the autumn sun hitting him straight in the face so it illuminated not just the hurt of the insult, but the confusion with it. My son was not just being tormented by the insult itself, but also his inadequacy of not understanding it. Inferior on top of stupid.

"Those kids must all need glasses. You're a boy. Of course you wear shoes. Now help me bring your dad his tea so he can feel better."

"They think—they—"

I took his shoulders. "Fearghus, let's decide something right now. Do we care what they think?"

In his eyes were the kind of tears that came on fast with a sting, unwanted and uncontrollable, giving more power to the people who caused them. *I will teach Fearghus to be strong.*

"What do you think? What do you *know*?" I placed my hand over his heart. "Right here?"

"I'm a boy."

"Then that's all that matters. Now let's get that tea to your dad."

Winter brought a shadow down on the house unlike any I'd seen. I took every opportunity to get Fearghus outside for walks among frosted trees in air so still our footsteps seemed like an invasion. Martin and I read the classics to each other by the fire each Sunday night—a new tradition thought up by Martin because he worked so much during the week I barely saw him. When he was in the house, he was in the training room with Fearghus. It left little time for the two of us. He was mine in bed each night, unless he was traveling, and I made that enough for me because it was all I could have.

One drafty January morning I awoke alone in bed well before the sun. I got out of bed to check on Fearghus next door, and after covering him and his cat with an extra quilt, the chill sent me back under my own covers. I couldn't fall back asleep with the house seething around me, so I scooted over to Martin's empty side to watch the windows for first light.

Martin came into the room in his robe and slippers. He stripped down and got back in bed with me. "Sorry, darling, did I wake you?"

"Something did."

He molded around me. "It's handled. For now, at least."

I pulled away to look at him.

"Paul and Pierce, at it again. Sometimes I wonder if we should just let Paul stay on the dope. He seems worse when he's clean."

I pressed the cold tip of my nose against his neck. "Maybe I should talk to him."

"No. Don't go near him. He's not very happy with me right now. And my father thinks this family is falling apart and we need to have dinner more often. We're having one tonight. So polish off your armor, it'll be a good one."

Fearghus and I were late for dinner, but not as late as Paul, who showed up during the main course. It was more of an insult to the master than if he'd skipped the whole dinner, and when I saw Rosemary shaking her head at her plate, I realized it was exactly the reaction Paul had wanted. His tardiness was not accidental.

The master took the bait. Paul smiled through the abuse without commenting until the end, when he dabbed his face, set down his napkin, and looked straight at Martin. "It's a real trip our old man's hounding me when his oldest son is fornicating with Bevan trash after adopting her bastard."

The shadow that had been hanging over the house swooped down onto me. I concentrated to keep my breathing steady, my face neutral. Fearghus perked up at the mention of our name, but he didn't know those words. If I didn't react, he'd have no reason to think we were the ones under attack by someone who'd once been on our side. Paul wasn't just baiting his father now, he was baiting all of us.

Fearghus had stopped eating. Rosemary mouthed, *Why?* at Paul, but he was locked in a stare down with Martin that only broke when Lewis ripped Paul out of his chair. I knew better than to think Lewis was coming to my defense, and I was proven right when Martin, Pierce, and the master stood simultaneously to follow them out of the room. Paul had broken the rule: no mention of anything that might inform Fearghus of his real family. They were taking him out to remind him. I'd come to Paul's aid so many times. I'd worried for him. I'd protected him. But this time, Paul deserved whatever they gave him.

"Trey Fearghus, you finish that supper and we'll go swimmin' in the heated pool. Just you and me." Rosemary was nodding at Fearghus, waiting for him to acknowledge her. "Maybe your momma will let you stay up late."

He glanced up at me, his forehead dimpled from the same mixture of hurt and confusion he experienced with the kids by the lake. Maybe he didn't understand the words, but he knew he and I were the target. I could no longer shield him from their malice. I had to teach him to shield himself.

When Martin joined me in our room that night, he swore they didn't hurt Paul. "Not that you should care, after what he said."

I'd promised myself I wouldn't say it, but out it came. "How can a family who *made* my child a bastard use that word to insult him?"

Martin hung his head. "I know, Sloane."

"And that idea—it's being taught to every child in this family. Not in the same words, but does it matter?"

He said nothing and sat on the edge of the bed, leaning onto his knees, staring at the floor.

"Those children—they're vicious, Martin. He's so little."

"What I want is to buy you a house somewhere and move you and Trey out of here, but I can't do that."

He'd just spoken my most realistic dream. All my other dreams were too far-fetched to give a moment's thought. But this one, it could happen. Now that it had been given life outside my head, it had inched so much closer to possibility it quickened my pulse. I had to be careful; these things were dreams, after all. It was dangerous bringing dreams so close to reality. The cost of disappointment was far too high. I sat on the bed next to him trying my best to appear merely interested and not over-the-moon giddy.

He took my hand, straightened the ring on my finger.

"Why can't you?" I asked.

He looked at me then, and when I saw the sadness in his eyes I realized the cost of disappointment was in a whole other galaxy. "I wish I could tell you."

Rosemary and I were in the library making lists of baby names the next day when Paul walked in and stood before us like we'd just called him for sentencing. His hair was mussed on one side. His puffy eyes squinted like he'd just woken up from whatever part of the floor he'd used for a bed that night. The boyish furrowed brow and extended lower lip were probably all an act, but he looked so much like the lost Paul I'd comforted so many times I had to look away.

Not Rosemary. She kept her icy glare on him. "Aw, come off it. Don't give us that bull. If there was a doghouse on this land I'd gladly show you to it. We ain't talkin' to you, so leave us be."

"You're talking to me now."

Rosemary huffed and turned away from him.

"What I said—it was for Martin, not for her. I was trying to make a point. I didn't mean to hurt her. You, Sloane."

"What letter were we on—M?" I asked Rosemary.

"We should ask Caroline what names she has for her baby. Think she'd tell us? I wouldn't want to have two little ones runnin' 'round here with the same name." She chewed the end of her pencil and I noticed the clean white moons of her nails.

I took her hand for a better look. "You stopped biting your nails?"

She pulled away to get a look at them herself. "You kiddin' me right now? I didn't even notice. Would ya look at that?" She flattened her hand like one might admire a new manicure.

Either someone else knew my nail-biting spell, or she'd worked out whatever had been troubling her weeks ago—enough time for her to heal and grow those pretty tips. I'd hesitate to use magic on unsuspecting people, but the Moores didn't observe such inconvenient morals. Only one of them was capable of healing Rosemary's nail-biting and her troubles.

I gave Paul my full attention then, and he looked as guilty as I expected. I'd been so often tempted to use that spell on her, I'd read it a thousand times. I had to know if he'd used it. "*Cén gheis a chuir tú uirthi? Geis lus na meala líomóide?*"

"*Ní dhearna mé tada.*" *Didn't do a thing.* Not quite the sentiment I'd use to express this situation.

He had to admit he did do one thing: He'd returned home. It was too much of a coincidence. "*Filleann tú ar an mbaile agus éiríonn sí as as a stuaim féin? An-chomhthárlú go deo é sin.*"

"*B'fhéidir nach ea.*" It wasn't a confession, but at least he acknowledged his return home had made some difference. As if to drive it in further, he smiled this broken half-smile that made me wince at the sadness packed inside it. Paul's heart was hurting in a way I'd never seen before. For the first time I was afraid to be his listener, to be the one to help him. To uncover why he agreed this wasn't a coincidence.

"Sloane, scold him in English so I can enjoy it."

But to uncover why, the answer had to have been buried. It was there before me, unearthed and lit by the light of a full moon, so from afar it might go unnoticed. Up close it was plain to see: Paul had simply returned home, and Rosemary's troubles had fled. There was no question she was worried about him while he was gone. So was I. He'd won her sympathy as he'd won mine, only in a fraction of the time. Worry for a friend didn't produce stress powerful enough to create a self-destructive habit of that nature. Rosemary hadn't been subconsciously chewing her nails bloody over missing someone who was just a friend.

How much of Paul truly cared for Rosemary, and how much of him craved the chaos their relationship would stir? The hunger for strife was an addiction, just like his attachment to booze and dope. The need for chaos was what drove him—it was what was destroying him one little piece at a time. Just when I'd thought Paul couldn't bring any more turmoil into that household, he had.

Rosemary gave birth at dawn on the summer solstice to a baby boy so fair she joked in her delirious post-labor bliss that he came from the North Pole where he blended with year-round snow. His hair was as white as the ripe seed head of a dandelion, his eyes so blue they seemed lit by sky from the inside. Admiring his little elfin lips, his velvet-soft cheeks, I was taken by a hefty guilt. When I was a new mother, I hadn't noticed one detail about either of my babies. I had no memories, no snapshots in my mind. I could describe the color of Fearghus' five-year-old eyes, but had no memory of his newborn self. And if there was an amount less than none, that's how many I had of his newborn sister.

I held the baby while Rosemary slept. I asked Fearghus to bring my honeysuckle oil and a frond from one of our balcony ferns. Fearghus helped me anoint the baby's fingertips and toes with honeysuckle. A witch's blessing, so wherever he walked, whatever he touched, he'd find peace as plentiful as the white and yellow blooms. In his powerful tiny hand, I placed the fern, for health and good luck. If I could've made him a bed of fern I would have. In that family he'd need as much luck as he could gather.

Pierce came to see him while I held him there at Rosemary's bedside, and although I knew I should offer him up, I couldn't command my arms to do it, and Pierce didn't ask. He gave his new son a casual look-over, his wife a quick glance, and went off to do whatever it was he did all day.

Rosemary awoke then, as if from a nightmare, knocking items off her bedside table and calling out for me like I wasn't beside her.

I took her hand. "I'm here."

"Sloane, promise me … if anything happens to me … promise you'll take care of him like he was your own."

"Of course. Don't even waste the words to ask. Sit back and rest." I handed her the baby and rearranged the pillows to cradle him. He blinked and wiggled from the disruption.

"Ain't he a prince?" she said, stroking his eyelids closed. "I finally got his name. A name for a prince."

And it was. She named him Christian Maximillian Moore.

CHAPTER 38

THE RECOGNITION OF Fearghus' gradually dimming spirit for the past couple years was a hot coal sprung from the fire at my back. How I hadn't noticed my son had fallen to sullen moods and frowns was yet another reminder of my failure at mothering him. His smile had all but gone out until Christian was born. Now his delight was new, in a body not used to its lift, and I had trouble dragging him away from that baby and calming him for meals, baths, and bedtime. This was a new human being who hadn't yet developed a voice to insult or a capacity to shun. I could see through Fearghus' eyes that this baby was his chance to win a human friend, and he was putting his all into it.

Whenever Fearghus was missing, I knew the first place to look for him was Rosemary's room. By giving birth to one child, she'd taken on two.

"It's really okay. You leave Trey Fearghus be. He helps me. He can change a diaper, ya know." Rosemary was feeding the baby while Fearghus played with his jacks on the floor at her feet. His coordination seemed a bit remarkable for a five-year-old. Perhaps playing jacks was what Martin had him doing all day long in the training room.

"You tell him if he's in your way. Send him back downstairs."

"He ain't in my way. I need his company. Ever since Pierce moved back to our old room I get lonesome up here."

When Rosemary had first come to the estate, she'd found it odd Martin and I had separate rooms. Now, because Pierce didn't like to be woken at night by a hungry baby, he and Rosemary had separate rooms. This house was turning her life into something she once considered odd. Her unease became more prominent every day. I had to help her expel it, to reclaim the life she wanted. We could succumb to the limitations of that house, or we could twist them to fit our needs.

"Let's go outside, go sit by the lake. I'll hold the baby while you and Fearghus swim."

Fearghus picked up his jacks in one fluid swipe. "Can the baby swim too?"

"That's a real groovy idea, Trey Fearghus. Let's teach this baby to swim."

Fearghus fell asleep in Rosemary's unoccupied arm that night, baby Christian in the other. When I offered to take him she shooed me away with her foot.

"This is heaven," she whispered. "Let him stay." She rested her cheek on his hair and closed her eyes.

I covered her with a blanket, tucked a pillow under each arm, and left her on her sofa drifting to sleep under two little boys. She'd been having trouble sleeping until I started hiding a sleep helper under her pillow. Pebbles soaked in lavender with a dab of belladonna contained only the magic of my blessing, which was more of a prayer for a friend than a spell, so my conscience was clear. I passed her bed on my way out, replacing the spent pebble with a fresh one from my pocket. In the hall I ran into Paul, who had no reason to be on that end of the house at that hour. "Paul, don't do this."

"Do what? He has her stowed away up here, like she's some princess locked in a tower. What happened to chess nights? Walks under the stars? Hanging out in the ballroom?"

I tugged his shirt to get him moving down the hall, away from Rosemary's room. "Things change."

He ripped loose from my grasp. "I can't even visit you anymore without Martin prowling your room like a guard dog."

I stopped there to look him in the face. My son had been called a dog, a mutt, *maistín*, so many times I had a fiery sensitivity to the word. Intentional or not, calling Martin a dog was poking the same wound. An argument so close to the rooms of the master and the mistress would not help my or Paul's standing in that house.

"You hate me," he said, studying my face.

"You're not making it easy for me to like you lately."

"Come to the ballroom and have a drink with me."

"I'm not drinking with you."

"Then just come. I'll play some Liszt. We can hang out like we used to."

Bevan trash. That's what he'd called me. I could forgive that, if he truly only used it to provoke Martin. But what he'd called my son—that insult served no strategic purpose that night. No one knew of Martin's fondness for Fearghus. No one knew that insult would provoke him. It was simply Paul's belief, slipping out behind the first vile comment like a drip after the faucet had been shut off. I didn't want to be around if that faucet ever turned back on.

I headed for the stairs and made it down three steps.

"Please, Sloane."

I could tell he hadn't moved, hadn't even tried to follow me, catch my arm, or block my way on the stairs. That's what the old Paul would've done. This new Paul didn't have the fight in him. I recognized the change then, just as I'd belatedly recognized the dimming of Fearghus, of his smile made so rare, of his melancholy.

I'd once considered Paul to be on my side, a victim of the Moore family instead of a willing member. Whether he'd strayed to their side or had been dragged there, I couldn't look the other way and allow the Moores to overcome him completely. I couldn't let them win him. Maybe he'd lost his fight, but I had enough fight in me for both of us.

We took turns playing Chopin and Liszt. He opened the ballroom's porch doors so the cool night breeze wound around our legs under the piano and teased my hair out of its pins. Only one lamp glowed softly behind us leaving the room dim and open like a cavern filled with the songs of frogs and Chopin's Nocturne in C Sharp Minor. I was whisked back to the day I was newly captive, frightened and alone, when Paul had taken me into this place where fear had no welcome, and time was a moment of music on air that found my lungs so I could finally breathe.

"Don't ever call my son a bastard again," I said to him.

He took his fingers off the keys mid-song. When he didn't look at me, didn't speak, I played the next few notes. He stopped me, his hands on mine, pressing out a discordant set of keys that shattered the lull of the night and echoed through me in the silence that followed.

He enclosed my hands in his. "I promise I won't."

I pulled away and began the song again. He got up and went to the bar. A light flipped on. Bottles clanged and ice clinked. The sound must have been like a dinner bell because it brought the three other Moore brothers from various parts of the house, and before I'd finished the song they all had a drink in hand.

My music-filled cavern became a different room—the frogs' song now an invasion instead of peaceful background noise, the lights by the bar too harsh. The shadow above the house had drawn over us, the seething quality of the air returned. I rose from the piano and pushed in the bench. Martin came over and put an arm around my waist, kissing my cheek with the lingering type of kiss that promised more later.

"Good night," I said.

He held on to me. "Stay. Play for us."

"You have Paul for that. Give me your tie, I'll take it upstairs for you."

Lewis had moved to the sofa near the piano. "Let her go, Marty. She's afraid to be in a room with all four of us."

Martin handed me his drink so he could take off his tie. "So am I."

"You look tired," I said, hoping to lure him up to bed with me.

He nodded. "Long day. But I'm too wound up. I need a few of these." He raised his glass.

I went upstairs to Rosemary's room to collect Fearghus. Her only light was the night light by the bed that held her, the baby, and Fearghus, all tucked in and too peaceful to disturb. I went to my room, undressed, and lay in bed watching clouds drift across the moon. Martin's arm had left a palpable imprint on my hip, his lips an unsatisfied charge on my cheek. I got up to open the doors wide, to breathe in the air, attempting to calm a need that could only be calmed by Martin.

Back in bed I tossed, turned, flipped covers off then back on. I switched on my lamp to read. I switched it back off. I put on slippers and a housecoat and went downstairs to fetch my husband.

I heard the raised voices from the main staircase. I stopped in the foyer to identify all of them, to be sure no new people had arrived. From the ruckus, it sounded like a hoard.

Paul's voice, yelling, "You've turned her into your—"

"I'd stop there—" That was Pierce.

A large piece of furniture rumbled across the floor.

"You *both* need to back up." Martin.

"No, I want him to finish. Into his *what*, Paul?" Lewis, in his most mocking tone, the one he'd stopped using on me when he realized it'd lost all its reach. I'd developed a shield, one I must lend to Paul.

I entered the room. The sofa was askew. Martin was standing between Paul and Pierce, a hand against each of their chests to keep them a safe distance apart. Lewis was sitting on the arm of the sofa.

Paul knocked Martin's arm away and took a step back, hanging his head. "You know—"

"Don't," Martin said.

Paul cast a dark look at Martin and spotted me standing in the doorway. "Don't—what? You don't deserve your wife either. Long vacations without telling her where you go, who you're with, how to reach you. Keeping her locked in this damn house like—"

"Maybe I *should* let you hit him," Martin said to Pierce.

I walked toward them. "Don't you dare."

Everyone but Paul looked at me.

"Ah, our lovely captive," Pierce said. "Maybe she can tell us why my brother Paul is so protective of my wife and newborn son."

"If you're going to carry on like children, perhaps I should tell you to go to bed."

"Paul's a bit protective of you too. Why is that?"

Martin turned to face Pierce squarely. "You're about to cross a line."

"Line's been crossed long ago. First with your woman, now mine. You don't want to teach him, then I will."

Lewis stood from his spot on the sofa's arm. The upward motion of his brawny frame disrupted the arrangement of bodies in the room, and I mentally stepped back to gain an overhead view, a better understanding of what might happen. It was this readjustment that caused me to see the shadow that haunted me was a real thing, an accumulation of anger pooling above us. Gaining mass. Becoming heavier—so heavy it now encroached into the room, skimming our heads. In a household incapable of forgiveness and full of distrust, it had ripened into an entity that now ruled the people who'd created it.

My practice of magic for my or Fearghus' good was certainly forbidden, but no one had ever warned me not to use magic that would benefit the Moores. If someone didn't neutralize the dark cloud over that house, we'd all be at the mercy of its influence. They'd created it; they couldn't see it. It was up to me.

"You want to hit me? Then hit me," Paul was saying. He opened his arms to give Pierce a clear shot. "Won't change a thing."

Martin wasn't interfering this time. He was too busy watching me. I worried he could feel my rapid pulse across the room, through the floor, like that night in the woods he pledged himself as half Bevan. If he'd opened that channel between us, I had to act fast before he saw what I was about to do.

I crossed the room, planted myself in between Pierce and Paul. "It's over. Go to bed."

"Won't change *what*?" Pierce said over my shoulder to Paul. He took a step forward, but I held my ground.

"The only person who can change this situation is you," I said to Pierce. Love and respect for his wife and brother, along with a little trust, could make all his problems disappear.

Pierce looked at me then. I could see the black blur of anger rising off him like steam, feeding the already impressive mass above us. I blinked. The image was gone. A new expression rose to his face, not of anger but of pure sinister satisfaction so unexpected I had to remember what I said. Surely nothing I said could generate such pleasure for this man.

"You're right." He turned to Martin. "This woman of yours, she has the best ideas."

Martin extended a hand to me, clearly not comfortable with my position between the two most volatile men in the house. I hadn't gotten three steps away before movement blurred past me, and Martin jerked me behind him as skin smacked bone.

"I still needed to hit him, though," Pierce said when I wheeled around.

Paul ran a hand across his face, smearing the blood running from his nose. He started laughing, wild and high, and Pierce was telling him to shut up, but Paul was only laughing harder. I surged forward. Martin held me back. All I could hear was the rush of blood in my head, the song of anger filling me, rising off me like I'd witnessed it from Pierce, who was now stepping toward Paul again, clenching a fist. Paul raised a finger and curled it toward himself in a gesture for Pierce to come closer, closer. I struggled against Martin but he was too strong; the harder I pushed away the tighter his shackle arms held. I didn't want to watch Paul be hit again, but I couldn't look away. Just as Pierce pulled his arm back, Paul bucked forward, the crack of forehead against nose driving through me.

Martin let go of me and I went to my knees, holding my ears to protect them from that awful sound that was long over but seemed to live on in my head. Martin barked orders over Pierce's yelling and Paul's cackling and the rumble of the sofa being shoved each time Martin pushed Pierce back. Pierce's nose was a smashed cherry pie, Paul's a river of blood. I dug both hands in my housecoat pockets, seeking the weight settled there—a stash of Rosemary's spent sleeping pebbles. They had little power left in them, but the memory of that sister oak's power was still alive in my bones. If I closed my eyes I could draw from that oak, turn a spent sleep aid into a spell strong enough to tranquilize a grown man.

Two pebbles in one hand, one in the other. Two men to take down. I doubted I could cast the pebbles fast enough before one of them grabbed me, but I had to try. I stood and walked into the chaos.

Paul curbed his laughter. Martin gave Pierce one more hard shove, and Pierce fell against the sofa and didn't bother to get up. I closed my eyes and walked my mind out the door, across the lawn, through the trees to the oak. Its power gushed in, as if it had been waiting for me. The pebbles warmed in my hands. I opened my eyes.

"Outside," Lewis said. "To finish it."

"No. It's over." Martin had his eyes on me. He shook his head, the motion so insignificant I may have imagined it, if his eyes weren't speaking an entire conversation. "Sloane, darling, could you get some towels from the bar?"

I released the pebbles back into my pockets and went to the bar. Paul refused a towel in favor of bleeding down the front of his shirt. Martin took one, tossed it to Pierce then offered him a hand up. Pierce needed more than a towel.

Pierce angled himself around Martin to point at Paul. "Someday you'll wish you hadn't done that. Someday very soon."

CHAPTER 39

ELEANOR PLAYED DOMINOES with Fearghus while I searched my family's texts for the cleansing spell powerful enough to banish the cloud of anger fed for years by the Moore family. To Eleanor, I was reading old books of poetry, and she didn't seem thrown by the spread of them on the bed, with me leaning over them like they were work instead of leisure. My texts hadn't been touched since Martin moved into my room. Although I knew the right thing was to keep them hidden, an excited anxiety was brewing in me at the thought of him walking in and catching me in the act. To fantasize that he could study them at my side was morally wrong, but I couldn't shelve the idea like the fiction it was, and I prolonged my task hoping he'd come to bed early.

And he did.

Eleanor started picking up the dominoes once he came in. I pretended to be engrossed in what I was doing. I had no time to cover my texts or hide them, which is exactly how I wanted it. He put his shoes in the closet, his watch on the bedside table. Every one of his movements was at the forefront of my awareness, yet I kept my attention glued to a page I wasn't reading.

"His eyes are different from ours," Fearghus was telling Eleanor.

"Are they?"

"Yeah, and he talks funny. He never knows what I say."

"Does he speak English?"

"Dunno."

"He's Chinese, Trey," Martin said. "Now help Eleanor pick up your toys and go to your room for bed."

"I'll give him a bath, sir, and tuck him in."

"Thanks, Eleanor," I said. She took the box of dominoes and led Fearghus out of the room. I looked at Martin. "Who's Chinese?"

"His new trainer. Doesn't speak a word of English. I need to hire a translator. What's all this?" He sat on the bed next to me.

Danger flamed heavy around me. It was too late to go back. I allowed a moment to pass so my heart would understand it had no need to pound. I'd willingly walked into this. I didn't need to escape. "My family's ancient texts."

He leaned back a little, staring at me like I'd spoken some threatening words that struck him low, with no time for him to prepare a defense. "They've been here—" He looked down at them like they were now the threat. "How did you get them here?"

"I had them sent years ago. To your Cambridge apartment. You brought them—"

"Yes, I remember." He rotated one so he could read it. "You really shouldn't let me ..." He leaned forward, too captivated to finish.

I started slapping them closed. "You're right. I shouldn't—"

"You can read this? No wonder you speak that strange language in your sleep."

I paused to gauge if he was kidding with me. He'd picked up the text and was turning pages like he was searching for something.

"It's just Irish."

"No, it's not. Maybe old Irish, but not the language we speak."

I took the text from him. The words on the page blurred and took on completely different letters than the ones I knew. I blinked. The correct words returned. I pointed to a line and read it to him.

"That's not what that says. Not even close."

I picked up a different text and read him another line.

"Are you translating or reading?"

"I'm reading what's on the page."

He laughed. "That's not what's on that page."

"It isn't funny, Martin." He picked up another one, and I snatched it from him as roughly as I could allow myself to snatch a family relic.

"You think I'm being a wise guy? Go get Eleanor."

I gave him a pained look. I wasn't sure what game he was playing, but I certainly wasn't going to drag poor Eleanor into it.

He left the room. I slid off the bed, gathered my texts, and piled them on the coffee table. Stored away from those poetry collections Mam had originally sent with them, they sat exposed, looking like their true selves. Martin had now seen them; those poetry collections would never steer his mind into seeing them as harmless books again.

Martin came back with Eleanor in tow. He picked up one of the texts and opened it up in front of her.

"I don't—"

"I know, just try to sound it out." He pointed to a word. "That one."

She squinted one eye and gave it her best shot. It was too bad a pronunciation for me to understand.

"Good," Martin said. "Now this one."

She tried again. Another indecipherable sentence. He nodded at me, brows raised, grinning like he'd just won a bet. He beckoned me over with a jerk of his head. "Now do it for Sloane."

I walked over. He pointed to another line, which she read in pure gibberish.

"Thanks. That'll be all," he said to her.

She gave me an amused smile, and Martin and I watched her leave the room.

"She was reading what I see," he said. "And I don't even think it's old Irish. I think it's just—"

"Gibberish."

Something made him look at me then, the tug of that channel he opened in the woods humming between us.

His lips parted and my realization mirrored itself on his face. The texts were affected by magic. Only a Bevan could see their true words. I took the text from him and flipped pages, trying to spot some break in the magic, but I could only see what I'd always seen—my family's spells, copied by hand by some ancestor from a book more ancient than mine. Passed through the family for millennia.

"That's—" He sat down weakly on the sofa, rubbing his face. He cursed under his breath. "I wonder if my ancestors knew that."

"Knew they couldn't read them?"

"No, knew no one but you—your family—could read them."

Was it true? Only my family could read them? Eleanor saw the gibberish. Rosemary—I don't think she'd seen the texts at all. Fearghus could read them; I was already teaching him. And his father—

"Fearghus. He could read them. Fearghus, my husband. He's not a Bevan."

He lowered his hands to the sofa cushion and gripped the edge. He wasn't looking at me anymore, and the shame that descended on me had me hearing my last uttered words again. I'd only meant to specify which Fearghus. I should've corrected myself. *Dead husband. Previous husband.* I couldn't do it.

"That's interesting," he said finally. The flatness of his voice made me wonder if it was my choice of words he found most interesting. If that channel had remained open before this exchange, it was now closed tight.

"I wanted your help studying them. I was hoping you could help me find a way ..." One glimpse of his face told me I'd made a grand mistake showing him those texts. I'd crossed a bridge that was now burning behind me. I couldn't go back. "Well, I suppose it doesn't matter. You can't read them anyway."

Damn the shudder in my voice. Damn it all. I scooped up the texts in my arms and took them to their spot between the two poetry collections on my shelves, now safe from everyone except Martin—the one person whose trust I depended on so heavily now had another burden to carry.

"There's no one I can ask without giving too much away." He was still on the sofa, staring coldly at the wall. "But I want to know if my ancestors knew those books were masked. Perhaps you could ask your mam?"

"I could, but why does it matter?"

He turned to me. "Because if my ancestors knew those books were protected, you and I shouldn't be enemies."

He left that statement to hang in the air, to prove how much more he knew about the war between our families. It may have been my fault. I'd never asked. More likely, it was yet another vital bit of knowledge kept from me by my own family. A detail that might have encouraged me to talk to my dead husband before he was killed, to inquire about his frequent trips with my brother, to convince him to stay home. To stay alive.

"I think we need to talk," Martin said, now standing close, his hands on my shoulders. "Outside, after moon-rise."

Fall swirled faintly on the summer air that night. Dew sprinkled my bare feet from the grass as we walked. Martin took us through the shadows, not once stepping into the white cast of moonlight until we'd been enveloped by the forest behind the lake.

"I'll tell you what I know. It isn't much, too much has been lost with time, but I have a feeling it's more than you know."

With the peace of night settled all around, I understood why Martin had brought me out there to tell our families' history. The house would've equipped Martin's story with claws that sunk into flesh, holding me with no room to fight free. Outside, I was already free. Even if the story had claws, it couldn't catch me.

The underwood was thick enough that Martin held branches for me as I followed him, the trail too narrow to walk side by side. Celestial light pooled on the path before us, cutting a way through the dark void of the forest.

"I don't know anything," I said.

He stopped walking and turned around. "If I'm upsetting some carefully planned Bevan balance, so be it. I can't go on knowing this, when you're in the dark."

"If my family planned all this, then you telling me is part of it. They don't make plans that can be so easily disrupted."

"My family lives to disrupt your family's plans. It's our business goal."

"It hasn't happened yet."

He smiled, wicked in the moonlight. "If I wasn't a traitor, I might disagree." He took a knife out of his pocket and flipped it open.

I halted his hand. "I don't need a blood oath to swear secrecy with you."

"Good. Nor I with you." He folded the knife and pocketed it. He took my hand and pulled me forward, our minds more bound by simple touch than any blood ritual.

Bats swooped overhead. The flurry of wings followed our trek down a path that continued for so long I was sure we'd soon round a bend and be flat against the iron bars of the north fence. Martin dropped my hand to hop a fallen tree, and when he turned to help me over I saw a looming ghostly shape ahead that pulled a gasp from my gut.

"It's a sacred stone. You'll feel it on the other side of this log."

As soon as my feet hit earth on the other side of the log, the tingle of sacred ground climbed my legs like a living thing.

"Three paths converge ahead at our hallowed ground. One stone to protect each path. We don't use this often anymore. Ever, really. But it's here."

The stone stood in the middle of the trail, guarding what lay beyond like a devoted soldier. As tall as my shoulders, its presence seemed much taller. An effect, and an old one, crafted to turn away those who weren't welcome. Martin went to his knees and bent to the ground, his forehead touching earth briefly before the upright stone. I did the same. He took my hand. Unsure what would happen if an unwelcome guest tried to pass, I braced myself as he led me around it. He kissed my hand before he released it. "You and Trey belong here as I do. There are no divides in this place."

On the other side of the stone began a moderate incline. We climbed to the top of a hill, the henge coming into view about halfway up.

"We should've feasted here for the solstice," I said, marveling at this sacred site that sat unknown to me for five whole years. Perhaps this is what drew me into the woods that rainy day when Fearghus was a baby wrapped against me, and Paul had saved us from the dogs they'd unleashed.

He stopped climbing, creating a tiny avalanche with his abrupt halt. "I'd like that. I haven't done that since I was a kid."

The henge consisted of a ring of oak pillars standing in twos, notched at the tops to hold a horizontal oak that latched against its horizontal neighbor to create a perfect circle suspended fifteen feet above our heads. Inside the ring of standing oaks sat three more sacred stones. One was aligned with our trail. The others were aligned with two more trails equidistant from ours around the circle, stretching away from the site like rays of sun. Martin went around the henge to the opposite side to enter the circle facing me—a practice that must be common to his family as it was to mine. To enter the circle in this fashion was a proof of trust and goodwill.

We met in the middle of the three stones. He handed me a crane-fly orchid on a long stem, an impossible wildflower to spot on a sunny day much less a moonlit forest.

"I should have married you here," he said.

A statement like that should have garnered a look from me at the very least, but the swell of emotion left me staring at the delicate blooms like I'd lost my understanding of language.

"Look at us, standing here. Our families have been at war for how long?" He ran a hand through his hair and shook his head like some mistake had been made and we were to blame.

What I felt for him wasn't a mistake. Not now, after our trust had been so painstakingly earned. Not with the oak pillars towering around us like witnesses to the secrets he was ready to divulge, secrets that would form another layer on the bond we already had.

I wrapped my arms around his neck. His remained at his sides, but he looked at me, the shame of betraying his family showing as clearly as if we were standing under a noon sun. These emotions he kept so well hidden weren't a surprise—I knew they were there—but they changed his face with such force it brought tears to my eyes. He was not any freer in that house than me.

He dipped his head. Before he could turn completely away, I kissed him. His hands found my jaw and he held me there, kissing me back, long and slow.

"Tell me," I said.

He tugged me down to the ground, and we sat facing one another, my crane-fly orchid lying across my lap.

"Our people—your ancestors, and mine—we were one. Other families, too. We traded and shared work, had a common primitive political structure. We shared magic. We agreed on many things, one more important than most." He looked me dead in the eye. "We agreed to never write our magic down. We passed it to our children only by mouth. We memorized everything. Writing it down put it at risk of getting into the hands of enemies."

I looked down at the crane-fly orchid, thinking of my family's texts. They sat on a shelf in the house of an enemy every day. Until that day, I didn't know the enemy couldn't even read them.

Martin put a hand on my knee. "Your family started writing things down."

"My books."

He nodded solemnly. "Something so simple, and it started a war."

"I'm sure we had a reason."

"Maybe. But whatever it was, it's been lost. To my family, at least. Yours might know. The thing is, if your family had simply told us you'd affected the writings so no one could read them but you …" He chuckled, looking away like he had to replace strong thoughts with gentler words. "If we'd have known, it would've prevented the whole damn war."

"Maybe not."

"What use is a book of gibberish to an enemy?"

"It might not be gibberish."

"It's not—to you. But to me, it's gibberish."

I picked at the blooms on my wildflower. "I wish we could show it to your mother. To see if she can read it." Órlaith Moore was still a mystery after five whole years. I could sense there was more to her than a bitter woman who never left her room.

He took me by the shoulders. "No. Don't even wish it."

In his unshielded eyes was a look of piercing alarm—fear I just might do it, and he couldn't stop me. I couldn't imagine doing anything that might put him in more danger. I'd had those books all my life. There were dozens of copies floating all around my family. As each new generation was born, unused copies were passed down, or a new set was handwritten by a group of the eldest members. No one had ever told me they were affected so only Bevans could read them.

"We'd have lost everything if we hadn't written it down. My grandparents had to flee Ireland because of you. Without those books, Bevans would be—"

"Not if you'd followed the rule. If you'd passed the knowledge only by voice, you'd never have had a reason to flee. You'd still be—" He stopped, as if waiting for me to finish the sentence. When I didn't, he said, "Your family wouldn't be called Bevan."

I didn't understand the care he took with those words. Not until the day I found a spell in one of my texts that turned my quest for cleansing the cloud of anger from the Moore estate into a new venture: righting a wrong committed by my very own family.

CHAPTER 40

I WAS ALONE WHEN I found the spell. Fearghus was in the library with his new tutor Martin had hired. I thought Fearghus was too young for school, but Martin disagreed, and I'd accepted just to give Fearghus something new to do. He was becoming more difficult to entertain, with Rosemary busy with the baby and Eleanor taking on extra work for a few maids who'd retired from the estate. What he needed was a friend, but none of the many children always visiting the house would have anything to do with him aside from planned, calculated torment.

I'd found the last component to my anger cleansing spell when a gust of wind from the open balcony doors blew my notepaper to the floor. After retrieving it I returned to my text but it had flipped to a new page in a section of curses

I rarely perused. I wasn't inclined to curse anyone, and I had no reason to read them.

As I pinched a chunk of pages to return myself to the correct passage, my eye caught a phrase on the page: *to blind a mother to her child.* I felt a new, imaginary wind blow through me. I read on, learning this curse would render a mother's children silent and invisible to her and only her. The timing could be instantaneous, or it could be tied to either the mother's age or the child's. It was the same curse currently infesting Órlaith Moore. *A Farrelly curse*, Martin had said. Then he'd asked me if I knew the name. When I'd told him I hadn't, that expression he wore should've been my clue.

I knew Mam's family had fled to Wales before she was born; I knew they'd all taken new names. No one had ever told me their original name. If they had, that conversation with Martin would've been different. Someone in my family put the curse on Órlaith Moore, and I now had the knowledge to undo it. There was no better bargaining tool to win my and Fearghus' freedom.

Empowered by a reckless thrill, I marched straight upstairs to the mistress' room and knocked on her door. My knock was politely soft and probably not loud enough for her to hear in her spacious room. I considered knocking harder, but before I had a chance the door opened, creaking slowly on its hinges as if pushed by a breeze.

"Hello?" I put my hand on the doorknob. It was clear no maid had opened it. No maid was there. But an open door was just that, so I stepped into the sitting room and shut the door behind me.

The double doors into her room were open just enough to cast a line of sunlight into the sitting room. Going close enough to knock seemed too forward when I wasn't sure if she was prepared to take a visitor. "Mrs. Moore, may I come in?"

The doors blew open with more force than the first, swinging to the wall and bouncing off the doorstops. What a mistake this was, to come up here unannounced with a wild notion I hadn't thought through. I had a bit of knowledge so priceless, to give it away so easily—even just to admit I *possessed* the knowledge—could only be a mistake.

Here I was, though, and it was too late to go back.

She was sitting in an armchair that faced her windows. She raised a hand, lazily beckoning me to the chair beside her. When I sat she put a finger to her lips. The yellow scarf was still being wrung in her hands like it hadn't left for years. We sat in silence, watching a heavy line of gray clouds overtake the blue late-summer sky. The passing time allowed too many thoughts to gather in my head. Too many worries. Just when I'd worked up the nerve to tell her I'd just come to visit, that I was sorry to have bothered her and I'd let myself out, she turned red-rimmed eyes to me and said, "There's a peace to your company I like very much."

"Thank you," I blurted.

"You have a reason to visit me."

The white lie I'd prepared to tell lifted away from me like a helium balloon rising into the sky, hopelessly out of reach. "I do. I think—I mean, I hope I might have a way to relieve you of the blindness you've been cursed with."

She lowered her hands to her lap, the yellow scarf lying idle in her palm. "Hope is a tricky thing. Tell me why you hope."

"I hope—well, I'm hoping I can craft a spell to undo it. I know the curse itself. I've reversed other curses before. I could try, if you'd like me to."

She watched the sky as she spoke. "You want something in return."

I held my breath a moment, wishing for her to look at me. I wanted to see her face when I made my request. Living with Martin had trained me to gauge a person's most subtle reactions, and I wanted to see her emotional response before she made her verbal one. The moment stretched too long. Her bargaining mask was cooler and more patient than Martin's. "I'd like to trade it for my freedom, and my son's."

She sighed, long and slow. "You've grown bold in your years here. I might say this house has been good for you. But tell me this: if you were me, would you want to see your sons again?"

I turned away from her. The gray clouds had triumphed, and the windowpane was sprinkled with the first drops of rain. The answer to her question was easy. The tone she'd used to ask it, however, a puzzle. It not only sounded as though she did not in fact desire to see her sons again, but also that the curse had been orchestrated, or approved, by her. Even the timing of it made sense. Children were the innocent products of their nurturing, or lack thereof. Fifteen-year-olds were no longer children. To a person with foresight, who'd see what her sons would grow up to be, a blind eye and deaf ear seemed a great act of mercy.

"Yes, I would always want to see my son."

"Your son is different from my sons."

But they were still her sons. Her flesh and blood. Two of them were evil through and through, but the other two … how could she disown them?

"Perhaps they wouldn't be, if they could talk to you."

She grew still, as if considering the statement I hadn't meant to say aloud. I was greatly out of my place. Bold, like she'd said. Too bold. She leaned forward in her seat, intent on something going on outside. I focused beyond the raindrops on the glass and saw Fearghus sprinting toward the lake and then a jump, a tuck of his legs, and a big splash. He came up several yards beyond, smiling at someone closer to the house.

I got up and went to the window. Rosemary was standing there in the rain, little Christian wrapped tightly against her. She hollered something to Fearghus then wrapped a shawl over her hair and around her shoulders, adjusting it to shield the baby's face from the sprinkling rain. Fearghus took off, swimming for the far bank of the lake as she headed on foot around it. She'd made it a race to the other side to get him out of the water before the lightning came. She was so good with Fearghus; she seemed to understand him more than me sometimes. She was going to be a great mother.

"If you can come up with a way to reverse the curse, I'll demand my husband release you."

"And my son?"

"And your son."

Her easy agreement made sense once I'd pieced together a spell to undo that curse. The spell's success depended on an ingredient that was impossible to gather: every child of the woman affected by the curse must be pure of heart. Not even Martin could claim that. His trips had become less frequent, but he was still apt to return home with a split lip or a black eye and a whole gang of men. Clean business didn't require so much backup.

I'd hit a wall. Mam was the expert I normally trusted to turn an impossible spell into a successful one, but I couldn't admit to wanting to undo my family's own work, even if it promised to bring me home. So I went to Martin.

"It's a bad idea," he said. "You don't know that spell in your book is the exact spell they used. A reversal could cause something worse, and I don't like the idea of you experimenting on my mother."

I followed him into the closet. He'd just come upstairs after a long day. Fearghus was in bed, and I'd waited up for Martin after deciding he was the only one who could help me.

"It's the spell. Listen." I retrieved the text from my bedside table and read it to him.

He stopped me halfway through. "And you'll do this for a woman who tried to imprison your son inside his own mind."

I closed the text. "If I do this, she'll set me and Fearghus free."

He paused to look at me, one arm in his shirt, one arm out. "She can't do that."

"She said she would."

He shot a resentful look in the direction of her room. "That's—" He tossed his wadded shirt onto the floor harder than he needed to.

"You could leave with me. We could buy a house somewhere, just like you said. We could be—"

He pushed past me, leaving me in the closet alone. I found him in the bathroom splashing water on his face. The tile was icy-cold against my feet. Fall had pushed in fast, and the heaters hadn't had a chance to warm the house yet. I wrapped my housecoat around myself and sat on the tub. Every movement he made with too much force—the yank of the hand towel from the rack, the angry twist of the faucet knob.

"Did you have a lousy day?"

"No, I had a fine day."

"Then—"

"We shouldn't be talking about this in the house." He left me again.

I followed him back into the bedroom. He'd gone to the windows, bracing himself with one hand high on the frame. The anger coming off him had me feeling wary of him for the first time in years. A sick feeling rose from my stomach, bringing with it a thought that turned me cold. He wanted me captive. Yes, he showed me the breach in the wrought iron fence, but only because he knew I'd never be able to leave safely. He liked being the one in control of my freedom.

"I need your permission to do some magic to help your mother." My voice sounded as cold as I felt.

Closing his eyes, he bowed his head for a few breaths before looking at me. "Then what, you leave?"

"I hoped you'd come with me." *Hope is a tricky thing.*

He hit the window with his fist. I braced myself for shattered glass, but all was fine. He put his face in his hands and rubbed down on it hard. "Sloane, I can't leave this house."

"We wouldn't have to move far."

"I can't go off the property. Not for longer than a few months."

The sick feeling returned with new dread and a question I didn't want to ask. "Why not?"

"Because I'm cursed. I'm bound to the house. I agreed to it so I could marry you."

"Whatever for?"

"Insurance. They couldn't trust I'd keep you here. They wanted to curse you, but I volunteered instead. If I leave this property for more than a few months, I'll die."

Hope. So powerfully positive until the moment it turns ugly, cackling wickedly in your ear at your foolishness. Tricky indeed.

He sat on the bed beside me, where I'd dropped a moment before. He took my hand. "I shouldn't have married you. If I'd waited, you would've won your freedom and I could buy you a house anywhere in the world. And marry you with no curse."

"I can remove your curse too."

He shook his head while staring at the floor.

"I could at least try, like I'll try for your mother. I'll find a way to clean all four of you up."

"What, kill us four and leave our bodies for the wolves? That's the only way you could clean us."

"If I could get you pure for just one day, trick the magic into thinking—"

"It wouldn't work. She only made the deal with you because she knows your end of it is a no-win." He appraised my expression. "She's *my* mother, after all."

I poured all my effort into the anger removal spell, it being the perfect first step to purify the hearts of the four Moore brothers. Sage and cedar were the easy choices. I decided to add black cohosh root to expel the toxin of anger and a thick helping of catnip to lure Fearghus' cat who'd chase it all away. And the wording from three separate texts, combined to create the most lasting effect. Fearghus helped me dig roots and bundle the sage and cedar into smudge sticks. We boiled the black cohosh root then soaked the sticks in the brew, allowing them to dry in a patch of sunlight the following day.

I gave Rosemary a hand in her room while Fearghus attended his lessons.

"It's downright stiflin'," she said. "I need outta this house. There's a demonstration in D.C. in a couple days. Paulie says I can take a car. Please go with me, Sloane. Will ya?"

She raised Christian up to burp. I reached for him. "Let me."

His hair had come in thick but was still as white as the day he was born. He cooed at me, taking a grab at my necklace.

"We'll take our boys. You and me, Christian and Trey Fearghus. I'm sure I remember how to drive. We can stop and eat at a greasy spoon, buy candy bars at a gas station. I miss all that so much."

I set Christian on my leg, facing me, and bounced him. His lips were as pink as watermelon. "I can't—"

"Don't say cain't. Let's just do. A nice little trip, just us girls and our babies. Four more voices to end this war." She bit her bottom lip, like she knew she had me. It would break her heart if I turned her down without an explanation.

"I can't leave this house without Martin."

She put both hands on her hips. "Well why the hell not?"

I hadn't prepared for this. Our friendship had demanded so little explanation from me for all the strange little things she had to notice but let slide by that I'd grown complacent. I surely couldn't tell her the truth, but what would pass for the truth without having to lie to her?

She came to sit beside me, probably sensing my struggle.

"I'm not sure I can tell you."

"Try me. I can keep a secret."

"I know you can, it's just … knowing this type of thing might put a person in danger."

She stiffened a little at that and looked around the room as if checking for a threat. "Okay, well if you ever need an ear, I'm ready and able and a dang good listener. You sure you cain't go?"

I shook my head. And she let me off the hook once more with a look in her eyes so keen I almost wondered if someone else had told her why I really lived in that house.

Fearghus and I searched the top floor of the house for access to the attic. We sneaked against the walls, trying not to squeak old floorboards. I got the notion Fearghus had explored these unused parts of the house before when he led me to a door that opened into a dark hall and pointed at the ceiling. I couldn't reach the pull rope so he promptly got me a stool, and I tugged down a folding ladder. Like my armored knight, he insisted on ascending first. The attic was as dark and dusty as any would be, so we ducked around spiderwebs and pried open all the windows, giving the anger an easy way to flee.

"Would Friend like to help us?" I asked.

He went to a west-facing window and stuck his head out. It took a moment for him to locate his cat with whatever power he normally used, then he pulled back inside. "He's coming."

With Fearghus armed with one stick and me another, we lit them in the basement in the witching hour. We worked our way up through the house, smudging every closet, stairwell, and room except those that held sleeping people. Friend had brought two helpers, and they'd split up, streaking past in an occasional blur of ghostlike white, orange tabby, or reflective eyes that belonged to an all-black female who was otherwise invisible. Fearghus whispered the chant along with me. The flicker of fire danced on his face, serious and so intent on the task. I couldn't help but worry he expected too much of this smudging, that he'd wake in the morning and find the Moore family as cruel to him as they always were.

When I tucked him into bed, I took a breath to explain that a smudging can't change people. The ease on his face took my voice. I couldn't rob him of one night of hope. In the morning I'd explain that a smudging will remove a lingering bad presence, that the people might feel relieved of its burden and choose be good, but it wasn't a guarantee. For this night I let him rest in relief.

I returned to my bed, next to the man who'd taken a curse for me. We were imprisoned in the same house, both our escapes punishable by death. He should have let them curse me. At least then one of us could be free.

CHAPTER 41

ROSEMARY AND CHRISTIAN were gone the next day. She'd left a note on her bed: *Onward to D.C. to help end this war!* I rushed outside to Paul's carriage house to demand he send someone after her. She couldn't go there alone, with a baby and no one to help drive the car or carry luggage. He didn't answer the door, so I went inside into a heavy scent of eucalyptus. One whiff and I knew right where to look—under the corner of his mattress—for a note of his own: *Went with Rosemary. Shh.*

I tore it into a hundred pieces and flushed it down his toilet.

Pierce didn't seem the least bit flustered she'd left. Ruby badgered him to go after her, but he said if his wife wasn't going to stay put like he'd told her, then it suited her right to be on her own with a baby and no help. When he said he hoped she met trouble, Ruby smacked him with a wooden spoon and told him to leave her kitchen and not return until Rosemary was safe at home. He wouldn't have been so nonchalant if he knew Paul was with her.

I closed the attic windows while Fearghus was in training. The burned herbs had left a fragrance throughout the house. Fran had a team of maids searching for the source of the smell. I called them off one by one until I realized I should go to *their* source. I caught her in the kitchen, rosy-cheeked from the strain of trying to locate a strange odor that might upset the mistress.

"Fran, I burned some incense last night. If the mistress complains, I'll talk to her."

She leaned against the wall and wiped her brow. "Dear, please warn me next time. I've never been so puzzled. It's gone through the whole house."

Rosemary and the baby returned in the car first. Paul arrived a few days later by cab. I couldn't have been the only one who knew they'd been together. Pierce didn't say a word but he didn't need to. The hate lightened by our smudging reappeared in short time as a permanent fixture on his face, so Fearghus and I made two more smudge sticks. Our job had only begun.

"This house ain't as stiflin' as it was," Rosemary said one wintry night. "I think that little trip did me some good."

The fire in the library was our only light while she rocked Christian in the creaky wooden rocking chair. I'd put Fearghus to bed hours before. I hadn't yet pulled myself away from the warmth to climb a set of chilly stairs into a chilly bed. Martin was due home in two days.

"I need to get Pierce used to the idea of me leavin' more often. I need to go home and see my momma and daddy. Let them meet their baby grandson."

I'd forgotten all about her family in Tennessee. Not their existence, but their hold on her. She was so much like a sister to me, I'd assigned my forbidden contact of blood relations to her too. Her family was perfectly in reach.

"You should go. Make Pierce take you."

"Sloane, get over here and listen to this. Is there anything sweeter than a baby's snore?" Distracted by the bundle in her arms, her expression was one of pure rapture. "I'll stay put in this chair all night. I cain't put this angel down."

I got up from the hearth to look at him. His eyebrows were raised in his sleep, his jaw slack, with a dribble of milk at the corner of his mouth. "He's a good sleeper."

"He and Trey Fearghus are gonna be best friends. I cain't wait to see 'em swimmin' in that lake together. Can you imagine?" She touched the tip of his nose, making his eyebrows waggle. She lifted slightly to allow room for the pillow I was sliding under her arm. "Go on up. I'll be fine down here."

In the quiet in my room upstairs I had a realization that left me numb. If I was able to undo both the mistress' curse and Martin's and win our freedom, the unintended consequence would be a new curse placed on another person I loved. Rosemary would be left alone in that house with Paul as her only ally.

Rosemary did go home to visit her family, in a car, with a driver and a maid. She told me she couldn't shake the idea the driver was more of a guard, and I explained Pierce probably felt more comfortable knowing there was a man to protect her. She left it at that, thinking I'd misunderstood when I understood completely. The guard was there to make sure she didn't get any ideas to stay in Tennessee, not to make sure she was safe.

Fully knowing I had work to do, I dawdled all winter and into the beginning of spring. Since I had no starting point for Martin's curse, awaiting inspiration made sense. The cure for the mistress, however, was a simple reversal. I had no excuse for putting it off.

By the time spring warmed to summer temperatures, I made a new commitment to my task. I set a goal: the mistress would be cured by the autumnal equinox. Martin, Fearghus, and I would celebrate in the henge on the hill in the woods. Then we would start a new life somewhere far away.

Fearghus and I were working in our garden one day when Rosemary showed up with Christian on her hip, red-eyed and shaky. I dropped my hoe, told Fearghus to keep digging, and took her out of his earshot.

"What happened?"

She scrubbed at her eyes. "Nothin', nothin'. I just had to get out of there. Fresh air." She forced a smile, which made her look even more upset.

Christian pawed at her face. "Ma-ma-ma?"

"When did he start saying that?"

She took his hand and kissed it. "Just now, on our walk over here. I know, ain't it grand?"

He spotted Fearghus and groaned, throwing his weight toward the ground. She set him on his feet, holding him up by the hands so he could practice walking. He wobbled a few steps before she let his arms down so he could crawl. He plowed a furrow in the grass over to Fearghus.

"Tell me what happened."

She shook her head, wiping her eyes. "It sure made his fits in the past look like a picnic. Aw, Sloane, I'm in way over my head. I don't know what to do."

"I'll talk to Martin."

"No, that'll make it worse."

She and I had developed this roundabout way of talking about Pierce. The house had too many nooks in which a person could hover and overhear. With so much forest and the east end of the lake between us and the back patio, if we couldn't speak plainly now we could never hope to.

"He's a bully, Rosemary. Everything he says is designed to rattle you. Empty threats. He can't hurt you unless you let him."

"I know he cain't hurt me. But—" She cast a look at Christian, who now had Fearghus' hand shovel and was trying to dig a hole while Fearghus patiently corrected his technique.

"He wouldn't dare."

"And Paulie. He could go after Paulie, and he already has, many times."

"Paul's a grown man who can take care of himself. But if he's threatening the baby …" I could talk to the mistress. If anyone had the power to control Pierce without telling him Rosemary had talked, it was her. Maybe she wanted nothing to do with her sons, but she couldn't refuse to help her ten-month-old grandson.

"He's not, not really. I'm just—he gets this look in his eye. He's changed so much. He's not the same guy who'd visit me in Tennessee before we got married. He's gone so cold and I don't get why. It's so much work to be mean. Love, it takes nothin'. People oughtta understand that, but so many don't. We just need to love each other and there's never any mess. If everyone would just understand that, think how easy things'd be." She took a shaky inhale and ran a hand across her nose. "And I don't favor that third-floor bedroom. It's so lonely and quiet, and it's like somethin's watching me all the time, waitin' for me to … I don't know. How silly." She kicked off her sandals and sat in the grass, elbows on knees and chin on fists.

I knelt beside her puddle of sunset-colored skirt. "Tell Fran to have someone move you back downstairs."

"Pierce don't want me in that room behind the kitchen anymore."

"Then to the second floor with me. Tell them to fix up one of those vacant rooms. Fearghus!" The boys were throwing dirt at each other, cackling each time one of them got hit in the face.

She headed over to Christian and brushed him off. She stood with her back to Fearghus, who was glancing between her and his unused fistful of dirt. Just when I saw what he planned to do, I hollered his name again but it did no good. He flung the dirt right at Rosemary's back end. She stiffened, turned slowly around. Fearghus met her eye squarely without even a flinch. Leaning down, she appeared to be going to his level to unleash a reprimand, but instead reached past him for a handful of dirt of her own. Fearghus bolted away, getting a clump of damp garden soil right in the back of the neck.

There was bound to be a spell in my family's centuries of knowledge to subdue a bully. I'd consult my texts first. If I found nothing to help Rosemary, I'd go to the mistress.

It was my lack of haste that left the door open for a crime so heinous it blew a rift through the five years of solid ground I'd built in the Moore household. It left us trembling with a quake that never subsided—one we'd feel for the rest of our lives. A crime awful enough on its own made worse by the fact it would forever go unpunished by any authority deemed fit to deal out consequences.

Except for me.

A person's best days remain alive in memories, but not as vibrantly as they could. Bad days—tragic days—are etched in memory with breathtaking detail, enough to overload our voracious minds, our fragile emotion. The slant of sun came through the trees one week later in such a way I'll never forget. Memory has it displayed as a harsh, unblinking beam so direct that one touch could propel a person back to its source, a plunge into heat so fierce the human brain could never understand it.

Fearghus and I were gathering acorn shells for my first attempt at a spell to encourage Pierce to be a better husband when we felt the sound. Rather than enter our ears, it burst from the ground into our bones. Fearghus looked at me for the last time as an innocent child. The big eyes, the ripe fear, the plea for understanding—three things I'd never see again on my son's face. From that day on he understood everything in his own way, whether his way was right or wrong. Big eyes became narrowed eyes, and all fear was replaced with hot anger.

He dropped his bucket and ran first, acorn shells scattering at my feet. Despite my longer legs, I never caught up. He was too fast, like a deer in the forest, hopping logs and avoiding limbs as if they weren't there. What was ahead I didn't want him to see. I yelled at him to stop, but he pushed farther ahead, across the back lawn, past the garden, the patio, and around the corner of the house.

When I rounded the corner, he'd stopped. One glance of the scene—light entering the eye for a fraction of a second, a picture painted, an image in the brain. I grabbed Fearghus' shoulders to turn him around, to spare him, but he was unmovable, a granite pillar anchored six feet into the ground. I repeated his name, over and over. He took no notice. He was still looking, as I was, though I had turned away. I could still make out every detail.

Waves of blond splayed on cold concrete. Rainbow colors of skirt twisted around a crumple of legs. A wrist bent in a very wrong way. A miniature pond of blood. Enough.

Enough.

I stopped trying to turn Fearghus and stepped in front of him instead. A block. A wall. His gaze didn't falter. He could still see her. My dear, sweet friend. My sister. Fearghus' beloved aunt. His only friend.

One person ran past us, then another. A group was gathering. Cries, exclamations, more feet running back into the house to call for help that could not help us.

And a presence coming from the carriage house lawn, a raw, unstable ball of energy. His body appeared roused from sleep: barefoot, shirtless, wild-haired. A slow, careful walk. His face, though, was the opposite of sleep. A fierce, determined set to his jaw, fists clenched tight enough to affect every muscle in shoulder, arm, and neck. His gaze planted on the ground where she lay; he was on the verge of war. He was the first to go near her, to kneel beside her. Everyone knew to give him the first touch. He straightened her neck, pressed her eyelids closed. Untwisted her legs, smoothed out her wrist. The blood pooled under his knees as he picked her up from the concrete, cradling her shoulders as he pressed his cheek against her forehead.

Sirens wailed on the road, up the driveway. As they cut off we heard another siren coming from the house, this one from a tiny body now left without a mother.

Fearghus broke into a run and leaped into the magnolia next to the house, snapping branches as he reached for stronger ones. He pushed from the tree and caught the downspout, took a grab of the second-floor balcony. I ran for the back kitchen door and collided with Martin.

"Find Pierce," I said, grabbing his sleeve as he made for outside. "No. Upstairs."

He followed me up three mountainous flights of stairs and down an unending hallway, into a room where a baby cried and a devil lounged on a sofa.

"It was too much for her," the devil said.

"What?" Martin said, eyeing him.

Outside on the balcony stood Fearghus, chest heaving, arms tight at his sides. Martin opened the door. "Go back down the way you came up."

Fearghus pushed past him into the room, and Martin went to the balcony railing to look down. When he turned around, his face had gone utterly neutral.

"Motherhood," Pierce said. "I tried to stop her from doing it. She scratched me, see?" He lowered his collar, displaying four long red marks.

Fearghus had already climbed into Christian's crib and picked him up, holding him under the arms like a big teddy bear. Seeing Fearghus had no way out of the crib with his load, I was riled from paralyzed shock into action. I took the baby; Fearghus climbed out. I followed him downstairs to my room and sat on the sofa, the baby on my lap, Fearghus facing me stoically like a soldier awaiting orders. Baby Christian's bewildered face stared up at me. The quake was vibrating low inside me, rising now, given freedom in the safety of my room. I shuddered under dry sobs.

"It's okay, *a Mháthair*, you can cry."

The imagery was too harshly detailed to process; Fearghus crumpled on our front porch, Rosemary broken on the concrete. I'd been thrust into the sun, the heat too fierce to handle.

"It's not okay, *a chroí*. It will never be okay." My eyes filled. There was nowhere for all the tears to go.

"It will," he insisted. "Because someday I'll kill that man."

In that moment, looking into his stone eyes, I believed him.

Martin took Pierce away, to where I didn't know. I did know now that Martin had a time limit away from the estate, and when he returned he was alone. Pierce wouldn't witness his son crying for three months straight, not that this would affect him at all. A man who killed a baby's mother wasn't capable of pitying that now motherless child. Fearghus, Eleanor, and I took turns trying to distract Christian from the gaping hole in his small world. Martin moved to his third-floor bedroom at night; there was no way to sleep in a bed with a baby who whimpered all night long. I used those hours when the rest of the house slept to research a fitting effect for Pierce Moore, not borne of vengeance, but necessity. I had to ensure no woman would ever fall for that monster again. With Christian moaning softly against my chest, I scoured my texts, collected ingredients, and planned.

Paul was unreachable behind a locked door and drawn shades no matter how long I knocked and pleaded. One lamp glowed in one window day and night. I wasn't even sure he was in there. I wasn't sure he was alive.

Rosemary's body had been returned to her family in Tennessee with a large sum of money affected by a Moore spell to help them keep quiet, but our family death ceremony awaited the return of her widower and killer. Martin left again and returned a second time without Pierce. He needed a dose of being on Moore land to keep the curse on him appeased.

I couldn't live with what I'd overlooked: the things she'd said, the little clues, that last conversation. Hindsight was the blueprint of my nightmares.

It was Fearghus' idea a month later that we stop being sad, that we start making Christian laugh like we used to. Like Rosemary would have. I took Fearghus and Christian to the oak henge, and we purged our sadness. We unloaded our regret: the clues I'd missed, the spell I'd delayed, my carelessness that lulled me into not cutting my amulet from the string around Fearghus' neck and forcing Rosemary to wear it. We cried it all out, into the ground, tears into earth where new life would grow. Two of us did, that is. Fearghus refused to cry.

We explored the other two trails. One led to a cluster of old stone buildings, a few houses, stables, and some crumbling outhouses. They appeared to be the original homes on the land, and I wondered if the Moores had built them, or someone else. Standing among those antique dwellings, Fearghus looked into the woods and said, "You should be my mother and his mother too."

Too consumed by grief to speak, I squeezed his shoulder in reply.

I followed him into one of the old buildings. Sunlight slanted through the cloudy window pane, lighting a dark patch on the broken tile floor that looked like a puddle of blood. A heavy chain sat near the wall like a dead snake. Fearghus knocked the lid off a bucket sitting by the doorway and dipped a finger in. It came out covered in tar.

"Put the lid back on that, now," I said. Tar had been used to persecute my people in less civilized times. Whenever the street crew would tar our street at home, Mam would burn every candle we owned to mask the smell coming into the house.

Fearghus was still peering into the bucket, so I put the lid on and steered him out the door. As we walked away from the cluster of buildings, I felt a stirring of something drawing me back. Fearghus stopped. He felt it too. I took his hand and tugged him away with him glancing over his shoulder until those buildings were out of sight.

The other trail dropped us into a clearing that held a stone altar, where we gathered two weeks later clad in burgundy cloaks to surrender our hold on Rosemary and release her into the elements. Moores had come from all around. Some I recognized, and many I didn't. The stone altar held only the white sheet without her body underneath.

Pierce had returned. I wanted to glare at him as deeply as Fearghus, but I had a role to play. The salve I'd prepared already soaking my palm, I left Fearghus with Martin and walked to the front with Christian on my hip. I took Pierce's hand, a gesture seen as comfort working undercover to mark this man with a blemish only women could sense to ensure no other woman would ever choose him as a mate. I held his big, evil hand long enough for the salve to warm and soak into him. It was eons longer than I could stomach, but for Rosemary I'd do it. For future Rosemarys I'd stand there forever.

The master was the one to light the sheet on fire as was custom without a body to bury. Into the air her spirit flew. Into Pierce's palm my magic soaked.

Christian buried his face in my neck, repeating his chant of the only word he knew, the one he'd learned just in time to make me certain of how well his child's mind understood the depth of his loss. There was no way to placate. All I could do was soothe until time could do its healing work.

"Shut him up," Pierce said.

He didn't look at me, so I didn't look at him and kept my grip on his ugly hand, my anger igniting that spell with a fire hotter than the one we watched. Christian quieted; he was old enough to understand the threat in that voice. And I made a silent pledge to that child to keep him safe from that man until the day I died.

When the fire dwindled I peeled my hand from Pierce's and turned, confronting a sea of burgundy cloaks when the familiarity of the ceremony had tricked me into expecting my own family's soothing brown. I choked back tears, putting a hand to my mouth as my eyes burned. A hundred Moores watched me, shoulder to shoulder in the clearing under a twilight sky. I glanced into the woods beside us to seek a more comforting escape. A single burgundy figure stood in the shadow of the trees' canopy. The hood covered most of her face, but a yellow tip of scarf peeked out from a sleeve. She'd left the sanctuary of her room to honor Rosemary, and I couldn't invade her peaceful space.

I faced forward and walked through the crowd. Beyond the cluster of people stood Paul, hanging far behind the last row of bodies like he couldn't trust himself to go closer. The relief to see him alive was a nauseating jab into my grief for Rosemary. When I stopped beside Martin he nudged Fearghus on the shoulder to follow me. Paul watched us approach with an expression so hatefully heated I shifted Christian to my other hip and took Fearghus' hand with my clean one. But I couldn't pass him by, not the old Paul, or the new Paul, and certainly not Rosemary's Paul, so I hesitated and looked at him with an offer of welcome. He could join us and leave this gathering, it said. *Come away with us.* He shook his head and raised his hood to shadow his face, but I saw the look he aimed at that crowd when he turned from me, and it hastened my steps away.

CHAPTER 42

I STUDIED EVERY CURSE in my texts. My fantasies of using them were my only solace. I wanted to affect Pierce with a slow, painful death. A lifetime of falls from a third-story balcony, one new bone broken each time until he was a crumpled sack of skin and bone fragment. Curses used in vengeance were likely to infect the caster, though, and I would never give Pierce that pleasure even in secret.

The house remained bloated with visiting Moores for weeks, and the voices and commotion left me with a homesickness as strong as the day I'd arrived there. I carried Christian everywhere to keep him out of enemy hands, and also because he refused to be put down. Fran said he'd never learn to walk, and I said that was fine as long as he was calm. We spent our days outside or in the kitchen, the safest place least frequented by Pierce. Or Paul, whose gloom was infectious and frightening and very much unwanted.

Christian was secured on my back one day, 'like Sacagawea's babe,' Ruby said, so my hands could be free to help her wash dishes.

"Care to tell me why my son is always sucking on a rag?" Pierce had come in unnoticed due to the running water and our backs turned to the room.

"Outta my kitchen," Ruby said.

He wasn't swayed by Ruby's suggestion, so I answered his question. "Because he was weaned too soon and he misses his mother."

"Ridiculous." He ripped the rag from Christian's mouth.

Christian cried out. I reached back to stroke his cheek, and Ruby went for her wooden spoon. "Out!"

On days like those, the curse fantasies didn't seem like enough. Pierce seemed to be riling me into a battle of wills each time we met. The real battle was against my temptation to fight him, for if I lost that, my already won victory would be forfeited.

In the heat of May while Fearghus, Christian, and I gathered peas from our garden, I discovered the reason for my newfound homesickness. I could never cure the mistress of her curse. Curing her would require purifying Pierce, and if it wasn't obvious enough what a futile task it was, it was more plain that I'd never do a thing to grant that man the happiness that swelled from a pure heart. Not even a day of it. I'd spend my time and magic on cursing him to protect others, but never would I clean his heart.

My family had done well to make sure Órlaith Moore's curse would go uncured. Fearghus and I would be prisoners in that house forever.

All my plans had lifted away. No need to make Pierce a better husband, or to purify the Moore brothers and relieve the mistress of her curse. No reason to unbind Martin from the house. I was lost, my powers stripped, made useless. Too broken to look for another way to help the mistress, I gave up. Too ashamed to tell her, I returned to my bedroom one morning to ask Martin to tell her for me.

Martin was in the bathroom at the mirror, the door standing ajar. Fearghus waited for him, restless. I walked Christian to the window to watch the birds bathing in the dirt of my pots. He started his *ma-ma-ma* chant, so I bounced him, blabbing mercilessly about those birds. Fearghus climbed onto the bed and started jumping. Martin came through the bathroom door, his face half-covered in shaving cream.

"Trey, off the bed."

Fearghus flopped onto his back as my bouncing went still. That vision I'd had so long ago had finally been given life. The baby I was holding, thought to be mine when the vision struck, was not mine but had become mine by some awful tragedy. Born on the summer solstice, the fifth anniversary of my imprisonment in the Moore estate, he was my reason to stay. Abandoning those spells I'd planned to win our freedom was not a surrender, but a renewed commitment to stay. To fight.

Christian did learn to walk and talk and become the friend Fearghus never had. Their brotherhood ran through their rival blood thicker than if they'd been true brothers. Five years of age didn't distance them, their loyalty an unbeatable opponent to the politics in the house. The external strain on their relationship created a stronger bond between them. I couldn't claim any role in bringing them together. They did it themselves.

Since Martin made the laws in the house, he had Christian's crib moved into our room, and he moved back in himself once I taught Christian how to sleep again. Fearghus came from his room next door to wake Christian in the morning and tuck him in at night, except for the one night he missed training and didn't show up for dinner. Martin released some men and dogs to search the woods, and I took Christian upstairs for bed and tried not to worry about the freeze of February and my always coatless child, who claimed he couldn't feel the cold. The lake was frozen solid. It had already been checked for holes near the bank.

"Where Tey?"

"He's missing, but your uncle will find him. Now, where's Fuzzy?"

"Fuzzy wi' Tey?"

I located the one-eyed bear under the bed and handed it to Christian. "Fuzzy's here. Lie down and I'll get your blanket."

He wobbled to the corner of the crib closest to the windows and strained to see out. Children his age didn't understand changes in routine, and I could see that settling him for bed wasn't going to happen until Fearghus came to say goodnight. I put on my warmest housecoat and slippers and took Christian out on the balcony wrapped in a blanket. Beams from the men's flashlights shot around in the nearby woods; the dogs' yips carried across the lawn.

"See the lights? Your uncle is going to get him. He walked far away, and he won't be back until you go to sleep. Now it's time for bed, so you'll have to see him in the morning."

He let me put him back in his crib and cover him up, but as soon as the light went off I heard the blankets shift and his uncoordinated footsteps over to the corner of the crib. I moved to my sitting room to read. The pages couldn't keep my attention, not with Fearghus missing on such a cold night. It was my fault; I should've punished him the times he'd wandered off on warmer days. He always had a reason. Checking on his garden. Following a rabbit. Looking for the moon. With so little to hurt him outside and so much threat in the house, those reasons sounded logical to me at the time. It was hard to punish him for wanting to venture outdoors. Once Martin found him, he'd probably punish him enough to cover all those times.

Christian still shuffled around in his crib. So my light wouldn't encourage him to stay awake, I turned off the sitting room lamp and went into Fearghus' room just in time to see a cluster of those flashlight beams crossing the lawn together. As they neared the house, I saw Martin in front, carrying something long-limbed and limp.

I ran down the hall and met them coming up the stairs.

The blood on Fearghus' face yanked me back to the day I found his father on our porch. I fell back against the wall, images from the past overlaid with the image I saw now: Martin reaching the top of the stairs, carrying a drooping, bloody little boy.

"He's okay," Martin said, passing me. "Just a nosebleed, I think."

Martin laid Fearghus in his bed and dismissed the two men who'd accompanied him. I sat next to Fearghus, who was breathing shallowly and covering his eyes with his arms. I needed to see what was bleeding. I moved one arm away, then the other. Fearghus groaned as if in pain, turning onto his belly on the bed and covering his head. "Ó *mo cheann, mo cheann.*"

Martin had shut the door and was now standing beside us. "He's chilled. We need to get him warmed up."

"Why's he complaining about his head?" I asked.

"This happened before. Do you remember? He was a baby."

"*What* happened? Where did you find him?"

"In one of the old stone buildings on the northeast end of the property. He was disoriented."

"From a nosebleed?"

"From the lunar eclipse."

Yes—tonight's eclipse. Martin and I had planned to go to the oak henge after the boys were in bed, but then Fearghus went missing and—

"Remember? He cried for hours and you brought him outside so we could see the lunar eclipse that night, that first year you were here. His ears bled. We called the doctor."

"And then he was fine."

"Yes, because the eclipse ended."

Fearghus tossed on the bed, begging us to stop talking. I sent Martin for some towels and got Fearghus free of his damp clothes and under the covers. He refused to be propped by pillows to ease the nosebleed; something about the angle made his head worse. So I got in bed to cradle him, blotting his face with a towel late into the night and into the early morning when his moans finally turned to soft snores and he fell into an exhausted sleep. With the bleeding stopped and his color returned, he looked like his normal self. I closed myself out of his room and went into mine.

Martin came inside from the balcony when he saw me, closing the door with minimal sound so he didn't wake Christian. "It just ended. Let me guess … he's fine now."

"He is. But how did you know it was the eclipse?"

"I didn't. It's a hunch that came to me when I was carrying him back. That night … I remember that night. And it's just too similar. He was too little to tell us about the pain in his head."

"So, every lunar eclipse …"

"I suppose we'll see, won't we?" He took me by the shoulders. "But here's the thing. If I'm right, then it has to stay between you and me. A vulnerability like this could be exploited. If anyone in my family finds out … well, it won't matter what you and I teach him. He can't protect himself when he's like this. Not with anything."

I pulled away from him to undress. "I want to know why. Mam—"

"You can't even tell your mam. If it leaves this room, my family will find out." He pulled the covers down on the bed and waited for me.

But I couldn't go to him. Maybe it was because I'd been up all night caring for a miserable child, but the scene around me had just become surreal. The mixed-up life I was living crashed down on me like one of my visions—

present colliding with future, dream colliding with reality. There was no way to tell which was which. So I stood there in my slip and let the raw panic overtake me.

"*A mhuirnín?*"

I stared at the man calling me 'darling,' the man who should hate my son but instead seemed to love him as much as I did. I trusted him more with this new secret than I trusted myself. Six years was not enough time for a person to adjust to an opposite world. The steps along the way—the little truths, one at a time—had gotten me to this place where I could see. I'd found an overlook, an unimpeded view. The original world and the opposite world were merged into one, each side as true as the other, each a part of my existence.

Only that day dawns to which we are awake. There is more day to dawn. The sun is but a morning star.

He came to me and put an arm around my shoulders to lead me to bed. He took the pins out of my hair, set them on his bedside table. And then he drew the covers over us and folded himself around me like we were made to fit that way, two complementary shapes that made one perfect whole.

Enclosing my hand in his, he kissed the back of my neck softly, the strength of his body tight behind me. "As tired as I am, your smell is all it takes to wake me up."

I reached back to find his rough cheek. When my hand made contact, he strengthened his grip around me. All the good he'd given me had absolved him from the bad, had banished the cruel man and created the one I loved. I turned my face to kiss him and felt him rouse against me.

We tumbled in the sheets as that morning star rose, my eyes ready and willing to take in all they could see.

"Trey needs to stay out of those old buildings," Martin told me over our late breakfast the next day. "And so do you."

It was the tone of voice he knew I didn't like. I wasn't one of his men to be ordered around. "We'll go where we please, thank you."

He set his coffee cup down. "No, you won't. Not there."

Again with that tone. Other women might let their husbands speak to them like that, but not me. Nor was I about to walk into the argument he'd so clearly laid at my feet. I set my napkin on the table and left the room.

I went upstairs to check on Fearghus and found him awake at last. I lay in bed next to him. "Are you feeling better?"

He didn't answer right away. His face had a pensive look, like he was trying to piece together the events of the night. "I don't like to get lost."

"Of course not. But you were sick, and I don't think you could help it." I knew my son wasn't like most children who don't like getting lost out of fear of being alone and away from their family. He loved being alone, lost in the woods, on his own. What he didn't like was failing at the challenge of finding his own way. It wasn't something he ever failed at, not in the woods, anyway.

Friend got up from the spot behind Fearghus' legs and walked up his body. Fearghus turned onto his back so Friend could lie on his chest. "I found a man out there, but I think he was pretend."

"It was probably your father, or one of the men who was helping him search for you. You were very sick when they found you."

He stayed pensive and quiet, stroking Friend like the act of it helped him think. I could see last night's blood caked in his hair and smeared on his neck.

"Let's get you cleaned up and fed, and you'll feel much better."

Eleanor brought Christian up for a nap while Fearghus was still in the tub. I left her in charge of both of them to do my daily check of Paul, to make sure he hadn't killed himself overnight. With it being nearly noon, I was feeling the pressure of the clock. In books and movies, tragedy always struck on the days when routine broke. I'm not sure if Paul overdosing would be considered a tragedy, though. Every day it looked to be more inevitable.

Martin caught me at the foot of the stairs. "I need to talk to you."

"Not right now. I'm—"

"Yes, right now." He took me by the arm into the parlor and shut the doors on both sides.

I stood and fumed, rubbing my arm where he'd gripped it. He was determined to get an argument out of me. It wasn't going to work if I didn't speak.

"Those buildings…" he paused to look at where I was rubbing my arm "…you and Trey need to stay away from them and I'll tell you why. If I don't, you'll get it out of Paul, and then—" He came over to put a hand on my arm where he'd hurt it, his grip now a warm and gentle apology. "I don't know my own strength sometimes."

"It's fine."

He glanced away as if reassembling his thoughts. "Can you just trust that I have a good reason for wanting you and Trey to stay out of those buildings?" He studied my face, not liking the answer he saw. "So I have to break your heart again? I've done it enough already. I'd like to avoid it, if you'll let me."

I remembered what Fearghus and I had seen in there: the bucket of tar, the chain, the stained floor. And the unsettling feeling all around that made me pull Fearghus away from that place. Rosemary's death had the sharp sting of a fresh wound that day. We were both in pain from her loss and a bit on edge. But if what Martin had to say about those buildings was going to break my heart, perhaps our intuition had some power to tear through all that grief.

"We keep prisoners in those buildings. Not often. But if we need information out of someone who's not cooperating that's where they go."

He was right about breaking my heart. "You kept Fearghus in there."

"Yes."

"You killed him in there."

"They killed him in the street in front of your house. But he was not in good shape when he was kept there, and it's not a place for you and Trey."

I sat down weakly on the sofa. Grief never left, no matter how much time passed, no matter how many tears were shed. It was always on standby, waiting to be called upon like the most dedicated laborer.

Martin sat next to me. "There's no end to it. You'd think there'd be no more things like this left to tell you, but there's always one more."

"I'll tell Fearghus to stay away from those buildings."

"Thank you." He reached to stroke my cheek.

I turned my face away and got up, my back to him. I had nothing to say to him. He must've sensed that because he let me go without any further discussion. I was glad he didn't ask me to forgive him. I wouldn't do it.

477

CHAPTER 43

P AUL'S CARRIAGE HOUSE had grown its nightly crop of empty liquor bottles. I saw no evidence of dope, but he was slobbering high, as incoherent as ever. I sat helplessly on his bed while he mumbled at the ceiling. He'd been okay for a week. Now this. It was his new pattern.

I loudly cleaned the room, tossing glass bottles into a trash can with a deafening crash. I shoved furniture back into place, stripped his bed, and did his dishes. By the time I was done, he'd sobered up enough to notice I was there. I took out his dirty sheets and returned with clean ones and made the bed under his fixed lifeless gaze.

"You're the only one," he said.

It was what he said a lot lately. I was the only one who cared.

"I am. Because they're all incapable, and you don't care about yourself. And that's a damn shame, Paul."

"I miss her so much."

The unexpectedness of it choked me up so badly I had to turn away to compose myself.

"You shouldn't have erased her memory that night."

"I never erased her memory."

"You did. That night she fell asleep here, and you made me take her back to Pierce's room."

I had to summon the memory of that night to realize he was right, in a way. I hadn't erased her memory, but I'd overwritten it with a new one.

"I finally had her convinced to leave. I was going to help her get a new name and a new place somewhere Pierce would never find her. She could've saved herself."

"I'm not doing this, Paul. You're stoned. You—"

He stood with a burst of energy and backed me against the wall. "I'm not making it up."

"Get away from me. I'm not talking to you until you're sober."

He punched the wall inches from my face. I didn't move away, just stared at him until he dropped to his knees and hugged my legs, apologizing and begging forgiveness in Irish. All it did was further my anger. I was no longer accepting apologies from a man who continued to attack me.

When he fell away from me, to his hands and knees, I was so mad at his weakness, his abuse, his total disregard for my love for him that I took a fistful of his shirt and towed him out the door. Still groveling, he didn't resist. I released his shirt and he continued to follow, coatless and barefoot on a winter day. The sun was warm, but frost still clung to the shadows.

I knew he realized I was taking him to the henge when he hung back, so I backed up and took him by the shirt again and dragged him all the way there. I knelt before the sacred stone. After a harsh look from me, so did he. We entered the center of the henge where I put my hands on his shoulders and pushed him to his knees.

"Release her."

He took a shuddering breath and held it.

"You want me to erase your memory too?" I asked. "Release her so I don't have to."

"You wouldn't."

"I'll do that before I watch you kill yourself."

A snowflake twirled down between us. He watched it land before turning bloodshot eyes back to me. "She was the only person—"

"Release her."

Snow was now falling all around, a puzzlement to my senses that so much motion could be completely silent. The cold encompassed me, sharp in my lungs and nipping my fingers and toes. I placed my palms against the ground and looked up at Paul, wondering if he could do what I was about to ask. "Warm. Count of three."

He mimicked my position without a moment's thought and counted with me. Warmth bloomed in the ground below us. He took my face in his hands. I stiffened, expecting a kiss I didn't want, but he drew my forehead against his. I was pulled outside of myself, then back inside something not of me but so familiar I grabbed him and clung on.

Grief due to violent loss. Paralyzing heartache. Leaden sadness. A biting fury that would never be quelled.

He tore me away and I was back in my own head, awash in my own mix of anguish so alike his.

I will not cry.

And I broke that damn rule, clinging to Paul in the falling snow as we both released someone who'd been ripped away from us by the Moores. A woman who never belonged to Paul, but should have. And a man who'd always belong to me—a man I'd thought I'd already released. I'd been so very wrong.

Paul got so sick from sharing his mind without a spell to ease the barrier that he was unable to drink or do any drugs. He was clean for three weeks.

It was a hopeful three weeks. But it was only three weeks.

When he returned to his routine it was more recreational than suicidal, and I eased up a bit knowing our day in the henge had healed as much of him as it had of me. Rosemary's death had not just given me new wounds, it had opened old scars that hadn't healed properly the first time. I couldn't decide if I was glad that Paul had made me aware of this, or angry with him.

The spring brought more hope when Paul showed up one day to help me, Fearghus, and Christian in our garden. Not getting stoned during the day was a big step forward, and

I gave him all the laborious tasks in an effort to wear him out enough that a shower and comfortable bed sounded more appealing than a hit of LSD.

The master was holding an extravagant May Day gathering, and the house was bursting with guests—family, extended family, and a wild gang of children running free at all hours. Fearghus had stopped making an attempt to be included, and Christian had all the friend he needed in Fearghus.

"I'm going to build a tent and move out here until everyone leaves," Paul said, leaning on his shovel. "My carriage house isn't far enough away from all of them."

I handed Christian a pack of seeds. His hair had gone blond on his crown, but it was still white at his temples where the baby hair still grew. He concentrated as he picked a seed loose from the packet. Instead of dropping it in the hole in the soil, he tried to eat it, and Fearghus laughed so hard he had to put his hands on the ground to keep from toppling over. Christian had learned the concept of an audience, and he used every opportunity to be goofy until someone laughed.

Their silliness lasted until bedtime, and I had to shoo Fearghus out of Christian's new room on the other side of the house so I could get him calm enough to stay in bed. I didn't like him rooming next to Pierce, but Martin had no way to fix it. Martin didn't know how often I found Christian curled in a ball with his blanket on the rug next to my bed. I usually woke in the night to find him and returned him to his room where I'd lay with him until he fell back asleep. Two long dark halls and a flight of stairs were quite a trek for a groggy two-year-old in the middle of the night, but I knew pushing the issue could jeopardize the time I already spent with him. Pierce could take it all away at any time.

Fearghus was reading a book when I reached his room. I made him scrub his fingernails and tidy his room, then I tucked him in and sat on the edge of his bed. Friend found his spot behind Fearghus' knees. I smoothed the furrow between my brooding son's eyes. "What's the matter?"

"That kid—Jared. He told me he has a baby brother."

"Oh? That's nice. What's his name?"

"Dillon."

"Maybe we can meet him tomorrow. Christian might like that, to meet a baby."

"No, he's not here. Jared said the baby and his mom can't come here anymore. They don't want that baby around me." He reached to stroke Friend.

"That's—" I couldn't think of a word that was appropriate for a child's ears.

"What's so bad about me?"

"Nothing's bad about you. People just like to keep babies home when they're little so they don't catch germs from other kids."

"He said it was me. Just me."

"He's playing a trick on you. Don't listen to him. Now, if Paul helps us again tomorrow we'll have two more rows put in. Think of what you'd like to plant. We don't have a lot to choose from since it's already May."

He turned over, away from me. I kissed his temple.

"Sweet dreams, *a chroí*. I love you. Your father loves you, and Christian loves you. And that's all that matters."

"And Friend loves me."

"He does. And every woodland creature out there. You're a very lucky boy, do you know that?"

I shut myself out of his room wishing I could tell him he had another whole family who loved him. All I could do was pass their love for him through my own and hope someday he could see that mass of people with his own eyes. I had to keep the Moores' hate and corruption from penetrating him until that day.

In my bathroom I turned on the faucet to fill the sink with water. The mirror fractured, the pieces turning white, and I entered a vision more vivid than all the others, with sound and touch and a firm footing on the concrete sidewalk in the city I once called home.

A woman with a baby on her hip walked toward me. I took a step that would impede her path, and she slowed, tilting her head as if she knew me but couldn't remember how. It was my doing, I knew. A simple effect to get her to stop. And she did, her blue eyes full of questions I headed off with a consolation for what would come. *You're a good mother. Accept no blame for the things you can't control.* I leaned in to kiss the baby's forehead to seal the spell. I knew this baby, knew she bore my name. I said to her, "*Faigh suaimhneas trí chodladh. Go gcumhdaí an chré thú go nglaofaidh muid aríst ort.*" I drew away, slipping off a tiny sock and hiding it in my fist. The woman tightened her hold on her daughter. A hint of worry crossed her face, making her so familiar it touched a memory that tugged me back into my bathroom with the running faucet and my own wild eyes in the mirror.

That woman, now in two visions. Sitting next to me on my sofa in one, walking down a Chicago street in another.

It wasn't the encounter of the same woman that had me rattled but what I'd said to her daughter. *Find peace with sleep. May the earth protect you until we call for you again.* Along with those words was my taking of her sock—a safeguard, a token tied to that baby so she'd know where to return.

The sink was nearing overflow, so I twisted the faucet off and splashed my face, shuddering under the cold water and the assignment of yet another duty. I was weighted by too many roles that were so often in conflict.

I undressed down to my slip and went onto the balcony. The sun had set but my western sky hadn't yet darkened to night. Orange mixed with indigo beyond the silhouette of my oak tree. A cool breeze swirled with air rising from warmed earth below. Strong hands took hold of my hips, a warm mouth settled on my neck like the breeze. "*A mhuirnín.*"

I turned around and hugged him, my cheek hard against his chest. It took him a moment to return the embrace— just long enough for me to regret my weakness, my need for him. But then his arms tightened around me, and his head bowed against mine with such tenderness it made that regret look like the mistake it was.

"What's the matter?"

"The world asks too much of me."

He pulled away to look at my face. "The world knows who's strong enough to take it."

"Well, I'm not."

His reply was a slow, sweet kiss—the kind that made me sink against him.

"I came up here for a break from socializing, but now I see I should stay."

"You should go back down. They'll wonder."

"Let them. *They* ask too much of *me*, and I just decided I'm playing hooky tonight. Are Trey and Christian in bed?"

I nodded, knowing Christian wouldn't be in bed for long. Once the quiet of night settled on the house, he'd be heading to the rug beside my bed. I went inside and locked the door to the hall and the door to Fearghus' room. Martin was loosening his tie when I returned. I stopped in the middle of the room, tempted to tell him about the vision, but I didn't want to relive it. I didn't want to think any more about how someday I'd have to put a death spell on another woman's baby. I just wanted to be taken away.

He came to me, still struggling with his tie. I went for the buttons on his shirt; he dropped the tie to the floor then he went for his belt. The effort against his clothes postponed the second kiss I needed, the feel of skin upon skin I craved. It added urgency to an already urgent matter, and when the oxford and slacks were finally discarded, we joined roughly instead of tenderly like we'd begun.

"Do you want to slow down?" he said, backing me against the bed.

I answered with a hard kiss, my teeth nipping his lip in an accident that had him taking my hips and tugging me against his pelvis. "*A bhean*, you do that and—"

I did it again. He sucked in a breath and backed off. "Sorry."

"Don't be. It's just—if you do that I won't last."

"You don't have to last."

He raised an eyebrow. I wiggled out of my slip. He stripped off his undershirt and shorts and melded with me. Our haste brought us crashing against the side of the bed. He got a knee onto the mattress and dragged me up with him, our hands too busy on each other to brace the fall onto the pillows that made his mouth yet even harder on mine. He pulled back briefly as if to check me for damage. I wrapped my legs around his hips. He gave me one gentle kiss before he rooted himself inside me, banishing the world long enough for me to be taken away.

In my dreams I held that baby's sock in my hand, and I knew to whom it belonged. I woke in the night, knowing the place where that baby should be tied. Someday I must give that sock to Fearghus.

CHAPTER 44

THE HOUSE WAS chaotic the next day with luggage thumping down the stairs and cars pulling up front and all the guests saying their goodbyes. Christian was extra clingy. When he wasn't on my hip, he was anchored to my skirt, and every time I pried his little hand free it found a new spot to hold on. I took him in the kitchen, sat him on the counter, and gave him a cup of dry cereal. Picking the pieces out of a cup occupied him long enough to forget what was bothering him until something walked in the room that bothered us both.

"Fearghus, what on earth?!"

I snatched a towel from the counter and held it against Fearghus' mouth. The blood was coming strong and fast, and I wasn't sure where from, so I steered him into direct light and peeked under the towel.

"It's my lip," he slurred. The detachment in his eyes gave me a chill worse than the sight of a bloody lip. Most children would be crying after such a wound. He wasn't just calm, he was preoccupied.

"It's your cheek too, up here." I put pressure on his cheekbone with one hand and his upper lip with the other. Christian slid off the counter and put one little hand over mine. "Fearghus, what happened?"

He was looking through me. I got an absurd notion the child had lost the ability to feel pain. I took another look under the towel. Two gashes, long and deep and still very much bleeding; one across his cheekbone, the other cutting into his lip. They lined up as if they were two parts of the same slice, like whatever had cut him had eased up in the middle of its work.

I returned pressure. "You're going to need stitches. Put your hand up here and press hard. I'm going to find someone who can call the doctor."

I exchanged my hand for his.

"Jared cut me with a piece of glass."

His steady manner deepened my chill. Lacking the anger and hurt that should've been combined with such a wound, his words felt expectant and ominous. They were more than an answer to my question—they were a motive. He was far away from me, possessed by something that wasn't my son.

Exactly one year later I was in the kitchen nursing Christian's wounds from Jared—a busted lip from being shoved to the ground. Three years old was too young for anything but accidental bumps and scrapes. No amount of time in the Moore household could change my mind on that.

Christian was grinning despite his mottled red cheeks from crying. The quicker he could let go of anger, the quicker he could go back to being goofy. When I checked his teeth, he pretended to bite me.

"Has my Christian turned into a wolf? Look, Fearghus, at what big teeth your cousin has."

Fearghus was watching the lawn through the glass door. "He'll have to come back. And when he does, I'm going to smash his hands with a rock."

"Oh, Lord," Ruby said from the stove.

"You'll stay away from him or you'll spend the rest of the day in your room."

Fearghus had a scar from Jared's piece of glass one year ago. The Moores had put their stamp on him in a way I could see every time I looked at him. Jared was now targeting Christian, it seemed. Christian had been joining Fearghus in their training in the basement, but a sweet three-year-old was still easier prey than my son after a growth spurt that started and hadn't yet ended. At almost eight years old he would soon be as tall as me.

"He needs to bring his little brother next time so I can beat him up like he beats up Christian."

"Fearghus, if I were you I'd not even think—"

"There he is." Fearghus yanked open the door and ran.

Ruby grabbed her wooden spoon, but I told her to stay, fearing I'd need something a little more powerful than that spoon, and I couldn't use it with her there. Fearghus already had a hold on Jared's collar and was landing short jabs into his nose. Jared sent an elbow into Fearghus' ribs and I set the grass on fire below them.

They burst apart, falling onto their backs. I walked onto the singed grass between them. The smoke was thick and earthy, alive with the static of spent magic. Jared spit. His nose was bloody but not running badly enough to need help. Fearghus got up first.

"To your room," I said.

He spent the rest of the afternoon in his room and the entirety of dinner that night glaring at Jared. Patrick took Jared home a few days later, but it didn't subdue the expectant look in Fearghus' eye. He no longer responded to my peaceful outlets to stress. Tending our garden was a relief, but not a lasting one. Chasing Christian around brought a grin but not a smile. When the fireflies came out later that summer, Fearghus taught Christian how to summon them into a jar. Upon their release Christian screamed with the abandon of his mother, and I had to turn against Martin's shoulder to soothe the heartbreak of her missing this moment.

Martin hissed instead of putting an arm around me. I'd spilled my evening tea down the front of him.

"It's okay," he said, grimacing. "I'll take on a mug of boiling water for you."

I set down my mug and started toward the door for a towel, but he swung me against the wet mess. Pressed against him, my blouse absorbed the tea, our skin damp yet warming with the contact. He tightened his hold and walked us backwards from the edge of the patio to the shadow under the eave.

"It's oddly arousing."

"Boiling hot tea?"

"Perhaps I just like to get you wet." He bowed his head to kiss my neck hard enough to leave a mark. When he rose up, I weaved my fingers in his hair and made him do it again.

"Oh, now you're just making a spectacle. Think they'll be okay out here by themselves for a few—"

Enraged voices resonated through the walls then burst onto the patio. Someone was shoved into the patio chairs. I recognized the master's voice, Paul's lunatic laughter. Fearghus and Christian were across the lawn, but heading toward the commotion.

Martin cursed, pecking my cheek before entering the brawl.

"See there?" Paul was saying. "Exactly what I was talking about. Your oldest son getting frisky with a Bevan. Everyone's cool with that."

"Enough," the master said. "Take a walk."

Paul brushed himself off as if resigned to the idea. But when he looked up and saw Martin standing there beside the master, his whole energy changed. I could sense it in my head, like we were still connected in the henge—Paul's forehead against mine, our shared emotion like a storm between us. I wished I'd held Martin back, kept him in the shadow with me. This humane, temper-cooling suggestion from the master was the first one I'd seen, and I could see Martin's presence about to disrupt it.

"I'll walk with you, Paul." I stepped onto the patio, offering my hand.

He homed in on it. The moment was a breathless inter-mission, a few seconds of tension packed to a state nearing combustion.

Martin was the spark. "Walk."

I could see Bad Paul settle in before he opened his mouth. "I'd love to, but the more time I spend with her, the more shit I get from the two of you. The more time I spend with her little *bastard*—"

I heard nothing after that. I withdrew my hand. With it, I withdrew so much more. He'd promised not to say that word again. A real promise, a heartfelt one. Martin had him by the collar, but I didn't care. I turned around, noting the frigid understanding in Fearghus' eyes, the stun of lost innocence on Christian. I took them both by the hand and dragged them upstairs, Fearghus stoically compliant, Christian asking too many unanswerable whys.

When I put Fearghus in bed and turned off his lamp, he flipped toward the window, the silver light of night making that expectation on his face more sinister. It was like a sickness I couldn't cure, a disease that was consuming my child before my eyes.

I went into my room and Christian was already snuggled up on the rug by the bed. "Uncle Paul's nice *some*times."

"Yes, but sometimes he can be very bad." I helped him up.

"He has a monster in him."

"Let's get you back to bed. I need you to stay in your bed tonight. Can you do that for me?"

He heaved a sigh and dragged his feet.

"Where's Fuzzy?" I returned to the rug and checked under the bed for the worn but loved bear.

"Dad threw Fuzzy away."

"When?"

He shrugged. His frown was so deep it was a perfect upside-down U. He hung his head like his sadness was not simply loss, but shame. He'd just turned four—only four—and that sick father of his was already trying to make a man out of him. How did he expect Christian to become a man if he wasn't first allowed to be a child?

"I'm sure he's not gone. I'll find him, and he can live in my room if you can keep it a secret. Classified *Fearghus Christian only*. Okay?"

Elated, he held out a hand for a shake—something Fearghus must've taught him. That type of becoming a man I could take. My nine-year-old was teaching manners and honor, and the grown men were teaching shame and aggression. Fearghus and I were clearly outnumbered, but we were stronger, and we had the backing of a family with power the Moores could only dream of.

When Martin finally came up for the night I took him fiercely in the middle of the room, ripping his already ripped shirt further. He picked me up, knocking furniture as he backed me against the wall. It was a fumbling of limbs, a clumsy mess of slipping holds, and too much gravity for what we needed to do. When his head struck the bookshelf, he cursed and took me to the floor. He paused then—me sprawled on my back, him on his knees between my legs. "I like this new side to you."

I reached for his belt but he inched away, raising my leg to kiss a trail down my inner thigh. I let out all my breath, felt my pulse thumping against his lips. The unwind was a much-needed bliss. The antidote to the turmoil of life. Love against anger.

He straightened above me, unbuckling his belt. "The more powerful you become, the more I want you." His voice was dark and deep, thick with a dangerous edge he found appealing in me that I now found so irresistible in him. "Is that possible?"

"Maybe we should move to the bed."

"Good idea."

He got to his feet and held out a hand. Standing there, all wide shoulders and strong arms, ripped shirt, unbuckled belt—the sight just about finished me there on the floor alone. My poor slip fell to the same fate as his shirt before we got in bed, and when he thrust into me, I dug my fingers into his shoulders because it was too much yet not enough. He put one hand against my lower back and the other behind my head and kissed me softly while driving into me hard. The perfection of the combination broke my grip from the world.

I left the bed later for the kitchen, to brew my tea since the first one had gone down the front of Martin. As much as I loved him, I couldn't bring another child into that toxic household, or another Moore into being. Not even a half Moore.

The door slid open behind me and I paused mid-sip, knowing exactly who it was. I was completely unprepared for dealing with him.

"I'm back from my walk. I'm better now," he began.

I stayed in place as if he wasn't there.

"Saw the light on," he continued. "Thought it might be you."

If I kept forgiving him, he'd keep hurting me. It was a truth, although an irrelevant one. I couldn't forgive him, not this time, and if it hurt him as much as it hurt me to know it, my damage would be irreversible. *I will not cry.*

I took my tea in one long gulp, wishing for an ability to stop time, to go through possible responses, to fully realize what lasting effect would come of my reaction in this moment. *I live for Fearghus.* And I lived for Christian now too. A broken promise to me was one thing, but it was Fearghus he'd insulted, and Christian who'd witnessed it. Forgiving him would make it acceptable.

"Sloane—"

I got up and pushed in my chair, leaving the room like he was a ghost in the night.

The next day I found Christian's bear in the trash, stinking of dirty rags and beer. Ruby helped me wash him up. He came out quite a bit fuzzier and missing his one remaining eye, so we sewed on new brown buttons and I set him on my balcony to dry. Christian visited him in my room for a week until I covered him with Discretion, a spell that rendered an object invisible to certain people but needed constant refreshing. It was a perfect task to teach Fearghus and Christian a little responsibility. The stakes were high. If Pierce saw that bear again, he'd be sure to burn it, which only made the task more rewarding for Fearghus.

I supervised the spell three times before he had it right, then I set them loose with their illegal bear. Martin couldn't figure out what was so funny the night it showed up at a family dinner with Christian. And I couldn't figure out what else I could do to make Fearghus so happy. His sickness had been momentarily cured. If these illicit little jobs were his medicine, I needed to come up with a list a mile long.

CHAPTER 45

SUMMER, 1974

CHRISTIAN'S FIFTH BIRTHDAY had the house in preparation for another party. Fearghus' tenth would be two weeks later, with no more than a homemade cake in the kitchen with Fran, Ruby, and Eleanor, but Fearghus was well past the age he'd first realized the difference between their birthdays and had already made his peace. Martin had spoken to him about this unfair circumstance years ago. He didn't share the conversation with me, and I didn't ask. Fearghus was content, which was all I wanted.

I was outside with Fearghus and Christian, watching the men erect a tent on the lawn. Storms were on the weather report, but the master was still determined to hold the event outside. When Christian got too close to the ropes and poles, I hollered his name. He was out of his mind with excitement, and since he didn't hear me the first time, I asked Fearghus to go down and get him out of the way.

We were too slow. Pierce had come outside. When his yell of Christian's name didn't gain a response, he crossed the lawn and jerked Christian up by the arm. My heart did a nauseating clench; Fearghus took a step forward and I grabbed his shoulder. Pierce slapped his little boy with the force a man would use on another man, not a child, spinning Christian so he wound up on all fours.

Fearghus twisted out of my grip. I got hold of both his shoulders and held him tight against me. "It's over. Don't make it worse."

He was breathing hard, as if he was already fighting that man.

"Calm down, *a chroí.*"

A curse unfit for Fearghus' ears came from behind us. I turned. Paul had seen the slap too. He looked so overcome by anger he'd gone numb. One fist clenched so hard the knuckles cracked. I caught his sleeve as he went by. He looked at me like I was a stranger who'd bumped him on the street.

"Paul, don't. It's over." It was the first time I'd spoken to him in a long time, and he swayed a little and closed his eyes. I waited until he looked at me. "If he knows you care, he'll be so much worse."

He gave me this little nod and shot a look toward Pierce that was so hateful, yet so resigned, I knew he was thinking exactly what I was: if Pierce knew he cared about Christian, it would be just like Rosemary.

Pierce left his little boy there in the grass, his return to the patio passing dangerously close to the three of us. I could hold Fearghus back, but I couldn't hold Paul. Once Pierce was back inside, Fearghus and I ran down the slope. One of the tent men had helped Christian up and was brushing him off. "Little guy might get hurt out here."

"I know. Thank you, we'll get him inside"

Christian's eyes were wet and his chin trembled. His big boy act crumbled as soon as I picked him up. He sobbed against my neck all the way back to the house, with Fearghus behind us kicking a rock so hard I was afraid he'd break a window. When we reached the patio, Fearghus kicked the rock with enough force to take down that whole tent on the lawn.

"Fearghus, that's enough. Come inside and help me with Christian."

Ruby cleared a spot on the countertop for me to set Christian. He raised a fist and opened his palm. In it was his tooth. With an abrupt cessation of tears, he gave me a bloody smile. "I been waiting for dis one."

"I'm sure the tooth fairy will have something very special for you." His skill at taking abuse was both a relief and a fright. It was an advantage to be able to take it so well and move on. It worried me that he felt no anger, that he considered it normal, that he saw no injustice. Ruby handed me some ice for his cheek, and I held it against the red blotch that swelled before my eyes.

He frowned then, as if reading my thoughts. "Will I have a bruise?"

I wished I could tell him no, but I couldn't lie to him. "I'm afraid you might."

"All the kids are coming tomorrow."

I kissed his forehead. There was no helping that. Kids could be cruel, but if he could withstand a slap like that from his father, he could take a few taunts from his birthday party guests.

"Tell them I hit you," Fearghus said.

"You beat me up? That's bad too." Christian sniffed and wiped his nose.

Children should not be burdened with these worries. I let the cold ice soak into my hand, cooling my fury. Ruby swatted at Fearghus, who stole a potato from her pile. Before I could tell him to put it back, he swiped the dishtowel from her apron and wrapped the potato like we hadn't just seen him take it.

And then it was swinging in the air, smacking Fearghus in the face with a blow that made me and Christian jump. I dropped Christian's ice and yanked the towel away from Fearghus, causing the potato to hit the floor and roll. "Fearghus!"

"It didn't hurt." He smiled. I could already see the blood rising to the surface of his cheekbone.

"What's the matter with you?"

"Now he can say he hit me back."

Ruby handed me two fresh towels full of ice, rocking with laughter she was trying very hard to contain. I handed one to Fearghus. He took it but set it on the counter. I returned to Christian.

Fran breezed in. "Well, what trouble found the two of you?"

"Trey hit me first," Christian said.

"Trey?" She stopped in front of them, surprised enough to take a pause on such a busy day.

Christian jumped into a meandering five-year-old's story of questionable logic involving a chase through the woods, several wild animals, and a blow-by-blow fight that had me forgiving both of their behavior due to how adorable he was even while spinning the tallest of tales.

Fran eagerly bought every word. "Well, I hope you apologize to your mother for the trouble you've caused."

"*Tá brón orm, a Mháthair.*"

"*Tá brón orm, a Aintín.*"

"I assume that was an apology," said Fran.

"It was."

Christian swung his legs, holding his ice against his swollen cheek. Ruby poked him in the ribs and he curled away, laughing, all worries forgotten—his cruel father no longer a point of pain. And Fearghus stood at the window, leveling a dark gaze toward the spot on the lawn where the slap had taken place. He shouldered enough anger for the both of them. The way he dwelled on it turned him into an unfamiliar, wild creature right before my eyes.

The storm blew in early that night. Thunder vibrated the house in soft grumbles while I prepared the boys for bed in Christian's bathroom. They stood side by side, Christian on a stool, admiring their faces in the mirror. Both their cheeks had turned a shocking purplish-red. Christian smiled at his reflection, his tongue peeking through the hole where his tooth had been. Lightning struck close, lighting the room with an electric blue burst. Its simultaneous slam into the ground rocked the house, and Christian toppled the stool and lunged for my legs just as the power went out.

"Nobody move." I felt for the sink and followed it to the wall then to the doorway. "Fearghus, take Christian's other hand."

We followed the wall, walking quickly with each burst of lightning that gave us a brief view of our way. I headed to the second floor knowing Christian would beg to sleep with me or Fearghus. After what happened that day, I was prepared to battle Pierce over his son's sleeping arrangements. Martin found us with a flashlight, which he gave to me, then left to find a better source of light.

When we reached Fearghus' room, we realized we'd left Fuzzy, so I left the boys in bed to travel back upstairs for the bear. Martin was lighting an oil lamp when I returned. The boys were out of bed, standing together at the windows to watch the downpour, Fearghus' arm draped loosely around Christian's shoulders.

"Back in bed, boys."

They grumbled, but complied. Christian was wearing Fearghus' amulet.

"Will that give enough light to read?" I asked Martin.

He turned the lamp's flame higher and moved it to the bedside table. "I'll be downstairs for a bit. Don't fall asleep without me."

I settled in between the boys with a copy of *Aesop's Fables*. We read and discussed story after story, until the thunder and lightning died down and only the rain remained. When the boys stopped their commentary, I read a few more just to settle them further. Fearghus' eyes became slits, his breathing slow. Christian was nodding off. When I closed the book, Christian mumbled, "You forgot the last one."

"Okay, one more." I opened the book and found the page. "The Oak and the Reeds. A grand oak stood at the edge of a pond where a cluster of reeds grew. 'O reeds,' the oak said. 'Why do you bend at the slightest breeze? Why not stand tall and strong, like me?' 'The wind,' the reeds replied, 'it is but a tickle. We bend, and it passes us by.' 'You are weak,' said the oak. 'Watch me, and learn to be strong.' 'You'll see,' said the reeds. At once there was a gust of wind, and the unbending oak stood tall but the wind was so strong it knocked the oak into the pond, its roots torn from the ground. The wind subsided, and the reeds once again stood tall."

I laid the book on my lap. I looked down at them, my oak tree, and my reed. There were terrors around us much worse than the wind.

I scooted off the end of the bed and went to extinguish the oil lamp.

"*A Mháthair?*"

I walked around to Fearghus' side and sat on the edge of the bed.

"Why is it 'The Oak and the Reeds'?"

I combed his dark hair with my fingers, unsure how to answer.

He didn't wait for me to respond. "Because I think it should be 'The Oak and the Moon.' Reeds can get stepped on. But the moon is high above everything. Nothing can touch it."

It was a glimpse of the things he pondered when he withdrew from me into that boy I didn't know. It made me so proud, yet so sad it brought a choke to my throat that left me mute for fear of crying. So I kissed his forehead instead and extinguished the light. By the time I made it back around the bed, I'd swallowed the sadness. The wind had subsided; I'd bent and I'd straightened once again. "I agree with you, Fearghus. It's just very hard to become like the moon. There is only one, after all."

"Some planets have more than one."

Soon he'd not only be taller than me, but also smarter. Perhaps he already was. I had no idea what went on in that head of his. "You're absolutely right."

A stray pulse of lightning lit the room just enough for me to see Fearghus' smile.

I took the flashlight into my room where another oil lamp glowed. I raised the wick so I could study the curses in my texts. If I found one similar to the curse that had been placed on Martin, I might be able to improvise a way to undo it. A long shot, of course, but I was ready to try again. I'd committed myself to staying there, to taking care of Christian. I could still do that and cure Martin. And I had a new form of encouragement: a new dream, even more far-fetched than the others. Martin and I would wake Fearghus and Christian and flee the estate under the cover of night, to fade into a place where the Moores couldn't find us.

Rain fell steadily all day for Christian's birthday party, but he didn't care. He got so many toys I wondered how they'd all fit in his room. Two weeks later we held a modest birthday celebration for Fearghus on the patio. After he opened his three gifts, Christian whispered a request in my ear that was so touching I hugged him for five straight minutes. That night I helped him wrap half of his new toys in birthday wrapping paper. He gave them to Fearghus the next day. I left them playing in Fearghus' room so I could sit alone on my balcony. I imagined calling Rosemary to tell her what a sweet boy she'd had, but there was no phone that could reach her.

I went to the kitchen later to help Ruby. Through the window I saw Paul on the patio with Christian, teaching him to tie his shoes. Paul showed him over and over, and corrected him so gently and patiently I wondered how much longer Good Paul would last. Even Ruby had her eyes glued to them as if prepared to rescue Christian at the moment Paul's personality flipped. As the lesson carried on, my anxiety rose. There was a whoop, and I dropped my knife and sprung to the door to see Paul mussing Christian's hair, Christian beaming up at him like a child to a superhero, and one perfectly tied shoe. I wondered then if Paul had found a phone line that could reach Rosemary, or at least a part of her, the only part that we had left.

When Christian started leaving for school in the mornings in the same car that took Fearghus every day, I had more time to work on Martin's curse. My research sent Eleanor to the library several times a week to collect books on subjects that varied from ancient Asian medicine to old European folklore. It was a serendipitous passage about Russian mysticism that gave me a clue.

"Mithridatism," I said to Martin when he walked in the door from a six-day trip.

He handed his jacket to the doorman. "Is that a greeting in that other language of yours? I'd prefer a kiss."

I headed toward the stairs. If he wanted a kiss, he'd have to follow me. In our room I handed him the book open to the page I'd marked.

"I've been thinking about your lips for a week and first you want me to read—" He flipped to the cover. "A book on venomous snakes?"

I wrapped my arms around his neck and kissed him. He set the book down to pick me up, drawing out a kiss I'd meant to be quick but now wanted to last forever.

He set me down to take off his tie. "Where's Trey?"

"Following the handyman around. He helped him fix our toilet then went off with him to do something else. He has a new fascination for how things work."

"He's missed six days of training. I'm thinking he's old enough to go down there without me."

"Sit down and read this." I picked up the book and handed it to him.

"Can you just tell me? I've been running for days without rest. I know it was less than a week but the strain this time was bad."

"That's what I'm trying to talk to you about. Mithridatism. It's the taking of small doses of poison in order to build a tolerance. An immunity."

He smiled at me like he wanted to laugh, but wasn't sure if it would go over very well.

"Your curse. Being away from the estate mimics being poisoned. You slowly get sick, until you return home and get a dose of antidote. Right?"

"Pretty close." He dropped onto the sofa, took off his shoes, and put his feet up.

"So, what if you practice mithridatism? Stay away a little longer each time to slowly build a tolerance."

"To leave permanently, I'd have to build a tolerance of what, fifty years? Sixty? And I just can't step away from my family's business. You know that, Sloane."

"Yes, but ten years from now Fearghus might want to move somewhere on his own. What if they allow it? We could leave. It might take you that long to build an immunity, so you need to start now."

"And you'll leave Christian here?"

"Okay, fifteen years."

"That's a long time. A lot can happen in fifteen years." He squeezed the back of his neck.

"Are you getting a migraine?"

"No, just stiff." He grinned at me, all lazy and sleepy-eyed, so I sat and tucked my legs, snuggling up beside him. He rested his chin on my head. "Why want to leave anyway? You'd miss the family dinners. Admit it."

"I'm just planning for the future."

"The future can't be planned. Not in this family, at least."

The future couldn't be planned, but it became predictable. When Fearghus and Christian weren't creating mischief together, Fearghus was getting in fights with his cousins. Some were more violent than others, and I tried not to think too deeply about why the more violent ones brought Fearghus into brighter moods. Teenage resentment came on early, aimed more at Martin than me, and Martin's cold way of responding to him only worsened things between them. The more resentful Fearghus was, the stricter Martin became.

Another total lunar eclipse proved Martin was right about Fearghus' weakness. Fearghus covered his head for its duration, moaning into a pillow. His nose and ears bled, and he was so weak he couldn't walk without stumbling. He stayed in bed the following day, too tired to do anything but frown at the ceiling.

I gave him his own copy of *Walden* for his twelfth birthday, hoping to remind him of the peace he could find around him in the glint of sun on the lake, the chatter of birds in the morning, the tickle of lilac on the air. There were days when even Christian couldn't jolt him from his dark place, and we learned to give him space and be there for him when he returned to us.

Sometimes it felt like Christian was my only son and Fearghus was a strange creature I'd picked up in the woods, hoping to tame. The detached way Fearghus would stare into the distance left me with a chill. I wanted to talk to him, to help him, but when I'd rest a hand on his arm or say his name, the look he'd fix on me would frighten me into silence.

The day Fearghus laid violent hands on Christian was the day it was time to intervene.

CHAPTER 46

AUTUMN, 1976

I WAS HELPING GRACE clean up dishes from the patio tables outside when the boys returned from their morning in the woods. Fearghus held an open hand to Christian before they went inside, and Christian dug in his pocket. What came out caught the sunlight in a way that went through me like a spear of ice.

I caught Fearghus' shoulder and spun him; he jerked his hand back, knowing at once what I was after.

"Let me see what you have."

With a glance at Christian, he opened his palm. Two silver rings caked with mud covering the engravings I knew by heart. Names of wives and daughters. My dead husband's ancestors. Those rings were missing from his fingers the day I'd found his body on my porch.

"Where did you find those?"

Fearghus closed his fist and held it down, like they were his find and he wasn't going to give them up. He set his gaze on my feet and held it there.

"Just tell her," Christian whispered.

Fearghus kept his eyes on the ground. "The woods."

"Liar," Christian said.

And then Christian was falling into the patio chairs, and it took a moment for me to realize Fearghus had shoved him so hard he'd shot halfway across the patio into those chairs. Fearghus had already covered the distance himself and was drawing back an arm, so I rushed between them. "Fearghus!"

He stepped around me to go for Christian again, and I took him by the arm and gave him a shake. "Fearghus, stop it."

Christian was whining, untangling limbs from the chair legs. I helped him up. His frown trembled like he wanted to cry but couldn't give in. He checked one bloody scraped elbow, then the other. He looked up at Fearghus. Then he charged him.

He was attached to Fearghus' waist, but Fearghus wasn't fighting so I pried them loose and stood between them to catch my breath.

"No lunch for either of you. You can spend that time in your rooms. Now, Fearghus, tell me where you found those rings."

He'd gone dead in the eyes and answered as if reciting lines. "In those old buildings we're not supposed to go in."

Now the fight was inside me, a struggle to keep my face clear of the sadness and anger tearing through me. "Give one of them to Christian."

To my surprise, he did it. I plucked a ring away from each of them, along with their memory of finding them. I took both boys to their rooms and the rings to mine, where I washed them in the sink and wrapped them in a handkerchief. I allowed myself to hold them against my heart for one broken moment. I knew why those rings were buried in the dirt in that building and not on my husband's fingers. He'd hid them from the Moores, buried them in the dirt of that place so the Moores wouldn't find them. I stowed them in the floor under my bed, with my illegal herbs, where they'd stay until I could give them to Mam. If ever a day came when Fearghus could meet his real family, those rings would be his, along with a trust in a family so absolute he'd never question his place again.

Later, I asked Christian why he and Fearghus would treat each other like that.

"I was bad to say it. I forget sometimes." Another missing tooth gave him a slight lisp.

"Forget what?"

"Not to call him 'liar.' He hates it. My dad says it to him in the training room. He says it to be mean." He shrugged weakly, like this situation bothered him deeply, but there was nothing he could do about it.

"How is he mean?"

"He says to Trey, 'Does that hurt?' and Treys says no, so my dad calls him 'liar' and hits him again."

I pulled Christian against me and hugged him hard. It was a hug I wanted to give to Fearghus, but I knew he wouldn't let me. "You go get Martin when that happens, okay?"

I met Martin in the foyer that evening as he was coming in. "Fearghus attacked Christian today."

He took off his jacket. "I'm sure it wasn't the first time, and won't be the last. Your son has a bit of a temper, in case you haven't noticed."

"*Our* son is becoming more angry and withdrawn, in case *you* haven't noticed. And I don't know what goes on in that training room, but it sounds truly awful and doesn't seem to be helping—"

He clamped a hand over my mouth and turned his ear toward the east hall. A door closed nearby then footsteps walked toward us. He slid his hand from my mouth to my cheek and drew me close for a kiss that was more an act of cover than love.

When we broke apart, Pierce was heading past us toward the stairs, and Martin looked at me like we'd just avoided death.

"You know how much heat is on me right now?" Martin said when we were closed inside our bedroom. "You can't talk to me about anything like that out in the open."

It was too easy for me to forget the delicate role he played. "I'm sorry. I—"

"And what happens in the training room is nothing to be concerned about. Yes, I'm hard on him. I have to be. You want him strong, right?"

"It's not you I'm worried about. It's Pierce."

"Trey's learning how to deal with Pierce. He's twelve years old. He's not a baby. And there are much worse things in his world than Pierce. I have bigger things to deal with right now."

"Bigger things than the well-being of your son?"

He tugged his shirttails out of his pants, like there was a more aggressive reaction in him and the shirt had to absorb some of its power. I crossed the room toward him and started undoing the buttons on his shirt. He stood still and let me do them all, his breath the only indication of how worked-up he was.

"Lewis is back on his crusade. He wants to kill you."

I let my hands fall away from him.

"He senses the power you have. Over Trey. Christian. Over the whole house."

"I haven't done anything lately."

"But he knows you can. And I think my father is moving to his side. I hate to say it, but Lew has a good argument. And you know who's his biggest resistance besides me?" He ran a knuckle along my cheekbone.

I shook my head.

"My mother," he said.

Protected by the woman my family had cursed. Perhaps she only wanted me alive because she knew I could undo that curse. If I had lifted it, she might have allowed them to kill me.

He went into the closet to undress. I walked on to the balcony and saw Fearghus on his balcony next door, sitting with his legs dangling through the railing, his forehead rested against a spindle. "Fearghus? You should go inside, *a chroí*. It's chilly out."

He got up without looking at me and went inside.

The seething black anger that I'd banished from the house so many times lingered in the air before the breeze took it away. There was so much evil in that house no smudging would ever draw it out. It had soaked into the woodwork, the plaster, the flesh and bones of my little boy. His dark moods and outbursts seemed like foreshocks, like the small releases of tension building up to disaster.

I went inside to Martin pouring himself a drink.

"Will you talk to Fearghus? Is there anything you can explain so he understands why they treat him the way they do?"

"Yes, I will. It's about time I do."

"What will you tell him?"

He poured more scotch in his glass and took a drink. "I'll tell him what your mother told me to tell him."

"Our prophecy?"

"Yes, but not your version. Our version."

"What's your version?"

"That his child will bring our end."

Martin took Fearghus for a long walk in the woods the next day. Christian and I heard the gunfire from the house. Target practice had become a daily event for my son. After the sound ended I expected them home, but it was hours later when I saw them crossing the lawn together. As they neared I could see visible relief on Fearghus' face. He finally had an explanation for all he'd endured. Even bad news could be a gift if it offered an understanding to a lifelong puzzle.

What scared me was what I witnessed at dinner that night. Fearghus gave Pierce a sideways glance no one caught but me. Even with Fearghus' relief at finally understanding, he still carried that anger. Only now, it was armed with motive.

Later in bed I put my lips to Martin's ear and whispered, "Will you show Fearghus the breach in the fence?"

He kissed my cheek. "I already did."

I lay awake listening to him sleep. Wind pushed against the house. I imagined a storm kicking up outside, bringing a cleansing rain that came on hard and dwindled to trickles in the gutters. If only the roof of that house would open, and that cleansing rain could pour inside. It was easy to wish for a magic cure, one that required no toil, no pain. A downpour to wash it all away. But the rain couldn't penetrate the roof, walls, or windows of this house. A fix must come from inside.

My struggle lay with being one meager step of this fix. All my toil and pain, with no timely gratification, no reward but the knowledge someday things would be made right. Not by me, but by a person whose place was partially created by me. A person I might never know.

I got out of bed and let myself outside to feel the call of the rain on the wind. I spotted the white coat of Fearghus' cat on the next-door balcony before I spotted Fearghus sitting on the floor with his legs through the railing again. I went back inside for two quilts, one I tossed to Fearghus.

He wrapped it around his shoulders. I sat at the edge of my balcony, wrapped in my own quilt.

"Do you feel the rain on the wind?"

He nodded, his profile a silhouette in the dim light that strayed from the house lights below. "The animals are settling in. They always know before us."

"They do."

A gust of wind tried to scoop us off our balconies. Fearghus sucked his legs under his quilt, and Friend took a spot on his lap.

"Dad and Pierce and all of them act like it's my fault."

"Like what's your fault?"

"My future. It hasn't even happened yet."

I wanted to hop the railing and sit next to him, but I knew the distance created by our separate balconies was the only thing allowing him to confide in me. "Your dad doesn't blame you for anything."

"He said—"

I felt, rather than saw, him tense. Martin didn't give the details of his conversation with Fearghus, probably because he liked to avoid breaking my heart. And Mam had asked Martin to tell Fearghus because she didn't want to put me in that position. Curiosity pushed me to ask Fearghus what Martin had said, but good sense prevailed.

"What he said will take time to settle in. Don't try to understand it now. Just give it time."

"You knew the whole time and you didn't tell me."

"What I knew—" I took my own advice and spent the time to phrase an answer that would do so many contradictory things: help Fearghus come to terms with what he'd learned, and tell the truth, while not disputing Martin. "What I believe might be different from what others believe."

He turned to face me. In his twelve-year-old face was a ghost of the baby he once was, and a hint of the man he'd soon become. "What do you believe?"

"That you're a hero."

He said nothing after that. I sat with him a few minutes then left the night to him so he could ponder that last line, let it soak in, hopefully believe it.

Christian was standing timidly at my doorway inside. I laid a hand on his back and steered him into the hall. "You're too big for this. You need to stay in your room."

"I know. I just … I was afraid my dad would come in my room and be mad."

"Why would he be mad?"

He took my hand on the stairs which slowed our progress. He was drawing out our walk. "I dunno. He's always mad. Why does he hate me?"

"Your dad doesn't hate you, he hates the world. It's a problem inside him that he takes out on others, even the ones he loves."

I lay with him in bed, this time making no effort to stay awake so I could return to my own room. I woke three times to him patting the bed, taking hold of my arm once it was found and falling back to sleep.

In the morning, he asked, "Did my mom look like you?"

I took him to my room where I showed him a photograph of Rosemary kneeling beside Fearghus with her arm around his waist. Two faces smudged with garden soil and two big smiles. A smile I never saw on Fearghus anymore.

I pressed the photo into Christian's hand. "It's yours now. But let's keep it here in my room, okay? This drawer." I pulled out the bottom drawer of my bedside table.

One week later I caught him alone in my room, studying that photo. He visited the drawer regularly for three years until I deemed him old enough to keep it safely hidden in his own room.

CHAPTER 47

SUMMER, 1979

AT FIFTEEN FEARGHUS was more man than boy. He'd surpassed my height and was on his way to surpassing Martin's. I rarely saw him. When I did, it was in the kitchen with Ruby offering him seconds and thirds. Ten-year-old Christian did all the talking and Fearghus did all the listening, nodding, and laughing. He'd developed a dry sense of humor out of the childlike one he'd lost years before, and he had a new way of hugging me with one arm that was so manly and grown-up I had to stifle tears every time he did it.

Those were the good things. The bad things were too abundant to name.

I'd lost my little boy. From him grew a young man so hostile toward his own father it had me questioning my decision to marry Martin every day. A young man who spoke his mind so infrequently I worried what was inside it. A young man who'd taken to training at all hours, without Martin, for spans of time that overlapped so I'd mix up my days when trying to determine how long he'd been down there. He'd surface from the basement with wounds so dire I'd call the driver to take him to the hospital, only to find Fearghus returning to the basement with a pack of ice for his face and a shrug for me.

Christian was often down there with him, or I'd have worried more. Christian was still young enough to tell me everything, including every outrageous comment from Paul, slipped into conversations Fearghus could hear as if a slur could ever be a joke. They clearly weren't, considering Fearghus' hostility had expanded to cover Paul.

"Every rude thing you say about my son, you're also saying to me," I told Paul one day I caught him playing piano in the ballroom, an event that had become rare.

"Oh, come on. Moody teenagers are too fun to harass. It's good for him."

"It bothers Christian too."

He pounded out the beginning of Beethoven's Fifth, an attempt to silence me that was so obnoxious I slid in next to him and elbowed him over for more room on the bench. He switched to some jazz of his own invention, a song I'd asked him to teach me but he refused. I watched him play, trying to memorize. When he stopped I played the part I remembered, and he caught my hands. "Don't. It's crap."

"It's really good, Paul."

"Crap." He went back to Beethoven's Fifth.

I ducked under his arm and put my arm around him. He took his fingers off the keys to pull me close. "You shouldn't be nice to me. I don't deserve it. But I won't stop you."

"Do you remember what it was like to be a teenager in this house?"

He chuckled. "Okay, I'll play nice."

"To Christian too."

He slackened his arm around me. "You know, sometimes it's hard for me to look at that kid. That new smart-alecky sideways grin he does—it looks so much like her. That's the kind of thing you learn, not something you're born with. It's like he's picking up her quirks, like she's still here."

A living, breathing, visual reminder of someone I loved who'd been stolen from me. I used to have only one. Now I had two. "I know what you mean."

"I'm sure you do."

The next afternoon Paul came through the back kitchen door with a bloody nose and a finger pointed right at me. "You need to get that boy of yours under control before someone puts him down like a rabid dog."

I walked around the counter and slapped him. It took several pounds of my heart to realize what I'd done, to feel the itchy burn in my palm, to draw it against me before I did it again. I couldn't form words. All I could do was breathe and stare into his hardened brown eyes as he stared into mine. He brought a fist onto the countertop hard enough to make dishes jump. Once didn't dispel the fury in his eyes so he did it again, then he grabbed me by the shoulders and the room burst into chaos.

Shouts from Ruby and Fran. The bang of the back door hitting the stop. Two bodies knocking into the table and chairs. I staggered back. Fran caught me and Ruby went in front of me with a rolling pin. I recognized my own voice in the chaos, screaming for Fearghus to stop, for Paul to stop. They were a scrambling mess, a wild movement of arms and knees.

Martin got a grip of Fearghus' arm and spun him away before I even saw him enter the room. Fearghus tried to go for Paul again, but Martin shoved him so hard he smashed backward into the wall several feet behind him. Fearghus sent an elbow into the plaster, a vicious look at Martin, and left the room.

Ruby hadn't yet yielded her position, so I put a hand on her arm, which she used to lead me around the counter, away from Martin and Paul. She fumed, mumbling about talking to the mistress about fights in her kitchen. I tried to walk away, but she pulled me back.

"I need to find Fearghus."

"Uh-uh. You leave that boy, let him cool down."

Martin and Paul were gone, the crack in the plaster wall and fallen chairs the only indication of trouble.

I found Fearghus sitting on the front steps of the house several hours later. He watched the driveway as if waiting for someone, and I got a chill when I realized Paul could have left and Fearghus could be waiting for him to return. I went outside and sat beside him. He didn't even turn to look at me.

"I don't think he would have hurt me, Fearghus."

He let that hang long enough for me to understand he didn't want to talk. I put a hand on his knee, wanting to hug him like I used to: his head on my chest, his tightly held breath finally releasing so I could feel the tension leave his frame. Instead, I stood and turned to go in.

"He told Christian what happened to Rosemary."

Her name gave me a little jolt in the chest like it always did, but this time it carried a deep dread. "It might be time Christian—"

"He didn't do it right. *I* was going to tell him. Was planning to, in the right way. It takes time to come up with the words, so it's not so bad. He did it in the worst way possible."

I sat on the step, all at once weakened by another oversight, another neglected responsibility on my part. I should've talked to Fearghus about telling Christian. I could've helped him come up with the words. He was absolutely right; there was a correct way to tell a child how his mother was killed, and a very wrong way.

"It wasn't even his job to tell him, but he did anyway, because he likes to pick at people."

"I'm sorry, Fearghus."

"Don't be. He'll pay. Maybe not today, but—"

He stopped when I covered my face, then he did that one-armed hug that made my eyes hot with tears. He took a breath and held it so long I looked up at him.

"Friend died. I buried him in the woods."

"Oh, Fearghus …"

"I'm going running."

He got up and sprinted away. Across the circle drive, down the driveway, and around the bend until I could no longer see him. He was moving farther away each day, and I had no idea how to bring him back.

I looked in all the obvious places for Christian. Someone told me they saw him go outside, so I walked around the house and spotted him cross-legged in the grass of the eastern-facing side of the house. As I neared, I followed his gaze to the third floor balcony. Rosemary's room. The balcony she fell from.

I sat beside him and put my arms around him. He was still a child at ten, and more affectionate than Fearghus ever was. I could still hug and he'd hug back.

"Friend died," he said.

"I know. Fearghus just told me."

"He was old."

"He was."

"My mother was not old."

"She was too young."

"She didn't just die though. She was pushed. From up there." He pointed. "Her head cracked open on that concrete. And nobody went to jail."

A tremble took over my hands. My field of vision went blurry at the edges. I squeezed my eyes shut. The tremble had traveled down to my legs, into the ground. Christian was patting my knee.

"Aunt Sloane?"

I could see it all again. Martin and me rushing upstairs to Rosemary's room. Fearghus on the balcony outside. Christian crying in his crib. *It was too much for her*, Pierce had said. *I tried to stop her from doing it. She scratched me, see?*

I tried to focus on Christian's face—the real Christian in front of me with the sunburned nose. His shaggy blond hair damp with sweat and a little curled at the ends. Past him a door opened on the side of the house and out came Pierce with two other men, handing out and lighting cigarettes. The tremble shot from the ground to my fingertips. I tried to make a fist, to contain it, but it was too late. Across the lawn, Pierce's head jerked to the side as if struck. He raised a hand to his neck to a set of fresh bloody scratch marks I didn't need to see to know they were there.

Christian had leapt up and away. He was now looking at me with a horrified awe. "What the hell, Aunt Sloane?"

"Don't say 'hell.'"

He'd turned his attention to his father who had now spotted me. "Oh, shit, he's gonna do something." All the awe left his face. Only the horror remained.

"Don't say 'shit.'"

If Pierce was going to retaliate, he'd have already been crossing the lawn. He had his two guests to consider, and any display would have to be dealt with by Martin or the master—two people Pierce wouldn't want involved in any battle between me and him. He took a long drag on his cigarette, his devil eyes still on me, a palpable assault even across such an expanse of lawn.

Christian took a few steps back. "I think I'm going in—"

"You stay right here. We do not cower to bullies."

Christian's hand went into his pocket where I knew he kept Fearghus' amulet when it wasn't around his neck. I didn't allow him to move until Pierce had tossed his cigarette, spit pointedly in our direction, and gone inside.

Christian went from fearful flight to jumping-up-and-down excited in one blink of the eye. "You *have* to teach me that. Does Trey know how to do that? If you don't teach me, he will, and he might do it wrong so you need to. Will you? Right now?"

"I'm not sure it's something I can teach."

He groaned and went slack, almost falling over until I caught him by the collar. "Come inside and take a bath."

After handing him over to Eleanor, I went straight to my room, hoping to lie down and subdue the stinging heat in my head and find a way to handle the anger that still lived in me over Rosemary's death. My entry into my bedroom must have been unexpected and forceful for the way Martin looked up from his desk as if startled, slapping folders closed and stacking papers like he was working on something he didn't want anyone to see. He never covered his work from me, even the most confidential documents. It was a sight strange enough to pause my hasty progress to the bed. "Would you rather not be disturbed? I can lie down in Fearghus' room."

"It's nothing that can't wait."

He didn't resume working after I lay down, just rearranged his desk a bit before leaving me so I could rest. That quick concealment of his work touched a deep distrust, the one that sparked those phone calls to his Cambridge apartment so long ago and led to my accusation of his infidelity. I couldn't let those questions linger. They turned harmless things into nightmares.

"Martin?"

He paused in the doorway.

"Are you working on something important?"

"Just a few trust funds. For Trey, Tara … it seems like the least I can do for what's been taken from them."

I reached out a hand for him, and he came to me and kissed it. "I won't say a word."

"I know you won't. Now get some rest. I'll wake you for dinner."

I couldn't grasp sleep due to one little word he'd used. *Few* usually meant three, and I'd seen three stacks when I walked in on him. Setting up a trust fund for a child he'd fathered before marrying me would make perfect sense. He'd never spoken of such a child, but I'd never asked.

I slid out of bed and took a peek at his desk. Sure enough, there were three stacks, crisscrossed on each other. The paper on top had a name written in: TREY FEARGHUS BEVAN. I could only see partial names on the second and third. One was clearly TARA. The third showed CHRIST before it was cut off. My shame was immediate and raw. Of course the third would be Christian.

When I lay back down I tried to put my mind at ease, but there was something wrong with that third one. It was the beginning of Christian's name but at the end of the line. Clearly I'd interrupted him printing his name and he'd left out the last letters. I was being silly. But I couldn't understand why it would be printed at the end of the line like that, with no room for the rest of his name.

He returned to wake me for dinner like he'd said he would, but I was already up. "Is the third trust fund for Christian?"

"Christian doesn't need one. He'll inherit all the money he'll need and they'll never have a reason to cut him out. Trey, I wasn't sure about. So I'm taking a precaution."

"Who's the third one for?"

"A baby girl we made an orphan." He picked up the third stack and handed it to me. The name on the top read LIV CATHERINE GILCHRIST.

CHAPTER 48

SUMMER, 1979

"COME LOOK AT this before we go down." Martin beckoned me toward the balcony.

I went out with him. Fearghus was on the side lawn playing fetch with the Moores' pack of Dobermans.

"Trey's trained them to take turns. See how they wait until he looks at them?"

Six dogs stood, tongues flopping and tails wagging, each waiting for their turn. As soon as Fearghus looked at a dog, it took a running start toward the woods and Fearghus flung a stick.

"I don't think he's trained them. They just listen to him."

Christian shot from the house below us. "I found a ball!" He waved it over his head. Six dogs turned to assess the commotion before taking off toward him, paws pounding ground, heads low.

"Oh my god, Martin, they're going to—"

Martin rushed to the balcony railing and gave a deafening whistle but the dogs took no notice. Christian had stopped. He took one step back. If he ran, they'd surely attack him. He was too far from the house to make it inside safely. Martin took a chest full of air for another whistle but stopped when Fearghus' low voice carried across the lawn. All six dogs skidded to a halt, kicking up chunks of grass. They all turned to look at Fearghus. He waved them forward and they ran back to him, Christian and his ball on their heels.

"Well," Martin said, "you're right. They certainly listen to him."

Fearghus declined dinner in favor of a walk in the woods with the dogs. I didn't demand he eat with the family after the distressing day he'd had. Christian wasn't given the same option, but his sulk only lasted until the food was set in front of him. Paul tried to catch my eye at the change of each course. I kept my gaze far away from his until he snagged my elbow on my way out of the dining room afterward.

"Your apologies mean nothing to me, Paul."

"I know. But I'm making it up to Trey. Okay?"

He could try. He knew my son could hold a grudge. Perhaps he didn't remember how potent those grudges could be.

Two days passed with so few glimpses of both boys I finally asked Eleanor if she knew what they were up to.

"They're probably in the garage with my dad, fixing up that car."

I helped her put away my and Martin's clean clothes then walked behind Paul's carriage house to the garage. Inside I didn't just find Fearghus, Christian, and Eleanor's dad, but a whole audience of men—all four Moore brothers, Lewis' two boys, a few of our drivers, and several members of the yard crew.

Fearghus was under the hood, leaning in, his cheek smeared black with grease. Christian sat on the counter with a heavy book open in his lap. Eleanor's father hovered nearby, giving Fearghus occasional direction while chatting with Lewis.

"I'm not involved in this," Martin said, coming up beside me. "Had nothing to do with it. It was all Paul."

"Paul got Fearghus a car?"

"Not just *a* car. A Chevy ZL1."

I heaved a sigh. "At least it's not a motorcycle."

"That'll be next."

"Absolutely not."

"Paul got it from a guy who was a bit rough on it. It needs a new engine and tranny and a little TLC. Turns out your son has a gift for fixing cars."

Every moment of the day he wasn't in training or school, Fearghus was in the garage working on that car. I started bringing him and Christian lunch and sometimes dinner. The two boys were mostly alone, Fearghus doing the work under the hood, Christian putting down his comic book to consult the manual in his lap when Fearghus hit a puzzling spot. On other days their project would attract the audience of men. The good-natured comradery was a magical force, a smudging of the room as effective as a bundle of burning sage. It swarmed me as soon as I entered the garage door. There was a visible lift to the air, an ease to everyone's smile, a warmth in their voices. One hunk of metal had united all four Moore brothers, paused an ancient feud, and affectionately joined Fearghus with an adoptive family who despised him.

The day I saw Lewis clap a friendly hand on Fearghus' shoulder was my first shudder of unease. It was simply too good to be true. I knew men bonded over cars, but what went on in that garage was more than bonding. It was an acceptance of my son by the men who lived to abuse him.

When Fearghus wasn't working on the car he was talking about it. He hadn't talked so much to me in years. I got a full education of horsepower, timing, and exhaust, and I ate up every word of my son's new man-voice and wished he'd never finish that car so he'd talk to me forever with such contagious enthusiasm.

He and Christian stayed up late one night they were so close to finishing it. I badgered them to go to bed, but after Christian begged for "five more minutes" about ten times, I surrendered and took a seat by the counter.

"That's it," Fearghus said, wiping his hands on a rag. He nodded toward Christian. "You wanna try it first?"

"You do it."

Fearghus got behind the wheel and turned the key. The engine turned over a few times, just to tease us before roaring alive. Christian jumped from his stool, whooping and throwing his fist in the air. Fearghus looked straight at me. Sheer delight beamed from the widest smile, breaking through every wall he'd built as protection in that house. I saw then what that car meant to him. It wasn't just a gift from his mercurial uncle, it was a challenge that was his alone. And he'd finished it, himself. Had he ever had something to be proud of, something that wasn't stolen away before he had a chance to enjoy it?

Paul had found a way to make his apology matter so much I forgave everything he'd done. It was dangerous, but it was beyond my control.

Christian hopped into the passenger seat. "Drive, asshole!"

Fearghus turned off the engine. "In the morning."

"Aw, what?!"

Fearghus messed Christian's hair and got out of the car. He came to stand by me and admire his work.

"You don't have a driver's license, Fearghus."

He draped an arm across my shoulders. "It's okay. I won't get caught. I won't drive it fast until the engine wears in."

Christian had shifted to the driver's seat to pretend to drive, sound effects and all. He seemed to be crashing a bit more than I'd prefer.

"If Christian goes with you, any trouble you get in—"

"We won't get in trouble."

He squeezed me against him. I couldn't remember the last affectionate gesture he'd made toward me. His tall, solid frame and easy confidence reminded me so much of his father I took a hit of guilt. He needed to know how the resilience of his father's spirit lived in him. The longer

I went without telling him about his real father, the larger the secret grew. I had to tell him before it turned to betrayal.

"Fearghus—" The hurt swelled, bringing its usual debris to score my heart, to sting my eyes. I'd pledged to only tell him if I could do it without passing along the pain. I could not burden my son with the nightmare I'd lived.

"Mom, please don't start with the girly stuff in the presence of a car like this."

"You need to thank Paul."

He gave a cool, lazy nod—another one of his new moves that had turned him from a boy to a man overnight.

"Both of you need to go to bed."

"Five more minutes," Christian begged, getting a friendly smack on the back of the head from Fearghus.

Martin and his brothers were drinking on the patio when I returned to the house. I didn't catch the rowdiness in their conversation until I'd already been spotted. It was too late to change my course to one that didn't pass by them. When I declined their welcome, Martin chugged his drink and got up to follow me, earning a bawdy remark from Pierce that got both Lewis and Paul snickering. Martin let it slide and so did I. It was too late to start trouble they clearly craved.

I grabbed Martin's arm halfway up the stairs when he stopped and swayed. He reeked of whisky; I could see he'd spilled it on his shirt. Inside our room I began to undress him but he stopped me clumsily. "No, I have to leave."

"To go where? It's past midnight. You're in no condition—"

He rubbed his face, shook his head to clear it. "I'm fine. Would you pack me a bag? I'll get my gun."

"Gun?"

"Briefcase."

"Martin—"

"It's only to Philadelphia. I have to close on a property first thing in the morning. Forge some documents. My father is asking where the money is going—the trust fund money. It's going to a construction project that doesn't exist yet. The whole thing's giving me an ulcer. I need to handle it."

"Can't you sleep first and leave tomorrow?"

"Tomorrow afternoon I'm meeting someone in Cambridge. You might want to sit."

He took my shoulders, pushed me backward to the bed, and sat me down with a strength he didn't need to use on me.

"A woman there—an ex-girlfriend—claims her kid is mine. It's a lie. She just wants our money."

I saw why he wanted me sitting, and I resented that hard shove even more.

"I can't exactly tell her the damn kid has no magic blood so I know he's not mine."

"How do you know he doesn't?"

He sat next to me. "We've tested him."

His eyes were closer now, a steady blue-gray gaze belonging to the expert liar I'd married. But I trusted he didn't use that skill on me.

"So take her memory. Turn the blackmail into something else."

"No one's been able to get close enough to her without an audience. And we'd have to take the kid or she'd remember. I'd rather not have to take the kid."

"Let me see her."

"Out of the question. Lew and Pierce already think you have too much power. You start cleaning up our messes? They'd have a field day."

"You can't drive as drunk as you are."

"I can't take anyone with me to Philadelphia." He took me by the shoulders—again, too hard. "If he traces this money, looks too closely, it's not just that orphaned girl they find. It's Tara too. And a shady stream of money no one knows about but me. I'm in deep shit and I need to work it out." He released me to go to his desk and pile paperwork into his briefcase.

"So, you have trouble you need to work out, know you have to leave, and you decide to get stumbling drunk?"

"I'll be fine in an hour when I leave. Pack me a bag. Then we'll have forty five minutes to say goodbye."

I dragged his suitcase from the closet. When I reemerged the fool was downing a shot from the liquor he kept in our room. From the way he dropped the shot glass and raised both hands, my aggravation must have smacked him in the face from across the room.

"Last one. I swear."

A noise woke me in the night, swooping around the house in a mad growl, and I reached for Martin but found his side of the bed cold. Worry deepened the more I loved, and oh how I worried for that man.

The next day was the first day of autumn, but the heat was the breath of a mammoth beast stalking my every move. My boiling herbs in the kitchen made an unbearable steam not even the ceiling fan could subdue. I was standing in the open door fanning myself when Fearghus marched across the lawn, Christian following behind, taking occasional glances behind him. I'd barely moved aside when Fearghus roughly pushed past me through the door.

"Car's gone," Christian said.

"Fearghus' car?"

"Yep. He's gonna—" He stared at the door Fearghus had gone through.

I didn't need him to finish. I was halfway to Paul's carriage house before Christian managed to stop me. "We already tried Uncle Paul. He's not in there."

"Where is he?"

He shrugged. "Dunno."

If Fearghus didn't kill Paul, I would. I returned to the kitchen and lowered the heat on my herbs, and Christian followed me through the house searching for Fearghus. We found him, along with Paul, on the front steps of the house, watching a tow truck coming up the driveway. I watched their backs, Fearghus' shoulders almost level with Paul's and just as broad. The truck made it to the curve, turning slightly so we could see the side. Fearghus' hands went to the top of his head. Something wasn't right about the car. Its wheels were turned at an odd angle, bringing it unusually close to the cab of the truck.

"Is it wrecked?" Christian ran down the steps to Fearghus' side.

The tow truck stopped. The car was a twisted mess, its hood buckled upward like a V, windshield smashed. One wheel bent upward into the frame, both tires flat. Paul descended the steps to sign the driver's clipboard. Fearghus had turned to stone, his hands still on his head, unresponsive to the exclamations coming from Christian next to him.

Paul gestured to the road that led to the garage, and the driver climbed into the cab. Paul took off on foot. And what came out of Fearghus' mouth sent an icy wave through me.

"You want to help me kill that asshole?" He was looking at Christian, who'd gone silent. When he turned around, I expected the subtle start of a child caught in a wrong. There was nothing. No start, no look of shame. He clearly didn't care I'd overheard, so much that he did me the favor of clarifying. "Uncle Lewis wrecked the car, and I'm going to—"

Fearghus' and Christian's eyes lifted to the doorway behind me.

"Going to what?" Lewis said from the door. "It was a great drive until that telephone pole. You're lucky I didn't get hurt worse." He swiveled his shoulder, wincing as he did it.

Fearghus started up the stairs toward him. I made a grab for his arm but only caught sleeve that ripped out of my hand with Fearghus' unaffected motion. The first punch landed before I, or Lewis, was ready, due to the sheer lack of sportsmanly pause that normally preceded a fistfight. Lewis touched a finger to his lip to check for the blood we could all see, cursed at Fearghus, and ducked too late for Fearghus' elbow. The spray of blood turned my stomach sick.

"Go—run, find Martin," I said to Christian before realizing Martin had left for Philadelphia. Someone had to stop them. Lewis' retaliation would soon begin. He was older, bigger—though not by much—and would not be gentle.

Christian gasped. I followed his gaze. Fearghus was now on the defensive, blocking blows with arms and knees, backing into the wall of the house with Lewis on top of him.

"Go get Paul!" I yelled at Christian.

The wet smack of flesh took our attention. Lewis was bent, stumbling, one arm extended to catch himself, the other cradling his face. Fearghus circled and locked an arm around Lewis' neck and began to deliver blow after blow to his face. I wanted to yell his name, but I knew he wouldn't hear me. I had to do something—a pop of fire on the grass like I'd broken up the fight between Fearghus and Jared—but they were on tiled porch. I spun around. I couldn't think. Magic so ripe and uncontained when confronted with anger, blasting out of me to scratch Pierce's neck, now absent. I kicked off my shoes and rushed on to the lawn, grounding myself to that sister oak.

The power was immediate, hot in my head, knocking me to my hands and knees. All power drained away, replaced by a heady lift, my vision going white. It was happening again—a vision at the worst possible time. I clawed the ground to return to reality, but it was already gone, replaced by my hand on a door frame, my careful step into a darkened room. A man—a much older, coarser version of Fearghus—leaning over a sleeping girl, his face grave. He drew her hair away from a pale cheek, and I recognized her at once. She was the young woman for whom I carved my amulet's design on my bedroom floor. She looked younger now. Frail. Her cheekbones sharp, her breath too weak. He took her hand in his and looked at me. I saw what my son would look like as a man. I saw heartbreak in his eyes, and his grief took me down.

My own grief greeted me when I woke in my bed that afternoon. Eleanor was humming softly beside me. I kept my eyes closed to dwell on that grief, to fully realize my failure to stop Fearghus from assaulting a man whose retaliation would make Fearghus' attack look like play. Perhaps my failure was in my own understanding that I couldn't stop Fearghus. I couldn't save him anymore.

"Is Fearghus—where's Fearghus?"

"He went for a long run in the woods. Been gone hours. I'm not sure he's back yet. Are you feeling better? Here, have some tea. It should still be warm."

"Lewis?"

She helped me sit up. "Not so good, madam. But we'll take good care of him."

I took the teacup and gulped it down. My head still swam with images of Fearghus' emotionless face while he pounded Lewis' bloodied nose, interlaced with his older self sitting at the girl's bedside, his expression too acute to bear.

I got up and went downstairs. Christian ran at me, colliding with his face buried against me and his arms tight. One sob escaped before he curbed it, fighting to hold it inside. "I'm sorry, Aunt Sloane."

"Oh, Christian, for what? It's not your fault." I tried to pry him loose, but he held on with a determination designed for more than just his need for comfort. He was too embarrassed to show his wet eyes.

"I should've stopped him." His words were muffled against my arm. "I will next time, I promise."

Next time came far too soon.

CHAPTER 49

AUTUMN, 1979

I HEARD THE SHOUTS while pruning roses in the garden behind the house. The noise carried on the breeze first before seeping from the open windows on the back of the house. I dropped my shears to run inside. From the amount of men swarming the hall and foyer, I knew the situation was inside the house. With Martin still gone I feared who was in charge, who was in trouble. History suggested the problem was Paul. Recent events proved it could be much worse—it could be Fearghus.

"Ready with the car!" someone shouted from the east hall.

I crossed the foyer, but there were too many bodies to pass through the hall. A man put an arm out in front of me. "Sorry, ma'am, it's best if you—"

He then had to back up for a group pressing through. Two men carrying a leg each, two more carrying a limp man's upper body. I didn't turn away fast enough from a sight so gruesome I had to hold onto the closest arm to me to keep from going to the floor. All I could think was *it's not Fearghus, it's not Fearghus* as my own blood pounded thickly in my head like I was the one so maimed. Blood-drenched from head to waist. A head sagged against a chest on a useless neck. Eyes open but rolled back. How I knew that, I wasn't sure, since they were as bloody as the rest of him. They carried him to the door and down the steps. He was a crippled man. A dead man. Even though I'd dreamed of his death so many times, I didn't want to see the gore that was once a man named Pierce.

I kept my hold on that strange arm. The sounds of slamming car doors and engines and shouted orders were consumed by a new ruckus coming from the stairs. The man I clung to towed me aside to make room for a second group. This time, it was exactly what I feared.

Fearghus walked in the middle, his arms held behind him by two brutes. His mouth was bloodied, his forehead gashed. He didn't struggle, but I could see in his eyes he wanted to. He was breathing hard and staring so violently ahead I got the sense he wouldn't see me even if I'd walked in front of him. As he was led past me, I saw fresh red drips on the floor and followed them to their source: his blood-covered fists.

I broke from my human support to follow. In the foyer they stopped him at the foot of the stairs but still held his arms. The master was descending casually, like he'd been called to receive a visitor. I stiffened my legs, my back. With no one to hold on to, the fear quaking through me threatened to render me useless on the floor.

The master reached the bottom of the stairs. "Knees."

The two men holding Fearghus kicked the backs of his knees, knocking him to a kneeling position.

"Bind his hands."

A man stepped forward with a rope. More men had gathered. Someone shut the front door, sealing the spacious foyer like a cage. Fearghus and I had never been so outnumbered, so hopelessly defeated.

"Get her out of the room."

Someone took hold of my arm but I shook it off.

"Madam, you must go. Don't stay for this." It was Fran's voice in my ear, her gentle hand again on my arm. "Christian—he's in the basement. He needs you."

The master snapped his fingers and lifted his chin toward me. The two closest men each took an arm. I was no help to Fearghus. Any power I had was illegal in front of so many eyes, and would only add to the crime Fearghus had already committed.

"I'll go," I said, twisting my shoulders. Not wanting to manhandle a lady of the house, the men released me. "But I expect you'll be merciful to your grandson, and save any punishments to be dealt by his father, who should be home soon."

I didn't wait for his response. I walked calmly back to the hall, where once out of sight I broke into a run, crashing down the stairs in search of the one I could help.

Christian was huddled on the floor in the far corner, hugging his knees. When he saw me he sniffled and ran a hand across his nose. I knelt in front of him. He trembled all over.

"Tell me what happened."

He shook his head before putting it down on his knees to hide his face. I stroked his hair, wet with sweat. He took in a gasp, creating a full-body shudder.

"Breathe, Christian. It's going to be okay."

"It's not. It's so, so not."

"Let's not decide until we calm down, okay?"

"They're gonna kill him." He looked up at me, and the confidence he had in that statement brought a shudder into me I had to mask by sitting beside him and putting my arm around him. I needed to be braced as much as he did. Mam told me long ago they were afraid to kill Fearghus. Martin had assured me they never would. But neither of them could have seen this day.

He laid his face on his knees again, and I saw a smear of blood on his cheek. I lifted his arm, prompting him to sit straight.

"Are you bleeding?"

"No, I just got it on me. All over." He straightened his legs against the floor, revealing a blood-soaked shirt. He showed me his bloody hands. "But I stopped him this time, just like I said I would."

"You stopped Fearghus?"

He scrubbed a hand against his snotty nose. "He was gonna kill my dad, and I stopped him."

When Christian and I emerged from the basement, the hall and foyer were empty. I took him to my room to bathe then left to get him a change of clothes. I scoured the house for any sign of Fearghus but found nothing, not even someone to ask. All the staff must have been released from duties for the day, or had retreated to hiding spots safe from the Moores—and my son.

Giving up, I climbed the stairs to Christian's room for a change of clothes and ran into Paul when I returned to my room. He pulled me inside and slammed the door. Beads of sweat clung to his brow.

"I got a hold of Martin. He should be getting on the road right now. He was back in Philadelphia, so it will only be a few hours—"

"Do you know where they took Fearghus?"

He ran a rough hand over his face. "Yes. You can't go out there, Sloane."

"To the woods?"

He turned to stare outside, as if debating whether he should answer. "Martin will be back—"

"Where'd they take him?"

He faced me. "You know those old buildings where they hold people? He's there for the next seven days ... unless Martin can talk my father out of it."

After putting Christian to bed with a thousand promises Fearghus would be okay, I sat on the front porch steps wrapped in a quilt because waiting inside the house lengthened the time between Martin's arrival and my speaking to him. Night slid over the land, darkening forest. The birds settled and the bats awoke to flutter overhead and give dimension to an overcast sky. I watched them hunt, drowning my thoughts of Fearghus chained in that evil shack where they tortured his father. Paul said the men would turn me away if I tried to see him, that Martin was his only hope.

Headlights blinked through the trees. I stood, raised my quilt over my hair, and descended the steps, but a twinge put me ill at ease. It wasn't Martin.

Lewis and some men unloaded from the car when it stopped in front of me. He was still black and blue from Fearghus' assault on him. "He didn't kill him. You should be glad to hear that. Because if he had—" He turned toward a car speeding up the driveway. This one, I knew to be carrying Martin, and his timing couldn't be better.

"I hope that's Martin because I'm in no mood to deal with this alone."

"It's him." I went forward to meet Martin at his car. He got out and took me by the elbows. "Martin, he's in those buildings—"

"I know." He kissed me as if it was a long-awaited reprieve, lingering too long when something so important was before us. He pulled away like it pained him to do it. "I'm heading out there now."

"Can I come?"

"No." He leaned into the backseat for his briefcase. His movements were measured and slow, like he was nursing sore muscles. He'd only been away from the house a few weeks and the curse had already started releasing its payload. He tucked a gun in the back of his pants and handed me the briefcase. "See that this goes straight to our room."

I took it and he kissed me again, his fingers weaving into my hair. "Don't worry."

Hours passed before he returned to our room nearly stumbling with fatigue. I helped him out of his clothes while he told me his news. Fearghus was guarded by three men, but he was okay.

"A little roughed up, and a lot pissed off. He gave me his word he'd behave—not that he'd be able to do anything. They tarred his hands and feet."

Just as I'd thought. It was a muzzle on our power. Unable to make any connection to earth, stone, or air, he'd been stripped of his magic. "Is he tied up?"

"Chained. But he's okay. I'll talk my father down from seven days. I just need to get some sleep first. I've been going nonstop since I left. And nothing's been settled, in Philadelphia or Cambridge. It's a huge mess."

He fell onto the bed and I lay down next to him. All night I was a rolling, tossing ocean next to a sound, stable rock. When I woke he was gone, but my curtains had been opened, revealing another overcast day that looked too chilly to be spending on the earthen floor of a crumbling old shack.

I dressed and went to the breakfast table, but all I could stand was tea so Eleanor cleared my place setting, and I sat until the cup cooled in my hands. I asked about Christian. She told me he went to the hospital to visit his father. I wondered if that was someone else's idea or his own, and I set the teacup down when it began to shake. The thought of Christian visiting his father all alone, with no one to hold his hand, no one to help him find the right room—it took me to the path that led to Rosemary, and I got up and went to the kitchen to find a task for my hands.

Martin finally found me around noon. His lips said nothing but his eyes said 'upstairs,' so I excused myself from my kitchen task and followed him to our room.

"I got it reduced to three days."

I hugged him so hard he winced. It normally took a few days before the curse released him from its grasp.

"But—no meals."

"No meals for three days? Surely we can sneak him something."

"No. He can handle a fast. It's something I've already taught him. Let's not screw this up; it's a good offer. My father wasn't easy to talk down, especially since Trey attacked Lew last week. Why didn't you call me?"

"Lewis wrecked Fearghus' car."

"I heard." He dropped onto the couch, his face in his hands. "There's just too much going on right now. We need to talk to Trey, tell him—I don't know. Because all I can think right now is that he went about it all wrong. That a premature attack only alerts the other side to your abilities, gives them a chance to figure you out before you've prepared a successful offense. He's letting his emotion rule him, and that's the worst thing to do."

"He's fifteen years old."

"He's a well-trained fighter. But like my father said, if he's going to act like our enemy, he'll be punished like one, and I hate to admit he's right." He got up to sift through his luggage. "Here, I got you something."

I took the white satin drawstring bag and dumped it out into my palm. It was a green aventurine, polished and hung on a pretty silver chain. He told me to turn around, and I lifted my hair so he could fasten it around my neck.

"It reminded me of your eyes. I couldn't pass it up."

When I turned around his mask had dropped, his hard edges now smooth. He studied me like we'd been apart years, not weeks, and the devotion that shone from him was a sentiment so rarely revealed I closed my eyes and drank it in, kissing him, hugging him so hard he had to unwrap me for the pain it caused.

Fearghus didn't return home after three days. When Martin went to retrieve him, he came back alone, saying Fearghus was stubbornly demanding to serve the full seven even though he'd been unchained and all his guards had been relieved of their posts. I packed a bag of clothes, water, and food and headed into the woods. Christian caught up to me, refusing to go back even after I threatened to lock him up next to Fearghus.

When the cluster of stone buildings came into view, Christian and I both stopped. The vile residue of the area crept around us like a smoke we could sense but not see.

"I hate this place," Christian said. "I want to burn it down."

In my silence I agreed. How perfect it would be to see it lit like a bonfire, burning away all the evil that had been performed there.

I wasn't prepared to see evil lurking in the form of my son. When we entered the building that held him, I drew back, first not recognizing his hunkered frame sitting against the far wall. I felt I'd instead stumbled upon a wild animal. He was patchy with the black of the tar. His eyes were sunken and dark when he looked up at me, and when Christian said his name he slid those blackened eyes over to him so slowly I got a tingle in my spine.

"I'm not leaving." His voice was rough with underuse, as sobering as the tar that streaked his arms.

"We're not asking you to. But I brought food, and some warmer clothes. Water."

"No food." He was now looking at a spot on the ground at my feet.

"We won't tell," Christian said.

"Yes, we won't tell anyone you ate. I brought sandwiches, apples—"

"I don't lie." Each word was a strike to my heart.

"Fearghus, you can't stay out here for seven days without food. He's released you at three days. You need to come home."

"He wants me to do seven, I do seven."

"That's stupid!" Christian shouted.

I got a napkin out of the bag and wet it with the water. Fearghus let me wipe his face and check the gash on his forehead, which appeared to be healing under the caked blood and grime. Christian unloaded the food, offering each item to Fearghus and helping himself to bites. I couldn't determine if he was hungry or had some kind of plan, but if he was doing it to entice Fearghus it was working. Fearghus had shifted his whole body away to better avert his eyes. A less stubborn person would surely surrender. I went to work peeling the dried tar from Fearghus' hands.

"I've never met a stupider person," Christian said after Fearghus ignored every piece of food I'd brought.

"Unload the candles, Christian, and I'll teach you to light them."

We spent the next couple hours like this, Christian slowly eating all the food I'd brought while I gave him lessons in Bevan magic. We tried to include Fearghus but he remained in his spot against the wall, glaring at nothing. Dusk came early due to the overcast sky. Christian lit the candles one final time, and we left Fearghus still refusing to leave his holding cell, firmly fixed in whatever angry darkness inhabited his mind.

Christian stopped me with a hand on my arm several paces outside the door. "Maybe I should stay with him."

"I don't think—"

"Yeah, I should." He turned back, his eyes white in the darkness. "It's just so damn spooky."

"'Damn' is a grown-up word."

"I know." He shivered. Everything in his life was grown-up. His worries, his pains, his responsibility. "He's just not gonna talk to me at all and it'll be like I'm alone in there too. I'll just have to talk for both of us."

He grinned at me until I smiled, partially because of how special he was, but mostly because I knew taking on both sides of a conversation was a task he could easily handle. I kissed his forehead. He scrubbed off the kiss, squared his shoulders, and walked back into that shack.

I brought them breakfast in the morning. When I delivered lunch, Christian followed me outside to tell me he'd gotten Fearghus to eat.

"I told him I wasn't gonna eat unless he did, and when my stomach started growling I knew he could hear it, so I whined about how hungry I was and the dummy started eating!"

Wind shifted the tree limbs above us, allowing a beam of sunlight through that hit him straight in the face. He squinted one eye and raised a hand to shield the sun, those blue irises like a reflection of the sky. He looked so much like Rosemary in that moment I had to seize him in a hug to cover the tears that gathered so fiercely. Her spirit lived on in this boy, who was such a blessing to me and Fearghus, some days I wondered if he was planted by my ancestors. I hoped they hadn't; his abuses were too great a payment for the relief he gave me and Fearghus.

But hope is a tricky thing. Imagining Fearghus' world without Christian wasn't something I liked to do.

CHAPTER 50

FEARGHUS RETURNED TO the house on the morning of the eighth day. To say he'd changed was a lie. For a change to take place, there must be evidence of a previous form. There was no hint of my son in the body that answered to his name. He was as different as the Moores' new treatment of him. Instead of the reluctant tolerance of the past fifteen years, they made every effort to shun him in ways that spoke of their hate while upholding the lie that he was very much still one of them. He knew as well as I did that they were experts at dispensing abuse against their own blood.

Winter came in fast and cold, freezing the last of our garden's unpicked harvest before we could save it. Martin returned home after a second trip to Cambridge and Philadelphia. His business wasn't finished, but it was handled for the time being, and he was so ill from being away I kept him in bed for two days. He hadn't stayed home long enough before he'd left the second time, and the curse was determined to punish him for it. Eleanor told me Pierce was also home, transferred from the hospital to finish his own recovery. I hadn't seen him, not until the night of the first family dinner in months.

Something wasn't right the moment I entered the dining room, but my confusion was replaced by the unease brought by Pierce's smile. His dinner jacket sat loose on a skinny frame. His face was drawn and angular, yellowed by old bruises, his eyes even more cutting than before.

"Welcome back," I said to him. "I'm glad to see you doing better."

He laughed, curbing it when Martin pulled out my chair. Instead of sitting beside me, Martin went to speak with one of the staff near the wall. Seats filled, the master entered, and Martin went to have a word with him. When he finally sat beside me, his displeasure was carefully held but so obvious to me it got my heart beating faster. I looked from one face to another, searching out the source of the problem.

Fearghus entered the room and that's when I noticed. His chair and place setting had been removed. He made it halfway to the table before he realized it himself. The silence was a living thing, sucking all air from the room, forcing all our eyes in the same direction. As Fearghus scanned each person I got an awful thought: he was sizing us up, determining whom to attack first.

Martin slid out. "Son, take my seat. I'm expecting a phone call."

"Sit down, Martin," the master said.

Martin hovered, halfway to standing. He seemed to wrestle with a decision, then he sat down.

Christian pushed out.

"Christian," the master said. He snapped his fingers at a member of the staff who came forward to scoot Christian back in.

The master's gaze was then on me, like I was the next one expected to defy orders. A flush rose in me and I shoved away from the table, meeting instant resistance as I was scooted back by the same man who'd scooted Christian. "Pardon, madam," he whispered.

I could see Fearghus leave the room even though I'd averted my eyes. I didn't want to witness my child take his own shunning. For so many years I'd been included in the treatment. To see him bear it alone was a new torment I never expected.

Martin leaned onto the table toward the master. "So this is how it's going to go? Fifteen years, all down the toilet? Ostracizing him will only do *us* harm."

"Eat your dinner. We aren't discussing this here."

Martin stabbed the table with his finger. "Then after dinner." He was rarely defiant, and it worried me.

As soon as dinner ended, Christian scurried from the room. I caught up to him and called him off. I needed to confront Fearghus alone. He was outside in the cold with no dinner jacket, as if daring the freezing air to overcome him.

He didn't look at me when I stood beside him. "Come to the woods with me. I have to show you something."

I started walking and he followed. We crunched through frozen grass, my dinner slippers turning cold and brittle.

My gown caught fallen branches in the woods, clinging helplessly until ripping free. Now robbed of all my warmth, I hugged myself, the air harsh in my lungs.

"Mom—"

"Hush."

He no doubt thought I was using Christian's trick on him—joining him in his self-torment until he surrendered for my sake and went indoors.

In the spot where Martin pledged himself as half Bevan warrior, I dropped to my knees and gestured for Fearghus to do the same. He faced me, his stoic detachment broken with such curiosity it summoned a memory of his child self.

"We don't feel warmth now, but it's all over this earth. In close places like heated homes, and far away on warmer lands. Overcome that distance. Seek out the warmth, feel it. Take a tiny portion from one place, a tiny portion from another, so each won't be missed. Gather them together until a powerful warmth rests at your feet."

I placed fingertips against earth. He did the same. I waited as he bowed his head to do what I asked. Heat surged in the ground below us, creating a wavy disturbance of air all around.

"Ease it back, Fearghus." I often forgot how much power he held with so little practice of restraint. "Magic is a balance. Draw too much and it will draw from you. What we've done here is a small act, but if we heated the whole forest we'd pay the price in whatever way the elements decide. Remember, our magic works best in combination with others of our kind. If we each add a small piece, the balance isn't tipped too much by one. Sometimes it's necessary to take more, and it's worth the price. Often it's not. You'll learn to determine that for yourself."

The blast of heat died to a subtle warmth, easing the burn on my cheeks.

"Magic must not be wasted, must not be called upon carelessly. It's only for the most dire of situations, ones where normal human action won't suffice. Overuse and misuse will wear on you. You'll become its slave. You'll be used as a draw for other forces beyond your control. It's addictive. It can control you. Never use it as a substitute for good sense. Never use it to cheat in life. Every spell we know has a price, some higher than others. Seek out the ones where the benefit outweighs the risk."

The ground thawed as I spoke, turning to mud that I spread on my arms in the Bevan war design. "You're a warrior, Fearghus. They hate you because they fear you. They know you're stronger and always will be."

"*Oderint dum metuant,*" he said. Anger creased his brow. Not because of my words— because of abuses we'd both endured, and new ones he'd have to bear alone.

"Your turn." I pointed to the mud.

He spread his arms. I placed my hand on top of his to paint the design, to transfer it through his hands into memory.

"Your ancestors live inside you, granting power I can't speak of. Remember this, what I've given to you now. Do you feel it?"

He nodded, reverence subduing the anger like I'd hoped it would.

"Bring it forth when you need to remember most. This is a gift known to my blood and yours, and no one else."

He studied his arms.

"Don't ever let them see this."

He looked up at me like I'd just given him the answer to a long-standing enigma.

"And don't let them pull you down into their darkness. Every hateful thing you do gives them pleasure. Don't let them get that from you. Don't let them win."

His face had gone hard again. I stood and kissed his forehead. "'What a man thinks of himself, that it is which determines his fate.'"

I didn't need to explain. I could see from his face he recognized the quote.

"I think I'll stay out here awhile," he said.

I left him there in the puddle of warmth, caged in by bare trees creaking in the cold. After smearing the design from my arms I returned to the house, climbed the stairs to the top floor, and knocked on the mistress' door. It opened gently this time, and I entered her room still shivering, the hem of my gown torn, arms covered in mud, my hair tossed by the wind. She remained in her armchair, studying my appearance, as stolid as her oldest son.

"I need your help." I paused to steady myself, now that speaking had revealed how breathless I was. "Your absence all these years has worsened an already grave problem."

"Do you think I don't know that?"

"I can't fix them alone. I've tried so many times. So many different—"

She abruptly clamped a hand over her eyes as if she'd just become gripped by a migraine. "Stop trying. Your wasted effort brings me pity I can't stand."

I sat on the edge of the chair next to her. "You won't help me at all?"

She lowered her hand to scrutinize me long enough for my question to die between us. Repeating it would turn it to the desperate plea I didn't want her to hear. Pity wasn't something I wished to empower in a woman whose help I sought. I wanted her to help me out of respect.

Finally she turned away to admire the tinkle of sleet hitting her windows. "You'd think weather like this would make your confinement here more pleasant."

"It would no longer be unpleasant if they weren't tormenting my son. I'm happy here with Martin, and I wouldn't leave him."

She brought both hands over her eyes then, as if blinded by bright light. "I'll offer you this. That stone you wear is capable of holding much power. Even the tiniest spell placed upon it will be magnified to a strength otherwise hard to achieve and impossible for most mediums to enclose and preserve."

I fingered my green aventurine pendant. "Martin gave me this."

"It was no coincidence."

"He didn't tell me that."

She breathed out heavily, like her next words were a new weight she'd have to take on. "He doesn't know."

That night I dreamed of collecting all the spent sleeping stones I'd hid under Rosemary's pillows. Their discoveries were unending—in the pockets of every article of clothing I owned and under every cushion in the house. Every stone I snatched up would be replaced with another, and the pile

I accrued was taller than the house. When I woke I remembered the day I'd almost used one to subdue that gory fight between Pierce and Paul. That stone didn't put one of them down before the blows began, but it could've been used to stop Fearghus from attacking Lewis, and Pierce, if I'd been in the room. Once out of bed I tripled my normal recipe and affected my aventurine with the strongest sleeping spell I'd ever done, deciding to wear it always so if I was witness to the next time my son turned savage, I could stop him.

My talk with Fearghus in the wintery forest that day brought fifteen solid years of his impassive obedience. He accepted his position as the shunned member of the family almost as if he favored it, and being exempt from family dinners was a perk envied by every one of us. They found new and sinister ways to shun him, and he shouldered it all. Whether he thought their response to his attack on Pierce was justified or inevitable, I did not know.

Pierce's cruelty toward Fearghus turned from a game to a war. The abuse I witnessed in the open left me helplessly livid. What Fearghus endured in private could only be reported by Fearghus himself, and he was coolly mute and dismissive if questioned. He quickly learned not to display interest toward any object that could be destroyed in front of him. He could no longer assume inclusion in the smallest, most casual of gatherings. And I warned him to never bring any living thing he'd raised or befriended anywhere near the house. Although his cat had died a natural death, I was certain no new companion of his would be that fortunate.

Like those of a common criminal, his room and body were regularly searched. Items were confiscated without explanation. Prized belongings he'd shifted to the secrecy of the attic were found and destroyed. All the newer staff were turned against him, either by orders from the master or by their own fear. His room became a shell of one, no longer cleaned and empty of everything but the few sparse necessities. Any new things Fearghus acquired were stowed in my room or Christian's. He learned to change his sheets, scrub his toilet, and keep up with other cleaning tasks I'd taught him over the years but he'd never had to regularly perform. The responsibility would make him a better man. There was good in every situation, and no matter what torment the Moores brought, we'd always find that one gleam in the darkness.

It was Fearghus' new uncomplaining nature that had me most worried. The obedience he'd found seemed more like a sheet slid over his temper. Although I couldn't see it anymore, I could sense it, and without an outburst now and then, I feared what was building. Speeding tickets, crashed cars, and school fistfights didn't count against his newfound compliance. They were normal teenage boy behavior as far as I knew, and Christian's teenage years following Fearghus' didn't prove me wrong. Christian was introduced to everything much sooner than most boys were, but his whole life consisted of growing up too fast.

School fights turned to bar fights in college, and my frustration lay more firmly with the police department's special rules for the Moore family than with my son. How was he to learn, if a fitting punishment wasn't ever granted? I was spared the news of most of the delinquent behavior, and for that I was grateful. Both Fearghus and Christian were old enough to get into this new level of trouble, and they were old enough to get themselves out.

With Fearghus at college, and Christian busy with school and girlfriends, my free time at the estate became unbearable. Martin agreed to practice mithridatism against the curse, so we travelled together, me nursing him in hotels, resorts, and bed-and-breakfasts when the curse took hold. I'd developed several recipes to soothe the curse's effect, ease his pain, and extend our days away. All the time I'd lost with Tara I was making up for in visits to her now that she'd made peace with our situation and outgrown her resentment that I chose Fearghus over her. Maturity helped her finally understand I'd have done the same for her, if she'd been the Moore's target.

Often we'd return home and find Fearghus out of town himself. Something kept pulling him to the big cities up north for a few days, only to return to the estate and sleep a few more. When Christian started going along, I demanded to know what they were doing. Christian was still young enough for me to have a small amount of say in his life.

"Tournaments," Fearghus finally told me.

"For what?"

"Fighting. It's good practice." He was standing at the kitchen counter, devouring a third sandwich.

"What kind of fighting?"

He raised his empty glass for Ruby to refill with milk. "You're asking too many questions." He smiled then and held it, fully knowing it would subdue me.

"I'm going to assume it's all completely safe and legal."

He laughed. It was so nice to hear a laugh from him I forgave that it was not the answer I wanted.

On our return home the summer Fearghus turned twenty-five, there was a girl staying in his room. With an apartment near the University of Richmond campus, he rarely spent time at home during the school year Now summer was here, and so was he, with this girl whose cool gaze could chip stone.

I heard Fearghus' voice from the hall as I helped Martin upstairs. After settling him in our room, I knocked on Fearghus' half-open door. I could tell he was on the phone with Christian. He told me to come in. With most of his attention on his phone call, he waved to me from the sofa. A girl sat beside him, her leg hooked over the top of his. She lowered her magazine and stared at me, unsmiling, in a way that made me feel unwelcome in my own house.

I crossed the room and offered my hand. "Hello. I'm Sloane."

She looked at my hand. Fearghus ended his call and got up to hug me. I'd never gotten used to the tower of a man he'd become, or how he seemed to gain twc inches and ten pounds of muscle every time I saw him.

"Christian's on his way. Should be home tomorrow." He turned to include the girl in our greeting. "Mom, this is Kate."

She set down her magazine and stood. She was model-tall with features strikingly similar to Fearghus: fair skin, dark, straight hair, lean yet athletic. The smile she unleashed seemed unattached to her and morphed her into a different girl than the one who'd observed me over the top of her magazine moments ago.

I took her hand. "Pleased to meet you."

She returned the sentiment in a rich southern accent and dropped the smile like a cigarette she wanted to put out.

"We'll have a little birthday party for Fearghus tomorrow. We'd love if you'd join us."

She made a face at Fearghus. "*Fearghus?*"

"It's nothing too exciting," I continued, "but Ruby's cakes are too good to miss."

She looked blankly at me. "I've already been invited."

"Wonderful. Then I'll put you in charge of making him come. He tries to get out of it every year." The conversation felt grossly out of tune. To avoid further dissonance, I retreated toward the door. "Fearghus, will you be around this evening? I'm sure your father would like to see you."

"I wasn't, but…" he cast a look at Kate's almost inaudible exasperated sigh "…I'll come by to see him before I leave."

As I passed through the doorway, I heard Kate again say, "*Fearghus?*"

I wanted so much to like her, but a feeling too strong to shake was screaming at me not to. The ridicule in her voice repeating his name carried no flirt, no friendly tease. I'd met many girls brought home by Fearghus, even more by Christian. This was the first time I'd been anything but pleased that either one of them had found a new friend, another road away from that house. Perhaps my uneasiness was due to Kate being the first who carried a hint of permanence. Or perhaps she was the first one who was so utterly wrong for him.

CHAPTER 51

SUMMER, 1990

ONE YEAR LATER my unease with Kate had not faded. She was no more familiar to me than one of the many men who trained with Fearghus in the room downstairs. Recognizable, yet strangers. Even if they spoke to me, they gave nothing of importance, no human connection I could carry in my memory. They spent more time with Fearghus than I did, knew things about him I'd never know. They had the capability and the opportunity to hurt him severely. They were just like her.

Christian's twenty-first birthday celebration had filled the house with so many people I found an exit early and escaped to my room. The summer solstice was again upon me, and I spent the anniversary of my captivity on my bedroom sofa with my feet in Martin's lap while he reviewed some documents.

Raised voices carried into the room through our open door to the hall. Martin looked up from his work just as I recognized it was Fearghus and Kate in the throes of a bitter argument. Into Fearghus' next-door room they went, slamming the door.

"I don't like him bringing her up here. I know he's a grown man, but—"

"I've told him to move into the room at the end of the hall. I'll have the staff move him tomorrow."

Our haven now unsettled, I put on *I Surrender Dear*, causing Martin to set down his work and gaze at me from across the room like we'd been transported to the past, his love for me raw and new again, but without the fear and guilt associated with that time.

"That's the one I won you over with."

"Not exactly. Well, maybe a little."

"All I could think about then was winning you over. I lived and breathed it."

We both turned toward a loud thud next door, followed by an angry female voice.

"I have good reason to tell him to move to his new room now."

I slid my feet into my shoes. "That would embarrass him. Let's just go downstairs."

The crowd downstairs had miraculously grown even more. We squeezed into the kitchen, where Christian's friends from Yale were playing a drinking game. I didn't see Christian anywhere. Twenty-one wasn't much of a milestone to a young man who'd been drinking since he was fourteen. Martin stole an unopened bottle of champagne and two glasses and pulled me outside. The patio was at full capacity. Another crowd had gathered by the lake.

"To the woods," Martin said.

Although it was still dusk, the heavy canopy brought the woods closer into night. Cool air lurked in the trees, untouched by the heat of the day. We walked the path to the bench within the woods, and Martin poured the champagne.

"I know you know the rules we've laid out for Trey, but you don't know what they'll do if he breaks it."

"You mean, if he fathers a child?"

"Yes. It won't live, if it's up to them."

"He won't break the rule."

"We've learned something that could make the rule more appealing. Do you know the effect that's been timed to his thirtieth birthday?"

We'd recently returned from Chicago, where Mam had locked herself and Martin in the kitchen for an hour. I wasn't pleased he'd waited so long to tell me what he'd learned that day, but I didn't want to be mad at him on such a balmy starlit night with the branches swaying gently above us, mixing the thick summer warmth with the idle forest-dwelling cool. The champagne prickled on my tongue and sent heat to my belly. I wanted a new topic of conversation, one that wouldn't turn the sweet night foul.

"Your family has affected him to stop aging at age thirty," he said. "We knew it would happen, just didn't know the timing until now."

I set my glass on the bench and got up. A few paces took me to a clear opening to the sky where the first stars twinkled.

"Your mam told me to use that information how I pleased. I needed time to mull it over, to find if there was some hidden meaning before bringing it to you."

"You did not. You should've told me."

"We have to use this, Sloane. Your love for him won't allow an unbiased view, but trust me on this."

"And what about *your* love for him?"

"I can keep it separate to work this out, which I've done, but you aren't going to like it." He took a breath and held it a moment before letting it out. "I've decided to go to my father with this, so we can use it to keep him straight. We'll tell Trey it's our gift to him, our exchange for following that rule."

"That's rotten, Martin. It's a sickening lie!"

He came to stand in front of me. "Do you want a child of his brought into this life? You've prevented a child of ours, yet you'd welcome his? To be raised in this house?"

"He could leave this house."

"He's not allowed to have a child, even if he leaves."

Martin was right to have kept Mam's news from me. Long ago he'd agreed to handle all the lying to Fearghus. I'd wanted no part of it. I didn't need to be made aware of information about my son that would only be twisted for their purposes.

"I'm out of this, Martin. Don't tell me any more things I have to keep from him. Now, and forever. I'd rather be in the dark."

He let me walk back alone. For that I was glad. I didn't want to argue with someone I knew was right. When he came to bed that night he was clumsy and slow, cursing each piece of furniture he ran into, cursing his pants he couldn't kick off. I'd been waiting to welcome him, but not if he was drunk. I didn't turn toward him when he got under the covers. He fell asleep a moment later, and I lay awake, consumed by the guilt of my son truly being the one in the dark and I was buried far too deep to offer him a hand.

Fearghus had signed up for classes that summer, and Kate spent a lot of time at the house waiting for him to come home. This had been Christian's job in the past, and he returned to it, with her. It seemed odd, since Fearghus' apartment was closer to his classes and where he spent most of his time. She'd be more likely to catch him there.

Kate and Christian wandered into the library one day where I was spending a rainy afternoon. Eleanor brought them snacks, leading me to understand it was the hospitality that made Kate prefer waiting at the estate. She and Christian already had a conversation going, and soon they appeared to forget about me.

"He doesn't get it. I tried to explain it to him, but—" Kate swiped a hand in the air over her head. They were talking about a movie they'd all seen. She apparently thought it had gone over Fearghus' head.

"He gets it," Christian said. "He just doesn't need to discuss it to death like we do."

"He doesn't discuss it because he doesn't get it. Ideas like that just bounce around inside that thick skull with nowhere to go."

I looked up at her, but she was oblivious to me. Fearghus had brought home so many girls who simply adored him. Why would he spend over a year with one who had no qualms about telling people how stupid she thought he was?

Christian laughed—his humoring laugh, not his real one. Then he changed the subject right before Fearghus walked through the door. Fearghus' eyes were faded; he looked worn, yet preoccupied. I got up to greet him. He let me kiss his cheek before turning those eyes on me. "I just talked to Dad. You knew?"

Martin must've told him about the immortality going into effect when he turned thirty. I shook my head, because even though I did know, I hadn't been in the know as long as Martin.

"Is it true?" he spoke low so only I could hear.

I nodded. It broke my heart.

"So I just have to accept it?"

"Yes. And be patient, because sometimes things we find unfair have their own way of working out."

"It's bullshit," he muttered, walking away. Immortality was a gift many would die for. But to Fearghus it was yet another one of their controls placed on him without his consent, when he was working so hard to be good, to obey, and hoping to someday be free of them. This unwelcome gift would drastically change his life. It was their side of a bargain he never agreed to enter.

He joined Christian and Kate on the sofa as I headed to the door. I took one glance before leaving, hoping Fearghus had relaxed now that he was with the people who loved him. He was as sullen as ever, staring at the floor as Kate tousled Christian's hair.

"Your hair is getting long," she said. It was a move so boldly flirtatious a foot away from Fearghus, I paused out of sheer surprise.

Christian squinted one eye and gave her a crooked grin. Fearghus continued his absent staring.

The threat of trouble there was thick enough to push me from the room before I witnessed more.

On my way to bed that night, I saw Christian standing at the window in the foyer, watching outside.

"Waiting for someone?"

He started so badly he dropped his keys. The Christian I knew should've laughed, but he cursed bitterly and stooped to pick them up.

"Everything okay?" I walked over to stand next to him.

Instead of the expected arm around my shoulders and kiss on the check, I got a blunt, "No."

"Can I help?"

He bowed his head, rubbing the center of his forehead. "What would you do if you wanted to stop doing something, and every time you think you're finally going to stop, you do it again?"

"It depends on what this thing is."

"It's something you really, *really* don't want to do."

"Something someone is making you do?"

"No, something you're just doing. Something you want to do." He cursed again, put both hands on his head, and gripped his hair. "I need to get out of this house."

I reached for his arm, but he was already out the door whistling for someone to bring his car. He had to be aware of how little what he said made sense, how contradictory it was. I hoped he knew how much I wanted to help him, if he'd only let me.

I climbed the stairs and found Martin sitting on the edge of the bed looking as tense as Christian.

"They're doing things without me," he said.

"Why is there a gun on the bedside table?"

He got up and put it in the drawer. "All the travelling we've been doing—they've started leaving me out of our plans."

"Maybe that's a good thing."

He went to his liquor cabinet and poured himself a whiskey. "No, it's not. We need to take a break from travelling."

"And disrupt our work at building your tolerance to the curse?"

"So be it. It's more important I'm here."

I exhaled at him, disappointed. I didn't want the tolerance he'd gained to seep away, all our work going to waste.

He tossed back his drink. "Come to bed."

"I'm not sleeping next to a loaded gun."

"Then we'll have to switch sides. I need to be by the door."

I woke that night in a sweat, a hand to my chest to slow my pounding heart. In my nightmare Paul was drowning, and I was running to the shore to save him. With each step I took, the tide went farther out, sucking him farther away from me. Now back in reality, I tried to gather my breath. My room around me was a void. I could feel my satin nightgown, the cool sheets, but I couldn't see my own hands raised in front of me. Instead, a fractured texture made a wall all around before my room reappeared. I realized in that nightmare Paul hadn't been in the ocean, but the lake outside, and I was running on grass in the blue slippers that were sitting at the bedside, the blue-flowered gown I was wearing right then flapping against my legs.

My feet hit the floor and slid into those slippers, and I ran down the stairs, through the foyer, down the hall to the kitchen. I flung open the door and tore down the hill. A patch of white lay at the shore. I headed for it, slipping in the wet grass. It was a person—a very still person. I knew it was Paul before I saw his face.

He was on his back, his upper body and head bent backward over the bank into the water. It lapped at his face, covering it, retreating. I tugged him up by the collar but his weight was too much and he went splashing back into the water, his head fully submerged.

I gripped his shirt and pulled to no avail. His waistband was no better for a handhold. I jumped into the water beside him. As soon as I got my shoulder under his neck, he jerked awake, clawing the air then clawing me. I hollered his name. His effort to fight sent him crashing into the water next to me. Pain flared in my cheek as I saw a burst of white. Then I was underwater.

I struggled free of him, but then he had me again, and I got a cold stab of fear that he didn't recognize me, that he thought I was his attacker. I inhaled water. It cut through my chest like a vicious burn. I didn't know which way was up or down. My feet found a solid plane and I kicked off, bursting out of the water to screams of my name.

I coughed and gagged, water pouring from my mouth. Paul trudged through the water toward me. I raised a hand and backed up, still coughing, my lungs on fire.

"I'm not going to hurt you. Sloane, my god, Sloane."

I took another step backward and tripped over something on the lake bottom. Paul lunged for me before I went under.

"Hold onto me," he said, but I was incapable. The coughing was all-consuming. He dragged me on to the bank and we lay there, me coughing up water while he cursed every sacred entity.

When I had my breath again, I stood up. Paul rose next to me. I cleared the water off my face with the back of my hand. He wiped my nose with his shirt. My throat felt raw enough to bleed.

I risked two words. "You okay?"

He nodded before hugging me hard enough to squeeze the remaining water out of my lungs. When he started to release me, I hung on, my cheek glued to his chest because if he let me go I'd fall apart. Someone had tried to kill him, and I wasn't going to give them the satisfaction of my breakdown.

"I'm okay, I'm okay," he said.

"What happened?"

"I don't know. I really don't—"

I let him go then so I could see his face.

"I was in my carriage house last I remember. Had some drinks like usual, must've passed out."

"And then someone dragged you out here to drown?" I spun toward the house, looking for lights in the master's room, Pierce's room, the mistress' room. All was dark.

He unloaded another set of curses.

"Paul, you have to get clean. Of everything."

He dropped to a squat, his face in his hands.

"Do you think you could have walked out here yourself?"

He shook his head, still in his hands. "Wish I could say no, but how could I? I'm a mess."

I knelt in front of him, lowering his hands from his face. He raised my fallen strap to my shoulder.

"That's why you need to stop all the drinking. All the drugs. This was bad, Paul. If I hadn't woken up—"

"Sloane, there's shit going on in that house you don't know about. Things they're doing—going to do—I need to have a way to turn it off."

"I can make you something less potent."

"Less potent isn't enough." He took my face in his hands and kissed my forehead. "Come with me and clean up. You can't go back in there like that. Martin will think I tried to kill you, and I don't think he'll be too far off."

He gasped when he flipped on the light inside his carriage house. He turned my cheek toward the light. "I'm a dead man."

I touched the spot. It was quite swollen and also felt like it had split. I went to his bathroom mirror and gasped myself. Now aware of the wound so hideous it rivaled one of Fearghus' worst, I noticed the throbbing pain that had been present since our struggle in the water but hadn't been important enough to dwell on after saving Paul's life.

"Please tell me you have some way to cover that up," he said.

I got some tissue to dab off the blood where the skin had split. "It was an accident. You didn't mean to do it."

"First of all, at the time, yes I did. And second—have you met your husband? Your son? Neither one of them will give a shit if that was an accident."

"Then I'll get rid of it, but you have to help me. I'll need some things from my room where Martin is sleeping." I leaned against the sink. It hurt to talk and my head felt foggy. "Give me something I can wear."

I dried off and changed into his shirt and pants. I did some folding and rolling so nothing would fall down. Then we walked across the grass under the stars. My head swam. I stumbled, catching Paul's arm. When it happened a second time, my vision darkened at the corners. We staggered in through the kitchen door I'd left wide open. I didn't know how we were going to get what I needed without waking Martin.

It was halfway up the stairs when I remembered Martin had stashed that gun in the drawer by the bed. And how he'd demanded to switch sides. The staircase pitched, and I tightened my hold on the handrail, but it slid through my fingers.

CHAPTER 52

I WOKE WITH SOMETHING heavy and cold on my face. I peeled it away, set it on the bedside table. I blinked my vision clear, and found myself in my bed, my room filled with sunshine.

"Madam? I think you should lay back down."

I was confused a moment, thinking it was Fran's voice I'd heard until I realized she'd retired from the estate long ago. Eleanor had replaced her, and this was the first time she'd had to nurse me.

"I'll tell Martin you're awake."

It was Paul I wanted to see, and I told that to Martin as soon as he came. Martin sat on the bed beside me, tilting my face so he could examine the wound. "I'd like to hear your side of the story before you talk to Paul."

"My side is the same as Paul's."

"I'll be the judge of that."

"Will you also be the executioner? I'm not going to play court with you, Martin, so—"

"Trey's also waiting to hear your side. He's not very happy with Paul right now."

The ache in my head was so deep it hurt to leave my eyes open, so I leaned back and covered my eyes with my arms.

"I'd like to know why you were wearing Paul's clothes."

"I'd fallen in the lake."

"In the middle of the night? I remember you going to bed with me."

I told him all of it—the vision, the near-drowning, the misunderstanding that led to the bump on my face.

"It's more than a bump," he said when I finished.

"Take it up with the person who tried to drown Paul."

"He's put his hands on you more than once."

"He'd never intentionally hurt me."

"I disagree. So does your son, and we don't often agree on things. But it doesn't matter. Paul's going away for a while." He checked his watch. "The car will be leaving in thirty minutes. If you want to talk to him, now's the time."

"Will you tell him to come up?"

He examined my face again, shaking his head. "Don't let him rile you up. You need to rest."

"Everyone's convinced I hit you," Paul said after he'd kissed my forehead, and both my hands, and apologized for five straight minutes. "I guess that's true in a way."

"It was an accident."

"Martin might understand that now, but Trey won't. His exact words to me were, 'I don't forget.' Next time you find me face down in the lake, you'll know exactly who did it."

"I'll talk to him. He'll listen to me."

"It doesn't matter. I'm leaving for a little while. Back to rehab, and I'm going to make an effort to get better this time. I'm tired of being their screw-up."

Christian and I were the only ones who saw him off. After the two of them traded some shoulder squeezing and back slapping, Paul started down the steps toward the car. Halfway down, he stopped. Then he turned around and came back up the steps to give Christian a hard hug that spoke of more than a simple goodbye. It brought to me all the times Paul had been a father to Christian when Pierce had failed. All the games of catch, the high-fives, the bicycle lessons. It brought forth Rosemary. Then Paul had me by the shoulders.

"Because I can't kiss that swollen cheek," he said, and kissed me sweetly on the lips. "I love you, Miss Bevan."

"I love you too. Don't come back until you're well."

"Yes, ma'am."

Paul got in the car. Christian linked his arm with mine and we watched the car drive away.

"Good thing they didn't see that, or we'd have a funeral to attend," he said.

I wasn't sure which act he was referring to: my kiss, or his hug.

Paul was still in rehab two years later when Fearghus came to my room looking more serious than usual. Fearghus' visits home were spent eating in the kitchen or practicing in the training room. Rarely would he come seeking me.

I was pleased with that, as long as he was busy and out of trouble.

"Kate and I are getting married," he said, with no lead-up to soften the surprise.

I didn't need time to prepare my response. "Do you love her?"

"Yeah."

I waited until he looked at me. "Does she love you?"

He gave me that special expression sons give mothers: *You're being paranoid. I know what I'm doing. I love you, but please butt out.* "She wants us to move back in here."

"Is that what you want?"

He shrugged. He knew the animosity he'd felt, the struggle he'd had with these people since he was a child. He knew his apartment gave him the distance he needed to keep the peace with them. And he was going to push it, like he pushed everything. Someday he would push too hard.

"I can't complain about my son moving back home." I took his hand. Children made mistakes. When they're young, a mother can correct them, steer them in the right direction. When they're grown, all a mother can do is take a seat and watch it happen.

"And you know the agreement you made with your father and grandfather. Are you okay with that? Not ever being a father yourself?"

He shrugged again. "I'm fine with it. I'd be a crappy father anyway."

"You'd be a wonderful father." I wanted to ask him if Kate knew of the rule, to gently suggest he have that conversation before they got married, but I knew it wasn't my place. If she loved him like she should love a man she'd agreed to marry, she'd stay with him despite that unfair rule, and hopefully also because of it. He needed her more than ever.

I took a breath and buried the store of distrust I'd collected for her. I forgave the countless twinges of bad character: the sideways glances, the rude comments to the staff, the rolled eyes, the words and gestures that straddled the line between friendly and flirty with Christian. I squashed my distrust under my trust of Fearghus. I hoped I was wrong about Kate.

I was glad to be wrong about the influence she had over him. Even as she pressed him to move back to the estate, he held his ground and bought a little house for them just outside of Richmond. According to Christian, Fearghus used his "fight money," to keep from being indebted to his father. Fearghus drove me to see his new house on my first day out of the estate without Martin in twenty-eight years.

Standing on the stone path in front of the white cottage with mint-green shutters and a swing on the porch, I saw a relief in Fearghus' face so profound he didn't need to speak. I knew exactly what he was thinking. His life had finally become normal. Had become his. He finally had something they couldn't take away.

"Seventy-five acres," he said. "All wooded. House needs a new roof and some remodeling inside, and I'll build a garage over there." He pointed to the side lawn.

"Is the backyard cleared for a garden?"

He grinned. "Sure is." There was an openness in his eyes I hadn't seen for at least twenty years. He kicked a rock free at his feet and scooped up a sample of the exposed dirt. "Check out that soil."

Kate never warmed to the cottage, even after the year of work Fearghus put into it. He worked beside the men he hired, replacing roofing and plumbing and light fixtures. Still determined to move into the estate, Kate went around Fearghus and talked to the master himself. The northwest bedroom was remodeled for her, and she moved in as a new bride whose husband lived with her part-time.

Fearghus dumped more money into the cottage, thinking perfection would attract his wife. He paved the gravel driveway, planted a rose garden, and built a screened-in porch off the back. He brought me to view the finished work before he showed it to Kate. I was the final set of eyes, employed to make sure he hadn't overlooked anything. He'd surpassed perfection, and I told him so. I couldn't stop myself from saying something else.

"If Kate's not satisfied by all you've done, then she simply can't be satisfied."

He laughed at that and muttered something under his breath I didn't hear. "She gets me though. She knows about us. And that's nice to have."

That was news to me. "How does she know about us?"

"I don't know. But I don't have to lie to her, and that's worth busting my ass to fix up a house she may never like."

I wasn't sure I agreed with him. And when I overheard her telling him she'd never move into that 'crackerbox,' I decided he was dead wrong. It wasn't worth it at all.

He divided his days between the estate and his cottage, pretending it didn't bother him, that he needed to visit the estate for training anyway, but I could see the slump in his shoulders, that new light in his eyes once again dim. His resignation to failure had killed the tiny sprout of enthusiasm. His short-lived taste of normalcy and freedom was over. She'd put roots into the estate, and she'd pulled him back to his prison like she was a natural piece of the family she'd married into.

It was an idea so powerfully evoked one year later, when he sought me out in my bedroom again with a bit of news to confound it all. He'd honored the bargain, he said. He'd been careful. He didn't know how it happened. It was impossible, but they'd checked and double-checked. Kate was pregnant.

Fearghus was sitting on my sofa, his face in his hands. I wanted to do the same but my feet were stuck to the floor where he'd dropped his news on me. I searched my memory for any mention of consequences of him breaking his bargain with the Moores. I couldn't determine if none had been set, or if I'd washed it from my mind as an impossibility.

"That's what a prophecy is, right?" he was saying. "I was stupid to think it could be avoided. I should've never—" He cursed, popping my sofa with his fist.

"We need to tell your father."

"No. That's one more person who'll know why I've left."

"You can't leave."

"I just need help convincing Kate to leave. She thinks we're just going to get away with it. She has no idea—" He focused behind me.

Martin had joined us. "Kate's just told the household your news. Come have a drink with me and your uncles and grandfather. We're discussing it."

Fearghus got up and followed him out. I saw Fearghus hesitate just outside my bedroom door, like he was buying time to gather his thoughts. Whether he was contemplating a plan of escape or attack, I knew neither could happen. Fearghus' good behavior should have allowed for an option besides fight or flight, but he'd have to remain calm long enough to receive it. I walked past him, and it was enough to rouse him. After a few paces he was ahead of me, moving with fierce intent. Kate waited at the bottom of the stairs, where Fearghus took her by the arm and walked her halfway down the hall. His tone was a hushed kind of angry; her words were clipped.

"You shouldn't come with us," Martin said to me. "It'll be fine."

"What are the consequences of Fearghus breaking the rule?"

"We're working that out now." Fearghus' attorney was present this time, prepared to plead for a lighter sentence.

Their conclusion was to do nothing. It took a day to fully absorb, for me to calm my jittery nerves that expected some violently performed punishment. I couldn't allow myself to be excited to have a grandchild, but the idea had already started to germinate. The stronger it grew, the harsher my fear set in. To watch my grandchild grow up in that house would be like starting over on the day I was first brought there, to relive the whole nightmare with the clarity of already having lived it. Another child to protect from harm, to raise with love in a household of hate.

Kate needed to move into Fearghus' cottage where their baby would be safe. Since he'd made no advances with convincing her, it was time to procure some help.

The tea I brewed was well-known among my people for its many uses. It had as many names: Lover's Tea, Honesty

Tea, Tranquility Tea. At its most practical it relieved stomach ailments and mental distress. I'd chosen it for its ability to break barriers between people, to open a line of communication too tight for falsehoods or facades. It left a drinker at perfect ease, trusting, and very agreeable. In the wrong hands it could easily be used for evil. In my hands it would be used to bring my daughter-in-law close enough for me to explain what her ego wasn't letting her see: the safest place for her, Fearghus, and their unborn child was away from the estate.

Knowing how addictive the tea could be, I cut the recipe in half. The taste was strong, so I added honey and brought Kate a mug one May morning when the bees were so plentiful in the gardens we could hear the buzzing on the patio. Through the tea I was able to convince her to move into the lovely cottage Fearghus had slaved to make perfect for her. What I didn't bargain for was the bare truth of her feelings for Fearghus.

"My oaf," she called him. "Loyal like a pet." When I told her he loved her very much, she blew out a breath and waved a hand to dismiss the sentiment. "Who needs love when you have money, and a man who doesn't question a thing you do?"

I ended it there, too brokenhearted to hear more. When I took her empty mug, I stole her memory of that last exchange. If she remembered revealing such ugly remarks, she'd question our earlier conversation. I couldn't lose her agreement to move to Fearghus' cottage. Getting it had cost me too much.

CHAPTER 53

WITH KATE AND Fearghus out of the house, I had a new set of problems. Christian had moved into Paul's carriage house while he was home for the summer and Paul was still in rehab. If the building had been affected to turn a man into a moody drunk, it had worked for one and now had a good start on another. Christian had a long way to go to reach Paul's level of drinking and emotional imbalance, but the last few years turned my sweet, charming nephew into a sour person on one too many occasions for me to ignore.

I also couldn't ignore how his sour moods coincided with the day Kate had entered the estate. Christian had so many friends it was hard to believe he'd be disgruntled over sharing Fearghus. If Kate had loved Fearghus like we did, I'd give Christian a good talking to. But Kate was Kate, and I couldn't blame him. I was disgruntled myself.

Lewis had taken a more active role in wanting me dead, and Martin's attempts to subdue him weren't working. Lewis didn't scare me, but Martin's anger did. For once he was letting it under his skin. Possession of Fearghus had been their goal, and that need was a safeguard to me as long as it went unfulfilled. Even though he was living outside of the estate, their hold on him was absolute. He had no reason to doubt his place in the Moore family. They no longer had a use for me.

"You've been Martin's toy long enough," Lewis said to me one day. "How do you want it? I could break your neck right now."

"Oh, Lewis. All the nice times you and I have had, and you're going to ruin it like this?" I tilted my head at him. A graying grown man acting like his sixteen-year-old self. It was impossible to see him as anything else. He hadn't matured a day beyond that age.

I rarely mentioned these threats to Martin. He was so preoccupied by the unexplained intermission of Moore-family business, the cessation of family dinners, the sheer lack of action in and out of the house. And the new vague way his brothers were speaking to him.

"They're planning something, and I have no idea what," he said in my ear one night in bed.

"Maybe they're going to kill me."

"Not funny."

We could've left, if Martin wasn't cursed. We couldn't travel to build his tolerance because he was convinced they were about to do something behind his back. We were stuck. And another curse was about to be invoked—one that affected our son.

Fearghus was unreachable on his thirtieth birthday. That evening I packed a piece of the cake Ruby had made and sent Christian to find him. Christian didn't return until the next morning. It had taken him all night to find Fearghus sitting alone in the woods on his property in a dark mood with an open cut running the length of his left arm.

"Self-inflicted," Christian said. "He was sitting there under the moon, watching his arm bleed. Can't believe I'm related to that freak."

Christian got him home, but Kate wasn't there, so Christian crashed on the couch. In the morning that long cut on Fearghus' arm was healed, and Fearghus was angry and silent, offering no explanations to Christian.

"Where was Kate?" I asked.

Christian looked away quickly, rubbing the back of his neck. "Don't know."

I saw a flash of that sourness in his face. It was hard to believe Christian disliked her. He'd forgiven every abuse from his father. He held no open grudge against any member of the family. For that, he was a better person than me. Whatever Kate had done to elicit such bitterness from Christian was not something I wanted to hear about. I had a hard enough time pretending to like her already.

Aaron James was born on an overcast November morning hours before the sun rose behind the dark veil of clouds. The phone call woke me from the light sleep of a mother whose daughter-in-law had started labor the night before. Fearghus sounded half-asleep himself and hung up before I could ask when we could visit. Forty-eight agonizing hours later, Martin drove me and Eleanor to the cottage with a trunk full of food from Ruby.

Fearghus had never looked so glad to see me. He dug into a casserole before we'd finished unloading the car and stood at the counter in his cozy kitchen with dish and fork, oblivious to the real reason Eleanor and I had come.

Eleanor toed him in the shin. "Where's the baby?"

"Sleeping with Kate. Finally both fell asleep."

She headed for the hall. Martin came through the front door with the last of the food. We rearranged the refrigerator to make room for it all while Fearghus ate, heavy-lidded and reserved. Martin caught my eye and I knew what he was thinking: if Fearghus and Kate had stayed at the estate they'd have so much help. I sent my own thought back to him: This was good for him. This was what he needed. Martin bowed his head and raised a palm, clearly not wanting to argue.

Eleanor returned with a bundle which she handed to me, whispering, "I stole a sleeping baby."

I settled him in my arm and turned the blanket down so I could have a look at his face. Miniature pink cheeks, button nose, and a light sheen on his head that was more fuzz than hair. His eyelids were taut, eyebrows raised, like sleep was a job at which he worked hard. One hand against his chin, fingers outstretched awkwardly as if seeking an enclosure that was no longer there. I kissed his little cheek. Downy soft skin, unspeakably sweet. One snuggle was not enough. I went to the sofa, settling him high on my chest so his head could tuck under my chin. He fussed, reaching again for those walls he missed, until Eleanor tucked his hands back into his blanket and he calmed, releasing a milky-sweet breath that left him limp against me.

"He's wonderful," I whispered to Fearghus. He'd followed us into the living room but kept his space, planting himself in the corner. My fearless son keeping distance from his own baby like a disturbance of air around his tiny frame might cause him to break.

"I'll have someone drive two of the maids over every morning," Martin said to Fearghus.

"None of their people are allowed here."

Martin opened the door that led to the backyard and tilted his head in a gesture for Fearghus to follow.

"I guess Trey doesn't consider me one of *their people*," Eleanor said. "Not sure if that's a compliment or not."

"You're like a sister to him, Eleanor."

"Then that makes this little one my nephew." She held out her arms, and we performed a transfer gentle enough not to wake him. "I can't decide who he looks like. Trey or Kate."

The phone rang. I made a dash for it before it rang again and woke Kate or the baby. I needed to tell Fearghus to lower the volume on the ringer. "Hello?"

"Hey—um, Aunt Sloane?" It was Christian's voice. "Did I just …" There was a rustling on his end, then a thump. "I think—I mean, I didn't mean to call you."

"Christian, I'm at Fearghus'. You should come—"

"Who?"

Cold liquid fear slithered down me on the inside, like I'd just swallowed an icy drink. It felt too much like a conversation I'd had with Paul, in one of his drunken or LSD-induced dazes.

"Fearghus. You called his house."

"Yeah, but I didn't mean to call him either. I don't know who I'm trying to call."

"Kate?"

He was silent so long I said his name again.

"I'm …" He sounded distracted and very confused.

I needed to get him out of that house. "Have someone drive you over. We're all here. You can meet your new cousin."

"I can drive. I'm on my way." He hung up.

I peered out the back window at Martin and Fearghus. They stood in the middle of the yard, facing the hibernating rose garden, the barren November woods beyond. Neither spoke; they were both absorbed in contemplation. I wanted to go to them, to draw them both back inside where it was warm, but the silence between them looked too special to disrupt.

Eleanor and I took turns holding the baby while he slept. The men came back inside. Martin sat and tried to take the baby, but he woke upon transfer to new arms so she took him to Kate's room to be fed. Kate joined us not much later in her robe, her hair brushed to a shine. Eleanor helped her to the sofa and found pillows to prop Aaron, a quilt for her lap. Once settled, Kate patted the cushion next to her and smiled sweetly at Fearghus, an adoring look in her eyes that reminded me of the nicer girls Fearghus brought home years before.

Fearghus' slow response proved he was as thrown by this uncharacteristic affection as I was. When he sat down she hugged his arm, laying a cheek against him like he was her treasure. If motherhood had taught Kate how to love my son the way he deserved to be loved, she'd be a new woman to me, and I'd welcome her like a treasure herself.

I heated some of the food we'd brought, and we waited for Christian, but he never arrived. When Martin, Eleanor, and I returned to the estate, Christian was drinking in the kitchen alone. He claimed he didn't remember speaking to me on the phone.

"The only person I've talked to today is myself." He raised his beer to me, clicking the corner of his mouth twice before leaving the room. I made a promise to myself to ask Fearghus if he knew why Christian was acting so strange.

Relatives from the north began to arrive in the following weeks while the staff prepared a grand party for the winter solstice. The house crawled with people. Spaces that had become mine for peace and solitude away from Lewis' noisy adult children and their friends were now invaded by guests with no understanding of our informal agreement: I'd leave them alone as long as they left me alone. This temporary disruption of my small claim of territory seemed to rouse Lewis even further into fulfilling his fantasy of my death.

"I'll let my boys do it," he said in my ear one day, his breath hot and body too close to mine. "One will hold you down, the other will smother you with a pillow. As soon as Martin goes out of town. We'll say you died in your sleep."

I took hold of his face before he could straighten back up, pulling his ear to my lips. "If your boys enter my room without my permission," I whispered, "they'll meet a worse fate than a pillow."

Like Martin's bedside table holding a gun, mine held weapons not as deadly, but twice as horrifying. Weapons built with the lowest magic. Most Bevans wouldn't touch it based on morals alone. I'd never used it for the same reason, but given the chance to fight evil with evil, I'd gladly take a walk onto the dark side. There was no better way to disarm an attacker than by tricking his mind into thinking the violence he planned to bring to another was directed at him. My magic would make him his own victim.

Martin was in bed before me that night. His migraines were coming often and hard. Thinking they might be the result of a decade-long buildup of that toxic anger I'd given up trying to expel from the house, I did another smudging while the dozens of guests and family members slept. All it seemed to do was turn their behavior toward me from avoidant to suspicious. My power was a threat to them. My knowledge a reminder of the war between my family and theirs—of the things my family still knew, and theirs had forgotten.

Knowledge was a threat to those who didn't have it. Violence was their knee-jerk attempt of subdual. They trained in it like my family trained in our texts. My son had been trained in both, and I worried if the training was at war with one another, and which would survive.

Fearghus burst into the formal dining room on the day before the winter solstice. Everyone had gathered, filling five rows of tables with at least twenty people each. It was the largest family dinner I'd ever attended. Banished from them long ago and now living outside of the estate, Fearghus was a stranger in that room.

He crossed the span of floor before anyone could react and jerked Pierce out of his chair by the collar. "Where are they?"

Chairs scooted back in a collective screech. The thud of a dozen feet pounded the floor. A mass of bodies descended onto one, and Fearghus was dragged backward. He slammed his head into the face behind him, threw an elbow into a neck at his side. They got better hold of his arms, and this time, he yelled it. "Where are they!"

Martin was in the crowd now, tapping arms and shoulders to send men back to their chairs. At last it was only Fearghus and him, and he said what only I could hear. "*A mhic*, let's talk outside."

Breathing hard, Fearghus studied his father. He surveyed every face in the room. I felt a hand on my back—Christian. He pressed me forward. When Fearghus' eyes caught us, I felt a stab in my gut. For the first time I was confronting him from their side instead of standing beside him.

"Fearghus, come," I said.

He took a step back. He bowed his head, shaking it as if to throw off a bad dream. Christian gave him a pat on the back and thumbed toward the door. I led the way and didn't look back to see if they were following.

"Kate and Aaron," Fearghus said when we reached the foyer. "Someone took them. Wrecked the house."

"*What*?!" Christian said.

Fearghus started pacing. Christian put a hand up to stop him, but he pushed past.

"Her car's there, her purse." Fearghus stopped in front of Martin. "Tire tracks in the grass."

"When?" Martin said.

"Just now, when I got home. I'll fucking kill them all."

Martin rubbed a rough hand over his mouth. "There won't be need to. We'll find them. They're okay. Someone's jerking us around."

"Someone?" Fearghus said. "Someone in there—" He made a move to return to the dining room, but Martin and Christian both grabbed an arm as I stepped in front of him.

"Let's stay cool until we find out what happened." I placed my hands on his sandpaper cheeks, hoping to spread some calm into him. Nothing would be solved if Fearghus attacked them. Their backlash would steal all chances of finding Kate and Aaron. My grandson was kidnapped and in their hands with his mother as his only ally. It was a repeat of history so dreadful a cold wave rushed through me. "Anger will not help us now."

He blew out a breath. The effort it took him to remain calm reminded me of all the things they'd taken from him. He had every right to his anger, and I was talking him out of it.

"Christian," Martin said, "take Trey back home. Look for clues. Tap into whatever you need to." He watched them leave before taking hold of my arm. "Could your family have done this?"

A queasy emptiness had me backing up to the bench in the foyer. I sat under a hot weight, an emotional chaos.

"I don't think they did," Martin said. "My father knew about this, or he'd have followed us out here, raising hell."

"Do you think Kate and Aaron are okay?"

He put a hand on my knee, his eyes on the front door. "We need to find them." He looked straight at me. "And I don't want you out of my sight."

CHAPTER 54

Unable to sleep that night, I prepared spells to aid in the hunt for Kate and Aaron. My fatigue was a curse. Nothing worked. The next day, the household celebrated the solstice around our frantic worrying and running about. Martin broke his pledge to keep me in his sight when he left to comb Fearghus' cottage for clues a third time. He called Arthur and Mam, who had no information for him and were as surprised by the news as we had been. Fearghus stayed away from the estate with a large help from Christian. His anger had turned into bloodlust.

Which is why I was so surprised when both Martin and Christian returned to the estate after spending the morning of the next day with Fearghus. They'd left him unsupervised.

"He's remarkably calm," Martin said.

Christian shed his coat and handed it to the man who came to take their car back to the garage. "And by 'remarkably calm,' he means the dude looks like he's cracked. He keeps going outside just to stare at the woods. We got him passed-out drunk and took his car keys. Let's hope he doesn't have a spare."

"We both needed a break." Martin took off for the ballroom, for his own drink no doubt.

Christian gave me a kiss on the cheek before departing in the same direction. Someone needed to stay with Fearghus. All I had to do was have the driver take me to his house, and I could watch over him until Martin or Christian could resume. I asked the maid to bring my coat and a driver, but when the front door opened it wasn't the driver I expected. It was Paul.

He closed the door and caught sight of me, his grin wide, his arms even wider. I ran into him and held on. He started laughing—a deep, full sound like a music beating through me, a laugh I hadn't heard in decades. I pulled back to look at him. A trim beard completely overtaken by gray, hair shaggy on his forehead and around the ears. He'd aged like the rest of us, but a youthful light shone from within, a rebuilt spirit that sent tears straight to my eyes.

"How'd you know I was coming? I wanted it to be a surprise."

I hugged him again, my face pressed against his chest. "It is a surprise. Such a needed surprise. And you look so well. Damn you for making me cry."

He laughed again—another shock that made me back up to look at him a second time. It had been four years since he'd left. He'd returned a different man. Part of the man he was a long time ago, part something new.

"They let me out, on a trial basis. Is everybody here?" he asked.

"Yes, only about a hundred of your relatives."

"Just my luck. Join me in my hellos. It'll be easier with you beside me."

I glanced at the door, where the driver stood waiting for me. "I was going to go check on Fearghus ..."

Paul told me he heard what happened. Then he talked me out of sitting watch over Fearghus. He reminded me how Fearghus needed time away from people to settle his mind and told me if he really was sleeping off some hard drinking, it would be hours before he woke up. I wasn't swayed until he promised he'd go with me later to Fearghus'. The idea I wouldn't have to go alone made it a worthy deal.

We never made it, though. I spent the rest of the evening taking drinks out of Paul's hand. I seemed to be the only one aware that Paul was a recovering alcoholic, that one drink might flip his switch and undo years of rehabilitation. I was the only one not determined to destroy him.

The household woke lazily the next morning. A harsh cold had blown in overnight. I'd heard every gust as I tossed and turned, worried now for both Fearghus and Paul, wishing all the extended family would leave so we could focus on finding Kate and Aaron. Martin had left the bed early, so I got dressed and went to the windows to investigate two sparrows that were hopping and chattering all over my balcony. Seeing me, they grew more animated. It was Fearghus they needed; I couldn't understand them. I wished I could send them to check on Fearghus. I had to find Martin or Christian to ask if he was okay. Upon descending the stairs, a shouting match carried in from one of the western rooms. I stopped, thinking a return to my room to be the ideal move, until I recognized one voice as Paul's.

He and Lewis were at each other's throats in the library when I peeked in. One glance at Paul's face told me all I needed to know. Less that twenty-four hours home and Paul was already being dragged back into his old habits. His old, broken self was rising. There was no longer room for his newfound spirit.

I walked into their midst and took Paul by the arm. "You're better than this, Paul."

Lewis clutched my shoulder and dug his fingers in. "Woman, you can get in line. After I cut his throat, I'll cut yours."

"*Cloisim arís uait é.*" I jerked my shoulder from his grip and tugged Paul's arm until we crossed the threshold into the kitchen.

He went to the window and rested his forehead against the glass.

I stood beside him, taking his hand, weaving my fingers between his. "This house is bad for you."

"I know. This time when I leave, I'm never coming back." He turned to me, took my other hand in his. "Come with me, away from this place."

"I won't leave Martin." There was a sudden cramping pain in my head. I'd slept too late and missed my coffee. And there were too many things happening, too many unresolved anxieties. The house was stifling me in a way it hadn't in years.

He released my hands. "And Martin can't leave because of the … where are you going?"

I buttoned my coat. "To go check on Fearghus." But that wasn't true. I'd come downstairs looking for Martin or Christian, not to go to Fearghus' house myself. And I didn't remember putting on my coat. Through the window, those two sparrows had landed on the patio and were hopping in circles, chirping at me like I'd seen them do to beckon Fearghus outside. "These two birds …"

One glance at Paul told me he was in no mood for a blustery December morning, so I went outside without him. The sky was a tapestry of varying grays rolling against one another. The air held a deep cold, unpenetrated by the sun. The sparrows alighted in a nearby tree. Perhaps someone had been feeding them and they were looking for a handout. One flew down and landed at my feet, and only returned to its perch when I took a step forward. They took turns with this technique until I'd walked halfway across the lawn. By then my head was throbbing, but I was too intrigued by the sparrows to go inside for breakfast.

My woods were encased in ice. The rain had ceased before the winds pushed in overnight, bringing frigid temperatures that had turned the stagnant water to ice. Between gusts of wind, the forest was silent except for my crunchy footsteps and those two incessant birds. Ice-sheathed branches clinked against one another as they hopped along. I hoped they'd stop soon so I could go home. My head was a pounding weight, too heavy for my neck. And I was getting so sickeningly hot I tore at the buttons on my coat to get it open, to get some air. I stumbled, going to one knee with a hand braced against the ground. When I looked up I was standing in front of the buildings where they held prisoners. Where they tortured my husband. Where they punished my son.

Pierce leaned against the nearest doorway like he was waiting for someone. Around his feet, symbols designed to draw the blackest magic had been carved into the earth.

Understanding swooshed in. The sparrows. The unintended walk outside. The pain in my head. Dirty magic had led me out there.

"Let them go." I gestured to the sparrows hopping nervously on the roof above Pierce's head. "They've served you as you asked."

"Oh, I didn't ask."

"Release them or I'm walking back." I braced myself for what a monster would do to helpless animals he no longer had a need for. He was in control of them—there was nothing I could do.

"Okay, I'll grant you a last request." He smiled and the birds flew off as if being chased by a predator. A gust of wind pushed through the trees, helping them on their way.

Something came crashing through the woods behind me. I backed in an angle away from Pierce, putting both him and the new arrival in my field of vision. Lewis slowed to a walk. "Sorry I'm late. I had a little incident with our favorite brother."

"We should've lured him out here too, but I only have one of these." Pierce produced a vial from his pocket. "So, *Miss Bevan*, your presence here proves you're the one who put a spell on me—how many years ago?"

"Twenty-four," I answered, even though his question was rhetorical.

Lewis spat on the ground. "*Dearg-bhitse.*"

"With the house so full of people, it could've been any one of them. I'm so glad it was you. So, Lew's gonna hold you while I force this down your throat, and what you'll get is the same curse, threefold."

Lewis circled around me. "Martin will finally be as disgusted by you as we are. And he won't care when I kill you."

"You lay one finger on me, I'll bring forth every element—"

A succession of snaps sounded far away. Gunshots, like when Martin took Fearghus and Christian into the woods for target practice. Pierce and Lewis were looking toward the sound, even more distracted from our current business than I was.

"Did they tell him?"

Lewis checked his watch. "Thirty minutes ago. Enough time for him to—"

"You don't think—"

Lewis cursed, staring into the distance. "One of us needs to go back."

"Go. I'll deal with her."

Lewis charged away. I couldn't entertain my relief until I saw him disappear into the trees. My aventurine lay idle on my chest—one powerful sleeping spell, now only one man to conquer. I'd worn the pendant every day, hoping I'd never need to use it on Fearghus.

"On your knees. Let's get this done. I think your son is causing some mischief at the house, and I don't want to miss seeing him gunned down."

"Fearghus knows not to cause trouble."

"I think he might've changed his mind when they told him they killed his wife and baby."

"Liar."

"This time, I'm not." The words had an honest passivity to them that were like slap in the face. He wasn't lying.

And my infant grandson—Fearghus' little boy—

I brought a fist hard against my mouth. An acid sickness was rising to my throat, and I wouldn't vomit in front of Pierce. I'd give no indication I believed him, that any words he said could hurt me, whether they were the truth or not. My fingernails dug into my palm, inciting the heat of a fury I couldn't contain. I backed under the canopy of the trees, seeking their calming spirit. I needed to think, to breathe, to solve my current situation before confronting another.

Pierce tucked his chin and began a low chant, his eyes growing distant as an unnatural stiffness settled on his frame. Turned devil before my eyes, he was the living representation of the build-up of evil that no cleansing agent could ever smudge from the house. Tree limbs cracked above me, popping under their own weight as they gave in to his control. I raised an arm, feeling the power of air collect in my hand and burst forth at my will. A shower of bark and twigs rained upon me, instead of the logs they'd been. They scratched my skin, but that was the worst of their damage. He didn't know I'd become sister to every tree in those woods.

He took three quick steps toward me—a human reaction that shot me full of fear. I couldn't overcome him as a human. He was bigger and stronger and willing to kill. I took hold of the aventurine lying against my chest. If there was ever a time to use it, it was now. I ripped it from its chain. A tremble vibrated the earth beneath my feet, but it wasn't of me—it was timed to a pounding coming through the trees, growing nearer. Pierce shouted orders, to what elements I wasn't sure. The aventurine warmed in my fist. It was syncing to me, reading my intent. I had to get closer to him. I couldn't miss.

A herd of black beasts surged from around the nearest building, coming to a halt just behind Pierce. It was the Moores' pack of Dobermans, and they weren't here to play. I didn't have a way with animals like Fearghus did, and I knew no spells to tame them. They were loyal to Pierce, and if they saw me hurt him, they'd attack me.

I looked at the trees all around. There were none to climb. All the low limbs had snapped off and were lying in pieces around me.

"My dogs are hungry," Pierce said. "So unless you come and accept this drink, I'll have to let them feast."

He was bluffing. They might bite, but they wouldn't kill. They weren't monsters. *He* was the monster, forcing innocent creatures to work his evil. I took a step forward to call his bluff, my arms open in offer to them. The dogs began a wild barking. They charged toward me but stopped as if held by an invisible wall. They bared teeth, snapping at each other in their excitement.

Pierce held up one finger, and one dog lurched forward, covering the distance before I could think to do anything but huddle. The impact knocked me onto the broken tree limbs. I felt the aventurine slip through my fingers into the debris. The dog circled, nipped at my clothes. I wished I'd paid closer attention to Fearghus when he spoke to animals. I wished I'd asked him to teach me.

I raised my head. Sharp teeth pinched my ankle. Instead of jerking away I offered my open hand to the dog's muzzle. The dog growled, snapping at me, jolting my already frantic heart. Every muscle shuddered, begging to run. I plunged my other hand into the mess of tree limbs around me, searching for that smooth stone that could save me from the man, but not the dogs. It had partially synced to me—if I could connect to its power, perhaps I could home in on it.

Another set of paws pounded toward me. The second dog collided with me teeth-first, ripping through fabric and flesh on my hip. The wound stung, its impact both on the surface and bone-deep. I ducked to avoid meeting the dog's eyes with mine.

"Easy," I said. "You know Fearghus, you know me."

A wet nose went under my chin, snapping my head up with a force that cracked my teeth together. The other dog rammed me in the side with its bony head. While they tried to get me upright, I grappled for my aventurine, searching by feel, discarding twigs and dirt and leaves. I conjured its image in my mind, its polished texture. The day Martin gave it to me, when I dumped it out of that satin bag into my palm. *It reminded me of your eyes*, he'd said. *I couldn't pass it up.*

A third dog attacked, this one with claws that tore strips through my pants. I felt the sting of the wounds, the cold rush of blood to the surface. It riled the other two into violence, and they were all upon me. My need to fight overtook me. I lashed out and was met with snapping jaws so close to my face I cried out against my will. One set of jaws got a firm grip of my arm, another clamped onto my shoulder.

I went still, and so did they.

A clamor broke out in the tree limbs above. Dead leaves and ice rained upon us. Both dogs released me, raising their ears as if being called by name. But it wasn't Pierce they were looking at. Two sparrows on the nearest limb had their unbroken attention.

All three dogs backed up. They turned their faces toward Pierce. My throat was dry from the scream I'd just released, from the breath coming so fast I feared I'd pass out. He must've thought I'd had enough, that I'd surrender. A rush of air came from overhead but it wasn't the wind. Hundreds of birds filled the branches, squawking and chirping and fluttering angrily. I couldn't see Pierce, but I heard him curse. He shouted at the dogs he'd just called off, as if they weren't following orders. But they had. They'd released me as he must've ordered. They'd even given me space to get up.

I saw him then—throwing an arm out to sic the remaining dogs on me, but they'd gone docile. They weren't following his command anymore.

The three dogs with me were still watching those sparrows chattering on the nearest limb, recognizable even though we'd been swarmed by a flock. I stood shakily, bracing myself as one dog came forward. It licked my hand.

At that moment Pierce unloaded the vilest slurs of my name, my family, my son. He'd gone more vicious than those dogs could ever be. He fell to his knees among those symbols of black magic and began a chant, charging the air with a desperate cold that spread against me like a mist.

Three sets of warm brown eyes were now upon me, as if pleading to help.

"Can you find something for me?" I offered the spot on my palm where my aventurine last lay, and each dog took a sniff before dashing off, nose to the ground. The remaining dogs rushed me to do the same.

The ground rippled with energy. I shouted at the dogs to hurry. I ran as close to Pierce as I could tolerate with the dirty magic seeping out of him. It was a heady toxin in the air, more foul than the darkness I'd tried to smudge from the house. My hands and knees shook. I could sense my connection to the earth weakening. My push to maintain it brought on a dizziness that pulsed against the backs of my eyes. I felt myself falling backward. I slapped myself awake.

The dogs swarmed me. One dropped a smooth green stone at my feet. It was so pretty I wanted to pick it up. It would make a lovely necklace. I was on my knees. Not to get a closer look, but because all energy had drained, and I had to sleep. Barking in my ears. So loud. But getting quieter. Moving far away.

It reminded me of your eyes. I couldn't pass it up.

Martin's voice. My aventurine. My salvation.

I jerked awake, my cheek against earth. My hand closed over the aventurine lying before my eyes, and I shoved myself up. Pierce was standing now, a perfect target, an evil asking for a deserved end.

I flung the pendant at him. It hit him square in the chest. The contact lit the air, knocking me off my feet onto the bed of twigs and bark. I scrambled to standing as the dogs scattered, yelping into the woods. Without a visual on Pierce he could be anywhere. He could be behind me. He could be unleashing his own attack.

I spotted him on the ground and tripped over branches toward his limp body, slowing as I closed in. He was playing dead—luring me closer to snatch my arm, to pull me down and pour that vial into my mouth. But his jaw was slack, his eyes closed. I nudged him with my foot. His body recovered its position. I plucked my aventurine from the ground by his neck. He'd skidded through the center of his evil symbols on the ground. It was a shame to see his work made so impotent. Perhaps I could remedy that.

Kneeling on his chest, I planted my forehead against his. The magic swelled into me, profane and powerful, as restless as unspent evil would be while trapped in a useless practitioner. I drew it through him and raised my arms, blasting it toward those grotesque buildings like a firehose of flame. They erupted so hotly I retreated to the trees, ready to protect them should the fire escape the clearing. It died to a controlled burn, to the bonfire Christian and I had dreamed of. I took off through the woods toward the house, leaving Pierce's body to the elements.

If he died, it would be his magic at fault. Not mine.

CHAPTER 55

I TOOK THE PATH toward the henge, planning to draw some power I might need once I reached the house. Instead of finding it empty, I found it guarded by the mistress. She stood barefoot in its center, her arms straight at her sides, her white hair loose and untouched by the wind that gusted around me.

I stepped inside the henge. "Órlaith."

"Sloane." She took a step back, a move that allowed me to join her in the exact center. She wasn't guarding the henge. She was waiting for me.

We were equals here. Two women, sharing a place of refuge while our home was seized by a violence we had not created but had allowed. We'd turned our faces away each time it grew, allowing it to live and mature beside us.

"Today is a day of death," she said. "My husband is dead. And two of my sons…"

"Come—we can go there and stop—"

"It's too late. It's not our job to stop a system they've set in motion."

"It *is* our job. We're the only ones who'll do it. We can end it now, stop it before it gets worse. Come!" I took off through the woods, unsure whether she was following but I couldn't wait any longer. Two of her sons were dead, but which two? Pierce burning in the clearing by the buildings? Lewis, catching a deserved fate on his return to the house? Or the two I loved?

A couple of Martin's men sprinted across the lawn to meet me. They each took an arm and hauled me in through the side entrance, straining the wounds from the dogs that must've been allayed by adrenaline. My protests were silenced by a finger over my lips and the sharp glance from a soldier that told me I was being shuttled to safety, and any noise could expose our position to the enemy. They hugged walls, aimed guns around corners before proceeding. The house was darkened and morgue-silent. A clock's digital display was blank. Two people lay on the floor in the library. The sight of blood made me gasp, earned me a hand over my mouth. They delivered me to another man in the parlor, to a protective arm I knew well.

Martin's face was so grim it snatched away my relief at seeing him alive. He'd seen something as terrible as death, and it was still around us. He nodded at me to get behind him, gave a jerk of his chin to convey our intended path. Then he raised his gun and led me forward. The foyer was lit dimly by what little light an overcast day could provide through curtained windows. Martin motioned to his feet, exaggerating a step he wanted me to mimic. Every sound in that cavernous room was magnified, and our goal was complete silence. When he stopped halfway to the stairs and looked behind us, my back crawled like something was surely there, but I didn't turn to see. A faint scuffle broke out somewhere in the house. Martin hurried forward and we ascended the stairs with more speed than before.

In our room he locked every door, took the gun from his bedside table, and dumped the bullets in the drawer. He handed it to me. "Pretend this is loaded. It's still as much a threat. I know you don't want to kill your own son."

He pushed me to the floor behind the sofa. "Now hold it like this, and if Trey comes in—"

"Fearghus won't hurt me." I let the gun fall into his hand.

"Maybe not, but everyone else will." He handed me his other gun. "This one's loaded. It's for anyone but Trey. They come in here, you shoot. Don't mix up the guns and don't leave this room until I come for you."

"Tell me what's going on!"

"Trey's snapped. He killed my father and Lew, and now he's on a rampage for everyone else. His guns are suppressed so we lost his position. He's probably looking for Paul, or—"

"Martin, stop him!"

"I can't stop him. I created him. They created him."

Gunshots popped somewhere in the house.

"They've found him. I have to go down there." He kissed my forehead and forced the empty gun back into my hands. Then he was gone.

I laid the weapon on the floor. Fearghus had to be calmed, not confronted by violence he'd surely fight to an even more brutal end. I had to find him before anyone else did. My aventurine had been used. I only had my voice, my bare hands. If anyone but Martin found him, they'd kill him. If they didn't, he'd kill more people. I had to find Christian to help me. I had to find Paul.

I tore out of my room and down the stairs. Across the vacant foyer the front door hung wide open, creaking in the wind. I crossed the room to peer out. A car was pulled up front, one tire in the grass and its driver's side door open. The driveway and front lawn were still. I heard footsteps; I spun around to see Fearghus stalking toward me.

He stopped in front of me. His face and shirt were splattered with blood, his hands wet with it. He coolly observed me. No sign of anger. No remorse. His eyes were somewhere else, a place I'd never reach. His mind had been disconnected, but it wasn't an effect from the mistress this time. It wasn't fixable by Martin. It was broken by everything. By his own will.

"A Fhearghuis—"

He tossed a gun to the floor. It slid away from us, then he was shouldering past me, through the door. Gone.

The sound of screeching tires curled in through the open door. He was leaving. He'd finished what he'd come to do. Impeded by upturned furniture, I rushed through the eastern rooms, each one littered with more bodies than the last. Bloodied bodies, crumpled bodies, twisted limbs and broken necks. None were the one I was seeking.

In the ballroom I halted to the sight of one lonely body lying as if in peaceful sleep. Halfway on the rug, Paul lay like I'd found him so many times he was too drunk or high to find his bed. The scene would be the same, if it wasn't for the circle of blood on his chest cascading to the floor. The red stain in his neat gray beard. The wet, labored breath I could hear from across the wide room.

I ran to him. His shirt was soaked, bloodiest at a rip near his collarbone. I tore it wider. It only exposed more blood and crimson ripples of skin and muscle. Blood oozed forth with the slow pulse of a waning heart. I pressed with both hands, the slippery texture underneath them creating a hysteria that buzzed from my core to my limbs. I screamed for Martin, for Eleanor, for every name I knew. For the healing earth, the cleansing water, the mighty oak that held our power.

He opened his eyes. They rolled slowly to catch mine. I bent to kiss his face, felt his hand slide on the ground against my leg. Too weak to raise a finger, he gasped out a breath and closed his eyes like it took too much strength to keep them open.

"Paul, you're fine. Someone will come help. Talk to me, just talk to me, and—" I screamed for Martin again. I got up and yanked the curtain until the rod broke off its hanger. I dragged the whole thing to him and wadded the fabric against his wound. "See? I'll hold this here until someone comes, and you'll be fine."

He swallowed a few times, choking until he found his voice. "Let me die."

The puddle of blood spread under my knees. I shook my head, blinking away tears that would only disclose how dire this was, when he had to stay strong so he could live.

"Don't bury me…" he choked until he found his breath again "…here. Bury me with Rosemary."

I sobbed against my arm, nodding my answer. I couldn't let that go unacknowledged even if he did live.

Someone hollered from the doorway. Martin and some men ran toward us. They parted me from Paul like a liquid force, their motion creating a tide that pushed me against the sofa and continued to beat against me as I watched them carry Paul away. And then I was beaten by my own sobs, a shuddering quake with aftershocks that lasted a lifetime.

When I heard the shouts of orders being given in the foyer, I gathered my shaky legs. I walked across broken glass, through spilled bookshelves, and around displaced furniture to join the gathering just in time to see the mistress' entry quiet a crowd of ramped-up soldiers.

"It's over," she said.

One man stepped forward from the crowd, but the mistress raised a hand to silence him.

"He's gone from here," she said. "Call off the cars and let him go. He's no longer ours. It's time to let what will be, be."

She started up the stairs.

"Mistress, we only want to—"

"I'll hear nothing," she said, and walked up the stairs to the whispered curses of a dozen men.

"Thank you," I called out.

She stopped and turned, meeting my gaze over the heads of the crowd. Our look was a connection of grief so thick it could have buried us beside the ones we'd lost. We wouldn't be counted as victims, but we'd suffer the pain of death longer than any who'd died that day. She bowed her head; I bowed mine. For the abuses her sons committed against my son, and the retaliation my son committed against hers, we forgave and we were forgiven.

I understood her then. Why she stayed in her room. Why she had accepted the curse that took away her sons. No mother wants to see the crimes her child has committed. But no matter how much my son's wrongs felt like they came from my own hand, they were his own. I would not take them on. I would not make excuses for them. He'd live with them, pay for them, make peace with them.

She extended her arm over the heads of the group as if handing the crowd over to me before climbing the stairs to her sanctuary. And every man turned to face me—twenty sets of eyes anxious for orders withheld by their mistress.

"Put away your weapons," I said. "We have a house to clean."

Reluctant yet obedient nods carried from man to man. Through the dispersing crowd I saw Christian in a squat, hands covering his face. I approached him. My legs were too numb to join him at the ground. I'd never get up again.

He looked up at me. "I couldn't stop him."

"No one could. Not this time."

My son had smudged the evil from the house in a horrifying way. He'd dismissed all I'd taught him. He'd followed Moore values as if they were his own blood. The Moores had wanted my son. Today they'd finally paid for him.

EPILOGUE

I FEAR THE DAY I must tell you your life has been a vicious lie. I have lived to protect you, but now I must forget you. My love will lead them to you. Today you have left behind a mountain of bloody bodies that will not go unavenged.

Their plans are already in action, and from what I've heard, it will not be easy for you. I can only hope you understand the magnitude of your actions and flee far away, to the most remote corner of the world, never to return. I can find the strength to let you go if I know you will be safe forever.

A goodness dwells inside you many do not see. Mingling with that goodness is a violent killer my denial has shielded me from all these years. I see it now. They have created it. And it scares me more than any of the other nightmares I have lived.

Should the day arrive that I must tell you the truth, I hope your scars have been healed, your heart has been mended, and your mind has found ease. I hope you have recovered enough peace to dissolve my grief with your forgiveness of my lies.

I live for the day the seeds I've planted will find light and burst through the layers of toxic soil the Moores have piled upon you. There's a secret waiting in the stars for you, one that will help you shovel off that awful soil, but you must be open, your eyes must be wide. You must find a way to live so your new life can begin. Your day will not dawn until you wake. Only then will your morning star find you.

DEAR READER,

Thank you for reading *The Oak and the Moon*! I know you're probably ready to continue with Liv and Trey's story, which will resume in the next book, *The Catalyst*. Subscribe to kaycamden.com to receive updates on my writing progress and other news.

If you liked this book—or even if you didn't—please consider leaving a review. All reviews help. And please tell your friends! All my ebooks are lendable, so pass them along!

Are you on Goodreads? Send me a friend request!

I love to hear from readers! Email me at kay@kaycamden.com

Again, thank you for reading. Our time is valuable and finite and there are far too many good books to read. Thank you for choosing mine!

—*Kay*

ACKNOWLEDGMENTS

My thanks go to—

Jackie at the Congress Plaza Hotel, who went above and beyond.

Montanna, who probably doesn't remember helping me with this book. Her advice added a dimension of character this story wouldn't have without her.

The ILF, speakers of the most beautiful language on Earth.

Rae and Ginny, for reading. And for everything.

Debra, the goddess of language, and saver of writers' butts.

My two boys, for showing me the real-life bond of brotherhood, and all the goofy fun, hot anger, and unconditional love that comes with it. I couldn't have written these two young fictional brothers without you two.

My husband, a part-time widower who never complains when I retreat below ground to my writing chair for hours every night.

My readers, who make the time I spend at the keyboard so completely worth it.

the

ALIGNMENT SERIES

The Alignment
The Two
The Oak and the Moon
The Catalyst
The Warrior

VISIT KAYCAMDEN.COM FOR MORE